The Forgotten Gift

KATHLEEN MCGURL

ONE PLACE, MANY STORIES

This novel is entirely a work of fiction. The names, characters and incidents portrayed in it are the work of the author's imagination. Any resemblance to actual persons, living or dead, events or localities is entirely coincidental.

HQ
An imprint of HarperCollins*Publishers* Ltd
1 London Bridge Street
London SE1 9GF

1

First published in Great Britain by
HQ, an imprint of HarperCollins*Publishers* Ltd 2020

Kathleen McGurl asserts the moral right to be
identified as the author of this work.
A catalogue record for this book is
available from the British Library.

ISBN: 9780008380502

MIX
Paper from
responsible sources
FSC
www.fsc.org   **FSC® C007454**

This book is produced from independently certified FSC™ paper
to ensure responsible forest management.

For more information visit: www.harpercollins.co.uk/green

Printed and bound in Great Britain by
CPI Group (UK) Ltd, Melksham, SN12 6TR

For my son Fionn, who always smiles when I send him a rough draft of each novel to read and comment on. Keep up the good work!

Prologue

George Britten, 1874

Extract from the last will and testament of George Thomas Britten

. . . and to Nathaniel Spring, Chaplain of Millbank Prison, I bequeath the sum of one hundred pounds and to Emily the wife of the aforesaid Nathaniel Spring I give my hand mirror with the silver frame that is inlaid with sapphires and pearls in recognition of his friendship and support during my time of greatest need . . .

George Britten listened carefully as his solicitor read out the section of the will that he had just completed writing. 'Does that cover it, sir?'

George nodded. 'Yes, I think that will do. So I am repaying in a small way the kindnesses shown to me by Nathaniel Spring. It's important to me.'

'Yes, sir.' The solicitor, Edmund Harris, frowned. 'It's not for me to comment, sir, but I can't help but wonder about your connection with these people?'

George stood and paced around the room. 'You are right. It is not for you to comment. Suffice it to say that without Nathaniel, I would not be here today. I owe him . . . my life.'

'Very well, sir. As to the remains of your estate: after your other bequests it is to be passed to your wife, and then split evenly amongst your children after her demise. Is that correct?'

'Yes, that is right.' George sat down again and leaned back in his chair as Mr Harris penned the next part of the will. It felt good to have this set down on paper. There'd been a time when he'd thought he would not need to write a will – he'd have nothing to leave to anyone. But now, at the age of thirty-three, he'd become well off, with a wife and family to provide for, and with personal debts to repay in whatever way he could. He'd come a long way since his youth, albeit by a roundabout route that he would never have imagined.

That mirror, expensive and beautifully made, which he'd bought so long ago as a gift that was never given – it was fitting that it should go to Nathaniel Spring's wife. She would treasure it. It had lain forgotten in a drawer for many years; it had not felt right to give it to his own wife.

George thought back to the boy he'd been at nineteen – that naïve young man who'd begun a journal in which to capture his hopes and dreams, thoughts and desires. How innocent in the ways of the world he'd been then, and how little he could have anticipated what his future held in store for him!

Chapter 1

Cassie, present day

The staff room at the sports centre was tatty and tired, its furniture functional at best, but it was one of Cassie's favourite places. That and the Red Lion pub where she and the other staff often adjourned to at the ends of their shifts. Today, Cassie was working the early shift. She'd started at seven a.m., acting as lifeguard to cover the early morning swim session. She was due to finish at four, and after a half hour in the gym and a relaxing swim, she'd be heading straight to the pub along with Toby and Shania, who'd worked the same shift.

Now, she was on her lunch break in the staff room, sitting on one of the plastic and steel chairs with her feet up on another.

'Shift your feet,' said Shania, arriving for her break. 'God do I need to sit down or what?'

'Tough class?' Cassie asked. Shania ran many of the fitness and Zumba classes. A more energetic job than being a lifeguard and general centre attendant, Cassie had always thought.

'Yeah.' Shania twisted open a bottle of fruit juice and downed half the bottle in one. Wiping the back of her hand across her mouth she looked at Cassie. 'Hey, did you see *Who Do You Think You Are?* last night?'

'The one with the fella off the soap opera? Yes, I saw it.' Of course Cassie had seen it. She was obsessed by genealogy – both watching the TV shows where experts traced celebrities' ancestry, and investigating her own. It's what she did on her days off. She didn't have much of a social life beyond the sports centre.

'His face, when they told him his great-great-grandfather, or whoever it was, had been convicted of murder! It was a picture!' Shania looked thoughtful. 'Wonder how it feels, though. I mean, what would you feel if you discovered one of your ancestors was a crook or a murderer?'

Cassie shrugged. 'Don't know. It'd be weird, knowing those genes are in you. But if the ancestor was distant enough, the genes would be watered down.'

'I suppose it's that old nurture or nature argument, isn't it? What makes you who you are – your ancestors or the way you were brought up?' Shania got up and went to retrieve her container of salad from the fridge. 'Anyway, would you tell me if you found a bad boy or girl amongst your ancestors?'

'Probably. You know I tell you everything, darling,' Cassie replied with a wink. As she said it, she wondered about the will of her great-great-great-grandfather that she'd recently come across in her latest genealogical searches. He, George Britten, had apparently bequeathed a valuable item – a mirror set with sapphires and pearls – to the wife of a prison chaplain, as well as making the chaplain a generous financial payout. Why, she had no idea, as yet. Presumably the chaplain had been a good friend. But if so, why did the will specifically refer to him as 'Chaplain of Millbank Prison' and not just by name? And what did it mean *in recognition of his friendship and support during my time of greatest need?*

It was possible, she had to admit, that George Britten had been an inmate of that prison at some point. Finding out if that was true, and if so, what crime he had committed, was high on Cassie's list of topics to research, when she had some spare time.

Shania laughed. 'Great – I will look forward to the juicy gossip, then. Speaking of which, are you going to the pub tonight?'

'Of course I am! I'm going to the gym and having a swim after work, then I'll be in the Red Lion by about seven. See you there.'

It was a regular event – at least once a week after work Cassie would meet up with her colleagues in the pub. Who turned up depended on who was working the evening shift, but today it was all her favourite people. Shania, of course, there before Cassie and already installed at their favourite table with a large glass of Prosecco for herself and a pint of Theakston's Old Peculier for Cassie.

'Cheers, mate,' said Cassie as she sat down and picked up her pint. You knew you had the best ever friends when they knew exactly what you liked to drink, and had the drink ready and waiting for you.

A few minutes later they were joined by Andy, the sports centre manager, who bought himself a pint of lager before pulling up a stool. 'Hey, my favourite girls. How are we?'

'Your favourite *women* are all good,' Cassie replied. 'Seriously, Andy, we are both in our thirties. Time to stop referring to us as girls.'

Andy grimaced. 'Oops, sorry. Lost a few feminist points there, didn't I?'

'You did, yeah.' Cassie put on a stern face. 'But we will let you off, if you buy the next round.'

'Sure. Want it now?'

'Definitely. Before you forget and try to wriggle out of it.'

'I'd never do that.'

As Andy got up and went to the bar to order the drinks, Shania turned to Cassie and laughed. 'You twist that poor man around your little finger, Cass. He'll do anything for you. It's probably actually my round – he bought two rounds last week and I bought none.'

'Ssh. Don't ever turn down the offer of a drink from the boss,' Cassie said, with a smile. She liked Andy – he was a friend and a good person to work for. Shania was probably right in that Cassie seemed to have a way with him. If she asked for a day off at short notice Andy would almost always grant her request, even if he had to work extra hours himself to cover her shift. Their previous manager had not been so accommodating and Cassie had been glad when he'd left and Andy, tall and skinny with a shock of black hair, had arrived in his place. Now, she had to admit, the sports centre was a great place to work, and that was largely down to the fun work ethic Andy had brought with him. Vicky, the assistant manager, was more strait-laced and never came to the pub, but was still a decent person to work with.

Occasionally Cassie wondered whether, at thirty-seven, she ought to look for a job with more prospects, greater responsibility and higher pay. Certainly her parents thought so. Cassie had tumbled into the sports centre job after dropping out of university, needing an easy job that would earn her enough to pay the rent and put food on the table. And there she'd stayed, for sixteen years now. Most of the other general centre attendants were part-timers – either students paying their way through university or older women working shifts during school hours or at the weekends. The other full-time staff were management – Andy, plus the assistant manager Vicky. And then there were the instructors like Shania, who taught classes at several sports centres, gyms and studios in the area, and topped up their income by doing a few general shifts at the sports centre. Cassie was the only full-timer with no teaching qualifications who only worked the general shifts, lifeguarding, setting up equipment, cleaning changing rooms and the like.

'Here we are then, ladies,' Andy said, putting their drinks in front of them, and earning himself a glare from Cassie. 'What? What have I said now?'

'We are women. Not ladies.' Shania stifled a giggle as Cassie rolled her eyes.

'Here we are then, *women*,' Andy said. 'Ah come on. That sounds ridiculous. If you were fellas I'd say, "here we are, gents," so why can't I say "ladies"?'

'OK, you have a point there,' Cassie conceded. 'Once again I will let you off.'

'My, you are magnanimous tonight,' Andy said. 'Anyway. How was your day, you two?'

Shania launched into a long story about a beginners' Zumba class she'd run, in which two of the participants had kept bumping into each other, one going left and one going right when both should have gone left. 'They're supposed to mirror me, but one thought she needed to do the opposite, no matter how many times I explained it. They ended up in a heap on the floor at one point, thankfully not hurt but in fits of giggles. As was I.'

'Ah the perils of a keep-fit class,' Andy said. 'And you, Cass? Anything fun happen to you today?'

'Ah you know, the usual. Watched The Back swim ten lengths of butterfly in the lunchtime swim session.'

'Ooh you should have said – I'd have come poolside to watch,' Shania squealed. The Back was the name the female lifeguards had given to a regular customer, a fit young man in his twenties who swam several times a week, showing off his rippling back muscles to great effect as he practised his butterfly stroke.

Andy leaned back and folded his arms. 'So I'm sexist and get told off if I refer to you two as "girls" or "ladies", but you're allowed to drool over a bloke's back muscles when he comes in for a swim? You'd be furious with me if I commented on a woman's body in her swimsuit. Doesn't it work both ways?'

Cassie fixed him with a stare. 'Yes it does, but women have been oppressed for so long. The pendulum has to swing back a little before it comes to rest in the middle, when full equality for all has finally been achieved.'

'Hmm. Think I'll put Toby and Ben poolside every lunchtime from now on.'

'Toby'd probably appreciate The Back just as much as we do,' Shania said.

'What? You mean . . . no, really?'

Cassie laughed. 'Yep. Didn't you know he was gay?'

Andy stuck out his lower lip. 'Perils of being a manager. No one tells me anything. I have to rely on you girls, whoops I mean women, to keep me up to date.'

'Also, Shania's an alien,' Cassie said, her face deadpan.

They were still laughing a few minutes later when Toby, Ben and a couple of other staff arrived. It was a good evening – a few rounds were bought and drunk but not so many that Cassie would have a hangover. A lot of banter and laughter and warmth. This, she thought, was why she was still in the job after so many years. Good people, good fun. Her colleagues came and went but they were always the kind of people Cassie got on well with, on a night down the pub.

So what if she'd never become closer to any of them. So what if none of her friends had ever been to her flat, or she to theirs. So what if when people left the sports centre they never seemed to stay in touch after a few months. So what if she'd never had a boyfriend who lasted more than a couple of months, not since . . . not since university. She was happy, wasn't she? Her life was good, wasn't it?

Cassie had a day off the next day. She'd planned to do some food shopping and go for a run – she was supposed to be in training for a half-marathon along with some of her work colleagues. They were going to run in T-shirts advertising the sports centre, and were raising sponsorship money in aid of the local children's hospice charity.

But the weather had other ideas. She liked to think of herself as not just a fair-weather runner, but she had her limits, and early autumnal torrential rain and gale-force winds were definitely beyond them.

'Hmm, two fish fingers and some manky potatoes for dinner, then,' she told herself, inspecting the contents of her fridge and freezer. 'Plus daytime TV or genealogy research. What do you reckon, Griselda?' She turned to address her elderly tabby cat who was rubbing herself around Cassie's ankles, clearly hoping for some tidbit from the fridge.

'Yeah, you're right. Genealogy it is.' She made herself a cup of tea then went through to her sitting room. She settled herself on a sofa, pulled the hand-knitted blanket her mother had made her over her legs and opened up her laptop. She had about thirty seconds of peace before Griselda jumped up and insisted on claiming some lap space between the computer and Cassie's stomach. 'For goodness' sake, Gris, don't you know how awkward it is to have to type around you?' Cassie grumbled, as she gave the cat a stroke.

Once settled, with the laptop precariously balanced on her knees, Cassie reread the transcript she'd made of George Britten's will. He'd been a solicitor and apparently quite well off, owning a large house overlooking Regent's Park. Most of his estate had been left to his children, with a number of small bequests to various charities. But then there were the two odd bequests to the prison chaplain and another one, to someone whose name Cassie could not make out from the looped, old-fashioned handwriting. This one was for five hundred pounds a year.

She googled to find out how much five hundred pounds would have been worth in the late nineteenth century. 'A good living, in those days. Whoever you were, you were important in some way to my great-great-great-grandfather. A lover, perhaps? Or an illegitimate child?'

The next job, of course, was to try to establish the link between George Britten and the chaplain, Nathaniel Spring, trying to work out what had made him so important to George Britten, and what his 'time of greatest need' referred to. Cassie opened up an ancestry website and began a search for Nathaniel Spring.

Chapter 2

George, 1861

30th January 1861

Why is it, having left the school room at long last, that now I feel inclined to start a journal? My tutor Mr Smythe was dismissed just last week, now that I am full grown and almost of age. I hated writing essays, practising handwriting and penning arguments whenever Mr Smythe asked me to do them, but with him gone I find I want to write, for myself. I want to put down on paper my thoughts about my childhood, my current situation, and my plans and dreams for the future, such as they are. This leather-bound, lined notebook is just the thing for it. Ironically, it was a parting gift to me from Mr Smythe.

I am ashamed to say I did not think to give him anything, despite his having lectured and harangued and cajoled me over the last ten years. I assume my father gave him a suitable bonus on leaving our employ. Or a good reference at the very least. Mr Smythe leaves our employment to take up a post in a school, in west London. Twickenham is the place I heard him mention. I believe he has a sweetheart there and may well marry her before too long.

Having begun in a rather odd way with my previous paragraph, I think it is time I started properly. As Mr Smythe was wont to say, begin at the beginning, carry on through the middle and stop when you reach the end. I don't know what awaits me at the end of this journal, but I assume I will recognise it when I meet it, so for the moment I shall just begin, and see where it takes me.

My name is George Britten, and I am nineteen years of age, the second son of Albert and Augusta Britten, and younger brother to Charles Britten. There, that is the beginning and serves as a form of introduction, (though who will ever read this journal I do not know. I have no intention of ever showing it to anyone. Perhaps my future self might look back on these words one day, and smile in fond remembrance). I live in my father's house in a village in the northern part of the county of Hampshire. It is a small estate but a comfortable one and serves us well. As well as my parents and I, the household consists of a cook who is also the housekeeper, a couple of house servants, a groom and his two lads. My elder brother Charles stays here sometimes when he is not travelling abroad.

I was born into sadness – my sister having died only days before my birth. She was just three years old. Mother said I came early. Her grief at Elizabeth's death brought on premature labour, but I was a good weight, and survived. When I was two there was more sadness for our little family, as my other sister Isobel also died, at the tender age of ten. There were no more children after me.

You would think, perhaps, that I was spoilt, being the last born, the youngest child, surviving infancy while my sisters did not. You might think my parents doted on me, pandered to my every whim, wrapped me in the softest merino wools to ensure my safety. But I am afraid you would be wrong. Very wrong. When I look back on my childhood, I don't see a happy time. I see a time when, try as I might, there was nothing I could do to gain my father's attention or my mother's love.

My father makes no secret of the fact that Charles is his

favourite. As Charles is his first born I suppose that is to be expected. But he looks upon me as though I am vastly inferior, as though he barely counts me as his son at all. My mother is withdrawn, cold and unfeeling towards me. The loss of her daughters was more than she could really bear, I believe. Perhaps in fear of losing another child, she hardened her heart against those who were still living, though not to Charles, whom she too favoured.

Mother loves Charles. He left home last year, to set off on his Grand Tour of France and Italy. Mother wept as he left, clutching hold of him until the last possible moment. 'You are leaving me all alone and childless,' she'd said, and Charles had shaken his head. 'You still have George, Mother. He will keep you company while I am away. Give him a chance – he is a fine young man.'

I'd preened a little at this compliment from Charles, and he'd smiled at me. But Mother just laughed. 'He's no substitute for you, dear Charles. Keep yourself safe, and return to me soon.'

'I shall return to all of you,' Charles had said, and then he'd bade us all farewell, his last and longest embrace being reserved for me.

An imaginary reader of this journal might think I exaggerate when I say my parents paid me no heed throughout my childhood, and indeed appeared to look upon me as one might consider a poor, distant relation. Someone to whom they had a duty to care and provide for, but for whom they held no love or affection. But I do not exaggerate. Just last week, I overheard a conversation after dinner, between my father and his friend the doctor Jonathan Moore. Let me set down here what happened and what it was that I heard. Perhaps in writing it down it might help me come to terms with it.

We had finished dinner – a small dinner party for just our family and the Moores. The ladies – my mother and Mrs Moore – had retired to the drawing room, while my father and Dr Moore lingered over the port. As a man, and almost of age, I wanted to stay too, but a stern look from my father told me I was not welcome. I pushed back my chair, nodded to Dr Moore and left the room.

In the hallway I dithered a while. The ladies wouldn't want me with them either. I felt caught in the middle, not wanted anywhere. A metaphor for my life to date, I thought, as I lingered, trying to decide what to do with the rest of my evening. I became aware that the men were talking about me, and as the door to the dining room was not quite shut (I had failed to pull it firmly enough for it to latch) I could hear every word. It was as though I was rooted to the spot. I am not normally someone who would listen at keyholes, and indeed Mr Smythe would say it is an exceedingly low thing to do, but in my defence I would say that their voices were loud, and who would not stop to listen, on hearing their own name mentioned?

'I don't know what will become of George,' my father said. 'It is a shame we are not at war. If we were, I would buy him a commission. Fighting for his country would toughen him up. Lord knows he needs it. That tutor we employed – Smythe – was far too soft on the boy. Never thrashed him once, as far as I could tell.'

A commission! I suppressed a gasp at this. While I did not know what I wanted for my future, a commission in the army was certainly not it. I had no desire whatsoever to become a soldier.

'Hmm. Not all boys need thrashing,' Dr Moore answered. 'He seems a pleasant lad, well informed and intelligent. I'd say Smythe was good for him, from what I've seen. You could still buy him a commission – we need an army whether or not we are at war. But is it the right thing for him?'

'What do you mean, the right thing? Something needs to be done to make a man of him. He's too soft and sensitive, always reading poetry and wandering about the countryside looking at flowers. Women's pursuits.' Father snorted, and there was a moment's silence in which I imagined him taking a sip of his port and shaking his head sadly. It is true, though, I do love to read

13

verse and seek out rare flowers in the hedgerows and meadows of our beautiful countryside.

'The world needs all kinds of men, Albert old chap. Not just the tough soldier boys. There'll be a place for him in this world. You just need to help him find it.'

'He'll get no help from me. The house and estate will go to Charles. There won't be enough money to keep George for life. He'll have to find some sort of profession I suppose. But he shows no interest in the clergy, or medicine. What else is there?'

'Oh, there are plenty of professions beyond those, Albert. Law, or teaching, or business. Perhaps you should send him to Oxford or Cambridge. He's bright enough.' I raised my eyebrows at this. I had never considered a university career. I wondered whether I would enjoy life in academia. Perhaps I might. My musings were cut short by my father's reply.

'I can't afford to send him to university, Jonathan. And I don't see the point. I never went, so why should he? Yes, I suppose he will need to make his own way in business. I just don't see how he'll be any good at it. His head's always too much in the clouds.'

'What does Augusta think?'

'Hmph. She has less time for him than I do. You know, she never got over losing the girls. If she hadn't been heavily pregnant she might have been able to do more for Elizabeth. And George was sick with influenza just before Isobel died of that same disease. He survived it while she did not. I think poor Augusta never forgave him for that.'

'Hardly the boy's fault, though, was it?' Dr Moore said. 'There was nothing that could be done for either of your little girls, unfortunately, or for the other child. Don't forget I tended to them all during their final days, the poor mites.'

'I know. No one's blaming you. I just think that Augusta blames George, illogical though that is. She wastes no love or time on him, I'm afraid.'

'And yet you don't try to make up for this?'

Father sighed and paused before answering. 'I should, I suppose. But I find the boy hard to like. I will keep him until he is of age. I will pay him an allowance until he is established in some kind of profession. And then he will need to make his own way in life.'

'Well, I suppose if you don't like the boy, that's as much as you can be expected to do. Parenting is a difficult task. I am glad Amelia and I never had any children. I'd have been no better at it.'

I raised my eyebrows again at this last statement from the doctor. I had never before considered that parents could be good or bad at parenting. I had always assumed I must be unlovable, and that is why my parents didn't love me. Could the fault actually lie with *them*?

At that moment the drawing room door opened, and my mother came out, calling behind her to Amelia Moore that she was just fetching her latest bonnet to show her. She pulled up short on seeing me lurking in the hallway.

'What are you doing here? I thought you were drinking port with the men?'

'They didn't want me. I was on my way upstairs to my room.' I stepped on to the first step as though to prove myself.

'Oh. Good.' She pushed past me and climbed the stairs quickly, no doubt wanting to get back to the drawing room as fast as she could.

I followed her up, and spent the rest of the evening in my room, reading the poetry that my father sneered at.

That evening, as I said, occurred about a week ago. I have replayed what Father said many times, praying that he does not buy me a commission, for I know I would loathe being in the army. I know I will need to think of some kind of profession and find a way to build myself a career, but for the moment I have no idea what that should be. I should like to be a botanist but I cannot see how I can earn a living following that pursuit. For the time being, and until I am of age, I shall just have to remain here.

Now, at nineteen, and no longer under the tutelage of Mr Smythe, I can use this journal to explore my feelings and try to decide upon a desirable future course for myself, knowing that these pages will only ever be seen by my own eyes. Setting everything down in words may help me to look deep inside myself and determine whether I should harden my own heart against my parents and their apparent lack of regard for me, or whether I should continue to do what I can to impress my father and win the love of my mother.

It is late and I grow weary of writing by gaslight. I will continue tomorrow, for something important happened earlier today which I need to capture in my journal.

31st January

We have employed, as of yesterday, a new upstairs maidservant, to replace one my mother had found unsatisfactory in some way, although quite what was wrong with the previous girl whom I'd thought was pretty and personable, was unclear to me.

The new girl's name is Lucy. She is the sweetest-looking girl one could ever hope to see. Her hair is a light brown, wavy tendrils of it escape her cap and curl about her heart-shaped face. Her eyes are wide, their colour is hard to describe – in some lights they look brown, in others blue, and in still others, green. Perhaps I shall call them hazel. They are intriguing, mystifying eyes like none I have ever had the fortune to gaze upon before. Her figure is slight, trim, neat and efficient. We call women the weaker sex, but Lucy's bearing suggests a hidden, exciting strength. Were I a painter, I would ask her to sit for me; I would try to capture that elusive eye colour, that regal bearing, that aura of mystical beauty she carries with her.

She arrived mid-morning. I was on my way downstairs, considering taking my father's bay mare Bella for a gallop across the bare fields. He rarely takes the poor creature out, and the groom and stable hands have enough work to do without needing to exercise his horse. I met Mother as she conducted Lucy upstairs to show her the duties that would be expected of her. I couldn't help myself. Lucy's face, her figure, her bearing – everything about her was mesmerising and I am ashamed to admit it, I stared as she approached and passed me on the stairs.

She noticed. A tiny smile played at the corner of her perfect mouth, and if I am not mistaken, she pulled herself a little more upright, her shoulders a little further back, her chin a little higher, as she ascended and I stood gaping.

Mother noticed too. While I was still sitting on a chair in the hall, pulling on my riding boots, she came back down, having presumably left Lucy in one of the rooms upstairs. She approached me and stood before me, her face clouded with anger.

'I saw the way you looked at that girl. You steer clear of her, you hear me?' Her voice was low and hissing. I supposed she did not want the other house servant, plain, simple Maggie, who was busy blacking the grate in the sitting room, to hear.

I was shocked but not surprised by the venom in her voice. It is not the first time she has spoken to me like this. I tried to appease her. 'Of course, Mother. I was just struck by her beauty. I meant nothing by staring at her. What is her name, please?'

'The girl's name is Lucy Carter, though why you need to know that is beyond me. I am warning you, if you go getting her into trouble, I will throw you out, and make sure your father leaves you not a penny. Do you hear? Do you understand me?'

'I hear you, Mother,' I answered. 'Please be assured I would never do anything to harm her, or any other servant we might employ.' It's not in my nature to harm another human. Did she not know that? My own mother? Did she not know my character?

'You say that, but you're a man, and I know what men are like and what they are capable of, when their heads are turned by a pretty face. She comes with good references and I don't want to lose her. You'll keep your hands to yourself and your eyes averted, my boy. Your brother would not have looked at her like that. He, at least, is an honourable man. You are too much like your father.' She turned on her heel and marched back up the stairs.

I sighed. This was not the first time she had turned on me like that, for apparently no reason. But perhaps I had stared too much, too openly, and perhaps she was justified in her admonishment. I pulled on my riding boots and took Bella for the hardest gallop she'd ever had. We both came back sweating and exhausted, our thoughts only on refreshment and rest.

I was late for lunch, and it was already laid out in the dining room – a buffet of cold cuts, scones, pickles and pies. With no time to change or freshen up, I went straight in, pulled out a chair and sat down. Father was already seated at the head of the table, his plate piled high, his wine glass part-filled with a deep rusty claret. Mother was hovering at the sideboard, picking the choicest morsels of cold beef and ham. And Lucy, sweet-faced Lucy, was going around the table filling water glasses from a large ewer.

She smiled at me as I sat, and then she was there, beside me, her hip pressing slightly against my upper arm. 'Water, sir?'

Her voice, in just those two words, was melodious, rich, and was I imagining it or did I detect a tiny hint of mischief in the way she raised her intonation at the end of the short sentence, as though she was offering more than a simple glass of water?

I nodded, unable to trust myself to speak, as my mother was glaring at me from across the table. What I was not imagining was the pressure of Lucy's thigh against my arm, as she leaned across me to fill my glass.

And so this evening, as I write my journal, I find myself pondering the events of the day and the attractions of sweet Lucy, and wondering whether her pressure against me was accidental or intentional. I can reach no conclusion. I find myself half wishing Mr Smythe were still here to work through the puzzle with me, as though it were a mathematical problem or a philosophical question. But I am grown now, and the problem is my own, and only I can solve it. Why is this girl who I have set eyes on only thrice (the third time being at the dinner table where she once again waited on us) filling my mind so, and leaving no room for anything else?

10th February

Lucy is all I can think about. She fills my senses, my waking thoughts and my dreams with her presence. I find myself prowling through the house looking for her. I stand and watch her at her work, as she sets the dining table for the next meal, or crouches by a fireplace to black the grates, or passes a duster over a mantelpiece. I try to catch her on the stairs, and pass her, uttering what I hope is a cheery 'good morning' with a smile. She smiles back, and dips her head, and occasionally says to me, 'good morning, sir,' in her warm, melodious voice that seems to melt my insides.

And I have begun wondering, what would life be like if she and I could . . . I know our stations in life are vastly different but does that matter? If two people love each other, why does it matter that one is a gentleman and the other a servant? I think she does like me. We have had a few conversations – just a dozen snatched words as she goes about her work. Comments on the weather, on how well she has polished a sideboard, how hard it must be to keep all Mother's ornaments dust-free. I speak and she responds and smiles at me, and my day is made. For the first time I have begun to dream of possible futures for myself, and, I confess, in many of those futures Lucy features.

But today, something more happened that I must write here. I came across her in the drawing room this morning, and stood by the door watching her as she bent to plump cushions and straighten antimacassars. Her slim figure stretching over the sofa back was something to behold. She spotted I was there, and stood straight, turning to me.

'Come in, sir, please don't let me stop you.' She curtsied as she spoke, and tilted her pretty head on one side, and I felt my heart flutter. I entered the room, and sat on the sofa she had just finished straightening. To my surprise she didn't continue working, but stood before me. 'You like me, sir, don't you?' she said, and I blushed to my roots.

'I-I think you are a very fine servant. And a most b-beautiful young woman,' I stuttered.

She took a step forward and to my surprise and delight put a soft, white hand on my shoulder. 'And I think you are a fine young man.'

I confess, my mouth flapped a little like a fish out of water, and then I managed to squeak out some words and bade her sit beside me. The door to the room was almost closed; no one would see us. My mother's wrath would be fearsome indeed if she'd caught a glimpse of us together. Lucy sat, smoothing her skirts beneath her, placing herself close to me – so close that I could feel the warmth of her leg beside mine, and she turned to look at me, her mouth ever so slightly open, ever so slightly smiling at me. And I was lost for words. I wanted to lean in to her, breathe her scent, kiss her soft lips.

She tipped her head to one side, regarding me. 'You are lonely, I think?'

'I-I am. Yes.'

'Your parents pay you little notice.' It was a statement, not a question.

'You are right. Th – they don't much care for me, I think.'

'I understand. I have felt it too, in my own family. It is hard to feel unloved.' And then she put her hand over mine, on my knee, and she leaned towards me and kissed me on the corner of my mouth. I confess, here in my journal, that I was too surprised to respond in any way, and so I just sat there, open-mouthed.

She smiled again and then stood, breaking the spell. 'I must continue with my chores, sir. It has been nice to talk to you.' She dipped in a small curtsy once more and then turned away to continue dusting, as I sat there mutely and wondering what it all meant and whether it would happen again and resolving if it did I should kiss her back. But just as I decided to call her back to sit with me again, the drawing room door was pushed open and my father walked in, a newspaper under his arm.

Lucy curtsied to him, gathered her cleaning cloths and brushes and hurried out of the room. My father, I noticed, kept his eyes on her the whole time, a smirk on his face and a calculating look in his eye. I left the room, hoping to find Lucy still in the hallway but she had gone. Perhaps tomorrow I will find her again and we will be able to interact some more, and maybe I will even kiss her properly . . .

Chapter 3

Cassie

Cassie was still curled on the sofa with Griselda and her laptop when she heard her letter box flap shut as the day's post was delivered. But she was comfortable, and so was the cat, so she didn't immediately leap up to fetch the mail. She was busy with her genealogy research, peering at George Britten's will, trying to make out the name of the person to whom he'd left an annual stipend. The first name began with an M. But the quality of the scanned document was poor at this point, and combined with the clerk's difficult handwriting, Cassie could get no further.

'Hmm. Well, it's a job for another day, eh Griselda?' Her leg was going to sleep where she had it curled under her. It was time to move, pick up the post, make another cup of tea. She closed her laptop lid, put it on the floor, then gently pushed the cat off her lap. Griselda immediately curled up again on the warm spot Cassie had left. 'Hard life, being a cat, eh?' Cassie laughed.

On the doormat were a couple of pieces of junk mail, an electricity bill, and a handwritten cream envelope. Cassie put the junk mail in the bin, the bill in her 'to-be-dealt-with' pile that really ought to be tackled soon, and sat at her kitchen table to open the more interesting-looking envelope. Inside was a letter, written in blue ink in a rounded, unfamiliar hand. As she read it, she felt her heart beat faster and faster. A flush rose up her neck and her breathing became light and shallow.

'Oh my God,' she whispered. 'Bloody hell. Is this for real?'

She put the letter face down on the table and stared out of the kitchen window, trying to drag her maelstrom of thoughts into some kind of order. Of all the people who might have sent her a letter, this was the last person she'd have thought of. Not that she hadn't ever thought about this person, over the last eighteen years. She had, very many times. Almost daily.

She'd been eighteen, in her first year at university, doing an engineering degree. She'd got straight As in her A levels and had sailed into her top choice university, to her parents' undisguised pride. She was happy in her course, loving the freedom that student life brought, enjoying going out with fellow engineering students for beer and pizza on a Friday night. She had a part-time job she enjoyed, working as a lifeguard at a sports centre, doing one day at the weekend and one evening a week to help pay her bills. She'd made plenty of friends, and the world was at her feet.

And she'd met Arjun. He was in his third year on the same course. They'd met in a student bar one night and immediately hit it off. He'd become her best friend, her tutor helping her to understand some tricky concepts, her drinking partner and eventually her lover. She'd felt as though she could drown in his huge brown eyes with their impossibly long lashes. She loved his skin, smooth and dark as a ripe conker. She loved the way he was different to her in so many ways, his looks, his background and upbringing; and she enjoyed hearing stories of his childhood in India, his family customs, his favourite stories of Hindu gods. And she loved their nights together, curled up under his duvet in his room at the top end of the university campus.

She'd known, all along, that his parents expected him to return

23

to India after graduation, and find a job there. She'd known too that they would arrange a marriage for him, to some suitable girl of the right caste and background.

'And is this what you want?' she'd asked him, early on in their relationship, before she'd gone to bed with him.

He'd shrugged. 'It is how it is done, in India. My parents will choose wisely for me. I trust them in this.'

They were in their favourite corner of a campus bar. She'd gone to buy another round, still considering how it must feel to know your future is mapped out for you at the age of twenty-one. Returning to the table she put a new pint down in front of him. 'Must feel odd though, I expect.'

'Hmm? What must feel odd?'

'Knowing someone else is going to pick your partner for life for you. Don't you worry that you might not like her, or that you might fall in love with someone else first?'

He smiled. 'If I fell in love before my parents found a match for me I am sure they would accept it. But it's not likely to happen. I will graduate in six months, return to India to work, and then the match-making will begin. I am lucky in that I should be able to meet my bride plenty of times before we marry. I have friends whose marriages were arranged while they were abroad, and they only met their brides once or twice before the wedding.'

Cassie pulled a face. 'That must be terrible. I can't imagine . . .'

'You do things differently here. Neither way is right or wrong. Just different.'

And the conversation had then moved on, but Cassie had never forgotten his words. When they first kissed, she knew she'd only have five months with him at best. When they first slept together, she had four months. When his parents sent a first batch of photos of potential brides for him, she had three months left. He showed her the photos after some persuasion, and they had a night getting drunk and considering which of them was the prettiest, which the most motherly, which had the most intelligent gaze.

And then they'd gone to bed and made love with an intensity they'd never had before.

It had been on the tip of her tongue that night to tell him she loved him, to urge him to stay in England with her. But she hadn't, and the next day she'd been glad she hadn't. It wasn't her place to disrupt his life. If Arjun decided he wanted to stay with her, that was up to him. She wasn't going to push him into it, and risk him regretting it and resenting her at a later date. She'd known the score, all along. He'd never hidden it from her.

With two months to go until his graduation, he'd said nothing more about his future life. 'Let's live in the moment,' he said. 'The sun's out, we're young, and do you fancy another pint?'

With one month left, and a job offer from an Indian firm accepted, he'd shyly showed her a new photograph his parents had sent. 'So, this is likely to be the one. She works at the same company I will be at.' Cassie had gazed at the photo, her eyes refusing to bring it into focus. 'She looks lovely,' she said. The girl probably *was* lovely, and would make Arjun a good wife, and he seemed happy with the arrangement. There was no chance for her. She realised she'd always known this even though a part of her had dared to hope things might work out differently.

'Yes, she looks perfect for you,' she'd said, and she'd smiled at him, with a genuine desire that he should be happy. She was losing him already. There was a distant look in his eyes these days, as though a part of him was already back in India with this girl, whose name he had told her but which she had instantly forgotten. And she began trying to distance herself too, to switch off from him, to stop thinking about him every waking minute. He'd be gone in just a couple of weeks, and she would likely never see him again. Perhaps she'd find a new boyfriend in her second year or third year. She had plenty of friends, and wouldn't be lonely.

That last month flew by, and Arjun's graduation day came around. Cassie didn't attend – his parents had flown over from Mumbai and she didn't trust herself with meeting them. She'd say something totally inappropriate. Better to let him begin his new life. He was due to fly back to India with them two days after the ceremony anyway.

But on his last night, the day after the graduation, he sent her a text asking her to meet him in their old haunt. 'I have something for you,' the text read, and she imagined a small farewell gift. She steeled herself for the goodbyes, armed herself with tissues and met him with a smile on her face. He did indeed have a gift for her – a delicate silver necklace with a blue stone. 'Blue for forget-me-not,' he'd said. 'I will never forget you.' They'd had a few drinks, he'd kissed her, and then without speaking, without thinking, she'd led him back to her accommodation. They'd tumbled into bed and made love, slowly, tenderly, knowing it was for the last time ever.

He hadn't stayed the night. He'd showered and dressed in silence in the early hours while she lay staring at a damp patch on the ceiling. Even now, nineteen years later, she could recall the exact shape of that patch – something like a truncated map of Italy. Eventually he'd leaned over and kissed her.

'I guess this is it, then,' she'd said, forcing herself to sit up and smile.

'Yes. I think this is goodbye,' he'd said.

'OK. Goodbye, Arjun. Have a good life.' What did you say in these circumstances? She would never see him again. Better that way than to make promises to visit or remain friends, which they'd never be able to keep. 'Be happy.'

'You too,' he'd said, and she could tell his thoughts had already moved on to the day ahead and his return to his homeland. She'd patted his shoulder, lain down and yawned, as if she was tired and ready to sleep even though she wasn't. It gave him a way out. 'You need to sleep, so I'll be off,' he'd said, and with a final kiss – a chaste peck on the forehead – he'd walked out of her life.

There were a few letters and postcards that followed, and a wedding invitation that she ignored. And a photo of him in a traditional Indian wedding outfit, standing beside a hennaed woman in a red and gold sari, both garlanded with flowers, looking beautiful and smiling happily for the camera.

And then there'd been a blue line on a pregnancy test. They'd always been careful, but that last time, that unexpected final time, neither of them had had any condoms and neither of them had mentioned it. By the time Cassie found out she was pregnant, Arjun was married. She knew she could never tell him. She never wrote to him again, and the cards and letters from him petered out in under six months.

Now, Cassie checked the postmark on the letter. Leicester. Her old university town. The place where she and Arjun had met and spent so much time together. Their old stomping ground. The fact the letter had come from there brought a wry smile to her face, even while her insides were in turmoil. How she would respond to this letter she had no idea.

'I don't need to respond right away,' she told Griselda who'd followed her out to the kitchen. 'There's no need. I can sit on this for a while and think about it. Talk to . . . people. Mum and Dad. Yes. Talk to Mum and Dad about this.'

She was lucky – her parents despaired that she was still in what they considered a dead-end job, they'd been regretful when she'd dropped out of university, but they had always supported her in everything she did. Supportive, loving parents who provided you with a stable foundation were essential in life, she'd always thought. It was the main reason she'd dealt with her pregnancy the way she had. There was no way she could have provided the child with that kind of foundation. It wouldn't have been fair.

'We're your safety net,' her mum had told her, back then when she was nineteen and the crisis was at its head. 'Whatever you decide, we are there for you and we will help you in every way possible.'

All thoughts of her genealogical research had drifted out of her head now. It would all have to wait. For now there were more pressing things to think about. She grabbed a tissue, blew her nose hard, and picked up her phone to call her parents. With a bit of luck they'd both be at home, hiding from the bad weather just as she was.

Chapter 4

George

17th February

Already I have missed a few days of writing in my journal, and who is there to blame but myself? Or perhaps I might lay the blame at Lucy's feet. She has quite bewitched me. Her image fills my head every waking hour. Her voice in my ear, her scent in my nostrils, the touch of her hand on my arm, the memory of her shy kiss – there is no part of me that has not been fully given over to loving Lucy. Yes, loving her, for I am beginning to recognise the emotion for what it truly is now.

She has been here three weeks now, and a full week has passed since that eventful meeting in the drawing room, the meeting in which I believe an understanding passed between us – that we are of the same mind, and waiting only until the time is right to make our feelings for one another public. We have stolen other precious moments together as she goes about her work – a look, a few words, a gentle brushing of shoulders as we pass on the stairs.

Sadly there have been no more chances to sit side by side. But I know she understands me, like no other person does. She cares for me. I have come to realise that the family I have need not be the only family I ever have. In time I can build a new, more loving family of my own, one – I dare to dream – which includes Lucy by my side. It will not matter if my parents do not love me, if Lucy does. I could be happy with her, in a way that I have never yet been.

Now I must write of the events of this morning. It is Sunday so of course, the servants had the morning off to attend church. My parents attend only monthly, as duty dictates. They are not God-fearing folk. 'Where was God when I needed him most, when my sweet babies were dying?' my mother has been heard to say, thankfully not in the reverend's hearing. But I have attended weekly all my life – first with a nursemaid, then with Mr Smythe, and now alone. The church, St Michael's, is but a short walk up the lane, in the centre of our little village. It is a fine church, built some three hundred years ago in the perpendicular style, and I have always found my Sunday visits there pleasant and comforting, if not inspiring.

Today I set off early, intending to take a brisk walk up the hill behind the village before going to church. It was a fine, bright winter's morning, the kind February occasionally manages, when there is an unseasonable warmth and a stillness in the air, and spring seems just around the corner. The hill is known locally as Fairy Hill, for there is a ring of rowan trees upon the top, and it is said that the fairy folk gather there on midsummer's eve to dance and sing. I am not sure I altogether believe that fairies exist, but oh how wonderful it would be to see them at play! Regardless, it is a beautiful spot, with views in all directions. I go there often to soothe my soul and let the wind blow away my worries.

But today I was not alone. I had barely turned up the track that leads to the hill when my attention was caught by scampering footsteps, closing quickly on me. I halted and turned, and to my astonishment and delight, there she was. Lucy herself, holding her skirts to avoid tripping on them, her bonnet sliding sideways over her head, her face flushed with the exertion of running. When she saw I had stopped she stopped too, straightened her clothing and smiled at me.

'Sir, Mr George, sir, I am so glad to have caught up with you. Maggie said she had seen you come this way, and that you sometimes liked a walk before going to church.' She was breathing heavily from running, and I was fearful for her health. I motioned for her to sit down – the lane was bounded on one side by a low stone wall.

'Please, sit and rest a while. I am delighted to see you.' I sat beside her, checking whether there was anyone around who might see us if I were to take her hand.

'Thank you, sir. Just for a while.' She glanced sideways at me, a coy smile playing about her lips. 'If you were going for a walk before church, I do not want to stop you, only I wonder if . . .' Her words trailed away and she looked up at me, her eyes catching the sunlight and twinkling from green to brown and back again.

'You wonder what, Lucy?' I asked, shuffling a little closer to her on our stony seat.

'I wonder if you would be so good as to allow me to walk with you? I have been here almost a month already, but have never been further than the village . . . I hear there is a hill where the fairies are said to play? I should so like to see it.' As she turned to look at me a tendril of glossy hair escaped from its bonnet prison. I wanted to twist it around my fingers. What would she look like with her hair loose and falling about her shoulders?

I was struck dumb for a moment with this thought, and had to cough once or twice before I could speak. 'I should love to show Fairy Hill to you, and it is in fact where I was intending on going before church. If you are rested, it is this way.' I gestured along the path, and she stood and took my arm.

And thus we walked up the hill quite as if we were social equals. I almost forgot she was but a servant girl and I was the son of the master of the house. She told me of her childhood, growing up in a small house on the edge of Winchester, the daughter of a railwayman and a washerwoman. Her brothers, four of them and all older than her, doted on their pretty little sister, though her mother seemed to only have time for her sons, ignoring Lucy.

'Just as my mother is cold and unfeeling towards me!' I exclaimed, and Lucy nodded in agreement.

'We have much in common, Mr George, sir.'

Now all her brothers had jobs, two of them on the railways like their father and two of them in one of the new engineering factories that seemed to be springing up in every town. Lucy described the little red brick house she had grown up in, the cosy kitchen always smelling of newly baked bread, the small but immaculate front room they only used when visitors came, and the two bedrooms upstairs where the family had hung sheets to separate the rooms so that she could have some privacy from her brothers. It all seemed so different from the privileged childhood I'd had. My parents may not have spent much time with me but I had never gone hungry or cold, or been in need of anything else. Except love.

Lucy too had been deprived of parental love, as she'd confessed to me, and had also had to deal with being brought up in poverty. I could save her from that – I might not be my father's heir but I had money enough, and I would love her, as she would love me. There was a future for us if only I was brave enough to reach out and grasp it.

Lucy chattered almost incessantly as we climbed the hill. I listened, making a few brief comments, but mostly I thought about the delightful warmth of her hand on my arm, the occasional bump of her hip against mine, the side-on glimpses of her sweet face, which I stole at intervals, whenever I could trust myself to glance at her without raising a blush to my face.

Truth be told I have had very little experience of the fairer sex, if I may employ the phrase Mr Smythe used to refer to women.

Apart from my mother and our female servants, the only glimpses of women I have had have been at church. We rarely have visitors at home, except for the doctor and his wife. We never go anywhere, and there are very few families of quality, as my father puts it, in the area. I have no cousins, and few friends. I have led a sheltered, socially impoverished existence – I am well aware of it.

When my brother Charles comes home for a visit, he tells me tales of the balls he has attended, the theatre visits, the pleasure gardens he has strolled in, the acquaintances he has made. It seems there is as yet no special someone for my brother, but I assume it is only a matter of time. How odd that it should be I who have been first to find his life's partner!

I digress. Returning to my feelings as I ascended Fairy Hill with dear Lucy – I became aware that what I felt for this girl whom I had only just met, must be nothing less than love. I could barely breathe in her presence. I felt as though she infused every cell of my body, as though her essence ran through my veins. Without her I would not, could not live. Life would be nothing without her in it, now that I had found her.

We reached the summit of the hill. The day was still bright although a few white clouds were beginning to gather, occasionally drifting across the sun. The view from the top, glimpsed between the rowan trees, is astounding – I have always thought so – and I was gratified to hear Lucy's gasp as she looked about her.

'All those houses, over there in the distance, where is that?' She pointed towards the south.

'That is Winchester,' I told her. 'Your home town. Your mother, even now, is in one of those houses, I imagine.'

'So small they look! And there, is that . . . could that be the railway line?'

I followed her finger, looking west, and indeed, a plume of steam gave away the location of the line as it ran through a cutting. We watched, and the train emerged, heading north towards London.

'It's like a toy! I could reach down and pluck it from the tracks with my fingers!' She clapped her hands like a delighted child, and turned north-wards, watching the train. 'Such little fields, like a patchwork quilt thrown at our feet. And there – that house – who lives there? From those upper windows surely people can gaze up at this hill and maybe see us standing here, gazing down at them!' She giggled.

'That, my dear Lucy, is my father's house itself. Your home. One of those upper windows is my mother's room. Above it, on the top floor, why, that is your room!' I laughed gently at her, for not recognising her new home. But then, why should she? She had only lived there for a couple of weeks and had never seen it from this angle before.

'It looks so grand from here, does it not?' She took my arm again and squeezed it. I turned to her and there was a question in her eyes, a slight parting of her lips and oh! The moment was so perfect, so absolutely right in every way on this fine bright day, and I leaned in to her, lowered my head and kissed those full, soft lips, the way I had been dreaming of doing for so many weeks now, and it was exquisite.

'Oh my dear, dear Lucy,' is all I could say when we broke apart. Words were inadequate to express the way I felt at that moment, and as she said nothing herself but just smiled shyly, I could only guess that she felt the same way. I wanted to seize the moment, ask her right then to come away with me, to be my wife. But I was not brave enough.

Suddenly I remembered what day it was, and where we were supposed to be going. I took out my pocket watch. 'Lucy, we have delayed too long. The service begins in just fifteen minutes and I am afraid it will take us rather longer than that to go back down and get to the church. Unless we hurry . . .'

'Well then, we had better run.' She let go of my arm, picked up her skirts and began to scamper down the hill, back the way she had come, laughing with the sheer joy of being young and alive. I had no choice but to run after her; but it was fun, I was exhilarated and I was with my love. Life was perfect in that moment. I hoped we would not meet anyone – surely it must look as though I was running after her, and that, I am sure Mr Smythe would have said, would not be quite the done thing.

We were halfway down, making good progress, when a terrible, awful thing happened. Poor, dear Lucy turned her ankle on a rock. Down she went, crying out as she tumbled. Her bonnet fell off and her skirts flew up around her knees. I rushed to her aid.

'Are you hurt? Can I help you to stand?' I asked. I was so concerned for her, but somehow all I could do was flap my hands rather ineffectually around, not knowing whether I should lift her, or sit beside her, or examine her ankle which she was clutching with both hands.

'I am hurt, my ankle, ow!' She began unlacing her boot, and easing it off the affected foot. I hardly knew where to look. Mr Smythe had always told me women's ankles were not to be thought about by young men if they wanted to remain pure at heart. But here she was, removing her boot, and then rolling down her stocking to inspect the damage. I blushed, but realised that now was not the time for delicate sensibilities. This dear young maiden, the love of my life, was in distress, and I – I had to become her knight in shining armour.

I could see her ankle was swollen, red and angry-looking. 'Lucy, you will not be able to walk on that,' I said, taking charge. 'You will have to lean on me, or I shall have to carry you if that does not work. Which shall we try?'

She regarded me, as if assessing whether I was strong enough to carry her. I could not blame her for hesitating – I am not the beefiest of men. 'I think if I lean on you, sir, and you hold me tight, I may be able to hop, and we should be able to get down the hill in that fashion.' She sniffed, and I was horrified to see a tear run down her face. 'We will miss the church service for certain, now, won't we?'

'Yes. It cannot be helped. In any case, I must take you straight back to the house, and then send one of the stable lads for a doctor. Come, let me help you stand.'

Somehow, we got her to her feet, and I wrapped my arm around her tiny, perfect waist as she wrapped hers around my neck. She leaned into me and I became a crutch, and she was able to make progress by way of hobbling and hopping, stumbling and shuffling. She winced with pain at every step, and I wished I could absorb the pain for her, have it transmitted through her to me, to save her from having to suffer it.

The walk seemed so much further than it was on the way up, when she had chattered non-stop and I had revelled in her company. At last we reached the end of the path, and turned up the lane towards home, which we entered via the kitchen door. There was no one inside, of course; they were all at church. I bade Lucy sit on a stool while I fetched a bowl of water and a cloth, and tried to soothe her ankle with a cold compress. I gave her a glass of water to drink, and found a wooden chair onto which I lifted her, so the stool could be employed as a footrest. I put a small cushion beneath her foot.

All these ministrations served only to deepen my love for her, especially as she gazed at me with tears and gratitude in her wide, hazel eyes. I longed to kiss her again, right there, and take away her pain in that way, but I stopped myself. It would not have been the right thing to do.

I wanted to fetch a doctor for her – my father's friend Dr Moore lived but five miles away and would come if we sent a pony trap to fetch him. Or there is another, younger doctor who lives in the village. But I did not dare to leave her, and there was no one who could be sent. There was nothing I could do but look after her, and stay by her side, until the rest of the household returned from church.

Those hours this morning (was it really only this morning?) were both the longest and the shortest I have ever lived through.

The longest – because every minute was a minute more that my beloved was in pain, and the shortest – because every minute was a minute more that I spent alone with her, with a good, sound reason to lay a comforting hand on her shoulder, or gently wipe away a tear, or press a newly cooled cloth against her ankle.

Finally, a commotion in the hallway and simultaneous rattling of the kitchen door told us the household had returned from church. Maggie, our simple-minded downstairs maid, was first to find us. She stood in front of us, gaping like a goldfish, until Mrs Peters, our cook and housekeeper, caught up with her.

'What are you doing just standing there, Maggie? Go and get the fire lit in the drawing room, where the master and mistress will want to be sitting. Go on with you, now, oh!' She gasped when she saw Lucy, her foot on the stool, her skirt pulled up to her knee and her lower leg bare. And I, kneeling at Lucy's side. 'Oh, Master George, whatever are you doing?' She calls me 'Master' George as though I am still a boy. She has known me all my life, so I suppose it is to be expected.

'I have hurt my foot,' Lucy said, 'and Mr George has been taking care of me.'

'We must send for a doctor immediately,' I said, standing up. 'Are the stable boys back? Maggie, go and tell one of them to run for Dr Madeley and tell him to come quickly.'

'Let me look, first,' said Mrs Peters, smiling at me kindly. She bent down and carefully felt around the injured ankle, causing poor Lucy to wince with pain. At that moment a bell jangled, and I looked up at the array of bells over the doorway. It was the drawing room bell. No doubt my father was wondering why no one had come to light the fire, or my mother was wondering where her post-church pot of tea was. 'Maggie, go and tell the master Lucy has had a mishap and then light the fire.'

All these conflicting instructions seemed to upset the poor girl, for she stood in the middle of the kitchen, flapping her hands and opening and closing her mouth. Mrs Peters, usually so kind and patient with her, shook her head in frustration and hurried out to the hallway herself. She was back a moment later with my father.

'A sprain, I think, sir, but best to let the doctor check in case there are broken bones,' she was saying as she entered.

'Broken bones? Oh, surely not!' I could not help myself from exclaiming.

'George, that's enough. Stand aside, and let me see.' Father bent over Lucy, and the poor girl had to endure yet another set of hands prodding and poking her swollen ankle. He felt all around, not just her ankle but further up her calf, to above her knee. She gasped, which he took as a sign of pain, and instantly apologised.

'I think it is not broken, but you will need to rest. Damned nuisance but I suppose it cannot be helped. We must get you upstairs to your room where you can rest. Come, put your arms around my neck and I shall carry you.'

'Father, I can help, she can lean on me,' I said, seeing the chance of having her dear slender arm about my waist once more disappearing.

'George, you may leave us now. Go and tell your mother what has happened.' Thus was I dismissed, like an errant schoolboy. I did as I was told, with a mere backwards glance at my beloved, hoping to catch her eye. Perhaps I could visit her in her room later, take her some refreshments, perhaps. But she was not looking at me. Her eyes were upon my father, and his, I saw with dismay, were upon her.

Chapter 5

Cassie

'Come round,' Cassie's mum, Shirley, told her, as soon as she'd managed to tell her why she was calling and why she was crying, after summarising the contents of that letter. 'You need us. Come and stay for dinner. Are you all right to drive? Or shall I send Dad to pick you up?'

Cassie wiped away tears and fought to get a grip on herself. 'I'm all right to drive. Thanks, Mum. See you in about an hour.'

She showered and changed then drove the twenty miles to her parents' house. They still lived in the house she'd grown up in – a detached villa on the edge of a village in West Berkshire. She'd never appreciated it when growing up, but as an adult, driving the quiet lanes back to the village and going for walks in the countryside direct from the house, she realised how lucky she'd been. She passed the village primary school, and the bus stop where she'd caught a bus to Reading every morning to go to secondary school.

Her parents' gravel drive was covered by a huge puddle – every time it rained this happened, and every time her dad would shake his head and mutter about getting something done about the drainage, as he'd done for the last thirty-five years. Cassie loved that nothing ever really changed here. Just like in the rest of her life. Nothing ever changed. Until now.

She parked her car and tiptoed over the puddle to the front door, which stood open, her mother waiting with open arms. 'Oh, love. What a shock it must have been getting that letter! Come on in. I'll make some tea and we can talk it through. Your dad's in the sitting room.'

Cassie kicked off her wet shoes and went through. Her father, Tony, was sitting in an armchair reading a newspaper. A log fire was blazing in the grate. He put his paper down as soon as she walked in, and stood up to hug her. 'Hey, Cassie. You OK? Your mum making some tea, is she? Come on, sit down by me. Such a miserable day – it's not that cold but I lit the fire to cheer things up a little.'

'Thanks, Dad. I love an open fire.' She sat on the sofa nearest the fire, and stretched out her feet to warm them. They made small talk for a few minutes, until Cassie's mum came in with the tea and a plate of scones.

'Made them this morning,' she said, placing the tray on a coffee table and taking a seat beside Cassie. 'So. This letter.'

Cassie took it out of her bag and passed it over, watching silently while both her mother and father read it. She kept no secrets from them. She never had. Unless you counted that slight pang of loneliness and dissatisfaction with life that she occasionally felt, and about which she had not told anyone, not even her parents.

'Bethany. A pretty name, that,' said Dad, as he passed back the letter.

'I always wondered what she'd be called.' Mum took a sip of her tea and looked over the rim of the cup at Cassie. They were waiting to hear her reaction to the letter before they said anything, she realised. They'd take their cue from her, and would support her no matter what. It's what they'd always done.

'She's eighteen?' Dad asked, filling the silence.

Cassie nodded. 'The age I was, when . . .'

'You were nineteen when she was born,' Mum said.

'Yes, when she was born. Still eighteen when I met Arjun and . . . well, you know.'

'Do you think she'll try to find him, as well?' Dad frowned a little. 'He has a family in India, doesn't he?'

Cassie shrugged. 'He does. I don't know if she will – she hasn't said. Or maybe she already has tried, and just didn't mention it in this letter. I mean, in her position, I guess I'd want to do one thing at a time. It must be pretty emotional for her, too.' She choked back a sob, and her mother leaned over to hug her.

'It's emotional all round, love.' Mum picked up the letter and scanned it again. 'Lovely letter. Warm and thoughtful. I imagine she spent a lot of time getting the wording just right.'

Cassie tried to picture Bethany – her daughter – sitting in a bedroom writing draft after draft of the letter. The letter said her adoptive parents knew she was doing this. Had she shown them the letter, to get advice or approval? If it had been her, she would have. Bethany had always known she was adopted, she'd written, and had used a family-finding service to track Cassie down. If Cassie would like to write back, or speak on the phone, or meet her, Bethany would be delighted, but she would understand completely if Cassie didn't want any contact.

The letter was neatly handwritten on good quality paper that Cassie imagined she'd bought especially for this purpose. She ran her hand over the page. Her daughter had held this letter, leaned over it, folded it, licked the seal on the envelope. Her daughter. Eighteen years ago Cassie had held her, looked after her for a few days in hospital, breast-fed her the first milk – colostrum – that was supposed to be so beneficial for newborns. And then she'd handed her child over to the social worker and turned to her mum and sobbed on her shoulder.

'We'd have brought her up,' Mum had said through her tears as the social worker left the room cradling the baby. 'Tony and

I – we'd have done it. You could have the life you wanted, go back to university, do all the things . . . and we'd . . .'

But Cassie had not wanted that. She knew her parents had enjoyed the freedom that came with middle age when children were grown – there was only her, but they'd always put her first. Once she'd left home for university they'd been able to put themselves first; do what they wanted to do. She couldn't send them back to square one with a newborn. She couldn't let them bring up her baby as her sister.

Over the years she'd wondered how it would have been, if she'd made a different decision. If she'd allowed her parents to do this for her; for her daughter. If she'd been able to watch her grow up, see her take her first steps, speak her first words, attend her first day at school. If she'd played the role of doting older sister, and bought her presents, taken her out, played with her . . .

But there was no going back. Her daughter had been adopted very quickly by an older, childless couple. She'd been sent one photo of them cradling her, a look of love so intense on both parents' faces Cassie had been almost unable to look at the photo. She'd tucked it away somewhere.

Now, holding the letter her daughter had sent, she had a sudden desire to see that photo again. She'd left it in her parents' house. In her old room. 'Excuse me a minute,' she said, putting the letter down on the coffee table.

Upstairs, she went into her old bedroom, which looked much as it had done on the day she finally moved out for good. After dropping out of university and having her baby, she'd lived back here for another couple of years, commuting by bus to her job in Reading just as she had done throughout her secondary school career. She'd since cleared out some of her old stuff so the room could be used by guests, but there was a lot still there. Including her old homework desk, with its lockable drawer, its key sellotaped underneath the desk in the back right corner. Here she'd locked her diaries, Christmas presents she'd bought her parents, a packet of condoms, her cigarettes during the brief period in her mid-teens when she'd thought smoking was cool.

The key was still there. And inside the drawer along with those old diaries and half a pack of condoms that were long past their use-by date, was an envelope with the photograph inside it. Cassie took it out, sat on the bed, and with shaking hands studied it closely. There she was. Her little girl, whom she'd just called 'Baby' for the few days she'd spent with her. There was Bethany, at two weeks old, with the parents who'd taken her in, raised her and loved her, and supported her in her quest to track down her birth mother. Bethany. Her daughter.

She stroked the photo with her thumb, as she sat there contemplating how best to respond to the letter. At last, she went back downstairs, clutching the picture. Her parents had been talking quietly, urgently, but stopped as she walked in and looked up at her expectantly, ready to take their cue from her.

'So,' she said, sitting down next to her mum again, 'I think I need to write back to her.'

'Will you meet her?' Mum took the photo from Cassie, to look more closely at it. Bethany was their grandchild, Cassie realised. A generation removed, but they must be going through the same tumultuous thoughts as she was.

She nodded, slowly. 'Yes. I think I will.' Out of the corner of her eye she saw Mum catch Dad's eye, and the two of them smiled at each other. She'd made the right decision, then.

But Cassie didn't want to rush a reply. Let it brew a while, she decided. Let the precise wording take shape, piece by piece, over a couple of days or so. She knew Bethany would be on tenterhooks waiting for her reply, watching the post and checking her email frequently. But it was important to get this right. Absolutely right. And she knew she needed to give herself a bit of time to get used to the idea that she was about to make contact with her daughter.

She talked all this through with her parents, over a roast

dinner, a bottle of wine, and an impromptu night spent in her old teenage room. Thankfully she had the next day off work anyway. It was the start of half-term, and at the end of the week and the weekend she'd be busy running holiday activities at the sports centre, and supervising hordes of children in the swimming pool.

She arrived home before lunch, promising her parents she'd keep them informed at every stage, and would visit them again on her next days off. Her laptop was still on the sofa where she'd left it, and Griselda was meowing crossly at her for having been abandoned overnight. 'Ah, poor sweetie,' she said. 'But one night alone hasn't hurt you, and look, you still have some dried food in your bowl. You didn't go hungry.' Even so, she threw out the remains and gave the cat some of her favourite pouched food. Griselda ate it hungrily, her back turned to Cassie in disdain.

Armed with a cup of tea, she returned to the sofa. Griselda would forgive her in about ten minutes, and would no doubt want a comfy lap for as long as possible. Cassie reread Bethany's letter for the hundredth time, then set it to one side. 'Give yourself time, girl. Don't rush a reply,' she told herself. To take her mind off it, she decided to return to her research. She was back at work the next day, and there'd be no more time to get back to it for a week.

In some ways, researching your family tree was only what Bethany had done. The difference was, Bethany had tracked down an ancestor, or set of ancestors if you included Shirley and Tony, who were still alive. Cassie was only looking for people and their friends and family who were long dead. That was easier. If you found them, and didn't like what you found, you weren't upsetting anyone, other than perhaps yourself. She found herself thinking about her genealogy hobby. All those episodes of *Who Do You Think You Are?*, all those celebrities finding their families – it was all connected in her mind. Tracing ancestors because she'd given up her only descendant, and as the years went on she felt unlikely to have any others.

She decided to spend some time checking back on George Britten. Where had he been living in each census? Maybe this would give a clue as to who those people mentioned in his will were. Perhaps he'd lived with them at some stage.

She logged onto a genealogy website and, beginning with the 1891 census, the one she'd first found him on, she worked her way backwards, noting down all details of each census entry. In the later ones George was living in a house near Regent's Park. 'The posh part of London, eh George?' He'd clearly had money. In 1871, however, he was living as a lodger, with a family named Smythe. In 1851 he was a child living with his parents Albert and Augusta Britten, in a house near Winchester.

But it was the 1861 census return that made her gasp. At that time George was an inmate of Millbank Prison.

'So I guess this is when you met the chaplain, Nathaniel Spring, then?' she muttered, noting down the details. What had he been in prison for? Were there prison records available online? If it had been a serious crime, it might have been reported in the newspapers . . . She opened up a newspaper archive website and searched for George's name, the word *Millbank*, and dates before the census of 1861. He'd only have been nineteen at the time. Young to have been in prison.

It took her a little while but at last she found a short article from *The Times* that made her gasp again and stare at the scanned document, unable to believe what she was reading.

Nineteen-year-old George Britten, the younger son of Albert Britten from North Kingsley, Hampshire, was yesterday sentenced to fifteen years with hard labour for the murder of a young woman who worked in his family home. The judge commented that Britten would have been given the death penalty, but for his youth and the fact that he had confessed and showed remorse. Britten is now incarcerated at Millbank Prison.

'Murder! And there was me hoping he'd just stolen something, or embezzled some money perhaps,' Cassie said to Griselda who'd come to join her on the sofa. She read the article again. George had been lucky not to be hanged. If he had been, Cassie, her father and even Bethany would never have existed. 'Thank you, unnamed judge, for your leniency.'

It was always a risk – when researching genealogy – there was always a possibility you might uncover a skeleton in the closet. Something that made you feel uncomfortable about your ancestors. George Britten was a good few generations removed – her great-great-great-grandfather. There'd been enough diluting of the gene pool since him – she wouldn't be carrying too many of his genes. But what about Bethany's search for her birth mother? For all Bethany knew, Cassie could be a murderer herself. Or simply a really unpleasant person. It had taken real bravery for her daughter to begin this search, she realised. She'd had no idea what or who she would find, and yet she'd taken that big step into the unknown.

She deserved a response from Cassie. Sooner rather than later.

Cassie closed her laptop lid and put her research to one side. She'd think more about George the murderer later. She grabbed a notepad and began drafting a letter to reply to Bethany. It would take several goes to get it right, just as she guessed that Bethany would have had several attempts at her letter. How do you even begin a conversation with the daughter you last saw at five days old?

Chapter 6

George

18th February

I was unable to visit Lucy again yesterday. I went to the kitchen and asked Mrs Peters if I could help with running up the stairs to take Lucy some refreshment, while she lay resting her injured ankle in her attic room, but the housekeeper smiled fondly at me and shook her head.

'Bless you, no, Master George. Maggie is perfectly capable, and indeed she has just been up with a bowl of soup for our poor invalid. 'Tis kind of you to offer, though.'

I was of less use than the simple kitchen maid. It was my father who helped Lucy up to her room, and then sat with her until the doctor arrived. I do not know what they talked about during that long time – it was over half an hour before Dr Madeley arrived – though I believe I heard giggles, and was pleased to think that Lucy was well enough to laugh. I confess, here in my journal but nowhere else, that I sat on the stairs to the second floor, within earshot of Lucy's room, while my father was in with her. I told myself it was so I could be of assistance, if called, but if I am to be honest, it was so that I could pretend I was still, almost, in her presence.

I leapt to my feet when I heard Maggie open the front door to admit Dr Madeley. He came bounding up the stairs carrying his battered leather bag, and I met him at the foot of the stairs to the attic floor. 'The room on the left,' I told him. 'My father is tending to her.' I like Dr Madeley. I don't think he is very many years older than me. He is only recently qualified and down from Oxford. He moved to the village last year, working for a brief while alongside Dr Moore who is my father's friend, but who has now all but retired from doctoring. His verdict was as Mrs Peters had suspected – a bad sprain, no broken bones. He prescribed bed rest for a week, followed by light duties for a week, but only if the ankle was bandaged and could bear weight without pain.

My mother grumbled. 'Only a month employed and now we have to feed and lodge her without getting any work out of her. We should send her home.'

'But she can't travel by herself, and I can't spare the phaeton or a manservant to take her. She will have to stay here while she recovers. She will be no trouble,' my father told her.

'Well, she'll have no wages while she's unable to work,' Mother said, and Father nodded his agreement. Thankfully all this took place downstairs, out of Lucy's sight or earshot.

I resolved to pay her wages myself, out of my allowance. I had money in a bank account that I could draw on.

22nd February

Lucy remains in her room. I am forbidden from entering, though I did manage to sneak up this afternoon, only to find her sleeping. How beautiful she looks at rest! Her cheek was soft and creamy against the rough blanket that covered her. Listening hard I could just hear the gentle sounds of her breath, her chest rising and falling in rhythm. I dared stay only a minute or so, but it was enough to refill my senses with her. There will come a time, I hope and dare to dream, when I will wake daily to the sight of her sleeping peacefully at my side.

I had not set foot in her room before. I glanced around, before I left. How plain it was! A small wooden chest sat under the window. On the washstand was her maid's cap and some hair pins. Hanging on a hook behind the door was her cloak and the dark dress she had been wearing yesterday. On the wall hung an embroidered sampler, instructing the reader to trust God in all things. I recognised it as one my mother had made some years ago.

I wanted to sit at her side and wait for her to wake up, but I heard someone's steps on the stairs, and quickly darted out before I was discovered. I hid in the darkened end of the corridor. It was my mother, bringing in a bowl of soup for Lucy. Unlike me, Mother had no qualms about waking Lucy up.

'Soup, girl. You need to build up your strength and get back to work.'

'Yes, thank you. It's a shame, though. I rather like things the way they are,' Lucy replied, to my astonishment.

'How dare you! I shall speak to my husband – we will send you home.' I was not surprised by the venom in Mother's tone, but it was Lucy's next words that made me gasp.

'Speak to him, by all means, madam. But I think he rather likes having me here. He has been very . . . *kind* to me.'

Mother sounded as though she was spitting with fury. 'Kind! Is that what you call it? I shall keep him away. And George, too. Thank goodness Charles is not here, though *he* would not be fooled by you.' At that she marched out of the room, her back ramrod straight and chin high.

I waited until she had descended the stairs before moving. And then I ventured into Lucy's room once more. She greeted me with a bright, wide smile, and patted the side of her bed.

'Please, Mr George, do sit down a while.' I wondered whether she had guessed I'd heard what passed between herself and Mother. If she did, she gave me no sign of it.

We talked for a little while, and then I inched closer and took her hand, wondering whether she would allow me to kiss her again. She regarded her hand in mine, and then looked up at me. 'Mr George, please tell me, who is Charles?'

'My brother. He is away in Italy at present.'

'Older than you?'

'Yes, by some years. He is not expected home until much later in the year, probably the autumn.'

I smiled at her, and once more shuffled a little closer, but she withdrew her hand from mine and turned her face away. 'I am a little tired now, Mr George. If you could pass me that soup . . . and then afterwards I shall sleep.'

I did as she bid, but confess I was a little saddened by her rebuff. I had thought – no, hoped – that we were reaching an understanding, but she had very clearly dismissed me. I left her, pulling the door closed after me. I had much to ponder on. Lucy's words to Mother about Father being 'kind' to her – is that where I was going wrong? I had paid her attention but . . . maybe there was some other way to win her love. A gift, perhaps. I should buy her something beautiful. Something that reflected the love I felt for her.

Yes, the more I thought of it the more I decided this was my best course of action, and resolved to follow through with this plan tomorrow.

23rd February

It was an early start for me today. I ate a hearty breakfast, following which I informed my mother I would be out for the day so I would need no lunch.

'Oh, really? Where are you going?' she asked, without so much as a glance in my direction.

'I have business to attend to in Winchester,' I told her, using the phrase I have so often heard my father say. He was not at the breakfast table. I wondered whether he was perhaps checking on Lucy's health this morning.

'Business?' At this, Mother did raise her head to frown at me. 'What business could you possibly have to attend to?'

'Just a purchase, Mama. I shall be back this afternoon.' I turned to leave before she tried to stop me. But it seemed she wasn't much interested, for she had resumed eating her breakfast and gazing out of the window.

I set off, with my cloak around my shoulders, my top hat on my head, and a walking cane of Father's which I'd borrowed from the hall stand. Looking in the hall mirror on the way out, though I say it myself, I thought I looked most grown up and dapper. If only Lucy could see me now; but I dared not risk a visit upstairs. Mrs Peters, my father and Maggie have been constantly in and out of Lucy's room, fetching and carrying, attending to her every need. She wants for nothing, and for that I am grateful.

I walked to the North Kingsley railway station. It was a gloomy day, with heavy clouds stretching from horizon to horizon, threatening to release their contents at any moment. I was glad of my cloak.

I had only to wait a few minutes for a train, and it is a short journey to Winchester. The High Street runs near to the splendid cathedral, which dominates the city. On another occasion I would have dropped in, to gaze at the stained glass, marvel at the ornate choir stalls and also to have a few moments alone in quiet contemplation. But there was no time to be lost today. I started at the station end of the High Street and called into every jeweller's shop I could find, looking for the perfect present.

Eventually, after much fruitless searching, I found just the thing. A beautiful, silver hand mirror, with sapphires and pearls set around the rim and in the handle. The stones sparkled as I inspected the workmanship – I could picture her smiling at me

51

out of the mirror, her eyes shining as bright as the sapphires. It was expensive – it would take several months' allowance – but Lucy was worth it. Worth every penny. The jeweller, a weasellylooking man with greasy hair and bad breath, encouraged me.

'A fine piece, sir, and guaranteed to impress any young lady who should be lucky enough to receive such a gift.' He coughed slightly. 'I take it the young sir is indeed buying this as a gift?'

I did not want to divulge my reasons for the purchase to a stranger. What business of his was it anyway? I had half a mind to leave the shop and try elsewhere, but the mirror was so perfect that I could not bring myself to do it. 'I'll take it,' I told him.

Initially the man would not accept my credit but when I gave him my address and asked him to send the bill there, he relented. My father, it seemed, had done business with him before. I made it very clear that this time the bill should be addressed to me, and not my father. I walked out of the shop with the mirror wrapped securely in waxed paper, and made my way to a coffee shop for refreshment before returning home. When I gave Lucy the mirror, she would understand. She would know then the depth of my feelings for her, and see that I was a generous man, one who would do anything for the woman he loved, and it would help her to realise she loved me too. Such was my plan.

I was back home by mid-afternoon. The promised rain had fallen as I walked home from the village station, so I was drenched by the time I got inside. My instinct was to run upstairs as fast as possible, burst straight into Lucy's room, and present her with the gift, but decorum told me to divest myself of my wet clothes, smarten myself up, and tap on her door before entering.

And so I took a few minutes to prepare myself before making my way up to the attic floor. Had I not, had I instead followed my instinct and gone straight up, how differently things might have turned out!

I had to change all my clothes, being so very wet. The paper around the sapphire mirror was by now torn and useless, so that had to be discarded. I had no other paper to wrap the gift in, so I used a scarf. I would unwrap it for her – I imagined her reclining on her bed watching me carefully unfold the scarf to reveal its contents. She would gasp and exclaim, both at its beauty and value and at my thoughtfulness for providing her with something she needed, for I had noticed there was no looking glass in her room. She would gaze at me anew, seeing me properly for the first time, not just as the young master of the house, but as her suitor. Never mind the class differences. There would be a way in which we could overcome those.

As I redressed myself in dry clothes I allowed my imagination to rush ahead, to see myself walking arm in arm with Lucy up Fairy Hill, her foot recovered; walking again to the church, then home from the church as newlyweds . . . I may be but nineteen years old but I know my own mind, and I knew that Lucy was the only girl for me.

Those thoughts, those hopeful happy thoughts for the future, were running through my mind just a few short hours ago. How quickly things can change.

So now, however difficult it may be, however tortured I feel, I must get on and put down in this journal what happened when I did finally make my way up to dear Lucy's room. With my clean clothes on, my hair smoothed and the mirror bundled up in the scarf, I tiptoed, heart pounding, from my room to the stairs that led to the attic floor, and quietly went up. I am not sure why I was trying to be so quiet, but that is how it was. On reaching her door I found it slightly ajar, and there were odd noises coming from within, panting, gasping, moaning. Fearing that she was unwell, perhaps choking or in pain, I pushed open the door without tapping first.

And oh, the sight that awaited me. I can hardly write these words. I was sickened to the core, to see my father, his trousers down, his buttocks exposed and pumping up and down as he lay on the bed. He did not see me – he was too absorbed in his act. Under him lay Lucy, her face buried in his shoulder, her hands clutching at his back. It was she who was moaning, and not in pain or fear. Thankfully she did not notice me either.

I left as quietly as I had arrived, pulling the door back to the position it had been in, and shakily went back to my room. I wanted to dash the mirror to the floor, let it shatter into tiny pieces just as my dreams of a life with Lucy now lay shattered at my feet. But it was too valuable. I hid it at the bottom of a drawer and sat down on a chair by the window. I stared out of the window, watching the sun emerge from the clouds now that the rain had stopped. A pair of amorous pigeons were cooing and showing off to each other on the garden wall. I envied them their simple life. They found a mate and that was that. They didn't have to watch their own father snatch away their love from under them.

The image of his white buttocks heaving away at her surfaced once more and I buried my head in my hands. One short hour earlier I had the world at my feet, but now I was drowning in grief, having lost everything. What was I to do? What future was there for me now?

Chapter 7

Cassie

'Good couple of days off?' Andy asked Cassie. They were supervising a dozen kids on a trampolining session, one of the many holiday activities the sports centre offered during half-term.

'Er, yeah. Went to see my parents,' she replied, keeping her eyes fixed on the child currently on the trampoline.

'Nice. How are they?'

'Fine, yeah. Whoa, there you go.' The little girl had misjudged a bounce and come too near the edge of the trampoline. Cassie put her hands up to gently nudge the child back to the middle. 'Small bounces, then build up; try to stay in the middle, OK?'

'You seem, I dunno, distracted?' Andy said.

'Distracted? Er, no. Just concentrating on . . . the job at hand . . .' She was glad she had an excuse not to look at him directly. Her thoughts were in turmoil since sending an email to Bethany, late the previous night. She'd spent hours drafting it, but had only sent it after drinking a couple of fortifying glasses of wine. There'd been no reply yet, but of course at work she couldn't easily check her emails.

'Well that's good, but if there's anything . . . I mean if you need to talk about anything, well, you know where I am.' Andy motioned to the child to stop bouncing. 'Right then, that's your turn over. Careful climbing down. OK, who's next?' A boy in his young teens was up next. He'd clearly done some trampolining before, and immediately began a routine of high bounces, sits and turns.

'Can I try a front somersault?' the boy asked.

'Have you done them before?' Andy replied.

'Yeah. They're easy. I'm in the club. Do them all the time.'

'All right then. Cassie, be ready . . .' She already was, standing at the end of the trampoline, ready to give him a nudge if he landed badly. There were deep crash mats all around the trampoline. The boy made a few more high bounces, arms neatly windmilling backwards, and then on his next bounce tucked in tightly and executed a perfect somersault.

Cassie and Andy both clapped, while the other children who were watching and awaiting their turn, whooped and cheered.

'Impressive,' Andy said, and the boy grinned.

Despite the theatrics, it was all Cassie could do to keep her attention on the trampolinists. Her mind kept wandering onto Bethany. Had she found the right tone in her email? She'd wanted to sound friendly, not pushy, willing to meet up but happy to follow Bethany's lead. When would Bethany reply? Had Cassie typed the email address in correctly? Maybe she'd mistyped it . . . Would she get a 'not deliverable' response? Or would it go to someone else? She'd included her phone number. Would Bethany ring her? What if she rang while Cassie was at work? What if she texted, and Cassie read the text at work and couldn't stop herself crying?

Yes, it was fair to say she was a little distracted. Should she talk to someone – confide in Shania, perhaps? But Shania was not working today. Andy, then? But Andy was the boss. You didn't tell the boss your personal problems. Her parents knew she'd sent an email. She'd sent a text to them immediately after clicking 'Send' on the email. And she'd had a 'well done, good luck, here if you need us' response immediately after.

She glanced at her watch. She was working until six today. Perhaps she'd phone her parents this evening and talk it all through. By that time she might even have had a reply to the email. The thought sent a rush of blood through her veins.

'OK, guys, we're out of time,' Andy was yelling. 'Your tickets cover you for a swim, and we'll have the inflatables in the pool in about half an hour.' He helped the last child off the trampoline, then turned to Cassie. 'You really are not quite with us today, are you? Should I get someone else to cover your poolside shifts? It's going to be busy in there with all this lot and the inflatables.'

'Yeah, I mean, no, I'm fine.' She forced a smile. 'I'll grab a coffee before I go poolside. Didn't sleep too well last night.' That was the understatement of the year. If it hadn't been for the wine she'd drunk she would probably not have slept at all.

'Ah, that'll be it, then,' Andy said, with a worried glance at her.

They packed up the crash mats and trampoline, returned them to the equipment store, and made the room ready for its next activity, which was a yoga class. And then Cassie headed up to the staff room for a coffee, and to check her phone.

There was no response as yet. Cassie wasn't sure whether to be relieved or disappointed. She drank her coffee quickly, then went to take her turn poolside, relieving Toby. And now, with hordes of children shouting and squealing and clambering about on the huge inflatable island complete with mud hut and palm tree that took up half the pool, she absolutely *had* to keep her mind on her job.

'Drink after work?' Andy asked her later on, when her poolside shift was over. 'It'll be just you and me. Toby's playing five-a-side this evening.'

It was tempting – Cassie always liked a drink or two in the pub at the end of the working day. But she had a feeling Bethany would send a response this evening. And she wanted to be home when it arrived, reading it in private. Bethany might even phone. 'Ah, sorry Andy. Got to . . . wash my hair.'

'Wash your hair? I wasn't asking you as a date – just as a work colleague. Oh well. An evening at home with the TV for me, I guess.' Andy shrugged and pouted, and left her alone.

Cassie frowned. Of course he wasn't asking her out as a date. They always had drinks out – there'd usually be several staff members in the pub. Had it ever been just her and Andy? She thought back – no. Never just the two of them although she'd often been for drinks with just Shania, or Ben. Why had he felt the need to say it wasn't a date?

She had another half hour before she could leave. Her time was spent swilling down the wet changing room floor, checking all toilets were stocked with loo roll, emptying waste bins, tidying up the equipment store. Menial jobs that didn't help her take her mind off Bethany.

At last the end of her shift rolled along and she changed out of her work tracksuit and into jeans. It was all she could do to stop herself checking her phone. 'Wait till you're home, Cassie,' she told herself. 'Half an hour.'

It seemed like the longest walk home ever. And then she forced herself to make a cup of tea, before finally sitting down on the sofa, joined within seconds by Griselda. She opened her laptop.

Yes, there was a reply to her email. With shaking hands she opened it and read the contents. *Awesome . . . so glad you responded . . . was really scared you wouldn't . . . would love to meet . . . any chance of Saturday . . . live in Leicester but happy to travel . . . where is best, maybe London? . . . maybe better to speak on phone first . . . whatever suits!*

The phrases washed over her as she read the email several times, taking in its chatty tone, imagining meeting Bethany at a London railway station, in a café or pub, or asking her to come to Reading, or travelling up to Leicester herself. What was best to do?

58

Or phone. Bethany had included a phone number. Cassie could just ring her, right now. *Any evening after six . . .* It was six-forty. Was Bethany at home, with her adoptive parents? Or in student digs? Apart from saying she now lived in Leicester she had given no clue as to her current lifestyle. Cassie did a quick calculation. Bethany had been born in March, and it was now late October. At eighteen and a half she'd have completed her A levels in the summer. So now she might be a first-year university student, or maybe she was retaking A levels, or maybe she'd started work, or maybe she was taking a year out.

Cassie reached for her phone and punched in a number.

'Hey, Mum. It's me. She's replied to my email. Wants to meet. Or to talk on the phone. What should I do?'

'Oh, love, that's marvellous. What do you want to do?'

'I don't know what's best! Maybe a chat on the phone first, and arrange a meet-up . . .'

'That sounds like a good idea. Probably better to talk first.'

'I hate the phone, though. Maybe if we met up and went for a walk somewhere . . .'

'Yes, that would work. Side by side is easier than face to face, and perhaps better than over the phone . . .'

The conversation drifted on, back and forth, for twenty minutes or more. Finally Cassie's rumbling stomach made her remember she had not yet eaten. And as usual her parents would not make a decision for her, but would clearly support her whatever she chose to do.

She thanked Mum, rang off, ordered herself a pizza and poured herself a glass of wine, left over from the bottle she'd opened the previous night. And then she sent Bethany another email, saying that Saturday was fine, and suggesting they meet at the café in St James's Park in London at midday. The weather forecast looked fine – they could have a coffee and then stroll through the park, sit on a park bench, and just chat.

Perfect! See you then! I'll be wearing a yellow coat. The response came within minutes of her sending the email. Cassie smiled, picturing her unknown daughter sitting in a student's room, clutching her phone as she awaited incoming mail. A yellow coat – a bold colour! If Bethany had inherited her father's dark colouring she'd look stunning in yellow.

Cassie pulled out the baby photo once again, and searched her memory. Bethany had been born with a shock of black hair, and skin just a shade or two darker than Cassie's own. What would she look like now, as a young adult? Well, in three days' time Cassie would find out. How she would get through the next few days she had no idea, but somehow she would have to.

Saturday inched around with all the momentum of a tortoise wading through treacle. Cassie spent half an hour deciding what to wear, eventually sticking with her usual attire of jeans, a jumper and a leather jacket. She drove to the station and caught a train to London Paddington, arriving far too early. She spent an hour mooching around some shops, before walking slowly through Hyde Park and Green Park and finally into St James's Park. Even so she still had plenty of time, so she sat on a bench overlooking the lake, watching children feed the ducks.

It was a peaceful scene, but Cassie did not entirely feel at peace. What would Bethany be like? What if they didn't get on? She found herself looking closely at everyone who walked past, peering especially hard at young women with dark hair. Was one of them her daughter?

At last, five minutes before the time they'd arranged to meet, she stood, stretched, and walked the short distance to the café where she picked a table on the outdoor terrace, from where she had a good view along most of the approaching paths. She sat down, tucked her bag between her feet, and prepared to wait and watch. Around her, the trees were just beginning to turn, promising glorious autumn colours in another few weeks.

'Excuse me? Are you Cassie Turner?'

The voice came from behind her, and Cassie realised she hadn't even looked at the other tables to see if Bethany was already there. She leapt up, knocking her chair over.

'Y-yes, that's me, oh, shit. Oops, sorry. Damned bag strap caught round my feet. God. Not usually so clumsy. Are you B-Bethany?' She kicked the bag away and looked up at the person who'd addressed her.

Tall, dark-haired, with smooth caramel skin. Beautiful, smiling broadly and trying not to laugh, but were those tears in her eyes? Cassie opened her mouth to speak again but no words came out. Bethany was feeling the same, it seemed, for her mouth dropped open as she mouthed the word 'yes' in answer, and then Cassie found she could no longer focus on the girl for the film of water that had gathered over her eyes.

'Oh my God,' she whispered, and then, almost as though they'd choreographed the moment, they opened their arms and fell into each other's embrace. 'Bethany. *Baby*.'

'Cassie. Mu . . . Mum.'

They stood clasping each other for a minute, Cassie breathing in the scent of Bethany's hair, but then the urge to look at her, really *look* at her, was stronger than the urge to hold her for longer. She gently pushed the girl away, to arm's length, keeping a light touch on her upper arms. 'Let me look at you. God, you're beautiful. This is so . . . so amazing . . .'

'I'm gonna need to find a tissue,' Bethany said, pulling away from Cassie to rummage in her bag.

'Yes, me too.' Cassie laughed, and found her own tissue, then picked up the chair she'd knocked over. 'Shall we sit down? Have a coffee? Or walk through the park?'

'I'm desperate for a tea,' Bethany said. 'Coffee for you?' Cassie nodded and Bethany went straight over to the counter to order. She was slim, wearing skinny black jeans and a yellow coat, and yes, the colour suited her. She was tall – far taller than Cassie. Arjun had been tall, she remembered.

61

When she returned with the drinks and sat down opposite, Cassie reached across the table to take her hand. 'I'm sorry, I just want to keep contact for a moment longer. This is so amazing. But . . . you must have lots of questions . . .' Like why I gave you up, she thought.

'I do, yes, but happy to just chat about anything, if that's easier. Or maybe I tell you my story and then you tell me yours?' Bethany smiled and gave Cassie's hand a squeeze, which brought tears to her eyes again.

She nodded. 'Yes, that'd be good.'

'Well. I always knew I was adopted. Mum and Dad are lovely – really nice people and I had a happy childhood. When I was tiny they used to say they'd gone to a hospital to get me, and that my real mum had been sad to see me go but wanted what was best for me. They never really changed from that story. When I turned eighteen I told them I wanted to find you, and they supported me one hundred per cent. They even sent me money for my train fare today.'

'Your parents sound lovely.'

Bethany took a sip of her tea – Earl Grey, Cassie noted, the same as Arjun used to drink. 'They are. Did you ever meet them? I mean, I don't know how it works, but when I was handed over . . .?'

'No. But they sent me this via the social worker, a couple of weeks after.' Cassie pulled out the precious photo – though it didn't seem quite so precious now she had the real, grown girl in front of her.

'Aw, I love that photo. I've seen it before – Mum and Dad had a copy of it on their mantelpiece for years.'

'It was the only one I ever had of you.'

There was a moment of silence, and Cassie picked up her coffee, cradling both hands around it. The day was sunny but there was a bit of a chill in the air and she welcomed the warmth in her hands.

'Anyway, to finish my story, I'm a student now, at De Montfort

University in Leicester. Studying fashion and textile design. Mum and Dad live in Warwick – that's where I grew up.'

'I love Leicester. All the history there, Richard the third and everything. I was a student there too for a while, at the other university. And your degree sounds fascinating.' Cassie had no artistic ability. She tried to remember whether Arjun had – not that she recalled. She swallowed. It was her turn to tell her story, and the first question on Bethany's lips was almost certainly going to be: why did you give me up?

Bethany was sitting, smiling expectantly at her. It was time. Cassie took a deep breath, and told the story of meeting Arjun at university, knowing all along their relationship could not last, getting pregnant by accident just before he left to start his new life in India.

'So he was Indian. I only knew he was Asian.' Bethany was silent a moment, and Cassie allowed her the time to assimilate this new information. 'Did he know you were pregnant?'

Cassie shook her head. 'I never told him.'

'Wasn't that a bit . . . unfair on him? Didn't he . . . deserve a say? I'm not saying you were wrong, but . . .'

'I felt at the time it would be unfair to burden him with the knowledge. We'd intended to end our relationship then. I didn't want him to feel guilt or responsibility . . . when he had someone else waiting and relying on him back in India. I . . . well I guess I wanted to give him the best chance at his new life. If I'd told him, he might have . . .'

'Decided to stay here with you?'

'That would have been the wrong thing to do. He was lovely, we were great friends, but I don't think we'd have lasted long term. The relationship was as good as it was because it had a time limit on it, I think. Does that make any sense?'

She shrugged. 'I don't know. I think I need . . . time to process it. So I suppose adoption was inevitable then . . . you were, what eighteen? Same age I am?'

'Nineteen by the time you were born. My parents offered to help me if I wanted to keep you, but I . . .' Oh God. How was she going to explain this? 'I wanted the best for you. And I didn't think I could offer you that. Even with their help. It was . . . not an easy decision.'

'I guess you wanted to go back to uni. I get that. I do. Maybe I'd even do the same in that situation.' Bethany smiled, her eyes full of tears and understanding.

Cassie shrugged and gave a half-smile. 'I never did go back, though.'

'Oh! Why not? I mean, if you want to tell me . . .'

'I don't really know why not. I felt different. I felt as though . . . I wouldn't fit in, anymore.'

'Because you'd had me.' Bethany made it a statement, not a question.

Cassie shrugged again. She didn't want her daughter to feel in any way responsible for Cassie not having finished her degree. After all, it didn't matter, did it? She'd managed all right without a degree. She was in a good job – well, good enough – and had a life. Of sorts. 'Because I was different. Anyway, now I live in Reading, in a little flat, and I work at a sports centre.'

'Cool job! And . . . sorry, Cassie, but I've got to ask . . . did you have any other children? Do I have any brothers or sisters?'

Cassie shook her head. 'No. Never met the right person. What about you – did your parents adopt anyone else?'

Bethany twisted her mouth a little. 'No. Wish they had. I always wanted a sibling. A big family.'

Was that part of the reason she'd wanted to find her biological mother, Cassie wondered, to see if she also had siblings? Cassie was herself an only child, but she'd always been so close to her parents, she'd never felt the lack of brothers and sisters. Maybe Bethany felt differently.

Chapter 8

George

1st March

I have been walking around in a state of utmost distress and confusion these last few days. If Mr Smythe were here, what would he advise? No, if Mr Smythe were here, I would not be able to confide in him. How could I tell him what I'd seen? That his employer was taking advantage of one of the servants in the most heinous way? A girl I had dreamed of building my future with? No. There was no one I could imagine telling, ever. I would have to carry this horrible secret to the grave.

Lucy. Could I confront her, ask her why she allowed it? Or did she allow it – perhaps, terrible though the thought may be, perhaps he forced himself upon her? I have veered from thinking that must be the case, that it is the only explanation, to remembering her moans of pleasure and the way her hands clutched at my father's shoulders, as if to pull him even deeper into her . . . the image, once more in my mind, makes me shudder. I decided not to confront her outright. But I would go to see her, start a conversation, perhaps steer it in that direction, and give her a chance to confess, to explain or apologise. I did not even know what I expected or wanted of her. But she deserved a chance.

I waited until my father left the house late this morning. Under no circumstances did I want a repeat of my last attempt to visit Lucy. I went first to my own room, where I took the sapphire mirror out from a drawer and gazed at it. Just two days ago I had purchased it, and imagined her delight when I gave it to her. There was still a chance – depending on if and how she explained herself. If she was sorry; if she'd had no choice, then perhaps we could start again, and put her affair with my father behind us.

I would have to take her away from here, I realised. Away from my father, as soon as possible. Though how I would manage to afford to keep us I do not know. My allowance is to remain small until I come of age at twenty-one. Even then, as the second son, I will not be very well off. I must take up a profession of some sort – though I still know not what – and earn enough to keep myself. My brother Charles will inherit this house and its lands.

When I heard the front door close, I ran to my bedroom window to peer out and saw my father mounting Bella. He had spoken at breakfast of paying some social calls in the area. I had at least until lunchtime. I tucked the mirror away again, and once more tiptoed up the stairs. This time Lucy's door was closed. I hesitated – perhaps she was asleep? But I had to see her. I tapped, gently, and received her answer, 'Come in.' The thought flitted through my mind that perhaps she would think it was my father. I would scrutinise her expression – see if she was disappointed or relieved when she saw it was me and not him.

'It is I, Lucy,' I called, as I entered. 'I have come to see if you are recovering, since your dreadful accident.'

She smiled kindly at me, as though I was a child. She looked neither disappointed nor relieved. I did not know what to make of this.

'I am recovering well,' she said, 'though I still cannot walk on my injured foot. I am glad you came up – I have been hoping for a chance to see you again.'

My heart soared at this. She wanted to see me! I looked about for somewhere to sit – it didn't seem right to sit on her bed. There was a small wooden chair in the corner, so I pulled that towards the bed and sat there. 'I have been waiting for an opportunity to come up again, Lucy,' I said. 'I have offered many times to Mrs Peters to bring you up your meals but she always sends Maggie.'

'Yes, poor Maggie. She is having to work very hard while I am unwell. I wanted to see you, Master George, to thank you for helping me home that Sunday. It is such a shame. We were having such a pleasant walk and chat, until this happened.'

'Perhaps when you are better, we could walk up there again?' And start again, I hoped. The feel of her hand on my arm might help to erase the image of my father in her bed.

'Ah, if only we could.' She sighed. 'But it will be a long time before I am able to walk that far. And a long time before I have another half-day off, and when I do have one, I shall have to use it to visit my family. We will have to postpone that idea until another day, Master George.'

I had the impression she was looking on me as though I was a child, and many years her junior. Yet at most she was a year or two older than me. I wished I could make her see me as a man. She'd cooled towards me, it seemed. Perhaps since hearing of Charles's existence. Perhaps since bedding my father. I was clearly the lesser catch. From her point of view, I realised, there was little to gain by her offering me favours or even befriending me. I could do nothing for her.

The idea flashed into my mind – I might sit on the bed after all, put my hand on her hip, lean over her and kiss her, maybe even push her back and do to her what I had seen my father doing. She'd allowed him, maybe she would allow me. Thankfully, I am glad to be able to write, no sooner had the thought formed than I banished it from my mind with extreme force. No, I wasn't that kind of man. I was not like my father. Though I longed to gain his respect, he had lost much of mine by his actions in this room.

'Tell me,' I said suddenly, 'do you like your master here?' The words slipped out before I realised what I was about to ask, and my tone was a touch harsher than I intended. I watched her carefully as she answered. This would give me clues as to whether we might possibly have a future together. My whole life depended on her response.

Her eyes widened. 'Your father? Yes, I think he is a fine man.' She stared towards the window for a moment, then smiled and shook her head slightly. 'A very fine man.'

I left her alone then, with a promise to send Maggie up with a fresh jug of drinking water. I was confused. Could she be in love with my father? But he was married, and much, much older than her, and he was her master, and it was all wrong. What did she want from him? I could have coped with the idea that he was forcing himself upon her. I could then have been her rescuer, taking her away from here, away from him, to a place of safety where she could perhaps learn to love me in time. But if she admired him and wanted him, then there was no place for me. I descended from her room feeling bitter and lost.

And what of my mother? What had she done to deserve such treatment – her husband unfaithful and her housemaid complicit? My heart broke for her. She might not love me but I did not want to see her hurt like this.

7th March

My mother and father had a disagreement today, over luncheon, and it was concerning Lucy. I fear something I said to Mother this morning may have been the trigger.

We had breakfasted, and I was lounging in the drawing room with a newspaper, uncertain what to do with myself. Since realising there is no chance for me with Lucy – and indeed, I am now unsure I would want her, even if she came to me begging and apologising – I have been unable to settle to any occupation, and today was no exception. I was flicking the pages of the paper back and forth, sighing and fidgeting. Eventually my mother, who was sitting in the window seat sewing a sampler, put down her stitching and regarded me.

'George, if you cannot sit quietly I would ask you to leave the room. You are disturbing my concentration.'

I folded the paper and placed it on a side table. 'Sorry, Mother. I'm distracted. Perhaps I will take Bella for a ride.' I glanced out of the window, only to note that it was raining heavily. I sighed again. The ride would have to wait.

'There you go again. Sighing like a consumptive girl. If you can't stop yourself then please leave the room.' She picked up her stitching once more.

I have never been able to confide in my mother. She has never seemed inclined to listen to my worries or woes, though she and Charles used to sit for long conversations in the afternoons. It is many years since I tried to interest her in my innermost thoughts. Today was no different – I was not about to tell her of my love for Lucy and how it had been thwarted by my own father, but nevertheless I wanted to say something to her, and gauge her reaction.

I recalled the conversation I had overheard after Mother dismissed Annette, our previous maid, only a week or so before Lucy arrived. 'If you can't keep your eyes off her, Albert, then the girl must go,' she'd said. 'I won't be made a fool of again. God knows the consequences of the last time, if it *was* the last time, have rumbled on down the years.' I had not spent much time thinking through what she'd meant by that.

Perhaps what I said next was capricious; perhaps it was a product of my heartbreak. Whatever it was, I could not help myself, and the words slipped out of their own accord.

'Mother,' I said, 'do you think Father is spending rather too much time visiting the maid, Lucy? It is kind of him to be so concerned for her well-being, but is it proper for him to be so often alone with her in her room?'

She put down her stitching and stared at me.

'What do you know of this?'

I stopped myself from telling her the whole truth, fearing what it might mean for Lucy. She'd rejected me in favour of my father, but despite that I did not wish to see her in trouble. 'Only that I have seen him several times on his way to her room. That is all, Mother. Think nothing of it.'

'I'll think what I like of it,' she snapped. 'If that girl has turned your father's eye, she won't be the first, but she will most certainly be the last. I won't allow such a thing to continue. I'll finish her. I'll . . .' She glanced at me as though she'd forgotten I was there, then stuffed her sewing into a basket and swept out of the room.

I sat for a moment wondering what I had done, then noticed the rain was easing off. I needed air and exercise, and something to take my mind off Lucy, so I spent the rest of the morning riding Bella hard over the fields.

By the time I returned, luncheon was already underway. As soon as I had removed my riding boots, I went straight into the dining room. My parents were already seated. Mother glanced at me, and then looked at my father.

'Albert, I have come to a decision. The new maid, Lucy, has done no work for a fortnight. What is the point of keeping a girl who cannot work? This afternoon I will instruct John Lincoln to take her back to her parents' house using the pony trap. I will soon find another girl to replace her. Someone older and more reliable.' She said this firmly, her gaze never moving from him. I realised she was telling him she knew what he was up to, and this was her way of saying *stop this now, and we'll say no more of it.*

But it seemed he didn't want to stop. He put down his knife and fork. 'No, Augusta. We will not dismiss the poor girl. It is not her fault she was injured, and we will not throw her out. We are good, fair employers and we will stand by her and give her a chance to prove her capabilities when she is fully recovered.'

'She is a waste of space. She is costing us money to feed and she is giving nothing back,' my mother persisted.

'She will repay her debts in time. She is staying.' He thumped the table. 'I want her to remain here. And that is my final word on the subject.'

Mother pressed her lips together, and glanced sideways at me. I did not know whether to be glad Lucy was to stay or not. A part of me now wants her gone, out of my life, so that I may try to forget her and move on. But a larger part of me knows I can never forget her. I still care for her, despite everything, and want to be sure she is safe and well. Even if that means enduring the knowledge that my father is visiting her room daily.

I find myself siding with my mother who is the victim in all this. It is unfair on her – she has to stand by in silence while her husband takes his pleasures elsewhere. Perhaps Mother is right – Lucy must go, for the sake of peace in our family. Perhaps I could persuade her to look for work elsewhere when she is better. Somewhere away from my father so she no longer turns his head, and our family can be at peace once more.

After luncheon was over I paid a visit to Mrs Peters, hoping that perhaps there was something that might need to be conveyed upstairs to Lucy, allowing me the opportunity to talk to her about my idea and warn her of what my mother now knows. But Mrs Peters seemed in a bad mood too – she was clattering pans around and muttering to herself, about 'that useless girl, no better than she ought to be, making more work for everyone.'

'Mrs Peters, do you mean Maggie?' I asked, gently. I was perplexed. Usually Mrs Peters had plenty of time and patience with our simple yet always sunny kitchen maid.

'No, Master George, I do not. I mean the other one – Lady Muck upstairs, expecting us to all run round after her. I confess

I do wish the master and mistress would get rid of her, one way or another, and let's employ someone more useful.'

'Is there anything I can do to help?' It was all I could think of to say. So now only Father's affair with Lucy was keeping her in her job.

'Bless you, no, child. But thank you for asking.' Mrs Peters smiled at me and shooed me out of the kitchen, as she had so many times when I was a young boy. When, I wonder, will anyone treat me like a man?

Chapter 9

Cassie

Sometimes Cassie really hated her job, when it meant she had to work at the weekend. And this week she had a Sunday shift, the day after her meeting with Bethany in London. A Sunday she'd rather have spent mooching around her flat, letting her thoughts coalesce into some sort of pattern. A Sunday of poring over the few photos she'd taken of Bethany, and the selfie they'd taken together – laughing, arms around each other, looking for all the world as though they were any other mother and daughter (if you didn't notice the film of tears in their eyes). She'd kept that selfie to herself so far. She'd sent her parents one of Bethany on her own in the park with a gorgeous tree in its autumn foliage behind her. She'd phoned them too, to give a brief account of the day, and promising to visit on her next day off to tell them more.

Today she'd rather be pulling both herself and her flat into order. But no – she was down for the early shift. A seven o'clock start, working through till three p.m. She'd stay on after for a swim. And maybe she'd go to the pub, if any of the others were. She had very little food in the flat and no inclination to go food shopping so a pub dinner appealed. And a few drinks would help relax her.

She tugged on her work tracksuit in the gloom of the late October morning, and walked to work through a grey drizzle. So different to the bright sunshine she and Bethany had had in London. Memories of strolling through the park, talking constantly, laughing a lot, grabbing sandwiches from a convenience store then taking them back to the park to eat as a picnic, hugging as they parted with promises to meet up again the following Saturday. A happy day with her daughter. And that was a sentence she'd never thought would apply to her.

It was a busy day at work. Being the last day of half-term and poor weather meant that every teenager in a twenty-mile radius had decided to come swimming. The pool was packed all day and Cassie had to use her whistle many times to admonish kids who were becoming too rowdy or doing something dangerous. Her head was pounding by the end of her last poolside stint. Thankfully the hour from three-thirty to four-thirty was adults only, so if she had a cup of tea in the staff room at the end of her shift, then dawdled getting changed, the pool would have thinned out and she'd be able to have a decent swim.

A good forty lengths of rhythmic crawl helped clear her head. When she finished her swim, changed and went back to the staff room to gather her belongings Andy was waiting for her. 'Fancy a pint? You can't use the hair-washing excuse today – you've just been for a swim!'

She grinned. 'Sure, why not. Who else is coming?'

'Ben, I think. Possibly the Sunday Girls.' He was referring to Belinda and Lorraine – two students who worked every Sunday.

'Great. Red Lion?'

'Where else?'

A short while later Cassie and Andy were sitting at their usual table in the pub, each with a pint. Cassie was perusing the pub menu, debating whether to go for pie and chips or a more healthy roasted vegetable salad.

Andy was peering at his phone. 'Hmm. The girls aren't coming, apparently. They have a house party to go to.'

'Aw, shame. Was hoping to catch up with them. Ben still coming?'

'As far as I know.' But a moment later Andy's phone pinged with another apology. 'Ah, no, he's not. His mum's summoned him.'

Cassie and Andy each rolled their eyes. Whenever Ben's mum called he would drop everything and rush round to do whatever it was she needed. Privately Cassie thought she took advantage of him. She'd call to say the grass was getting long, and he'd drop his own plans so that he could drive a fifty-mile round trip to cut it for her. And yet the woman could easily afford to pay a gardener, or at least wait until Ben's planned next visit. But, each to their own. 'Poor Ben,' she said. 'His mum wiggles her finger and he goes running.'

'Could be an actual emergency this time,' Andy said. 'We shouldn't judge. Everyone has their own particular relationship with their parents.'

'No, you're right. So just you and me, then.' Suddenly she felt shy. She'd hoped for a night of laughter and banter in the pub. A night going back to her old, simpler life. Now she felt it was only a matter of time before she blurted out to Andy that she had a grown-up daughter whom she'd met for the first time yesterday. But would that be such a bad thing? He was more than a good boss. He was a friend, and he was always sympathetic and kind and wise.

'So, what did you get up to yesterday?' Andy asked, as though he'd read her mind. 'Anything exciting?'

'Exciting – yes. You could say that. Buckle up, it's a long story.' And then she told him about Bethany, and her letter, and their meeting. He listened carefully and in silence, a small frown between his eyes, and didn't interrupt her at all, just let her tell the story in her own way and in her own time, even when she stumbled trying to find the right words. Even when unbidden tears came to her eyes, as she related how she'd felt seeing Bethany in her yellow coat.

75

At last she fell silent, and picked up her pint for a long pull. It felt good having told someone the whole story. Andy kept quiet for a moment longer, as though he was waiting to see if she was going to say anything more. When she didn't, he said quietly, 'Wow. Wasn't expecting that. So . . . you're seeing her again?'

She nodded. 'Next Saturday, in London again.'

'That's fantastic. You're really making a connection.'

'She makes it very easy.'

'Have you told your parents? They're her grandparents, of course.'

'Yes. They are happy to meet her, if or when she wants to meet them. That'll be weird for them, I guess, as they'd offered to bring her up.'

'The grandchild they never had.'

'Mmm.'

'And will you meet her adoptive parents?'

Cassie shrugged. 'I don't know. Right now I don't think I could, but one day, maybe. It's all early days, yet.' She took another sip of her beer then realised Andy was looking at her with a quizzical expression on his face. 'What?'

He shook his head. 'Sorry. Just . . . it's big news, and I'm trying to take it all in. Like, when you think you know someone and they really surprise you . . .'

'In a bad way?'

'Not at all. I've known you, what, four years now? Worked with you, been down the pub with you, got drunk with you after Emmy dumped me, thought I knew all there was to know about you. But I was totally wrong.'

'No one knows everything about another person though, do they?'

'No. And it's made me realise that we all have hidden depths.'

'You'd thought I was shallow?'

Andy shook his head again. 'No, no. That came out all wrong. I mean . . . well I guess I mean . . . I'd like to get to know you better. Thought I knew you after four years working together but

76

I don't, and I'd like to.' He picked up his own pint and turned away a little as he drank from it.

Cassie didn't respond. Was he saying . . . that he wanted a closer relationship with her? One that went beyond co-worker friendship? That was not something she felt she could deal with right now. Although, his words had sent a little frisson of excitement through her. She glanced at him. Was he blushing? He was. Oh God. She looked away, and found a TV screen showing a rugby match in her line of sight.

'Munster have just scored,' she said. Anything to change the subject.

'What?' He turned to see what she was looking at. 'Oh. Didn't have you down as a rugby fan.'

'Me? All those men in tight shorts? What's not to like?'

He laughed, and they were back on track, bantering and joking and relaxing into each other's company. Cassie felt relieved, in a way, that someone unrelated to her now knew about Bethany. Someone she'd be able to talk to, share each step of the journey of getting to know her daughter. As to what she felt regarding what he'd said about wanting to get to know her better – well, she wasn't thinking about that. Who knew what he meant. She decided to forget he'd ever said it, and just continue with things the way they had always been.

Saturday rolled around and Cassie set off by train to London for her next meet-up with Bethany. This time she wasn't as nervous – she was simply excited to be seeing her daughter again and spending time with her. They'd arranged to meet in Kensington this time, and visit a museum or two. Bethany wanted to go to the Victoria and Albert design museum as she was doing a module on nineteenth-century design trends as part of her degree.

Meeting her again was as lovely as Cassie had imagined it to be. They hugged, Cassie complimented Bethany on the striking red jacket she was wearing this time and Bethany commented

77

that Cassie looked glowing and happy. They had a coffee in a nearby Costa, then headed off into the museum.

Cassie found she was only half concentrating on the exhibits. She was far more interested in chatting to Bethany as they wandered around, swapping stories and anecdotes about their lives. Bethany stopped in front of a few exhibits in the fashion rooms, taking diligent notes in a sumptuous notebook with a deep red velvet cover.

'That's gorgeous,' Cassie said, reaching out to touch the silky cover.

'I know. I have a bit of a thing for lovely notebooks,' Bethany said.

'I'd be too scared to actually write anything in it.'

Bethany smiled. 'But then it's just a piece of clutter. If you don't use it, it doesn't fulfil its purpose and then it's not a notebook, but just an object. To me, it's more beautiful for having my notes written in it.' She scribbled a few words and made a quick sketch of the late Victorian bustle dress they were standing in front of. A lovely attitude to have, Cassie thought, delighted that she'd found she could learn something from her daughter.

After spending some time in the fashion rooms they went to the museum's café for lunch, chatting continuously about what they'd seen and what they liked.

'I'm not much into clothes for myself,' Cassie admitted. 'I spend half my life in a tracksuit at work. But I've enjoyed seeing this exhibition.'

'If you want to, can we have a wander around the jewellery collections next? Again, it's the Victorian stuff I most want to see. All those detailed, fussy designs. They're not my taste but it's so interesting seeing how designs evolve over time.'

'Sure, happy to do whatever you want to,' Cassie replied.

As they headed off towards the jewellery section, Bethany turned to Cassie. 'Can I ask you something? I've been wondering about it all week.'

'Go ahead.'

'Why didn't you return to university? You could have completed your degree after having me easily enough, couldn't you?'

Cassie didn't answer for a moment, using navigating their way through a crowd of school children an excuse. Once they were in a quieter area she stopped walking. 'I couldn't face being at university and pregnant. I thought people would judge me, keep asking questions. So I never went back for my second year.'

'Students wouldn't judge – they're generally liberal and accepting. But even so, you could have negotiated a year out and picked it up the following year?'

Cassie nodded. 'I could have. But somehow my heart wasn't in it. I worked in a supermarket while pregnant, on the tills, living with my parents. Went back to that job after you were born. My parents thought it was just for the summer, and I'd be back at uni in the autumn. But then I got a new job at a sports centre. I liked working there – the camaraderie of the staff, drinks after work, free use of the pool and gym. So I stayed on. Found a flat to rent, and later bought one. And just kind of shelved the whole idea of getting a degree.'

'Were your parents disappointed?'

Cassie shrugged. 'Not that they've ever admitted. They were supportive. Actually they've supported me in everything I've done.'

Bethany smiled. 'They sound like mine. I'd like to meet them.'

'They'd like to meet you, too. Shall I set something up?'

'Yes please. Oh, here we are.' Bethany led the way into the jewellery collection and they wandered amongst the displays, peering into glass cases and exclaiming over the intricate designs and lavish settings. 'Wow. Would you wear something like this?' She was pointing at a tiara, encrusted with pearls and diamonds.

'Oh yes. Wear one just like it every day to work,' Cassie joked, and Bethany giggled. Something about the way she giggled, putting a hand up to her mouth as she did so, reminded Cassie of Arjun. He'd made the same gesture whenever he laughed.

'Mmm, it'd go well with a tracksuit,' Bethany said, and then the tone was set for their next half hour as they bantered and giggled about what outfits to team with each piece of jewellery; the more outrageous the better. A ruby and emerald butterfly brooch with a pinstripe business suit. An elaborate diamond choker with a wetsuit. A long mother-of-pearl pendant with a Barney the Dinosaur costume.

In one room was a collection of trinkets and accessories adorned with precious stones – not jewellery as such. There were belts and sword hilts, trinket pots and dressing-table sets, all made from precious metals and set with all manner of stones. Many were from the Victorian era, so Bethany pulled out her notebook to make a few sketches and notes. Cassie left her looking at a dance-card holder set with diamonds and moved over to another cabinet. In it was a couple of silver-backed hairbrushes with elaborate engravings, and then, in the corner of the display, a hand mirror framed in silver and set with sapphires and pearls.

'Bethany? Come and look at this,' she called, and her daughter came over to see what she was pointing at.

'Mmm. Pretty.'

'It is, isn't it? And what's weird is . . .' Cassie frowned '. . . I've come across a description of something very similar in the will of an ancestor of mine.'

'An ancestor of mine, too, then?' Bethany smiled.

'Well, yes! My great-great-great-grandfather, so add another "great" on for you, left a mirror of that description to someone in his will.'

'Nice thing to be left! Who got it?'

'That's the odd thing. He left it to the wife of a prison chaplain. Turns out he'd been in prison and must have befriended the chaplain.'

'Ooh, naughty fellow, what was he in prison for?' Bethany looked genuinely interested in all this.

'Murder, apparently. He escaped the death penalty because he was only nineteen and also he confessed.'

'But then ended up with items like that to bequeath in his will? Did he get out early for good behaviour or something?'

'Must have. He was in prison when the 1861 census was taken, and aged nineteen so can't have been inside for long at that time. By 1871 he was out and living in lodgings. I don't know how he got out so soon, especially as he'd actually confessed to the murder.'

'Interesting. Wow, I'd love to see all your research at some time. So, do you think this is, like, the actual mirror from his will?'

'I don't know. Looks pretty unique to me – not a mass-produced piece. What does the ticket say?'

Bethany leaned in close to read the caption beside the artefact. 'Silver, sapphire and pearl hand mirror, made by Franklin and Son, Winchester, 1859. Bequeathed to the museum by Winifred Spring, 1947.'

'Spring . . . oh my God. The chaplain's name was Spring. Yes, I think this could well be the actual mirror!' Cassie pulled out her phone and took a photo of it, earning herself a frown from a museum attendant who was sitting on a plastic chair by the wall. 'That's incredible!'

'So, how can you discover why he got out so quickly if he'd been done for murder?'

Cassie shrugged. 'Maybe newspaper reports? It's likely I'll never be able to find out. But I'll have a go. Wow. Can't believe we've found the actual mirror.'

Bethany grinned. She was sketching the mirror and making some notes. 'I'm totally going to use this in my essay on Victorian design trends. Unbelievable that it used to belong to an ancestor. Can't wait to tell Mum and Dad all about this.'

'Um, how do they feel about you meeting up with me again?' Cassie tried to imagine herself in their situation. She was sure she'd feel jealous. What rights did a birth mother who'd given up her child at just a few days old have over that child eighteen years later? None at all.

'They're cool with it. I spoke with them after seeing you last week and they know we were planning to meet again. When they're back home, maybe we'll all get together some time? If you'd like?'

'Are they on holiday at the moment?' Cassie imagined Bethany trying to plan a visit within a couple of weeks.

'They're in Australia on a three-month trip.' Bethany grinned and rolled her eyes. 'As soon as I left home for uni they arranged career breaks and buggered off to see Mum's sister who's lived in Sydney for twenty years.'

'Oh! Are you on your own for Christmas?' Cassie wondered whether she should invite Bethany for the holiday period.

Bethany shook her head. 'No. They'll be back by then. My grandparents will come too. And my aunt and a bunch of cousins, aged fifteen down to three. It'll be crazy but fun.'

'Lovely! Our Christmases are always just the three of us, Mum, Dad and me. You must miss your parents while they're away?'

'Yes, but they're having a great time and they deserve it so I'm happy for them. Mum says, when children grow up the parents have to learn to let them go, but the children must also learn to let go of their parents, so those parents can do their own thing while they're still fit enough to. And I've got loads of family around should I need any help or support.' She looked sideways at Cassie. 'And now there's you, too.'

On impulse, Cassie reached out and pulled Bethany towards her in a hug. 'Yes. You've got me, now.'

'And you've got me.'

Chapter 10

George

15th March

Oh Lord, where to begin with today's journal entry? *At the beginning*, I hear Mr Smythe say with a sigh, but no, I think in this case I must first state where we are at the end of this momentous, horrible day. As I write this, by gaslight at around a quarter past midnight, my one-time love Lucy lies terribly sick in her room. My mother is tending to her, mopping her brow, holding her still while convulsions rack her poor dear body. I have never seen my mother show such kindness towards another human, and yet it was only a few days ago that she was arguing with Father, saying the girl should be dismissed and sent back to her parents! Today she could not be more attentive if she was Lucy's mother herself.

I will not sleep tonight. Not while poor Lucy is suffering so, and the outcome is uncertain. Whatever can have struck her down so badly? I fear the worst, and while I no longer dream of a future with her, I still care, and wish more than anything to see her recovered.

But now, I must pull myself together and set down in writing the events that have led to this terrible state of affairs.

* * *

83

Over the last few days my father has continued to visit Lucy in her room. He has not even tried to hide it lately, but has openly gone up the stairs to the attic floor even when people such as my mother or I are watching. Indeed, I saw him smirk at my mother as he came down from Lucy's room once, as if to say, I'm having my fun and you can't stop me. Her mouth was set in the thinnest line possible, as she raised her head high and walked away, making no comment.

My heart went out to her. Why does he treat her so? I am sure they must once have been in love, in the early days of their marriage at least. It was the loss of my sisters that turned my mother cold towards me, I believe. Perhaps it also made her cold towards Father. Perhaps that's why there were no children after me, and why Father has been driven to look for his pleasures elsewhere.

Mrs Peters too saw Father coming down the stairs yesterday, adjusting his clothing, his face flushed. She turned away and I think it was only I, on my way to my own room, who saw the tiny, disapproving shake of her head and pressing together of her lips.

I heard Mother in with Lucy too, telling her she would not be paid, and Lucy responded that the master was 'seeing to her needs', and my mother walked out with a face like fury. She went straight to Father who was in his study, and I, justifying to myself that I needed to know what was happening in the house, followed at a distance and listened outside.

They had the most almighty row. I could not hear every word – some were hissed as though they feared a servant might overhear, but Mother accused Father of being 'so blatant, you don't even try to hide it.' She said too, something about 'the girl says she's . . .' and 'this cannot happen again!' I had to duck away quickly before Mother left the study, slamming the door behind her so hard that a small picture hanging on the wall outside fell off, bringing a small chip of plaster with it.

* * *

84

And so, to the events of today. This morning I visited Lucy. I had persuaded Mrs Peters to let me take her breakfast up to her room, rather than entrust Maggie. She has dropped the tray on the stairs a couple of times this week, and Mother has been cross, telling Mrs Peters that Maggie must not be trusted to carry anything breakable. Mrs Peters does not like having to climb all the stairs to the top of the house, so was only too happy for me to do it today. I wanted to see if Lucy still seemed cool towards me.

I found her smiling and happy, and apart from her injured ankle, in good health. She was standing by the window when I entered, but quickly hobbled back to her bed and lay down again.

'You are improving,' I said. 'It is so good to see that you can now stand and walk a little.'

She blushed. 'Yes, but only a very little. If I take more than a couple of steps my ankle is still very painful. But it is slowly improving.'

I placed the tray on a small table beside her bed, which my father had ordered to be brought specially to her room for her to have her meals on. She watched as I laid out the plate of bread and bacon, a knife and fork, a dish of butter and a mug of hot chocolate. It was quite as though I were the servant and she the mistress. A small smile played at the corner of her mouth, and I suspected she was thinking the same thing.

'Thank you, Master George. You do that so much better than Maggie, who slops the chocolate all over the floor, if she hasn't dropped the whole tray on the way up. Such a clatter there was, when she let it go yesterday.'

'Well, that's why Mrs Peters allowed me to do the job today,' I replied. 'I had offered before but she hadn't allowed me. I wanted to see whether you were improving. I feel guilty, you see. If I hadn't encouraged you to climb the hill that day, we would not have been late for church, you would not have needed to run down, and you would not have been hurt.' And, I thought, your affair with my father might never have begun.

'Nonsense. It's not your fault, Master George. And I haven't really minded being hurt. It's been pleasant enough staying in my room, having my meals brought up and receiving . . . um . . . occasional visitors.' She propped herself up on one elbow to reach her food, and I leaned over to adjust her pillows.

I understood immediately what she was referring to regarding her occasional visitors, but of course, I could say nothing, though I could not prevent my eyes from narrowing. It was clear to me that Lucy was enjoying her position in our household – lying abed as my father's invalided mistress, with no work to do. It could not last forever. It must not; I would not allow it to.

I left her soon to her breakfast. The sun was shining, and after several days of rain I was keen to get outside and go for a walk. I had in mind I might climb Fairy Hill again, for the first time since that fateful Sunday morning. I would be back for lunch, so there was no need to tell anyone where I was going.

And so I put on a jacket and a hat, slipped out through the kitchen door, and walked up the lane towards the village. As I reached the path that led up to Fairy Hill, I hesitated. I had not been to church for a few weeks. Instead of going up the hill, I decided to sit in the church for a while. It might help, I thought, to meditate a while on Lucy, my feelings for her, and the uncomfortable situation in our house.

The village church is built of grey stone, has a spire that houses a clock with a single bell, and is surrounded by a pleasant, grassy graveyard. It is an inspiring place to sit and think. I pushed open the heavy wooden door and entered. The pews smelled of beeswax polish and dappled light shone through the stained glass windows, one of which had been sponsored by my own father.

I took a place near the front, knelt for a moment, then sat back in the pew, my eyes raised to the depiction of Christ on the cross, on the window above the altar. I prayed silently for guidance. Should I try to do anything about the situation at home? Should I confront Father, tell him I knew what he was up to? I suspected he wouldn't care if I knew. He didn't seem to care that Mother knew. Should I find a way to get Lucy away from the house? She didn't seem unhappy. On the contrary – she seemed very content with the way things were. But they could not continue. Soon her ankle would be healed and she would need to resume her duties. She would then not be available for Father to visit so often. Oh, it was all so awful, so horrible.

Christ on his cross gave me no answers.

I became aware that someone else had entered the church. Glancing round I saw Maggie, her round face gazing in awe at the coloured windows as though she had never seen them before. I recognised her expression – it was the one she always wore upon entering the church. She carried a basket over her arm, with a cloth covering its contents. Probably a joint of meat from the butcher for our dinner, I thought.

She startled when she saw me. 'Oh, Master George, I didn't see you there, I didn't. I am only fetching the meat for the dinner. Mrs Peters sent me, she did. May I sit here a while and look at the pretty windows – may I?'

'Of course you may, Maggie,' I told her. The poor girl gets little enough rest. Mrs Peters keeps her busy in the house always. Her thinking is that the more jobs Maggie does, the less likely it is that she'll get into trouble and break something. I'm not sure that follows but it's true that the more Maggie does a task the better she gets at it, so perhaps there is something in it.

Maggie sat down in the second pew on the opposite side of the aisle from me. She raised her eyes towards the end window and let her mouth fall slightly open. She remained thus, absolutely still and silent, for the next twenty minutes.

I envied her simplicity. Her head, I supposed, was empty of everything except contemplation of the pretty colours. Unlike mine.

At last I felt at peace enough to continue my walk. I rose and quietly left the church. My movement woke Maggie from her trance, and she left too, curtsying clumsily to me as we emerged into the sunlight and went our separate ways.

I took my walk up Fairy Hill as planned, and spent some time at the top, admiring the view that spread at my feet in all directions. I could never tire of it. Distant fields shone bright green with new growth of wheat and barley. Winchester's chimneys emitted curling tendrils of smoke, white against the stunning azure sky. Below me, my father's house stood proud in its small estate. One of those windows on the top floor was Lucy's. Was she, perhaps, standing at it, as she had been this morning, gazing up at the hill? Or was she entertaining my father?

That last thought made the bile rise in my gut, and spoilt my peace once again. I descended the hill quickly, though careful not to turn an ankle, and made my way home, just in time for a late luncheon.

All was commotion back at the house. I entered through the kitchen door, to find Maggie standing and flapping her hands in that helpless way she does when her equilibrium is upset. Mrs Peters was bustling about filling a bucket with water and finding cloths.

'Oh, Mr George, sir, it seems that girl Lucy has been taken sick, and has vomited all over her bedclothes, and worse besides. Your mother is up there with her. I think we will need a doctor. Is there someone outside who can be sent?'

'I'll find a stable boy,' I said, as I turned to go out again. Poor Lucy, not more suffering! What could have afflicted her so quickly? She had been perfectly well when I took her breakfast up this morning.

One of the lads was polishing tackle in the stables, and I sent him to run for Dr Madeley. His second visit here recently, and to see the same person!

Back inside, I bumped into Maggie, who was still flapping. 'Maggie, sit down, please, if you can't be of any use,' I said, rather more crossly than I meant. I pushed her into a wooden chair and rushed up to the invalid's room, to say that a doctor had been sent for.

Mother was there, cleaning up. Lucy lay on her bed moaning and clutching at her stomach. The smell of the chamber pot's contents mingled with vomit made me gag, and Mother looked at me with annoyance. 'George, if you can't be of use, get out. If you want to help, open the window.'

I did as she bade, and took a few deep breaths of fresh air before turning back to face them.

'What has happened, Mother? What has made her so ill? She was very well this morning when I brought her breakfast to her.'

'What, you've been visiting her too? Like father, like son, is it?' She tutted and rolled her eyes.

I began to protest, but realised there was little I could say. I was saved by a tap at the door. Mrs Peters entered, carrying a bucket and a pile of clean towels. I took them from her, and put them beside Mother.

'Take that pot and empty it,' Mother said to Mrs Peters, whose wrinkled nose showed her distaste at the task assigned.

'Pardon me, ma'am, but should your son be in here at a time like this?' she asked, glaring pointedly at me.

Mother glanced swiftly at me, her face expressionless. 'Perhaps not, but in the absence of more staff, he'll have to do. Maggie is no good in emergencies and you have enough to do. Until the doctor gets here, he can stay and try to be of use to me.'

'Very well, ma'am, whatever you say.' Mrs Peters nodded and left the room, taking the covered chamber pot with her.

'Fetch another pot, the one from Maggie's room,' Mother told me. 'I fear she may need it again very soon.'

I ran and fetched the pot. I did not want to have to witness Lucy on it, but truth be told, I did not see how she would manage to sit on it, in the state she was in. She was rolling around on the narrow bed, groaning, clutching her stomach, barely registering our presence. Her breath was coming quick and sharp, as though each inward gasp was a struggle. I hated to see her like this, and feared greatly how things would end. I found myself praying aloud that the doctor would come quickly, and would be able to save her.

'Stop your muttering, George,' my mother admonished. 'It does not help. Dip that cloth in the clean water and pass it to me.'

I was glad to have something useful to do, and passed her the cloth. She used it to mop Lucy's brow, murmuring soothing words to her all the while. You would think Lucy was her own daughter, not a servant who just a couple of days ago she was trying to dismiss. I had never seen my mother act so tenderly towards another person. I must admit, it made me feel insanely jealous. If only *I* could be the one lying sick and in pain – thus saving Lucy from her agony and feeling the blessing of my mother's love, for the first time. But we cannot swap places with another, however much we might long to do so. All I could do was pray, silently now, and help my mother with her nursing duties.

A half hour later, thankfully, Dr Madeley arrived. I heard him on the stairs, probably taking them two at a time as was his custom. He tapped on the door and entered without waiting for an answer. Mrs Peters was bustling up the stairs behind him, short of breath from having hurried to keep up with him.

'Ah, the same patient I was privileged to attend the last time I was here. What have you been up to, poor girl?'

'I think it could be the cholera, perhaps. She is vomiting, and worse, and has stomach pains.' Mother stood back to let the doctor near the bed. I was unsure what to do, but wanted to know his verdict, so I lingered quietly near the door of the room.

'More than pains, I'd say. She's convulsing. Hmm.' Dr Madeley felt Lucy's skin, probed her stomach, and stroked his whiskers thoughtfully. 'What was the last thing she had to eat or drink?'

'I brought her breakfast this morning,' I said. What was he implying – that something she had eaten had caused this? It seemed far more severe than any stomach upset I'd seen or experienced.

If Dr Madeley thought it odd that our servant should have been waited on in her room, he made no sign of it. He picked up a mug from Lucy's bedside table, which contained the dregs of some drink, and sniffed it. 'Was this part of her breakfast?'

'Yes,' I said. I assumed it was the mug I had brought, though her other breakfast dishes had been cleared away.

'Chocolate?' he asked.

'Yes.'

'Hmm.' He frowned, then pulled a small glass flask from his case, emptied the cup into it and pushed a cork stopper firmly in place.

'What are you doing?' Mother asked. Her eyes were wide, and fearful.

'Her condition is very serious. We will need to run some tests to see what has caused this, in case it is from something she ate or drank.' The doctor turned his attention back to his patient. 'Now, my dear, can you hear me? How did this all start?'

But Lucy was unable to respond. Her eyes rolled back in her head as she writhed in agony.

'Isn't there something you can give her, to ease her pain and make her well?' I said.

Dr Madeley looked at me. 'Ease her pain – yes, I can try. Make her well – I don't know. It depends what she's ingested and how much of it.' He took some medicines from his bag and prepared a draught of something. 'Help me; hold her head while I try to get this into her,' he said to Mother.

'What are you giving her?' She took hold of Lucy's face and held her jaw open, while the doctor inserted a tube and began to pour the liquid down it via a funnel.

'Laudanum. It'll ease the pain and perhaps let her sleep while her body fights this.

Mother nodded, and between them they managed to get some of the medicine into her, though she coughed and spluttered and much was spilt.

'There. I don't think there is much more we can do for her but keep her comfortable, and let this run its course.' Dr Madeley replaced items in his bag and stood to leave. 'I must be frank with you. I fear the worst. I will return in the late afternoon and see how she fares.' He raised his hat to my mother, and with a sighing backwards glance at Lucy, bounded down the stairs as quickly as he had come up.

'Why did he take the hot chocolate?' my mother muttered, though I realised she was not expecting me to answer. Why indeed. I had no idea.

It was a long and weary afternoon. I was kept busy fetching and carrying. As I did not object, and Maggie could not be trusted, and Mrs Peters was too stout to be running up and down the stairs, it was inevitable that I should end up doing it. Mother stayed at Lucy's side for the entire day. My father looked in on us a couple of times, standing white-faced in the doorway, and unable to offer any advice, sympathy or aid. Mother dismissed him with a curt word and a wave of her hand on each occasion.

Lucy did not improve at all. The laudanum Dr Madeley administered calmed her somewhat, and I thought she was sleeping, but Mother said no, she was unconscious rather than asleep. To be sure, we could not rouse her by shaking her or speaking loudly, though the rasp of her breathing and rise and fall of her chest showed she was still with us. If this is indeed the cholera, what a very dreadful disease it is. I was – and still am as I write this – frantic with worry. It is one thing to lose her to my father, and quite another to contemplate losing her altogether. I wanted her gone from our house, it is true, but whatever her sins, her faults, she does not deserve this.

Dr Madeley returned at five o'clock, as he had promised. He ran up the stairs and straight into Lucy's room, where he checked her pulse, felt her breath on the back of his hand, sighed and shook his head. 'The poison is winning, I fear.'

'Poison?' Mother gasped. 'Is it not the cholera?'

The doctor shrugged. 'It may be cholera. Or it may have been caused by something she has ingested.'

Mother shook her head. 'No, no. She has not been poisoned. I expect her bacon at breakfast was off. No one else ate it.'

'Mother, I—' I began, about to contradict her and tell her I had eaten bacon cut from the same joint this morning. But she held up a hand to silence me.

'Hmm. I'm referring to whatever bad thing she has eaten or drunk as poison, you understand,' the doctor said. 'I don't mean to imply deliberate poisoning. Please accept my apologies.'

Mother pressed her lips together. I said no more. Something about the doctor's tone belied his words. I suspected he meant the opposite of what he said – that he did think she'd been poisoned and he was not really offering an apology of any kind.

Once again, the doctor did not stay long, after attempting and failing to get more laudanum into Lucy. He gave Mother some instructions of how to keep Lucy as comfortable as possible, and left with a promise to send someone to help share the nursing duties overnight, and a further promise that he would return first thing in the morning.

At seven o'clock a woman from the village turned up, sent by the doctor, and relieved Mother in the sick room while she ate dinner and had a rest. But Mother insisted on returning to nursing duties afterwards. The woman took over my duties as deputy nurse, fetching and carrying, freeing me to go to my room to fret. And to write my journal.

And now, at midnight, there is no change. Lucy lies in a coma, her forehead constantly sponged by my mother, her breathing shallow and irregular, her pulse weak. I do not want to go to bed or sleep, for I greatly fear Lucy will not survive the night. She has torn our family apart, and her death, if or when it comes, will not help to heal the rift.

Chapter 11

Cassie

It was two weeks after their trip to the V&A before Cassie and Bethany met up again. The two weeks had passed uneventfully, with Cassie swapping shifts to free up as many weekend days as she could, and working weekdays instead. Thankfully that fitted well with the part-time student staff who were free at the weekends to work but not mid-week. She'd had a few nights out in the pub as well, with Andy there, but had not had any time alone with him. And maybe it was her imagination but apart from a few quizzical looks he seemed to have cooled towards her. Whatever it was she thought he'd said, about getting to know her more, he'd clearly thought better of it, which suited her. She had no time for messing around wondering whether he liked her as more than just a work colleague or not.

She'd told Shania about Bethany, during one of their lunch breaks.

'You're a dark horse,' Shania had said. 'Awesome to have a ready-made teenage daughter. I'd love one. You can be more like friends than mother and daughter.'

And yes, that was the relationship Cassie was hoping she could build with Bethany. She'd missed the baby and childhood years. But there were the adult years, plenty of them, ahead. With that in mind, she wanted to see Bethany as many weekends as they could manage.

This time, Cassie and her parents drove to Leicester on a Saturday morning. Cassie drove, and the idea was to have lunch in a pub with Bethany and then visit the cathedral with its newly built tomb of King Richard III, which had been installed since Cassie had been a student living in the city.

'Will she like doing that sort of thing?' Cassie's mum asked, as they were part-way up the M1.

'She loved wandering around the V&A,' Cassie replied. 'And she seems easy-going – she'll fit in with anything.'

'I wonder what it would have been like . . .'

Cassie glanced at her mother, who was biting her lip. 'What do you mean?'

'Oh, nothing. Just thinking how differently things might have turned out.'

'You mean if I'd kept her?'

'Shirley, love, don't go there.' Cassie's dad leaned forward from the back seat and put a hand on his wife's shoulder. 'Choices were made back then and they were the right ones at the time. Let's focus on getting to know the girl as she is now.'

'You'll like her, Dad.' Cassie knew her father would have been an excellent granddad, if he'd had the chance. She was thirty-seven now. She might still have a child or two, she supposed, if she met the right person to have a family with. But it all seemed a bit unlikely. She'd never been sure that she wanted children. The idea of being pregnant again, giving birth, and this time keeping the baby had always left her terrified she'd spend a lifetime regretting having given up her first child. She'd be always wondering what that child had been like at each stage of her development.

Maybe she'd feel differently now, now that she knew the

grown-up Bethany. If she wanted to know what Bethany had looked like aged three, or what her favourite toys had been, or whether she'd preferred football to ballet, Cassie would only need to ask.

Life was different, now that she was a mother in touch with her student daughter.

'It's a form of genealogy research, what she's done, isn't it?' Cassie's mum said suddenly. 'Except instead of searching for distant, long-dead relatives she was looking for close relatives who are still alive. Us.'

'Yes, that's what I thought, too. A bit more emotional though.' Cassie smiled, remembering how she felt when she first clutched Bethany to her. 'Talking of genealogy, I've been doing some. Found something interesting the other day. On Dad's side.'

'Oh yes?' Something about her dad's tone made Cassie glance at him in the rear-view mirror. He was frowning.

'Yeah. My great-great-great-grandfather, so your great-great-grandfather, George Britten, was convicted of murder and imprisoned, when he was only nineteen. But somehow he didn't stay in too long as I know he was out of prison in under ten years, judging by his addresses on the census returns. Do you know anything about it, Dad?'

'Er, well, no. I've never looked into all that.'

'Just wondered if your granddad had told you any stories about his grandfather that you remember? It's weird thinking I'm descended from a murderer. I know it's a few generations back but even so, feels strange. A murderer's genes in me. Do you know what I mean?'

'Oh, I don't think genes make you a murderer or not, darling. It's more about how you're brought up, surely?' Mum reached out and patted Cassie's leg, as though to reassure her.

'Nature or nurture. That age-old argument. You'll have to see what you think of Bethany. If she's lovely and kind and adorable, then she gets it from me, yes?' Cassie laughed. 'But seriously, Dad.

How do you feel about having a murderer in the family? And you'll have passed those genes to me . . .'

'Hmph. Like your mother says, I think it's all rubbish.'

Cassie glanced at him again in the mirror, just as her mother twisted round to catch his eye too. He pressed his lips together indicating he did not want to talk about it anymore. An odd reaction. Dad was usually interested in everything she was doing. When she'd researched her mother's side of the family he'd wanted to know all the details. He just seemed to clam up about his own family. Was he hiding some sort of secret?

'This is the turn-off for Leicester, isn't it?' her mother was saying, and Cassie needed to concentrate on driving as she took the slip road and headed into the city. Bethany had suggested they meet in a pub in the older part of the city, and Cassie was heading for a multi-storey car park not too far from there.

Soon they were making their way through the maze of twisty, ancient streets. Cassie had her phone in her hand and was navigating a route to the pub using Google Maps.

'Isn't it lovely here?' Mum said. 'I've never really explored Leicester before, other than brief visits when you were here. I love all these little old buildings and cobbled streets.'

'Yes, it's really pretty.' Cassie was finding it strange being back in the town, for the first time since she'd been a student here. Parts of it she remembered well but other parts had changed a lot over the years. It made her wonder what life would have been like, if she'd stayed and finished her degree. But that was not something to dwell on, today.

'Ah, here's the pub.' Cassie opened the door of a pub in a Tudor-style building, on a street corner. She stood back to let her parents enter first, but they hung back.

'Oh God, love, I'm suddenly really nervous,' Mum said. 'How on earth must you have felt when you first met her!'

'Come on in. It'll be fine. She's lovely and really easy to get on with.' Cassie gave them both a nudge and then followed them inside. She checked her watch. They were about ten minutes early – time to get a drink and find a suitable table. She glanced around the pub, remembering that Bethany had been early to the St James's Park café. And yes, there she was, sitting at a round table in a corner, with a glass of Coke in front of her. She was fiddling with her phone and hadn't seen them come in. Cassie called out to her. 'Hey, Bethany!'

Her daughter looked up, and broke into a wide smile when she saw them. 'Cassie!'

They hugged, then Cassie beckoned her mum and dad forward. 'And these are my parents – Shirley and Tony.' Her dad shook hands with Bethany rather awkwardly, but Cassie's mum leaned in and gave the girl a hug, with a few tears in her eyes.

'I'll get us all some drinks, then? You sit down, Mum and Dad. Get to know your granddaughter.'

The day went as well as Cassie could ever have hoped. Bethany was bright and sparkling and easy to get along with. Her parents liked her instantly and they had a day of warmth and laughter. In the end the only sightseeing they did was the cathedral, having spent too long over lunch and then wanting tea and cakes. 'It doesn't matter what we do today – it's all about us chatting and getting to know each other, isn't it?' Bethany said, as they decided to dip into another pub for a final drink before splitting up.

'Absolutely,' she replied. 'And it's been great, hasn't it?'

Bethany nodded, and linked her arms through Shirley's on one side and Tony's on the other. 'A whole extra set of grandparents! I keep looking at you and thinking, well, my nose comes from Shirley, and perhaps something about the shape of my forehead is from Tony. Do you think,' she said, turning side-on to Cassie, 'that Tony and I have the same profile?'

Cassie considered. 'Possibly, yes.'

But Tony was pulling his arm out from under Bethany's. 'No, love. We're not at all alike. You're pretty and I'm an ugly old brute for a start.' He smiled, tightly. 'Anyway, let me get this round in. What does everyone want?'

'Um, half a lager for me,' Bethany said, frowning slightly at the way he'd pulled away.

'Coffee for me. Long drive ahead,' Cassie said. Why had her father brushed Bethany off like that? It wasn't like him, and it had left Bethany looking confused and a little bit hurt. 'Let's sit here,' she said, leading them to a table, where she made sure to get a seat next to her daughter. 'You OK?' she whispered, as they sat down.

Bethany responded with a too-bright smile. 'Yes, fine. So, what are you up to tomorrow? Working again?'

Nice change of subject, thought Cassie, as she answered. 'Yep, usual Sunday shift for me and the Sunday Girls.'

'She loves it at that sports centre,' said Mum. 'Though I keep hoping she'll get a management position there some day, and earn a bit more. She's worth it, and she'd be good at it.'

'I'm happy as I am, Mum,' Cassie said, wanting to shut down that line of conversation before Bethany started thinking of her as a loser.

'That's what's most important, isn't it? Being happy in whatever you do.' Bethany squeezed Cassie's hand, and she felt grateful for the support.

'What are you hoping to do after university, Bethany? Or is it too early to know?'

'Something in the fashion world, hopefully! A job with one of the big houses, designing textiles would be my dream. Shallow, I know, but someone's got to do it.'

'Not shallow at all – the world needs beautiful things,' Cassie said.

'Yes . . . but I suppose sometimes I feel I should do something more worthwhile. Something to help save the planet, you know? Talking of which, there's that climate change march in London next Saturday. Won't be able to see you next week, Cassie, as my

99

flatmates and I are planning to go on the march, do our bit, make our voices heard and all that.'

'Oh, wow, good for you! Good to stand up for things you believe in,' Mum said, and Cassie nodded her agreement.

'All part of the student experience, going on a few marches,' Dad added. 'Just, be careful, keep out of trouble, eh?'

'Of course! That's what my parents said, too, when I told them I was going. Anyway, it'll be peaceful. Just a bit of marching through the streets with witty placards, starting from Hyde Park and ending up at Parliament Square. Look out for me on the TV!'

'We most certainly will,' Mum said. 'It's a good cause.'

The rest of the day in Leicester passed far too quickly, and then it was time for the long drive home. Cassie found herself wishing they'd decided to spend the night in a cheap hotel in Leicester. They could have had a night out with Bethany, met her flatmates, perhaps. But no doubt Bethany would rather spend her Saturday night out with friends of her own age, not her mother and grandparents. Besides, Cassie had to be at work in the morning – though thankfully she was not on the early shift.

As they drove home the chat was all about Bethany, of course.

'It's amazing. Can't believe we've met her now, and what a lovely young woman she's become,' Mum said. 'I hope when her parents are back from Australia we'll still get to see her now and again – hope they don't put a stop to it.'

'It's not up to them, Mum. She's eighteen, she's an adult and can do what she wants. Anyway, she said they've been really supportive of her tracing me and everything.'

The following week passed as usual. With no chance to meet Bethany on Saturday (though Cassie did consider going up to London to join in the march) she spent the day cleaning the flat, and going out for a run, as the day was one of those gorgeous bright cold autumn days that just have to be made use of.

She got back from her run in the late afternoon, had a shower, put on pyjamas (oh, the decadence of getting into pyjamas while it was still daylight!), made herself a cup of tea then sat down, switching on the TV to provide some background noise. Soon after, a news programme came on, reporting about the climate change protest march in the capital. Cassie sat up to take notice – this was what Bethany said she was planning on going on, though whether she actually had or not Cassie didn't know. It seemed many thousands had turned up, and in a few areas there had been some trouble – protesters locking themselves to railings; eggs thrown at politicians' vehicles entering and leaving the Houses of Parliament.

'Bethany, keep out of all that,' murmured Cassie. 'Keep yourself safe.'

She spent a quiet evening watching TV, went to bed around midnight and was on the point of sleep when her phone rang. It was Bethany.

'Cassie, oh thank God you've answered. It's horrible, I've been . . .' And then she broke down in tears.

'What? What's happened? Bethany, are you all right?'

'No, I mean, yes, I mean I'm all right, not hurt much but . . . Cassie, I need help . . . can you . . .'

'Of course, what do you need?' Cassie switched to full alert. Her heart was racing, blood pumping. Her daughter needed her.

'Come and get me?'

'Where are you?' Cassie sent up silent thanks that she had decided not to open a bottle of wine that night. It looked like she was going to need to drive.

'Police station. The one near Charing Cross.'

'Police station?'

'I-I got arrested. Wasn't doing anything wrong!' Bethany let out a wail. In the background Cassie could hear raised voices, people arguing, shouting, doors being banged closed. 'It's awful here. They're letting me go but I don't think there's any more trains to Leicester tonight . . . and . . .'

'I'm coming. It'll take me about an hour to drive there. Find somewhere safe – an all-night café perhaps, or stay at the police station. Text me.'

'Oh God, will you really?'

'Of course. Right, let me get off the phone. You can tell me the full story when I get there.'

Cassie threw some clothes over her pyjamas, grabbed her keys and purse and a pack of chocolate biscuits, and ran down her apartment stairs out to the communal car park. At that time of night there was very little traffic, and she broke every speed limit there was, slowing down only for speed cameras. In London she crossed into the congestion charging zone, feeling thankful it was outside of the chargeable hours, and then pulled over to search on her phone for the police station and directions to it, courtesy of Google Maps.

Bethany had texted to say she'd found a café around the corner from the police station and was sitting there waiting. It wasn't far. She found a parking place, albeit one that was supposed to be reserved for taxis, and spotted the brightly lit café over the road. A group of young men were jostling each other on the pavement and Cassie felt a rush of fear – was the café really a safe place for Bethany to have waited? Would she be all right? At that moment, Cassie realised, the most important thing to her was her daughter's safety. She may have only met her a month ago but that girl meant everything. Was it maternal instincts that made her prepared to do anything to help her? Whatever it was, Cassie hurried across the road, ignored the taunts and lewd comments from the drunken youths and pushed open the door to the café.

'Cassie!' Bethany called out from her table at the far end, nearest the service counter, and Cassie ran over to her, enfolding her in a hug. Her daughter's face was drawn and tear-stained, and there was a bruise developing on one cheek. She was wearing her yellow coat, and it looked like one sleeve was torn. As Cassie held her, she broke down into sobs.

'Ssh, it's all right, I'm here now. Ssh. Do you want a cup of tea or . . .'

'Just want to get out of here,' Bethany sobbed.

'OK. My car's over the road. Come on.' Cassie put an arm around her and led her out, running the gauntlet once more of the drunken men but thankfully with one stern glare at them they left her and Bethany alone. She ushered her daughter into the passenger seat of the car, got in herself, and started driving, in no particular direction.

'So. Want to tell me everything that's happened? Or should we just get somewhere we can sleep and you tell me in the morning?'

'I'm so blinking tired,' Bethany said.

Cassie glanced over and noted the dark rings under her eyes. 'All right then, let's find a Premier Inn or something.' They were away from the café and police station, in a quiet road now, so she pulled over, locked the doors, and ran a search on her phone for a nearby hotel with parking. There was one just outside the congestion zone, about twenty minutes away. It was two a.m. before they got there but thankfully the reception was manned all night and soon they were in a cosy twin room, with a few supplies from a vending machine and the packet of biscuits Cassie had grabbed from home.

'Here, eat something,' Cassie said, pushing the stack of food towards Bethany. 'I'll put the kettle on.'

Bethany picked out a pack of crisps and opened the biscuits. 'Healthy dict, this. But thanks. God, thanks so much, Cassie.'

It was on the tip of Cassie's tongue to say, what are mothers for? And then she realised that she wasn't really Bethany's mum. If the girl's parents hadn't been in Australia no doubt she'd have called them for help. 'It's no problem. So, what happened?'

Haltingly, Bethany told the story of the march, which had started out peaceful and good-humoured, but which had then somehow got entangled with a group of far-right neo-Nazis who'd jeered at them and picked fights. It was that group who'd thrown eggs and stones at politicians' cars, Bethany said, even though the media had said it was the climate change protesters.

With things turning ugly Bethany and a group of girls she'd been marching with had run down a side street, right into a brawl that was just starting between more neo-Nazis and police. Her sleeve had been torn as one thug grabbed hold of her. She'd lashed out instinctively and been punched in the face ('but it's not too bad, honest,' she insisted) and then felt a policeman's arms around her from behind, pulling her wrists into a set of handcuffs. Before she knew what was happening she'd been bundled into a police van along with one of the other girls and three neo-Nazis. Bethany had suffered a tirade of verbal racial abuse from the thugs on the journey to the police station, leaving her feeling shaken.

At the police station she and the other girl had been put into one room, thankfully away from the others who'd been arrested along with them. They'd been given a cup of tea and then left for hours, awaiting 'processing'. There'd been endless forms, statements to make, and questions to answer. Eventually the police had accepted the two girls were innocent and not to blame for any of the violence and had let them go. The other girl lived in London and went off straight away to get a late-night tube home.

'Through it all, Cassie, I'd kept myself together. Even when those Nazis were shouting at me in the police van. But then, when that other girl left, I felt so alone I just . . . broke down. That's why I rang you. None of my friends in Leicester have cars. My parents are away. My aunt and grandparents are in Sheffield. I don't have enough money for a hotel or taxi home – oh God, I'll have to owe you for this room, sorry. And you came.' She reached out and took Cassie's hand.

'You don't owe me for this. Tomorrow I'll drive you back to Leicester. I'm glad you called me. I'm glad I've been able to help. You've had such an ordeal. Come on, let's get you into bed.' Cassie cleared away the remains of the junk food from the beds, and turned them down while Bethany used the bathroom. Bethany stripped down to T-shirt and knickers and climbed into bed. Cassie sat for a moment on the bed with her, tucking the duvet up under her chin and stroking her hair. 'Sleep well,' she whispered, as the pain of having missed eighteen years of bedtimes threatened to engulf her.

Chapter 12

George

16th March

I did, eventually, sleep. Still dressed, I had lain on my bed, trying to listen out for any commotion that might indicate a change in Lucy's condition. Despite my best intentions, sleep overcame me at some point in the small hours. I woke after seven in the morning, when sunlight was streaming in through my window, birds were singing and a fine new day was promised.

Except it was not to be a fine day. As soon as I opened my eyes, the events of yesterday came flooding back to me, and I leapt off my bed and rushed straight up to the attic floor. Dr Madeley was already there, and my mother, looking tired as though she had not slept. I arrived just in time to see the doctor gently close Lucy's eyes with his fingertips, as he shook his head.

'No, please Lord, no!' The scream was out before I had chance to stop it. 'It can't be! She can't . . . Tell me she is only sleeping!'

'I'm sorry, George. She has gone. But be thankful she is at peace and no longer suffering.' Dr Madeley patted my shoulder sympathetically. He must see so much death, I suppose he is immune to it. But has he ever been at the death of someone he once loved, as I had loved Lucy with all my heart?

I sank to my knees. I could not help myself. It was as though all strength had poured out of me, leaving nothing but a shell. My face in my hands, I curled up on the floor beside Lucy's death bed, and wept.

'Get up, George. You are making a fool of yourself. Such a display is not seemly.' My mother poked at me with her foot, and I was reminded of where I was, and of my station in life. She was right. My behaviour was not appropriate for someone of my position. I dragged myself upright, apologised, and with an anguished final glance at the girl on the bed, I went downstairs to my own room.

Once there, I pulled out the sapphire mirror I had bought for Lucy. I counted the days back – was it really only three weeks ago that I had shopped in Winchester, so full of hope for my and Lucy's future? Later that same day the future I'd dreamed of was smashed into pieces by my father's actions, and now, with Lucy's life extinguished, I wondered what it would all mean, not just for myself but for my family. Would we, could we return to how we were before she came? Was that possible, or would my mother, understandably, never again trust my father? Could I ever respect him again, knowing what I now knew of his morals?

I put the mirror back and left my room. Dr Madeley was now in the hallway, speaking with my father. Mother had also come downstairs, and stood by the hall table, her hand resting upon it as though for support.

'I will send a cart for the poor girl,' Dr Madeley was saying. 'The autopsy will be complete by tomorrow, and we can then arrange for her family to collect her body for burial. Someone must notify them as soon as possible.'

'Why does there need to be an autopsy?' Mother asked.

'To determine the cause of her death, ma'am,' he replied.

'It was the cholera, I am certain of it,' she said, firmly. 'I have seen it before – the stomach pains, the gasping for breath, the convulsions. There is no need for an autopsy, surely? The girl has suffered enough; there is surely no need to violate her body?'

'I am sorry, ma'am, but there is every need. There have been no other cases of cholera in this area lately. As I'm sure you are aware, cholera tends to strike in clusters. This is an isolated case. It bears all the hallmarks of a poisoning, whether accidental or deliberate. And so it is imperative we find out exactly what caused her suffering. She will be returned intact for burial, I assure you.' He nodded, retrieved his hat from the hat stand, picked up his bag and left.

The rest of the day was the most difficult few hours I have ever endured. The doctor's cart came for Lucy's remains before lunchtime. I watched, horrified, as two rough-looking men carried her down from her room, wrapped in a coarse blanket, and loaded her into a dogcart. It seemed such an undignified way to leave the house.

Mother was watching too, from the drawing room window. I know not where my father was. He had taken the news of Lucy's death with apparent calmness, and had gone out for a ride. Whether that was intended to help clear his head and collect his thoughts, or because he felt unaffected by it, I do not know. I assume, though perhaps I am naïve in these matters, that if you have had carnal knowledge of someone then you *cannot* be unaffected by their demise a few days later. I am certain I could never act so nonchalantly about such an event as my father has.

A visibly shocked Mrs Peters, aided by Maggie, stripped Lucy's bed and deep-cleaned her room. Mother wanted it ready for a new maid by the morrow. A new maid, just like that. As though Lucy's loss was nothing more than a minor inconvenience requiring replacement, like a broken chair or a chipped plate. As though her life and her demise meant nothing.

* * *

18th March

I must set down events that occurred two days after Lucy's death, although I write these diary entries very much later, and seated in very different surroundings, as I will tell. I fear I will no longer count the years *anno domini* but the years *post* Lucy, as nothing will ever be the same. We had not long finished breakfast: a subdued affair, as all our meals had been lately, where neither I nor my parents said a word to each other beyond 'Good morning', and which was punctuated by Maggie's constant sniffing as she attempted to serve us and clear the dishes.

She could not have known Lucy well, but even so she appeared vastly distressed at her loss. I felt sorry for her. Being of such simple mind I wondered if she truly understood what death meant. I wondered too, do any of us truly understand it? Are the dead still with us, watching us and perhaps influencing our actions? Sometimes I feel that must be the case – it's as though I sense Lucy's presence behind me in the dining room, or catch a glimpse of her on the stairs, a mocking smile playing at the corners of her mouth.

The front doorbell jangled before the breakfast dishes were even cleared. Mother looked at Father. 'So early! Who can that be?'

'The doctor with the autopsy results, I should imagine,' he replied, without even glancing in her direction. 'Let us all hope it was the cholera after all.'

Mother opened her mouth as if to say something more, but obviously decided against it. She sat at the table, her back ramrod straight, until Mrs Peters entered.

'Sir, ma'am, it is the doctor and another gentleman. I have shown them into the drawing room.' She looked flustered, as though she knew or suspected something about the visit but didn't want to say anything.

My father pulled his napkin off his lap, dabbed at his lips and stood. 'Well, I'd better go and see what they want.' He left the room, and I followed, but he closed the drawing room door firmly behind him. Clearly my presence was not required.

Not wanting to return to the dining room, or go upstairs, I lurked in the hallway. On the hat stand was the doctor's top hat and another, a bowler. Beside the hall table was the doctor's bag. It had fallen open. I don't know what made me do what I did next. I crossed over to the bag, crouched beside it and peeped inside. All manner of instruments were jumbled together, along with vials and boxes and pots and little linen bags. I touched nothing.

Or rather, I touched nothing except for the publication that protruded from the bag and was the reason it would not close. I pulled that out. It was a medical journal, folded back on itself on a page headed *On the Diagnosis and Detection of Poisoning by Arsenic*. I read it quickly. The doctor had underlined a few phrases – *symptoms superficially similar to cholera; sample combined with zinc and acid produces arsine gas with a garlic odour*. It became clear to me that he thought Lucy had been poisoned with arsenic.

We keep arsenic, in a small brick shed next to the coal shed, at the back of the house. It is used as rat poison. As a child I was told repeatedly never to go in that shed. My nursemaid and later Mr Smythe warned me of the dangers that would befall me if I so much as touched the contents of the earthenware pot stored within. Even now I am grown, I feel a frisson of fear whenever I pass by that shed.

I could not believe it. Lucy, poisoned! Had she been in that shed, perhaps? But how, with her injured ankle, could she have descended two flights of stairs, gone out through the kitchen door and round to the back of the house? Besides which, I knew the shed was always kept locked, and the key stored in a drawer in the housekeeper's room. Lucy had surely not worked here long enough to know where the key was kept. Why, anyway, would she have wanted to enter that shed?

But the alternative was that someone else had deliberately poisoned her. Who, and why?

The drawing room door opened, and I quickly stuffed the journal back into the doctor's bag. My father and Dr Madeley came out; the other gentleman stayed inside. Father shook the doctor's hand and bade him goodbye. The doctor then retrieved his bag and left the house. Father turned to me.

'Well, it seems foul play is suspected. We are all to be questioned. The gentleman who has called on us this morning is a detective from Scotland Yard. His name is Watling. This is outrageous, but there we have it. We must comply, he says, or else it looks even more suspicious.' Father was trying, and failing, to suppress his fury, pacing about the hall as though he didn't know where to put himself.

I didn't know what to say. 'But, Father, surely . . .' I began, but he interrupted me.

'Well, we may as well get it over with. Servants first. Fetch the men from the stables. He can start with them.' Father stormed off into his study and slammed the door behind him.

I couldn't believe it. So they did suspect someone of poisoning her! In a state of shock I went out to the stable yard and called in our groom John Lincoln and the two stable lads Tom and Isaiah. They shuffled in behind me, clearly uncomfortable at being in the main part of the house and looking completely out of place in their rough tweed work clothes. They lined up in front of the drawing room door. Father was still shut in his study so I guessed it was down to me to show them in. I opened the door and ushered in John Lincoln.

'Sir, here is our groom Mr John Lincoln,' I said, to the gentleman within. He was sitting at a small side table, an open notebook in front of him, an air of expectation surrounding him. He was tall and gaunt, with sparse whiskers, and I judged his age to be around forty.

'Thank you. And you are?'

I bowed slightly. 'George Britten, sir. You have spoken with my father.'

'Yes, that is right. I am Inspector Watling, of Scotland Yard. Has he explained what I am here for today?'

I nodded. 'Yes. He asked me to fetch the outdoors servants for you to question first.'

'Question? Mr George, what do he think we have done? We ain't done nothing, surely we ain't. I can speak for the lads too – none of them done nothing.' Poor John was quite agitated.

'Of course you haven't,' I soothed. 'But you must answer Inspector Watling's questions, the same as the rest of us. Now stand there, in front of him, and it'll be all over in a few moments.'

I stood back out of the way, and ready to escort him out once the detective had finished. But Inspector Watling stared at me, and then waved his hand towards the door, dismissing me. 'There can be no one else present,' he said. 'Otherwise people might think they can't speak the truth openly.'

I nodded again and left the room.

Mother emerged from the dining room. She looked pale and on seeing the stable lads in the hallway she called me in to see her.

'What is happening, George? Who is the man, and why are those dirty stable boys inside?'

I quickly explained everything to her – well, except for what I'd found out by snooping in the doctor's bag. Father clearly had not kept her informed. Though I wouldn't have thought it possible, she paled still further, and sat down heavily.

'This is horrible. To think he suspects someone here of hurting the poor girl! Who could it be? Mrs Peters, perhaps, or Maggie, or perhaps a stranger sneaked into the house when our backs were turned . . .' She shook her head. 'George, you must do something for me. I will be so grateful. Go out to the hallway, and listen at the door, find out what everyone says to him. I – we must know what they say, before we too are questioned. Murder is a hanging offence . . . Oh, dear son, will you do this for me?' She took hold of both my hands and gazed up at me, her eyes pleading and brimming with tears.

I could not recall a time when she had held my hands like this and spoken to me thus. She needed me! She wanted me to do something for her! Me, her son – her *dear* son she had called me! She had never asked me for help before, never needed anything from me. She had suffered so much lately through my father's actions. And she had so selflessly nursed Lucy as she lay dying. Mother deserved my help. I felt overwhelmed with love for her. I would do anything, anything at all if it would win me her love in return.

'Of course, dear Mama,' I said, and I squeezed her hands. I longed to kiss her cheek, but she pulled away and I realised there was no time to lose. I needed to hear as much as possible of what passed between Watling and his interviewees. He had already started talking with John Lincoln. I hurried out to the hallway, where Tom and Isaiah were still waiting, twisting their caps in their hands. They would realise I was listening in, but there was nothing for it. I nodded at them and approached the door.

Inspector Watling's voice was strong and clear, and I could hear everything he said, if I stood close by. John Lincoln's was more muffled. I suspected he was mumbling somewhat, perhaps due to his extreme discomfort at the situation. Nevertheless I could hear enough to determine that he knew nothing of Lucy's death. He and the lads had been out in the stable for the entire morning of 15th March and had seen and heard nothing suspicious.

I stood back from the door when I heard Watling draw the interview to a close. John Lincoln emerged, blinking, and nodded to Tom. 'You're to go in next, lad. Just tell the truth, is all.'

Tom swallowed, his Adam's apple bobbing in his throat, and went in. His was a very short interview, and he must have mumbled even more or perhaps only nodded or shook his head in answer to the questions for I did not hear his voice at all. Isaiah followed him moments later, and again, there was nothing of interest.

I began to wonder what Mother thought we might learn from

113

these interviews. After Isaiah's, I heard the inspector scrape back his chair ready to leave the room, and I darted into the dining room where Mother was still sitting. It would not do for the detective himself to catch me listening at the door.

'Well? What has been said?' Mother asked, as I pushed closed the dining room door.

'Nothing of interest yet. I believe Inspector Watling is to speak to Maggie and Mrs Peters next.'

'And then it will be us,' she whispered. 'You, me and your father.' I nodded, and placed a comforting hand on her shoulder. I did not know what was frightening her so, but whatever it was, I wanted to do my best to help her.

'I can hear Maggie going in. Let me go and listen again.'

'Thank you.' She smiled weakly at me, and I returned a reassuring smile to her. Oh how good it felt to be performing a useful service for my mother and to have her gratitude for it.

In the hallway, Maggie was flapping her hands frantically, as she followed Mr Watling into the drawing room. I felt sorry for her. She probably did not understand what was going on at all. Unnoticed by the detective, I took up my place again beside the door, after Maggie closed it behind her.

Thankfully her voice, which only had one pitch, that being strident, was easy to hear through the door. Unfortunately, she was not making a lot of sense. On being asked to recount her movements in the morning four days earlier she answered:

'I cleaned the grates but didn't set no fires cos there weren't no need for no fires and then I were in the kitchen but Mrs Peters said as there was meat to be got and there was none else cos of Lucy's foot and I know the way to the butcher's I do cos she has shown me it afore now and so that's what I done.'

'You went to the butcher's?' I imagined Mr Watling frowning and scratching his head as he tried to make sense of her babbling.

'No yes I done that and I were in the church but only a minute or an hour I don't know the time I don't and then I were back here and all were a commotion and it were such an upset it were, and Mrs Peters told me get out of the way and that's what I done.'

'Very well. Thank you, um, Maggie. You may go and send the housekeeper to me now.'

'Yes, sir. I will, sir. Who be the housekeeper?'

'Mrs, um, Peters, is it?'

Maggie must have run out of the room for she almost knocked me over in her haste. Her face was bright red, and tears streamed down her cheeks. Judging by the rate of her hand-flapping, Mrs Peters would get no work from her for the rest of the day at least.

A moment later, Mrs Peters emerged from the kitchen corridor and crossed the hallway. Her back was ramrod straight, her cap neatly pinned and her apron clean. She obviously intended making a good impression. She nodded to me as she passed me.

'Terrible business, this. To think, poor Lucy!'

'Indeed,' I replied, and showed her into the drawing room.

I had to lean close to the door to hear what was said in this interview. Thankfully no one passed through the hall to see me eavesdropping. But what I heard made me gasp with horror.

Chapter 13

Cassie

Cassie awoke early the next morning, despite having not got to bed until well after three a.m. For a brief moment she wondered where she was, then looked across at the other bed where Bethany was still sleeping. With a start she remembered that it was Sunday and she was due at work. 'Buggeration,' she muttered, and got up, taking her phone into the little en-suite bathroom, where she called Andy. He was on the early shift and would already be at the sports centre.

'Andy? Listen, I'm so sorry but I'm not going to be able to work today. I know it's short notice and all, but . . . something came up that I had to deal with.' It had crossed her mind to say she was unwell and take the day off as sick leave, but she didn't want to lie to Andy. She had the feeling that sooner or later she'd want to talk through the events of the previous evening with someone, to explore how she felt about it all, and that someone would probably be Andy.

'Is everything all right, Cassie? Are you OK?' He sounded concerned.

'I'm fine. It's . . . kind of a long story, but honestly, I wouldn't be doing this if it wasn't important. Maybe you can get Ben or Toby to cover? Belinda and Lorraine are due in anyway.'

'Don't worry. I'll sort something – can always do the pool cover myself. I don't think we'll be busy today. Do whatever you need to do, but Cassie?'

'Yes?'

'You owe me a pint and the full story . . . That's if you want to tell me, of course . . .'

'Yeah, sure. OK, so I'll see you tomorrow, then.'

'My day off. And Tuesday's yours, so I think it'll be Wednesday before our shifts coincide. Red Lion after work?'

'Sure. Thanks, Andy.'

'No problem. Hope whatever you need to do goes well. Bye, then.'

As she ended the call Cassie smiled. Good old Andy. No questions, he'd just accepted that she needed the time off. She realised she was looking forward to working with him on Wednesday, and better still, having a pint with him afterwards. If it was just the two of them, she'd be able to tell him all the details. But if Ben, Toby and Shania were there, it'd have to wait. For the first time ever, she found herself hoping the others would cry off going to the pub, leaving just her and Andy. It'd be cathartic to offload on him again. He was a good listener.

In the bedroom, Bethany was still fast asleep; the bruise on her cheek beginning to come out. She'd have a corker of a black eye soon. The poor girl needed to rest, so Cassie climbed back into bed and tried to sleep herself, with no success. Eventually she got up again, made a cup of tea, and sat sipping it, scrolling through news reports of the climate change protest march on her phone. It seemed some journalists had got hold of the true story about the violence having been caused by far-right thugs rather than the marchers.

* * *

117

Later, once Bethany had awoken, showered and dressed, Cassie took her for breakfast. Bethany was subdued. 'Still tired, I think. And I've got a hell of a headache.'

'Paracetamol?' Cassie rummaged through her handbag and handed Bethany a battered pack of pills, which she took gratefully.

'Thanks. You don't have to drive me to Leicester, Cassie. Just drop me at the nearest train station. You've done enough.'

Cassie shook her head. 'I'm taking you right back to your door. No arguing.'

Bethany smiled. 'You sound like my mum.'

'I *am* your mum,' Cassie said, then blushed and clapped a hand over her mouth. 'Oh God. No I'm not. Well, I am, but I mean . . .'

Bethany took her hand. 'I know what you mean. I'm so lucky. I've got two mums.'

'Better not say that in front of your parents,' Cassie said, trying to lighten the mood.

'They're the ones who said it to me, first. When I told them about our first meeting and how lovely you were, Mum said, "well, you're lucky, you have two mums now, so make the most of both of us!"'

'You'll tell your parents, about last night, will you?'

'Yes. I don't keep any secrets from them. They knew I was going on the march, anyway.' Bethany frowned. 'Unless there's anything you don't want me to tell them?'

Cassie shook her head. 'I'm like you. I think honesty and openness are always best. So, will you mind if I tell *my* parents about it all?'

'Not at all. I did nothing wrong.' Bethany touched her bruised cheek. 'Quite proud of this shiner, actually. It'll impress my university friends. As will me telling them I got arrested. Student kudos.'

'Well, when you've eaten let's get going. Although, I might have one more coffee first.' Cassie stifled a yawn. She had a long drive ahead – London to Leicester, then back to Reading – and she'd only had around five hours' sleep.

Bethany slept for much of the journey. At her student accommodation – a standard block of modern student flats, with ten students sharing each kitchen – she invited Cassie in for a cup of tea and something to eat before she headed back. 'I've not got much in, though. Will cheese on toast do?'

'Perfect.' Cassie sat at the cheap kitchen table while Bethany made the food. Other students bustled in and out, all asking Bethany about her bruise and about the march, and nodding greetings at Cassie when Bethany introduced her (simply as 'Cassie', without elaborating on their relationship). Cassie felt a little out of place. Being in that shared kitchen reminded her of her abortive time at university – the similar-style student accommodation she'd lived in where Arjun had been a frequent visitor. She'd enjoyed herself so much that year. The life had suited her well.

Now, witnessing the student lifestyle for the first time since those days she found herself wondering, for the first time, whether it had been a mistake not to go back and finish her degree after having Bethany. She could have just deferred it a year, so easily.

'Here you go,' Bethany said, placing a plate of cheese on toast and a cup of tea in front of Cassie. 'And if you're really knackered, feel free to stay here tonight. I can sleep on the floor and you have my bed – I have a sleeping bag.'

Cassie smiled at her. 'Ah no. I need to be at work tomorrow. I'm on earlies, too, so I need to get back today. But thanks. I'd better be on my way after eating this.'

'OK. Well, thanks again, so bloody much, Cassie! You have been amazing. I'm going to have a really early night tonight – still feel exhausted.'

'If you still don't feel right tomorrow, go to the doctor, perhaps?'

Bethany shook her head. 'I'll be all right. And there you go again, sounding all mumsy.' She impulsively reached over to Cassie and put her arms around her. 'I hope you do have children one day. You'd be an amazing mum. You *are* an amazing mum.'

'Oh God, don't set me off, I won't be able to see to drive,' Cassie said, tugging a tissue out of her pocket to dab at her eyes. 'Just promise me you'll take care of yourself? You've had a horrible experience and sometimes it can take a few days to properly get over it.'

'I will, I promise.'

Tuesday was Cassie's day off, and she'd agreed to meet her parents for a pub lunch. It was a couple of days before her dad's birthday so they were using the excuse to celebrate ('not that I really want to celebrate being sixty-five,' Dad had said. 'Qualifying for a bus pass!'). She'd done some shopping first and left it in the boot of her car while she met them. Her parents were already in the pub, seated at a dining table that overlooked the pub's well-maintained garden. It was a changeable weather kind of day – one minute grey and squally, the next bright sunshine.

'Hey, Mum, Dad,' said Cassie, as she approached the table and leaned over each of them to kiss them. 'And happy birthday, Dad!'

'Not my birthday yet,' he replied.

'You won't be wanting this then,' Cassie said, holding up a gift bag in which she'd put his present – a new high-tech cycling top that was supposed to be windproof yet breathable. Her father was a keen cyclist, heading out most Sundays with a group of friends and she knew he'd been eyeing up these tops but not wanted to spend that much money on them.

'Ah, I'll take that, thank you,' he said. 'Can I open it today?'

'No. Not your birthday yet, is it?' They all laughed, and Cassie pulled out a chair to sit at the table.

'So, love, how's Bethany? Heard from her recently? She was going to go up to London for that climate change march, wasn't she? We saw that on the news. She wasn't caught up in any of the trouble, was she?' Mum looked worried.

'Yes, she did go up to London for that. Kind of a long story. Let's order first and I'll tell you it all,' Cassie replied.

By the time the starters arrived Cassie had given them both a rundown of the events of the weekend. They'd listened in silence, with just a few gasps and requests for reassurance that Bethany was all right.

'She's got a black eye and a bruised arm, but yes, she's all right. I think she slept most of Sunday. I've had a few texts from her.'

'It was good of you,' Dad said, 'to do all that for her. All the way to London, put her up in a hotel, drive her back to Leicester.'

'It was nothing. You'd have done it for me, wouldn't you?'

'Yes, of course, but that's . . .'

'That's what being a parent is all about,' Mum interrupted. 'Being there when they need you. Being a safety net. Well done, Cassie. We're that proud of you.'

Cassie blushed and turned her attention to her food.

The conversation pottered onto other subjects, but as they finished their desserts Cassie found herself talking about her genealogy research once more. She remembered she'd been talking about it in the car on the way up to Leicester to visit Bethany, and they'd never really finished the conversation.

'Remember I told you about that chap, our ancestor, Dad, who'd been imprisoned for murder but then let go? Did I tell you Bethany and I found what must be the jewelled mirror he mentions in his will – and bequeaths to the wife of a prison chaplain – in the V&A museum? Honestly we were gobsmacked when we saw it. Of course it might not be the actual one, maybe they were mass produced, but it's just like the description in the will and also it was donated to the museum by someone who has the same surname as the prison chaplain. We reckoned it has to be the same one.' She paused to take a sip of coffee. 'Bethany's thrilled I'm into genealogy. She's not only found her birth mum and grandparents but also the whole line going back nearly two hundred years.'

'Mmm. Well. Is she going to look for her birth father too?' Dad said.

Cassie frowned at the change of subject. It wasn't the first time he'd done this, when she'd talked about her research. 'I don't know – not yet. But anyway, this George Britten – Dad I wanted to ask you, whether you'd heard anything about what happened? Wondered if you remembered your grandfather saying anything. I mean it's a big thing to happen in a family and maybe there was some sort of family legend . . .'

'No. Nothing I remember.' Her father's expression was closed.

Cassie glanced at her mother, who was wearing an odd expression on her face. Questioning, wondering. Mum reached across the table and took Dad's hand. 'Tony, do you think, now that we have Bethany in the family, we should . . .'

'Should what?' Cassie asked, but her mother's eyes were focused on Dad and she didn't turn to look at Cassie.

Cassie's father sighed, and looked down at his empty dessert plate. 'Probably. Probably should have done it long ago. Bethany said, she always knew, and it was better that way . . .'

'Always knew what? Mum, Dad, what are you two talking about?'

But still her parents gazed only at each other, reading something in each other's eyes that was hidden from Cassie. At last her dad looked at her. 'Cassie, there's something we need to tell you. Well, I need to tell you really, I suppose. Here's the thing. These ancestors, this George Britten you talk about – he's not . . . related to you.'

'He's your great-great-grandfather! Of course he's related to us!'

Dad looked uncomfortable. 'To me, yes. Not to you.'

'What? Oh God, don't say you're about to tell me I'm adopted!' Cassie laughed but her stomach was turning over.

'No, not exactly . . .'

'Mum, what's he trying to say?' Cassie was seriously scared now.

Her mother took her hand. 'Perhaps we shouldn't have done this here, in the pub . . .'

'Too late, you've started now,' Cassie said. 'Come on. Tell me, whatever it is.'

Dad took her other hand. 'Cassie, love. You're the best daughter any man could ever have, and I love you so much. Just remember that when I tell you . . . oh God, there's no easy way, after all these years. Shirley, will you . . .?'

Cassie stared at her father, then at her mother, questioning.

'The thing is, you know how I was already pregnant with you when we married?'

'Yes?' Cassie had always known this. The wedding photos, where an eight-months-pregnant Shirley grinned at the camera in a dress that didn't even attempt to hide the bump, were a bit of a giveaway.

'Well the thing is . . . Dad wasn't your father. It was . . . someone else. Dad always knew.'

'Dad? You're not my dad?' Cassie couldn't take it in.

'Cassie, I'm your dad in every way that matters. Just . . . you came from someone else's sperm, is all.' He looked anguished.

'Is all? But . . . that's huge . . . I can't . . . Oh Christ.' Cassie got up from the table and ran to the ladies' toilets. Why had they chosen to tell her this here, now? In a pub dining room? With people sitting at the other tables, beginning to stare at them? Why now, after all these years? There was no need for her to ever have known . . .

She crashed open a cubicle door, went inside and locked it, sitting on the closed toilet lid. She grabbed a handful of toilet paper ready for the tears she expected to fall at any moment, but realised that what she mostly felt was anger. Fury at her parents, her wonderful, supportive, kind parents who'd always been the best anyone could hope for, but who had been living a lie all these years. For thirty-seven years. No wonder they'd only ever shown her a short-form birth certificate. The long-form one would have shown her real father's name. They'd always said it was lost. Who was he? How had it happened? Where was her real father now?

'Cassie? Are you in here, love? Look, your father's paying the bill and maybe we should just go home, have a cup of tea and talk about it all?' Shirley's voice sounded as though she was crying. 'You'll probably have loads of questions. Just like Bethany had for you.' When Cassie did not answer her mother continued talking. 'We thought . . . as things have gone so well with you and Bethany, this would be easier . . .'

'Bethany always knew she was adopted. This is different, so very different,' Cassie said, fighting hard to control her voice. 'You lied. I can't . . .'

'Oh, love. Please, come out; let's talk . . .'

Cassie took a deep breath, unlocked the toilet door and came out. Shirley was holding out her arms for a hug, but Cassie couldn't . . . not now. 'You've lied to me all my life. I can't even . . . no, Mum. Sorry. I'm not coming back with you. I'm just going to go home by myself, work out what I feel about all this . . .'

Shirley let her arms drop to her sides. 'All right, love. Whatever you think best. Then, when you're ready to talk . . .'

'I'll call you.' Cassie walked out of the toilets, past her mother, back to the table where she grabbed her handbag and jacket without even glancing at Tony, who was busy with the waitress, paying the bill.

'Cassie?' he said, as she turned to leave. His voice broke on the word.

She felt a wave of emotion wash over her, and nearly, so nearly turned to look back at him. But if she had, she knew she'd have broken down, here, in the middle of the pub, with the waitress and other customers looking on. She knew it'd hurt him. But she was hurting too. Her life was a lie. She pulled herself together, walking fast, out of the pub to the car park, into her car. For some reason she seemed unable to get the key into the ignition and had to jab at it a few times, swearing, before it would go in. She didn't dare look back at the pub door, in case her dad – no, *Tony*, he wasn't her dad – had come out after her. Right now, before she'd had time to think about this, she didn't want to even look at him, let alone talk to him.

At last the key found its slot, and she started the engine, rammed the car into reverse out of her parking spot, and was away, back through the village and out into the countryside where at last she could let out the choking sob that had been building. She dashed away tears with the back of her hand so she could see to drive. Thankfully it wasn't far, and soon she was back in her flat, ignoring the blink of an answer-phone message, and turning off her mobile.

'Fuck,' she said, collapsing full-length onto her sofa, her forearm across her eyes to cut out the world. How was she supposed to deal with all this? Her world, the world she thought she knew, was not the same. Would never be the same.

Bethany. How would she tell Bethany? You've found your birth mother, but not your grandfather, because he's lied for thirty-seven years. But Bethany would understand how it felt to be brought up by someone not biologically related to you. Cassie reached for her phone. Maybe she'd call Bethany now, talk it through, maybe her daughter would help her to come to terms with it – now that it seemed they'd both been adopted . . .

She stopped herself, while her phone was in the process of turning on. No. It wouldn't do to tell Bethany this right now. She needed to think about it herself first. And Bethany was too close – it affected her too. She'd need to talk to someone unconnected.

Tomorrow was Wednesday. Work, and then the pub. Andy. She'd already promised him the full story of why she'd had to miss work on Sunday. Maybe he'd be treated to this story too.

She imagined how Andy would sit and listen carefully, a concerned look on his face. She pictured him quietly fetching another pint when hers was finished, and letting her talk as much and for as long as she liked. Yes, Andy was the right person to confide in. Suddenly she felt she needed to see him, as soon as possible. Maybe she'd call and see if . . . no. It was Tuesday. He worked on Tuesdays, and played five-a-side football in the evenings, with a session in the pub with the footballers afterwards.

No, she couldn't break into his Tuesday night plans with her needs . . . They were friends, work colleagues, but not close enough for that.

She realised she had no one close enough that she felt she could call them and they'd drop everything and come to her aid. In the past she'd relied on her parents in these situations. Or rather, her mother and *step*-father.

She rolled over onto her side, clutched a cushion to her face and drew her knees up into the foetal position, and at last, she wept. For herself. For the undermining of her foundations. For what she'd lost. Because although she still had Shirley and Tony, it felt as though she'd lost something profound.

Chapter 14

George

18th March

I listened carefully, ear pressed to the door, as Mr Watling first asked Mrs Peters to recount everything she had done on the morning of 15th March. She obliged, telling him in great detail how she'd stoked up the range, sent Maggie to clean the grates, prepared the breakfast dishes and laid them out on the sideboard in the dining room, and then put together a tray of breakfast things for Lucy.

'And who took this tray up?'

'Master George, did, sir. He has, I mean, he had, a soft spot for the girl. He was always wanting an excuse to go up to her room if he could.'

'I see.' It was awful, hearing my love for Lucy described thus, as nothing more than a *soft spot*, and imagining the detective stroking his whiskers thoughtfully as he considered the possibilities. 'And did that breakfast tray include a cup of hot chocolate?'

'It did, sir, yes.'

'Who collected the breakfast things? The hot chocolate cup was left in Miss Carter's room, as I understand it.'

'Maggie collected the breakfast things, sir. But she brought down everything, including the cup. Lucy had a second cup of chocolate later.'

'Who took one that up to her?'

'Um, that was the mistress, Mrs Britten.'

'Does the household keep a supply of arsenic?' the inspector was now asking.

'Y-yes, sir, in a locked shed.' Mrs Peters' voice cracked as she replied.

'Who keeps the key to this shed?'

'I-I do, sir, in my room.'

'Who made the second hot chocolate? You, I would suppose?' The inspector sounded as though he was making an accusation.

'No, it was Mrs Britten who made it.'

I remembered how the doctor had poured the dregs of the hot chocolate into a flask and taken it away. Suddenly my blood ran cold when I thought about the paper in his bag I had glanced over – the tests for arsenic poisoning. Was it the hot chocolate that had poisoned her? Is that what they suspected? The hot chocolate Mrs Peters says *my mother* made for her and took to her? Mother, who had not taken any trays of food to her before, and who was furious with Father for his affair with the maid? I recalled her words when she heard of his visits to Lucy's room: *I'll finish her.* With horror, I understood why she had wanted to hear what passed in the drawing room this morning, and why she seemed so agitated at the arrival of the detective.

Surely not? I did not believe – did not want to believe – that she could be capable of such a thing. My own mother – who I loved dearly, and would do anything for – a murderer? Surely she hadn't meant to. Perhaps she'd only intended to make Lucy sick, so that Father would be put off from visiting her. That must be the reason. I recalled an overheard conversation between Lucy and Mother. Lucy had taunted her, I realised. She must have felt her position in the household was secure as Father's mistress. How could Mother have borne it?

If Inspector Watling questioned her and my father, as he surely would soon, he would find out about my father's visits to Lucy's room. That would give my mother a motive. He would arrest her. Our family would be in ruin – an adulterous head of the household, a murderous wife. My father's reputation would be in tatters, and my mother in prison, perhaps to hang.

Hang! I bit on my knuckles to stop a cry escaping my lips. I could not bear to think of that fate befalling my dear mother. And then it hit me. The answer, the only answer, to this terrible situation. If I truly loved my mother and would do anything for her, here was the thing I needed to do. Perhaps it would help me win her love, and my father's respect. Mother hadn't meant to kill Lucy. She did not deserve to hang. And only I could prevent this from being her fate.

The drawing room door opened and Mrs Peters emerged, in tears, her fist rammed up against her mouth. I realised I had listened to no more of her testimony since she'd revealed who made the second hot chocolate, but it mattered not. She almost bumped into me in her haste to leave the room, and she apologised.

I did not answer her, neither did I respond to Mother who had come out of the dining room and was frantically beckoning me to go in and update her. Instead I went straight into the drawing room and stood before the detective.

'Ah, Mr George Britten,' he said. 'I would like a few words with Mrs Britten next, if you would be so good as to send her in.' His voice was matter-of-fact, betraying no sign of his suspicions, though I knew they must be there.

'Sir, I would prefer you to talk to me next,' I said, trying desperately to keep the tremor from my voice. 'It might save you time.' What I was about to say would change my life forever. There would be no going back. I swallowed hard. Could I do this? I pictured

129

my mother gazing at me with love and gratitude, and my father regarding me with pride, and it strengthened my resolve. It was a path forward. A way to save my mother. With the future I'd once dreamed of no longer possible and none other presenting itself, I had nothing to lose and everything – my mother's love and respect – to gain. Watling stared at me a while, frowned, and then nodded.

'Very well. So, first I need you to tell me your movements on the morning of 15th March.' He turned a new page in his notebook, wrote my name at the top of the page, and waited expectantly.

No one knew I had been out all morning, except Maggie, and I knew she had not mentioned seeing me. So I told the detective I had stayed at home, moping in my room, for most of the morning.

'Moping? Why?' he asked.

I took a deep breath. Time for the lies to begin. 'Lucy had turned me down.'

'Turned you down?'

'When I took her breakfast up, I propositioned her. I asked her to come away with me, when she was well enough. I wanted us to marry and set up a modest home together. I loved her. You can ask Mrs Peters – she knows how I felt.' Of course I knew Mrs Peters had already said I had a 'soft spot' for Lucy.

'And Lucy said no?'

I made myself appear bitter and frustrated, consumed by hate. 'She laughed at me. She said she would no more look at me than she would a ten-year-old farmer's lad. She poured scorn on my love for her, and for that I immediately hated her, with even more passion than I had loved her.'

'I see.' The detective made a few notes in his book. I waited for him to ask me about the hot chocolate, or ask me what happened next, but he said nothing more. 'Well, George, she is gone and you can no longer either love or hate her. Could you send your mother in to me next?'

'But, I haven't finished.' There was nothing for it. I had to deflect attention away from Mother and onto myself. I had hoped to be more subtle about it but with the detective apparently dismissing me already I realised bluntness would be the only way.

'If there is something more you need to say, please say it,' Inspector Watling said, as he continued scribbling in his notebook.

'There is. Later in the morning, I heard someone go past my bedroom door and up the stairs to the attic floor. I believe it was my mother, taking Lucy a cup of hot chocolate.'

'Mm hmm,' Watling grunted. I knew my lies needed to chime with the facts he had already heard, to make them more believable.

'When I heard her come down again, I went up. Lucy was asleep, her face turned to the wall. It was then that I did it.'

'Did what?' I had his attention now. He put down his pen and looked straight at me.

'Oh, Inspector, I am sorry, so sorry, I didn't mean to kill her. I just thought I'd pay her back for rejecting me. I wanted to give her some discomfort for a few days perhaps, not to kill her outright.'

'George, calm down please, and state the facts clearly. What did you do?'

'I got some arsenic, and slipped it into her hot chocolate.' That should do it. He had not mentioned poison to me. And indeed, he raised his eyebrows at my words.

'And where did you get the arsenic?'

'From the shed. We keep it for rat poison. The key is kept in the housekeeper's room. I didn't know how much to use. It seems I used too much and I am so sorry! I was consumed by hatred and wanted to punish her, but I never meant to kill her!' I wrung my hands to act out regret at my actions, but the tears I shed were genuine. No matter what Lucy could have said or done, she had not deserved to die.

'I see. Well, you leave me with no alternative. I must arrest you for the murder by poisoning of Lucy Carter. If you are willing to write and sign a confession it will spare your parents the agonies of seeing this go to trial. I will then need to take you to the county jail to await sentencing.'

I breathed in deeply, and steeled myself. This is how it would be. I agreed to write the confession – a trial would be too dangerous, in case more facts came to light, perhaps about my father's affair with Lucy. Inspector Watling then furnished me with paper and pen, and bade me sit at the table where he had been, to write my confession. I made sure to write it exactly as I had told him, changing no details whatsoever. In the meantime he rang the bell, which was quickly answered by Mrs Peters. He asked her to send in my father. Her eyes widened to see me sitting at the table, writing, but she nodded and left.

A moment later both my father and mother entered the room. I looked up from my writing to watch their reactions as the detective told them of the latest events.

'Sir, madam, it is my unpleasant duty to inform you that I have now determined the cause of death of the maid Lucy Carter and the person responsible for it,' he began.

'Well, go on then, man,' said my father, impatient as ever. Mother looked white and shaky. I wondered if she thought Watling was about to accuse her.

'Your son, George, has confessed to adding arsenic to Lucy's hot chocolate,' he summarised. 'The girl died of arsenic poisoning.' Mother gasped and her hand flew to her mouth, before she sat down heavily on a sofa.

'But, George, why?' she asked.

Only I understood that she was not asking why I had poisoned Lucy, but why I was confessing to a crime I did not commit.

'I wanted only to hurt her, not to kill her. To make her ill for a while . . . because . . . she'd turned me down. I declared my love for her but she laughed at me. I want *only to be loved and respected*,' I said. Would she understand the subtext to my words, which I had stressed especially for her? She stared hard at me, and for a brief instant I thought she was going to confirm that

I was loved by her, and respected by my father. But it wasn't to be. She opened her mouth as though to speak, but then shook her head slightly and looked away.

'You've brought shame on us, George,' said my father. 'She was a mere servant girl and not worthy of your attentions. But no matter what she did or said, to kill her is beyond belief. I'm ashamed and horrified by your actions.'

'But, Father, she was worthy of *your* attentions, was she not?' I could not help myself. The words slipped out, but I muttered them, so that only he would hear.

'I don't know what you mean,' he replied, quietly. As he gazed at me I nodded slightly, to let him know I knew his secret, but that I would not tell it.

'Well, George, at least you have done the honourable thing now by confessing,' Father said. I don't know if I imagined the slight break to his voice as he said this. He coughed, nodded to the detective and then took Mother's elbow to lead her out of the room.

And so it was done. Whether Mother would love me or Father respect me for it, no longer mattered. It was as if a big, well-oiled machine had been set in motion, and I was powerless now to stop it. Having written and signed my confession, I was taken with Inspector Watling to the county prison, where I was held for two days. During this time I had only the Bible to read, and was fed just bread, gruel and water. I had time enough to reflect on what I had done, and what fate might await me. Most probably it would be the gallows, but this did not frighten me for I could picture no future life for myself anyway.

But the gallows was not to be my fate, nor transportation. At my sentencing, the judge read out my confession and set great store by the fact that I had only meant to cause Lucy some discomfort to punish her for spurning me. I had not wilfully committed murder. He also mentioned my previous good character and my youth several times. And so my punishment was set at fifteen years imprisonment with hard labour. I was to be conveyed to Millbank Prison in London the next day.

I was taken by train and closed wagon to Millbank, accompanied by a police constable at all times. I could not see the prison as we drove in through its gates. I had only an impression of high, soot-blackened walls, imposing gates and a terrible clang like the gates of Hell as they closed behind me. I was taken initially to a room fitted out as the prisoners' reception office. A framed poster on the wall advertised the prison rules, and those were read out to me by a warder. I can read, I wanted to tell him, but thought it better to keep quiet, nod and agree. I was made to leave all my personal property. I gave my name, age, place of birth and other details and was weighed and measured.

Then I was sent to have a bath. I'd had one at home very recently, being in the habit of taking one every few days, but it was prison regulations so I complied. I was issued with carbolic soap and a scrubbing brush, and sent in to the bath room. The water had already been used by the last several men to be admitted that day, and was far from clean. I feared I would emerge dirtier than before, but bathe I must. And then I was inspected from head to foot to ensure I was clean enough to enter the prison. I was issued with prison clothing – a rough shirt, trousers and jacket in grey wool with a design of black crows' feet. As I stood there thus attired, a woman came and sewed a number to the breast of my jacket. This was my prison number – 7565 – and was what I was to be known by.

The prison medical officer saw me next. I was pronounced fit and healthy, and cleared for hard labour. What that would entail I did not know, and neither did I care to dwell on it.

Next stop was the barber's, where my hair was cropped and my whiskers, such as they are, shaved.

Finally I was led along miles of corridors, all smelling of

carbolic mingled with unwashed bodies – a paradoxical combination, I remember thinking – and through no fewer than seven iron doors (I counted them), each of which had to be unlocked to allow the warder and myself to pass through, and then relocked behind us. At the end of this broken journey was my cell. I was pushed into it, and the door locked behind me.

That was, I think, the very worst moment of all. It was the moment when I realised this was all real, and this small cell, barely six feet square, was to be my home for the next fifteen years.

There was a raised wooden platform with a thin mattress upon it, and a roll of woollen blankets. A block of wood placed at one end of the bed I assumed was intended as a pillow. A small scrubbed table and stool. A bucket, with a fitted lid. A Bible, a bar of soap and a small wooden box, which contained a white substance. I tasted it – it was salt. As I was to learn, prison meals needed seasoning to make them palatable. There was a gas jet for lighting protruding from the wall beside the door – its tap on the outside and its use controlled by the warder. And that was all. The sum total of my creature comforts could be counted on two hands, with room to spare.

The warder called an hour later, informing me there would be no labour for me that first day, but I would start on oakum-picking on the morrow, and would also be visited by the prison governor and the chaplain. It was the chaplain who arranged for me to be furnished with paper and pen, that I might continue writing my journal.

My meal that first night, taken in my cell, consisted of a watery broth and a hunk of dry, gritty bread. When the bell rang to tell us to unroll our bedding and make ready for the night, I crept into my bed feeling wholly sorry for myself, and beginning to wonder whether I had made a terrible mistake. But then I imagined my mother in this cell, eating gruel and trying to make herself comfortable on this narrow, hard bed with a wooden pillow, and I realised things could be no other way than this.

Chapter 15

Cassie

When Cassie woke up on the day after her lunch out, for one blissful moment she forgot all about her parents' momentous revelation. And then, as she rolled over in the dark and switched her alarm clock off and her bedside light on, she remembered. Tony was not her father. At once a pounding headache began, and then she remembered she'd drunk a couple of glasses of red wine in the evening to take her mind off it. Her eyes were sore too. She groaned and rolled out of bed. She needed to be at work in an hour.

There was a text from Andy on her phone. *Still up for the pub after work? Want to know what happened on Sunday.*

Sunday? For a moment Cassie was confused. What had happened on Sunday? Sunday was before she found out that her father was not her father. Sunday was another planet. She went through to the bathroom and got in the shower, and then remembered. Of course, she'd had to miss work on Sunday because of collecting Bethany after the climate change march. She'd promised to tell Andy all about it. And last night, she'd decided to tell him too, about her parentage.

Once out of the shower and dried, she texted him back. *Definitely. Lots to talk about, if you can bear to listen to it all.*

A text pinged back. *No problem. Should we go somewhere quieter if you need to talk?*

She wasn't sure how to answer that and eventually settled on a non-committal: *Possibly, see you soon.*

Forty minutes later she looked presentable for work. Thankfully it wasn't the sort of job where you needed to be well groomed in tights and heels and lipstick – she knew she wouldn't have lasted five minutes in that sort of job. But her hair was washed and tied back in a ponytail, a bit of make-up covered the worst of the redness around her eyes, her stomach had settled after a bit of breakfast and her tracksuit was clean. As she walked to work she debated whether to tell Shania what she'd found out yesterday. Shania was her best friend at the sports centre – or so she'd always considered. By the time she'd reached the centre she'd made a decision – she would keep this quiet from Shania until she'd come to terms with it herself.

'Morning, Cass! How's things? Did you see *Who Do You Think You Are?* last night? That story about the great-grandmother and her first baby she gave up for adoption – made me think of you and your daughter! Then it turns out the grandfather was adopted too! Made my head spin, I'm telling you.'

'Hey, Shania. No, missed that one.' Cassie put her bag in her locker and hung up her coat.

'Missed it? Who are you and what have you done with Cassie Turner?' Shania widened her eyes in mock horror. 'You *never* miss an episode. Unless – ah, were you out? Who with? Some new fellow? Must admit you look a bit tired this morning. Was he good?'

'Ha ha. No such luck. I just . . . well I'd been out for lunch with my parents, for D-dad's birthday and I kind of . . . fell asleep on the sofa after.' Sort of true. She'd lain on the sofa with her wine and her churned-up thoughts.

'Oh well. You'll probably catch it on iPlayer later anyway. It's a good one.'

Cassie smiled. 'Sure, will do.' She checked the rota for the day. Good. She was on pool duty first thing. Time alone, when she could let her thoughts wander as long as she kept half an eye on what was going on in the pool. It'd be quiet this morning. There was an over-sixties aqua-fit class and then school lessons, and then the lunchtime public swim. The staff alternated between poolside and dry-side duties, an hour at a time. Ben and Toby would be in later, but for the first pool session it was just her.

She stripped off her tracksuit so she was in just shorts and T-shirt, hung her whistle round her neck and went through to the pool, climbing up to the high observation chair. The aqua-fit class was due to start in five minutes and people were already coming through from the changing rooms and waiting on the benches that lined the poolside.

Two minutes later Andy came to the poolside and approached her chair. She leaned down to hear what he had to say.

'Hi, Cass. I'm going to be busy most of the day – got some council bigwig coming for a meeting and then interviewing for a new receptionist. You still want to go somewhere other than the Red Lion? Ben, Tobe and Shania will be asking if we're going out. I was going to say I've got something on; if I say I'm going somewhere with you they'll jump to conclusions . . . maybe we could go to the Three Crowns – that'll be quiet. Shall we meet there at six – give you time to pop home and change if you like?'

'Er, yeah. Sure. Three Crowns at six. Yeah I'll tell Shania I'm a bit tired tonight or something.'

'OK, it's a date, then.' Andy smiled and wiggled his fingers at her in a wave as he walked away.

Cassie decided to yawn a bit in Shania's company so her cover story of being 'a bit tired' would work. Shania had already commented she looked exhausted anyway. Cassie hated lying but Andy was right – if the others thought for a moment that she and Andy were going out somewhere, just the two of them, there'd be innuendos and ribbing about it for weeks. Which she wouldn't mind if it was actually a date – but it wasn't. It was a friendly drink, a chance to offload on someone who was a good listener. Nothing more.

The aqua-fit class members were getting into the water so Cassie turned her attention to watching what was going on. Her greatest fear, all these long years of working in the centre, was that she'd go off into too deep a daydream and not notice someone in trouble in the water. She'd perfected the art, she thought, of keeping enough of her attention on the pool while still being able to think about other things while she sat and watched. And today's topic of thought was: how to come to terms with the fact that Tony wasn't her dad.

Why did it matter so much to her? She was surprised at her own reaction to the revelation. Tony was still the man who'd brought her up, who'd taught her to ride a bike and helped with her homework – the one who'd always been there for her. And yet . . . now it all felt so different. Picturing his face, knowing that genetically he was nothing to do with her. She wasn't who she'd thought she was. It was different for Bethany who'd always known, but for her, Cassie, it was going to take a while to adjust to this new truth.

The day dragged on – somehow it seemed much slower than usual. At lunchtime Cassie noticed she had texts from both her mum and Tony, both urging her to ring them or go round to see them whenever she was ready. That they understood it had been a shock but that it didn't need to change anything about their relationship. That they loved her, and always would.

She read them, knowing they'd see that the messages had been read, but still couldn't bring herself to reply. She realised she needed to talk it all through with Andy first, get his advice on how to respond. She muted her phone and put it back in her bag.

'Problem?' Shania asked, over the Coronation chicken sandwich she was eating.

'No, no, nothing,' Cassie responded, realising she'd been frowning at her phone. 'Just some marketing rubbish. I don't know how they get the number.'

'I know. Really annoying, isn't it? So, you going to the pub tonight? Haven't been out for a drink with you for ages!'

'All of a week, Shania. No, sorry, not tonight. I still feel wrecked somehow. Gonna go home, eat some dinner and have an early night.'

'You can still do that and fit in a swift pint first, Cass. Come on. It'll do you good. The boys were saying you look like you could do with a good laugh.'

'Ah, no. Thanks, but honestly, if I go for one I'll be there all night and I need to sleep.'

'You sure you're all right, Cass? All these years I've known you I don't think you've ever said no to a pint.' Shania looked concerned.

'I'm fine. Well, probably fine. Might be coming down with a cold or something. Yes, I think that's it. Nothing a quiet night in won't solve.' Cassie gave what she hoped was a sick-but-brave smile and turned her attention to opening her ready-made Caesar salad pot. 'God why does the lid always rip when you pull it off? Can't they invent something that comes off in one piece without you having to pick at it with your fingernails?'

Shania laughed. 'I know, right? OK then, just me and the boys in the pub because apparently Andy's had something come up that he can't get out of. Lightweights, the both of you.'

At last the day was over. Cassie walked quickly home as rain was threatening. There was time for a quick shower. After, she put on black jeans and a brightly coloured loose tunic top. Usually she'd be in the pub in her work tracksuit – but that was the Red Lion. Tonight she was going to the Three Crowns, which was a smarter kind of place. She wondered whether to have a quick bite to eat before she went out, but decided against it. She wasn't hungry. She could always get some crisps and nuts in the pub anyway.

She grabbed an umbrella for the walk to the pub, but thankfully the rain held off, and she reached it just after six. Andy was already there, and had secured a table in a quiet nook near the fireplace where a welcoming log fire was burning. 'This OK?' he asked. 'Or do you think we'll get too hot here?'

'It's lovely,' she said, as she removed her jacket and tucked her umbrella under the chair. 'Pint?'

'I'll get them,' he said, easing out from behind the table to get to the bar. 'Usual?'

'Please.'

He was back a couple of minutes later, with the pints and a couple of menus tucked under his arm. 'Thought we might want a bite to eat?'

'Ah, why not?' She smiled and took a menu from him, suddenly feeling hungry. There was an enticing range of food – not just regular pub classics but some more adventurous dishes. 'Looks good.'

Once they'd ordered food, Andy sat back and looked at her expectantly. 'So. I'm dying to know what it was that kept you from work on Sunday. If you're still happy to talk about it, of course.'

'Yeah. Of course. But . . .' Suddenly she felt she wanted to talk about the bombshell her parents had dropped on her first.

'But?' His eyes were concerned, sympathetic.

'But there's something else, first. Something I kind of really want . . . no, *need* to talk about. Do you mind?'

'I'm told I'm a good listener.'

'You are. So . . . I just found out, yesterday in fact, that my dad isn't my real dad. And I'm still trying to process that fact.'

'What? Were you adopted or something?'

'Mum's my biological mother. She was pregnant when she married, but Dad's not my biological father.'

'Whoa. Who is?'

'Don't know. Haven't asked her, yet. Dad knew, apparently, but was happy to marry her and pretend I was his anyway.'

'Why did they suddenly decide to tell you now? Is it because of Bethany?'

She nodded. 'Yes, I think mostly because of her. Because she was commenting on whether she looks like him or not. And because I've been researching our family tree – what I thought was our family tree – and was asking him about his great-great-grandfather.' Cassie felt annoyed that her research had turned out not to be her own family. George Britten had seemed such an interesting character, yet he wasn't even related to her! At least it meant she wasn't descended from a murderer after all. She'd hated that thought – that an ancestor might have killed someone.

'And how do you feel about this? Must be a bit of a shock.'

'Definitely a shock.' With horror she felt tears welling up. She took a deep breath and looked away, so he wouldn't notice the telltale sparkles in her eyes. 'I don't quite know how I feel about it. I still love him – he's still the same person who taught me to climb trees and played endless games of Cluedo with me when I was obsessed with it at fourteen and all the rest of it – but somehow I don't feel as though my foundations are as solid as they were. It's like there's some sort of shadowy presence there now – my biological father. I feel I don't quite know who I am, anymore.'

'Have you told Bethany?'

'Not yet. She's just found us – I don't want to have to say actually there's a plot twist and your granddad isn't your granddad after all.'

'From what you say of her, she'd cope all right, I think. When she did her research it was to find you, not your parents.'

'True.'

Their food arrived then, and they fell silent for a while, commenting now and again on how good it was. Cassie went to the bar to buy another round, choosing wine for herself this time to go with the meal.

'Thing I find a little bit odd, if you don't mind me saying so,' Andy said, as they perused the dessert menu, 'is that you took Bethany getting in contact so calmly and yet you're thrown by your dad's revelation. To me, a daughter turning up out of the blue would be the bigger event.'

Cassie shook her head. 'But I always knew I'd had a daughter, and had imagined many times what it would be like if she contacted me as an adult. So although it's a huge thing to happen – and by the way I was not at all calm when I got her first letter – it was less of a surprise. Getting to know Bethany has added to my life. Whereas finding out about Dad has kind of taken something away.'

'If you found who your real dad was, and got in contact with him, wouldn't that add something the way Bethany has?'

'I don't know. Maybe. But I'm worried Dad – by which I mean Tony – would still seem diminished in my eyes somehow. God I wish I'd always known this. If I'd grown up with it the way Bethany did I think it'd be easier.' Once again, tears came to Cassie's eyes and this time she was not quick enough looking away. Andy's expression softened – he'd obviously noticed.

He reached across the table to her and took her hand. 'Ah, Cass. I can't know exactly how it feels but I imagine it's like having the rug pulled from under you. Listen, I think you need to talk to your parents again. Sit down with them, hear the full story, assuming your mum's prepared to tell you it all. Maybe just see her on her own. When you know it all, maybe you'll understand it better. Ask all the questions you need to – from what you've always said about them, they're great parents who'd do anything for you. That won't have changed.'

He looked at his hand holding hers, as though he'd only just realised what he was doing, and took it away, lifting his pint for a sip. Cassie's hand felt strangely cold and empty.

'Then when you know the full facts, take a few days to assimilate it all, and perhaps book a day out with them. Not to sit and talk any more, but just to enjoy their company, the way you always have done.'

Cassie pulled a tissue from her pocket and wiped away a stray tear. 'Could go and see a film with them, I suppose. We used to go every month.'

'Perfect. Suggest that, and a drink after, when you can discuss the film.'

'Dad would like that.'

Andy smiled. 'You're calling him Dad again. Not Tony.'

'I don't think I could get used to calling him anything else.'

'And there's no need to.'

'Cheers, Andy. You're very wise.'

'Huh. Am I really?'

'Yes,' she said, firmly, smiling as she picked up her wine. 'Thank you.'

'You're very welcome. So, what about last Sunday then? What happened?'

The tale of Bethany's anguished call, the late-night dash up to London to rescue her, the night in a hotel and the drive to Leicester the next day all seemed so distant now. Cassie told him the whole story, trying to find the fine line between making it amusing but also ensuring he understood that she'd simply had to do what she did. At the end, he picked up his glass, clinked hers and said, 'You are one awesome mother, Cassie, you know that? Not everyone would have done all that, not even for a daughter they'd brought up.'

Cassie's next day off was Saturday. She'd made no plans to see Bethany and in any case, her daughter had texted to say she was invited to a family event – a cousin's birthday party. Cassie felt a pang of jealousy but remembered that of course Bethany had a whole family that she, Cassie, was not a part of. She decided to carry out the first part of Andy's advice – to meet with her mother and hear the whole story. When she phoned to arrange a meeting it was as though her mother had been waiting by the phone for exactly this call.

'Of course, dear. Wherever and whenever you like.'

'Come round to my flat for coffee on Saturday?'

'Yes, that's fine. Do you want both of us, or . . .'

'Just you, Mum, if that's all right.'

'Of course it is. Your dad's longing to see you again, but it's completely up to you.'

Cassie felt a pang of guilt at what she was putting him through, but it was quickly followed by a flash of anger. If they hadn't lied about her parentage all her life they wouldn't be feeling this anguish now, would they?

Saturday rolled around at last. Cassie had cleaned and tidied her flat and bought pastries for them to eat with their coffee. Mum arrived precisely on time – at eleven as they'd agreed – bearing a large bunch of flowers. 'They're actually from your dad,' she said. 'Shall I put them in water?'

'Yes please,' Cassie replied, knowing full well that the flowers would have been her mum's suggestion, but appreciating the sentiment.

They busied themselves in the kitchen for a few minutes – Mum with the flowers and Cassie with the coffee. When it was ready Cassie led her mother through to the sitting room, where they sat at opposite ends of the sofa.

'So,' Cassie began, 'I guess, basically I'd like to know . . . everything. Who's my real father. What kind of relationship did you have with him, how come he didn't stick around and how come Tony was happy to just pretend all these years.' She noticed her mother wince as she called her dad Tony, but didn't comment on it.

'OK. So – let me start at the beginning. I'd met Tony, and we had dated a few times. I knew he really liked me, and I liked him. But then . . . he went away for a few weeks. On a short work contract – in the US. We kept in touch – there was no email back then and calls were expensive but we wrote letters every week. In one letter he wrote about a woman he'd gone to a gig with, and afterwards they'd had a few drinks. In his letter it sounded to me like they were dating. So I thought, well, that's that then, and began considering myself unattached.'

She took a breath, picked up her coffee and sipped it. 'During that time I went to a few parties. Looking back I suppose I was hurt – I'd thought I was waiting till Tony came back but he didn't seem to want me. So, I guess I was a bit wild. Sorry, love. You probably don't want to hear all the sordid details.'

'I think I need to, Mum,' Cassie said quietly.

'All right. Well, at a couple of parties there was a fellow called Jack. He was tall, good-looking, bit of a bad boy, and . . . well I suppose I quite fancied him. Then he asked me out. I was flattered – of all the available women in our set he'd picked me. I realised later he'd also picked several others – some turned him down, some went out with him just once or twice, like I did.'

Cassie was listening intently, staring down into her coffee cup as though her mother's story was playing out in its depths. Jack. Was that her real father's name?

'So anyway, Jack took me to a pub where we had a dinner. Just pie and chips – I remember thinking it was cheap and nasty food. Then we went on to another pub, closer to his home. He was driving and I thought he'd had too much to drink, but I was too scared to say so. I thought, well I'll have one more then get a taxi home. I even checked in my purse that I'd have enough cash. But he talked me into having a couple more drinks – he paid so I thought well, I can still afford a taxi. I suppose I was a bit drunk by then. When he suggested leaving the car in the pub car park and going up to his flat for a coffee I thought it was a good idea and would help sober me up, and I could call a taxi from there. Of course there were no mobile phones in those days.'

She broke off to sip her coffee again, and Cassie dared not look her in the eye, terrified of how this story would pan out.

'In his flat, which was messy and masculine and smelt of unwashed damp towels, he put the kettle on and then sat with me on the sofa waiting for it to boil. Then he started kissing me, and, oh dear, I'd had that much to drink I was not really thinking straight. I kissed him back, and one thing led to another. You know.'

Cassie nodded. She'd had a few such evenings herself, in the years since her relationship with Arjun. He'd been her only proper boyfriend. No one else had lasted more than a few dates. 'So, was that when . . .'

'You were conceived. Yes. I was ashamed at first but actually it was the best thing that ever happened to me.' Mum tentatively took Cassie's hand and squeezed it. 'It resulted in you.'

'Did you see him again?'

'At another party, where he cornered me and tried to get me into a bedroom, but I'd decided I didn't want to see him anymore. I'd realised we didn't have much in common, and ever since our date I'd only been able to think about Tony. So I pushed him away and he just went off and found someone else. I left that party early. I never saw him again.'

'Did you tell him when you found out you were pregnant?'

Mum pinched her lips together and shook her head. 'I agonised over that for ages. I talked it through with my parents and my best friend. They all said I should tell him. I'd just about decided to, when two things happened. Firstly Tony came back, and wanted to see me, and it was clear he was still very much interested. Secondly, I heard via another friend that Jack had moved away, and no one was sure where to. So I decided that was a sign – he wasn't going to be around so there was no point telling him, even if I could find him.'

'But you told Tony?'

'Yes.' Mum smiled. 'And he was amazing. I told him I was

pregnant on our first date after he came home. We were walking through a park; it was one of those bright autumn days when the leaves were crunching underfoot. I told him the whole story as we walked along, and then he caught my hand and made me stop, and asked if I wanted to marry him. Just like that.'

Cassie smiled too. She'd heard this story before, but a different version in which her mother had been pregnant by Tony. 'And you said yes.'

Mum shook her head. 'Not immediately. Oh I know that's what we always told you, but it was more complicated than that. I had to be sure he wouldn't regret taking on another man's child. We walked and talked for hours that day – thankfully the weather stayed fine. In the end I'd agreed we'd become an "item" as we used to say back then, and if we still felt the same in a couple of months then we'd start planning a wedding. And in that time I grew to love him deeply, and he stayed certain that I was the one, and so . . . the rest is history.'

Cassie nodded. Her parents had a solid, loving marriage. The kind of marriage she'd always hoped she might have herself, one day. 'Did Da . . . Tony . . . never want children of his own?'

'He did, and we tried, but it just didn't happen. But right from the start, when I said I was not going to tell Jack he had a child, Tony said he'd be your father in every way but biologically. I left the father's name blank on the birth certificate. Of course we then hid that away and only used the short-form certificate to get your passports and so on.'

Mum fell silent for a moment, then took Cassie's hand. 'Love, he'd be so hurt if you start calling him Tony and not Dad. After all these years, all he's done, he's still your dad in every meaningful way.'

'I know. I don't want to hurt him. It's just . . . somehow, knowing he's not biologically related, it all suddenly feels so different.'

Mum squeezed her hand. 'It doesn't need to be different. It's up to you. It'll take time.'

'Yes. I suppose so.' There were just a couple more questions Cassie needed to ask. 'Did you ever hear from Jack again?'

'Never. Heard on the grapevine he'd moved to London; that was all.'

'What was his surname?'

'What?' Shirley seemed surprised by the question. 'What do you want to know that for? You're not going to . . . try to find him, are you?'

Cassie shook her head. 'No, not interested in finding him. Just want the complete picture.'

'Oh. Well, it was Wilkins. No, Wilkinson. Yes, that was it. Jack bloody Wilkinson.'

'Thanks.' Cassie stored the information away in her memory. Her father. Jack Wilkinson.

Chapter 16

George

Late March (I am no longer sure of the date)

I have been here for some time now. I am settling, if that is the right word, into a routine. Here's how the days at Millbank are spent.

The bell rings at a quarter to six, whereupon I and, I suppose, the other inmates wake up cold and shivering, roll up our bedding, clean out the cell, slop out, dress and await inspection. Breakfast is dry bread and water. We make a brief visit to the chapel at eight o'clock, then we are returned to our cells and locked in. And then a pile of old ships' rope, tarred, matted and ingrained with salt, is delivered, for picking to produce oakum. The idea is to tease apart the fibres with your fingers, so it can be used again, usually for caulking ships' timbers. The work cuts your fingertips and strains your eyes and your back, as you lean over it in the poor light. You unravel each strand, rolling it back and forth on your knee, separate the strands and clean them. You must produce three to four pounds of picked oakum every two hours, and the pickings are weighed at the end of each day. If you have not produced a satisfactory amount you are punished.

We have an hour's exercise in the late morning, which consists of walking around the prison yard. The prison exercise yard is a bleak place, bounded on all sides by high, featureless brick walls, which are topped with metal spikes. The other inmates look to be a fearsome lot – dirty, smelly, wearing ill-fitting prison garb and the wildest collection of footwear I have ever seen. I have been allowed to keep my own boots, being a first-class prisoner – that is to say: a prisoner who can read and write.

Exercise hour is the only hour of the day when I am out of my cell, and the only chance I have of getting a look at my fellow inmates. A look is all I can manage – we have to walk in line, no closer than six feet apart. If anyone catches up with the man in front a whistle is blown, and everyone has to stop and realign themselves. If the same man is caught walking at the wrong pace three times he is subjected to the silent system: solitary confinement for a period of a few weeks. I make absolutely certain to keep my distance, although I allow my eyes to roam freely.

The little irregularly shaped patch of sky above, that is sometimes blue and sometimes grey, the occasional sound of sweet birdsong, the scents that reach us from outside – these are my only interaction with the outside world and although they are few, I relish them and look forward to the exercise hour.

Lunch – thin gruel and weak tea – is at midday, and supper – a feeble stew – at half past five. Between these times we are back in our cells picking oakum or taking a turn on the treadwheel. This is a contraption on which six men stand side by side, climbing a never-ending staircase, which turns a wheel to grind corn or pump water, or very often, for no useful purpose other than to punish the inmates. We do an hour at a time. It is hard work and after my first few turns my thighs were burning. Then I worked out the best technique – it is all about the timing. Step up too soon and you are pushing the wheel around by yourself with no help from the other men. Step up too late and you almost fall onto it, painfully jarring your back in the process. Get it just right and it is like climbing a staircase.

At eight o'clock a bell rings to tell us to cease work, and then any tools we have been using are removed from the cells. There is a free hour for reading or writing in our cells, and lights out is at nine o'clock, the gas lights turned off on the outside of the cells by the warders as they do their evening rounds.

As a new prisoner the chaplain made a point of coming to visit me in my cell during my first day, while I was working on the oakum. I was about halfway through my pile, feeling almost proud of the way I was beginning to get into a rhythm with the work, when the door opened and the chaplain was admitted. His name is Nathaniel Spring, and he is a man of about thirty, tall and well-built, a handsome man with an open, kind face. I warmed to him instantly, before he'd even introduced himself.

'You must be George Britten, I presume?' he said, holding out his hand. I was faintly amused – who else might he expect to find in this cell? And so I shook his hand with a smile on my face, which was echoed on his. 'May I sit down?' He indicated my platform bed, and I nodded.

'I like to meet all new inmates,' he explained. 'You'll already have been told how the prison operates, and the governor will meet you later if he hasn't already. My job is to ensure your spiritual well-being of course, but also to loan a friendly ear, and give you a shoulder to cry on, as it were. For someone as young as you, from your background, prison can be a frightening and daunting place. You must accept your lot, but it does not need to break you. I am here to make sure that you get through this period of your life and emerge at the other end as a better man.' He smiled warmly at me, and his eyes crinkled at the edges. He gave the impression of being a proper friend.

'Thank you,' I said. 'It has been a shock arriving here and I fear it will take some time to adapt. Any help you can give me will be much appreciated.'

'And will be offered gladly,' he said. 'I teach some men to read and write, but of course you won't need that. I'll ensure you have access to books to read. Is there anything particular you would like?'

It was then that I asked for pen and paper, so I could continue with my journal. It was not usual for inmates to have access to such equipment but as many prisoners were illiterate that was not surprising. Nathaniel Spring readily agreed to my request, and offered to apply to the governor on my behalf.

'It will help you immensely, I think, if in your writings you are able to work through the thoughts and feelings that led you to commit your crime. I do know, by the way, what it is you did, what put you here. And I very much hope that during our chats, and through prayer and contemplation, you will eventually repent of your sins and cleanse your soul sufficiently to allow God to forgive you.'

I was tempted at that moment, sorely tempted, to confess to him. What a confession it would have been – not to admit to what I had done, but to tell the truth about what I had not done. To confess that I had allowed myself to be arrested and charged with murder, convicted of it and imprisoned for it, when all along I was innocent, and guilty only of wanting to spare my mother from the gallows. But I could not admit my innocence without incriminating my mother and ruining my father's reputation. No. It was better this way.

I wondered what my brother Charles would think when he heard what had happened. No doubt my father had written to him by now, to tell him of his brother's disgrace. But he too, if he knew the truth, would agree that it was better for the family if I shouldered the blame. I wondered for a moment if he would have done the same thing, himself. To protect me – I think he would have. To protect Mother or Father, I am not so sure. My resolve wavered at this thought – had I, after all, done the right thing?

That thought must have been visible on my face, for the chaplain looked concerned, and reached out a hand to lay on my arm. 'Be strong, my son. It is hard to bear this new life, but you will become accustomed to it. The first days are the worst, and you will soon be over them, and it will then be easier. Trust me.'

The kindliness and concern in his eyes made me want to weep, and bury my face against his shoulder, as though I was a child and he was my mother. Though I did not recall ever having been held by my own mother in such a way. I pulled myself together. His presence in my life could become, perhaps, more like that of Mr Smythe's. A wise, older friend who would help advise me and shape me through the years to come. I had a strong feeling I would be in deep need of him at least until I had adjusted to life in prison. The fifteen years ahead of me seemed to stretch to infinity.

Later I was taken to meet the governor. This meeting was in marked contrast to the one with the chaplain. Instead of him coming to my cell, I was taken to the governor's office. There I had to stand in an iron cage, locked and chained, while the governor sat across the room at his desk. His name is Major Freeman – an ironic name for the governor of a prison! He is retired from the army, having fought and been injured during the Crimean War. He walks with a pronounced limp and puts up with no misbehaviour from his 'boys', as he calls the inmates. I had the distinct impression he would prefer to still be part of the army, fighting, issuing orders, engaging the enemy rather than running a prison.

'Britten, is it?' the governor said, referring to a sheet of paper.

'Yes, sir.' Do not speak unless spoken to, I'd been advised by the chaplain. It was just as though I was a child again, standing in front of my father awaiting punishment for some minor misdemeanour.

'Here for murdering a poor innocent young girl. That right?'

I swallowed, and nodded.

'Speak up, boy.' He barked these words at me.

'Yes, sir.' He'd barked, but I could only manage a squeak.

'You were lucky to escape the hangman's noose, boy. You'll find life hard in here, after your pampered upbringing. It's what you deserve, after ending a poor girl's life, just because she spurned you. Right then. I inspect the prison every day. Your cell is to be tidy. You stand to attention when I am in your sight. Don't expect any concessions due to your class – I'll see you don't get any. Put your nose out of line just once and you will be punished.'

Punishment, he told me, was the birch for assaulting a prison officer, or for a less serious offence a spell in complete isolation, with privileges such as access to the exercise yard, the comfort of a mattress and blankets, and the evening portion of soup, withheld. Isolation, it seemed, meant exactly that. For the entire punishment period, the convict would see or hear no other human at all, and have no access to any reading material. Meals – just bread and water – were pushed through a slot in the door, and the slop bucket would exit the same way. I knew without a doubt I would not last a week under such conditions and made a resolution never to do or say anything to upset Major Freeman.

And with that I was dismissed. I don't know what I had expected – a cosy chat over a cup of tea, fatherly advice on how to survive, promises to help me however he could – no. I have a friend in the chaplain, but not in the governor, it seems.

At last the first full day of incarceration finally limped to an end, with a meal of weak broth and bread, an hour of free time in my cell in which I began writing of all the events since the doctor and Inspector Watling called at our house (the chaplain having followed up on his promise to furnish me with pen and paper) – how long ago that all seems! – and then lights out at nine o'clock.

Since then, the days have continued as described, relentlessly unchanging. I suppose I will get used to it, but when I look ahead and imagine myself fifteen years hence and still here, I despair. I do not know that I can last that long.

14th May

I have been here two months. It's hard to believe. I thought I would write my journal every day, but every day is the same, and there is no point repeating descriptions of monotony. Only the Sunday sermons from Nathaniel Spring serve to break up the week a little. And there is the occasional small drama: the man who collapsed in the exercise yard and had to be carried inside to the infirmary; my visit to the prison surgeon with cut and bleeding fingertips after a week of pulling oakum (they were cleaned, bound with strips of cloth, and I was sent back to work with the advice that they would harden in time); the day the governor was replaced on his rounds by a senior warder, the governor being indisposed.

This warder's name was Plaistow, and if I'd thought Governor Freeman was harsh and unfeeling he is nothing compared with Plaistow. The warder kicked my slops bucket over intentionally when he inspected my room, for no reason I could discern other than that I briefly made eye contact with him. He then threatened me with three days' isolation as punishment for having a dirty cell. Thankfully the punishment never materialised. I wondered if the chaplain, who witnessed what really happened, had perhaps intervened on my behalf. Since that day I have kept as far from Plaistow as possible, keeping my eyes down, hoping not to be noticed. Plaistow is not a man of whom to make an enemy.

The only respite from the tedium is my occasional meetings with Nathaniel Spring. My initial feelings about him have turned out to be correct, and he is becoming a true friend. Whether other inmates find him thus I do not know; all I know is that without him and his words of comfort, both from the pulpit and when he visits my cell, I do not think I could have survived. He continues to tell me things will get easier, but in truth, they do not, as the 'novelty' wears off and I begin to realise that this is how things will be for the next fifteen years. Transportation would perhaps have been easier, were it still routinely employed as a punishment. Hanging too – as it would have soon been over. But I was not sentenced to either of those, so endure prison I must.

I write my journal today because I actually have something to report. I was visited today by my brother, Charles. I received a letter from him a couple of days ago to say that he was making arrangements to come as soon as was possible, having returned to England from his tour of the Continent. A warder came to fetch me, and given my brother's status in life he was allowed to see me, with the governor's office put at his disposal. I was made to stand in the iron cage, as before when I met the governor on my first day. A warder was present throughout, and Charles was instructed not to approach the cage, but to sit in a chair beside the governor's desk and no nearer.

But oh, how good it was to see him! He is the one member of my family who has always had time and affection for me.

'Dear George, what a horror it was to hear what happened, and to see you here!' he exclaimed. He shook his head sadly, and once more, as with Nathaniel, I so wanted to confess my innocence. When we were children, Charles – being several years older than me – was my teacher, my confidant, my friend and my protector. When I broke a window bowling a cricket ball to him, he took the blame for it, knowing that as Father's favourite, his punishment would be far less severe than mine. Would that he could protect me now.

'Charles, my dear brother, thank you so much for coming to visit me. But I thought you were in Italy?'

'I was, but when I received Father's letter reporting the horrific news I rushed home at once. I am only sorry it took me so long to get here. I was in Naples, and it is a long journey. Oh, George. What did you do, and more importantly, why?'

I could only shake my head sadly, as if the memory were too much to bear. Which, in fact, it is. As time goes on and I live the lie, I am beginning to muddle fact and fiction, and wonder if perhaps I did poison Lucy after all. And then I come to my senses and remember that it is not in my nature. I would never have harmed a hair on her head, no matter what she had done. I am not that kind of a man.

'Father said you put poison in a serving girl's drink. George, is that true?'

'That's why I am here, yes,' I answered. 'I loved Lucy, but she had rejected me in favour of another.' Who that other was, I would not tell Charles, ever. He worshipped our father, and that respect was returned. I would not spoil their relationship, even though I was jealous of it. Mr Smythe had taught me to control and bury any feelings of envy towards my brother. We were separate people, and I had no rights to what my brother had. As the eldest it was only natural he would be favoured over me by our parents.

'Oh, George,' he said again, his eyes regarding me with extreme sadness, and disappointment. I was dismayed. While I knew his reaction to the news would be one of sadness, I did not want him to feel disappointed in me. After all my actions were designed to spare our parents from ruin. Their reputation could survive having a younger son in trouble – they only needed to disown me, as indeed it appeared they had. They could not survive having Mother in prison and Father known as a philanderer. The urge to tell Charles the truth, only so that he would understand and not think badly of me, was almost overwhelming.

'It is not quite as you might think,' I whispered. 'There were reasons, good ones I assure you, behind what I did. I wish none of it had happened. I wish I was not in here, and that we could turn back time to . . . to a Sunday in the middle of February, when I was as happy as I have ever been in my life.'

He shook his head. 'We cannot turn back time. I just don't understand it at all. More than that, I don't believe it. I simply cannot believe you, sweet George, capable of such a terrible crime. You do not have it in you to hurt another human being. You were always the gentlest and kindest boy who ever lived.'

A gentle cough alerted me to another man's presence in the office. I had not noticed, but Nathaniel Spring had entered and was standing just inside the door, on the left of the cage.

'I am sorry, Mr Britten, and George, but we must cut short your meeting. The regulations state that visits may only last ten minutes and no more. Would you please make your farewells, and then, Mr Britten, if I might have a word?'

Charles stood, and approached the cage, his face twisted in the agonies of farewell. I assumed my own carried much the same expression. The warder took a step forward, as if to prevent him moving closer, but a small gesture from my brother stopped him. 'George, dear brother, stay strong. I believe you are innocent of this crime, and are perhaps protecting someone else, though who that might be I cannot guess. If there is anything I can do to get you out of here I shall do it, rest assured.'

I opened my mouth to reply but Charles turned and followed the chaplain out of the office. And then it was my turn to leave, following the warder back to my cell and the pile of oakum that awaited me. By now I can accomplish this task without really thinking about it, so I was able to ponder my brother's words as my fingers picked their way automatically through the fibres. Why did he suspect my confession was false? What could he do about it? I had been convicted and imprisoned, and until my sentence was complete here I would stay. Unless the true murderer confessed, and she would never do that. Nor did I want her to. If she did, I would say she was lying, and would do all I could to keep the blame on myself. I could bear the punishment far better than my dear mother would.

I wondered if she would ever visit me here, even though as yet she hadn't. Did she think of me at all, her youngest child, and wonder how I fared behind bars? She did, I was sure; she must do. She could not have borne me within her womb, given birth to me, watched me grow up, without now sparing a single thought for me as I languished in a prison cell. The idea that I was in her mind was comforting and gave me the strength to bear my fate, though I wished she might write me a letter to prove she was thinking of me.

Charles would not be able to change the course of events. Much as I would like to be free, and hated prison, I would not wish that at Mother's expense.

Chapter 17

Cassie

A few days after hearing the full story of her beginnings from her mother, Cassie judged the time was right to tell Bethany. They weren't due to meet – but had fallen into the habit of having a long phone call at least once a week, catching each other up with everything that they'd done. Cassie looked forward to these calls. She'd curl up on the sofa with Griselda, a cup of tea and the phone, and enjoy listening to her daughter chattering on about what she'd studied at university that week, the gossip about her student mates, where her parents were on their tour of Australia. In return, Cassie would regale Bethany with anecdotes from work.

But this time she needed to be more serious. After the initial chit-chat she found a way to broach the subject. 'Remember that jewelled mirror we saw at the V&A?'

'The one belonging to my four-greats grandpa? Is that the right number of greats?'

'Yes, but . . . well, listen. My parents told me something a bit . . . surprising the other day.'

'About George Britten?'

'Not exactly. Just – turns out he's not our ancestor at all.' And then she told Bethany the full story.

'Wow! So . . . you're adopted too, in a way. By Tony, anyway.'

'You OK with this? I mean, you'd just found us and now . . .'

'Cassie, it gives us something more in common. We were both brought up by people not biologically related to us. Must have been hard for you to hear it though, after all those years thinking Tony was your dad. I'm glad I always knew I was adopted.'

'Yes, it was a shock. And I'm still . . . you know . . . working through it. Had a long chat with Mum where she told me the whole story. Haven't seen Tony again since I heard, though.'

'You should. You must. He's still your dad, in all the ways that are important.'

Cassie nodded, considering Bethany's words. Her daughter was only eighteen but so wise.

'Hey, are you going to trace your birth father?' Bethany asked.

Cassie stuttered a moment before answering. 'I-I'm not sure. I wouldn't have the first clue how to go about it. I only know his name, nothing else.'

'And that he lived near your mum around the time you were conceived. I can help you trace him, if you want. There are online services – that's what I used to find you.'

'Oh, Bethany, I don't know . . . Mum seemed horrified I might want to find him.'

'With respect though, it's not up to her. He's your dad, and you have a right . . . I mean, look at us! Aren't we a walking, breathing advert for getting in touch with a birth parent? It's been, what, six weeks or so, and we're best friends! My life's been so enriched by meeting you, Cassie.'

'Aw, yes, mine too. So glad you found me.'

'Well then, if you find your birth father it could be the same, all over again!'

'It's a bit different though – I mean I knew you were out

there somewhere. This man – my biological father – doesn't even know I exist.'

'Like my father, Arjun, then. He doesn't know about me.' There was a silence, as though Bethany was weighing something up. 'What was your real father's name? Did your mum tell you?'

'Jack Wilkinson. Don't go putting it into your family finder thing yet though . . .'

'Of course I wouldn't. It's for you to do, not me. But I'm hoping you will. And talking of fathers, I'm wondering about my own . . . thinking of having a go at tracing him. But I don't want to do it if you're not sure. Ha! I've just contradicted my own advice to you, haven't I?'

'You have, a bit,' Cassie replied, biting her lip. No, she wanted to say, don't try to trace Arjun. Please don't.

'So . . . would you be happy if I tried to trace my real father?'

'Um, I'm not so sure. Don't rush into it. He never knew about you. Can we perhaps . . . talk about this more the next time we meet up? Rather than over the phone?'

'OK. Sure. Whatever you want.'

As the call ended and Cassie hung up, she frowned, trying to imagine how she'd feel if Bethany went ahead and traced Arjun, imagining scenarios where Arjun came to the UK to meet his daughter, and she saw him again. She'd successfully boxed up and put away all the feelings she'd had for him – as she'd once said to Bethany, she'd always felt the relationship had been as good as it was only because there was a time limit on it. But she had no idea how she'd react if she ever actually met him again.

And Arjun – who was married, with children – how would *he* feel if a daughter he never knew he had got in touch out of the blue? What about his wife, and their children? It could all be very messy . . . but if Bethany wanted to try to find her father she had a right to do so, didn't she?

* * *

163

Cassie used her next day off, Tuesday, to meet up with her parents again. Andy had suggested a trip to the cinema or something like it – the kind of thing they used to do as a family quite often. But there was no film on that they'd all enjoy. Instead she suggested they visit a Christmas market that had opened up in town. They could do a bit of shopping, have a mulled wine at a stall, chat as they wandered around. Christmas markets were more her mother's scene than Tony's, but he'd go along with the plan, she knew.

It was a blowy day though not too cold when they met up. Cassie was bundled up in a scarf and woolly hat. Her parents were already seated at a table at an outdoor café, sipping hot chocolates. Tony's expression was wary but hopeful, as though he wasn't sure how she would react to seeing him again.

'Hello, love,' he said, half-getting up as though to kiss her but stopping part way, so he was left hovering awkwardly neither standing nor sitting. Cassie gave him a quick kiss on the cheek, her hand on his shoulder. His expression was part relief that she was there and had greeted him in a friendly manner, and part hurt that she'd only pecked his cheek rather than give him a full-on dad–daughter hug as she usually would.

'I'll just get myself a coffee,' Cassie said, and went over to the bar. She was aware that her mother had leaned over to whisper something to Tony behind her. As she returned with her drink they broke apart, looking vaguely guilty. They'd been talking about her. Discussing how Tony should behave, perhaps. She smiled tightly at each of them and sat down, unwinding her scarf. The seating area was well sheltered from the wind and she felt warm.

'So, how's things?' Tony asked.

'Fine. Good. I . . . er . . . had a chat to Bethany the other day.'

Tony nodded. 'Good, good.'

'I told her, about you, and everything.'

Her mother shot her a glance. 'Oh . . . well yes I suppose she needed to know too . . . just . . . I suppose I feel a little uncomfortable thinking my granddaughter knows about . . . my one-night stand.'

Cassie shrugged. 'She had to know. She's OK with it all.'

'Good,' said Tony, again.

They fell silent, sipping their drinks.

'Windy day, isn't it?' Tony said, after a while.

Mum nodded. 'Not too cold, though.'

Cassie didn't respond. Talking about the weather, when really they should be talking about their new relationship to each other. She tried to formulate something to say, that would test the water, see if they could get back on track with the warm, loving relationship they had always had. But no words came to mind.

'Another hot chocolate?' she said, eventually.

'Ah, not for me, love,' said Tony, and her mother shook her head.

'So, shall we look around the market then?'

'Yes, come on,' said Mum, sounding relieved. 'There was a stall selling leather goods. I like the look of a handbag there – maybe I can persuade your dad to buy me it for Christmas. Tony, I mean.' She blushed.

'You can still refer to him as my dad,' Cassie said, and both parents smiled with relief. But even though she'd said it, Cassie wasn't sure she meant it. Was he still her dad? Bethany considered her adoptive parents to be her parents, and had somehow easily slotted Cassie into her family circle as an extra mum. Why couldn't Cassie do the same – keep considering Tony as her father but also allow space for the shadowy figure of Jack Wilkinson? It wasn't easy. She felt tears well up – yet again! All she did these days was cry! She turned away and busied herself wrapping her scarf back around her neck so that they didn't notice.

But her mother clearly had noticed, for she felt a sympathetic touch on her upper arm.

'Right then, handbag shopping,' she said, forcing a jolly tone into her voice. Any other year this trip would have been fun – it was the sort of thing they'd always done together. This year it was clearly going to be strained and awkward. Well, if she at least managed to get some Christmas shopping done, that would be a result.

Gain a daughter, lose a father. How quickly life could change!

Chapter 18

George

15th May

Nathaniel Spring visited me in my cell today – just one day after Charles's visit. I was expecting a follow-up of some sort. He is the conscientious type. And prison being such a lonely place, I was hoping and praying that he might call on me soon. I was glad not to have long to wait.

I put aside my oakum picking to speak to him. (Oh, how tedious that task has become! Although I am getting skilled at it, and can allow my mind to wander while my fingers deftly unravel the fibres, I am bored stiff of it and find myself wishing I could do a turn on the old treadwheel, or sew some mailbags or some other such task just for a spot of variety.)

Nathaniel perched, as always, on my platform bed. It is so low he might as well be sitting on the floor. I offered my stool but he would not take it.

'Did you enjoy seeing your brother yesterday?' he asked, when he was settled in a half-squat, half-sitting position. 'He seems like a sound, well-meaning chap.'

'He is one of the very best of men,' I replied, feeling a little puff of pride at being related to such a fellow.

Nathaniel picked up a shred of oakum and began twisting it around his fingers. I watched, itching to show him how to pick it properly. 'You know, of course, that any conversation you have with visitors cannot be fully private. I was listening throughout, and I do apologise, but it is part of my duty. I have to report back to the governor if anything untoward or suspicious is said at such meetings.'

'I understand.' I nodded, wondering where he was going with this line of conversation.

'I was especially interested in what your brother had to say about your character – his belief that you are too gentle and mild a boy ever to be capable of murder. I questioned him further on this afterwards.' He raised his eyes from the oakum he was still fiddling with and regarded me carefully. His eyes were a green-grey colour, and eyelashes long and tawny. His expression was one of curiosity and compassion. 'Your brother not only believes you aren't capable of the crime for which you were imprisoned, George, he believes you didn't do it. He told me you must have confessed to it in order to shield someone else, though whom and for what reason he cannot begin to guess. From what little I have learned of you since you have been here, I think he may be right.'

He dropped the oakum, and took hold of my hands. His palms were smooth and warm. With a start I realised it was many weeks since I had felt the kindly touch of another human being. The last hand I had held was Lucy's.

'George, your brother told me he has reason to doubt your confession. Now, do you want to tell me the truth?'

Did I *want* to tell him the truth? Yes, of course. But would I, knowing what it would mean for my family? No, of course not. I forced myself to meet his gaze. 'I have already told the truth. Lucy – the servant girl – spurned my advances. I was so furious I decided if I couldn't have her then no one would, and so I added arsenic to a cup of hot chocolate the housekeeper had made for her. I took that up to her room and watched her drink it. She became ill within a couple of hours and died the next day.' I sighed, and looked away. 'There is no more to be said. I appreciate your concern, but I am where I should be, in this prison. I must accept my punishment and repent of my sins.'

It was Nathaniel's turn to sigh. 'Usually those are precisely the words I wish to hear from inmates, though they are rarely uttered. But today I do not believe you. Your brother does not believe you. Although family members may be biased and blind to the truth I do not think that is the case here, and neither does Mr Britten. He tells me he is going to get the case reopened. He hinted at new evidence, which would negate your confession. Now, George, I shall ask you once again. Do you wish to change your story and tell me the truth? It might help if someone other than yourself knew what really happened.'

I pulled my hands away from his and resumed picking oakum. 'I have told you. There is nothing more to say.'

He pressed his lips together and stood. 'You are not helping anyone by continuing with this charade, George. I am sure you have what you think are good reasons for taking the blame but you are misguided. May God forgive you.' He left me then, with a sad shake of his head.

I had come so close to telling him or Charles that I was not to blame. But if I said that, then they would want to find out who the real culprit was. And that must remain a secret.

Though sometimes I confess I wonder – I have put myself through so much to earn Father's respect and Mother's love and gratitude. Might it end up being all for nothing? Is it worth it?

26th May

Today is a Sunday and throughout the chapel service, Nathaniel kept glancing in my direction with a strange gleam in his eye.

I could not concentrate on his words, comforting though they usually are, as I knew it meant he was going to come and see me and once more urge me to recant my confession. I must remain strong. I have come this far. Instead of listening I found myself gazing around the chapel, with its high, barred windows, its plain cross over the altar, the undecorated wooden pulpit with three steps from which Nathaniel delivered his sermons. It was all so plain and austere, as befitted a prison chapel, and so very different from St Michael's back in our village.

I recalled my last visit there with a jolt. It had been the day before Lucy died – the day on which she was poisoned. I had sat in quiet contemplation for a while, admiring the stained glass and intricate carvings on the rood screen and choir stalls, which I had always loved. As I half-listened to Nathaniel today I tried to overlay St Michael's glorious beauty onto the prison chapel's functional austerity. Would I ever again see St Michael's? It was when I thought of all that I missed by being in prison – the scent of springtime blossom, the feel of the wind in my hair as I rode over my father's fields, the sound of skylarks above Fairy Hill on a summer's day – that I felt most weak and in danger of breaking my resolve. And now, with thoughts of home running around my head and a no-doubt imminent visit from Nathaniel I felt particularly vulnerable.

I'd been back in my cell only five minutes after chapel when he arrived. His face was flushed with excitement. I bade him sit down, but he wanted to remain standing.

'I have had a letter, from your brother. And it states as we both thought but you would not admit – you *cannot* have been the poisoner. You were away from the house that morning. Mr Britten says he has found witnesses who will testify that they saw you in the village and that you could not possibly have been the person who put the poison in the poor girl's drink. You are innocent, as we knew you must be.'

I could not believe it. Who would testify? I had seen Maggie in the church that day but surely she was too simple to be believed. And after all this time how could she be relied on to know what day it was that we'd sat together in the church? All days merged into one in her head. I sat down heavily on my stool. 'Who, Nathaniel? Who says I was out of the house?'

'Your brother does not go into details about who the witnesses are, but he says there are more than one and that they are reliable. He has written also to the detective – Inspector Watling was it? – who carried out the investigation. The case will be reopened. You will be found to be innocent and you will be released!'

He said this triumphantly, with a grin and sparkling eyes. He expected me, no doubt, to leap to my feet and cheer, perhaps hug him or at least shake his hand, but I did no such thing. I shook my head in despair. 'Nathaniel, this is not good news. The witnesses are misled. Although I did leave the house that morning it was only for a few minutes, and I was, I assure you, back in enough time to put the poison in the hot chocolate and take it to Lucy. I did this. No one else.'

He sat down now, on the platform bed, and as he had done once before, took my hands in his. 'Stop it, George. Stop it now – this ridiculous lie has to end. You are protecting someone, but who? Another servant? A friend? Someone in your family, perhaps? I can't guess at the truth. You would have to tell me. Or perhaps you want to wait for Inspector Watling to find out the truth? As he will do. Your brother seems convinced the new evidence is enough.'

I stared at the chaplain. Charles may well have discovered that Maggie was with me that morning in the church, but she could not be relied on. What other witnesses did he have? And surely he hadn't found evidence that implicated Mother? Reluctantly I realised I would have to say something. Perhaps Nathaniel would be an ally here. If we were Catholics I could have told the truth in the confessional. I would have felt safe knowing he was bound by God not to repeat it. But we were not Catholic; there was no confessional box and iron grille between us. All I could do was stick to my story. 'There is no evidence that anyone else committed the crime. There is only my confession. Dear Charles is a loyal brother, trying to help me, but he is deluded.'

'Well. We shall have to wait and see. In the meantime, George, if you want someone to talk to please send word to me by one of the warders and I will come. I will return in any case as soon as there is more news. Meanwhile I urge you to think this through carefully. You cannot persist with this charade indefinitely. What will you do when the inspector discovers the truth?'

With these words he left me, and I did as he had asked, and spent the rest of the day thinking it through. Was there some way in which my innocence could be proven but the blame still not be cast at my mother's feet? If there was, I would happily accept it and would revel in freedom once more. But there was no way I could think of. I realised that—

27th May

The chaplain returned to my cell late last night, as I was writing the above entry. That is why it is broken off. As he entered I hurriedly hid my pages under my Bible, it being the nearest thing to hand. He raised his eyebrows.

'What I would give for a glance at your journal, young George. I'll wager you have poured out your innermost thoughts onto those pages. You have no doubt told the truth there, while still concealing it from me.'

'I write what has happened to me each day. That is all,' I told him. If he insisted on seeing it, as he was within his rights to do, then all would be lost. My heart was pounding as I tried to look him in the eye and convince him I was hiding nothing.

'So every day you write that you rose, washed, breakfasted, exercised and picked oakum?'

'Yes.'

'A dull narrative then. Occasionally enlivened by recounting visits from your well-meaning chaplain. Whom I hope you consider your friend, as well.'

'Yes, I do, indeed.' My only friend, other than Charles.

'And yet you won't confide in me. I could confiscate your journal, you know, and read it from start to finish. If you've poured your heart into your words then it will tell me what I need to know.' He rubbed his chin as though considering whether to take it or not. I was momentarily terrified, and kicking myself for writing with such honesty. (Yet here I am, still relating what happened with one hundred per cent honesty!) It would ruin everything. But finally he shook his head. 'I would not intrude on you in that way, George. You must know that. I believe you are entitled to some privacy, within the bounds of your journal. I live in hope that one day you will come to me and tell me the truth of your own accord.'

His eyes questioned mine. I realised I had to say something – something to make him understand why I had done what I had, and why the truth could not surface.

'Very well. I will tell you some of what you want to know,' I said. 'Please sit down.'

He did so, and waited expectantly.

Where could I start? How much could I say without incriminating my mother? I gaped like a goldfish a few times while I formulated my words.

'I will not tell you who I suspect of adding the arsenic to the hot chocolate,' I said, as an opener. 'I do not know for sure, and I will not accuse that person of something I cannot be sure they did. I did not witness the arsenic being added.'

'Very well.' He nodded. 'But you are admitting it wasn't you.'

I regarded him for a few moments. Although I had started speaking, it was hard after so long to refute my confession. 'I do admit that,' I said, finally. 'I was away from the house that morning. I had taken Lucy her breakfast tray and then went out. By the time I returned she was already very ill.'

'Can someone vouch for you being out of the house?'

'One person saw me, yes, but she is not a reliable witness.' I pictured Maggie's round, moon-like face and imagined her flapping her hands in anguish if she were to be asked to recall what happened that day.

He stroked his chin. 'Hmm. I wonder if that is who your brother is referring to. Though he stated in his letter there was more than one witness.'

'I do not recall seeing anyone else that morning.'

He watched me for a moment then nodded as if satisfied I had finally told him the truth. 'May I ask one more thing? I understand you do not want to say who you suspect of the murder. But why have you persisted in taking the blame for this? You could have hanged for it – only your youth and the judge's leniency prevented you from an appointment with the gallows. Surely it would have been better to let justice take its course?'

In answer I merely shook my head. There was nothing I could say in answer to that which would not endanger Mother.

He stood to leave. 'Well, at least we have made progress. I shall write to your brother.'

At the door he turned back once again. 'Whoever it is you have been protecting, I hope they are grateful to you.'

I hoped so too. That had been the whole point. But I had not received so much as a single letter from my mother or father during my incarceration.

Chapter 19

Cassie

Once again Cassie found herself longing for the next time she would see Andy and could talk things through. The whole day out with her parents had been horribly stilted and awkward. Every time she looked at Tony she couldn't stop herself from thinking: *You're not my dad.* Every time she looked at her mum she remembered she'd been lied to all her life. She kept turning the name Jack Wilkinson over in her mind. Who was he, what did he look like, what kind of life had he made for himself? Did she have half-siblings out there somewhere, people just a couple of years younger than her perhaps, who had no idea she existed? Were Jack's parents still alive – were there elderly grandparents she might meet? Aunts and uncles, cousins?

Did she want to trace Jack? She still didn't know. All she knew was she couldn't wait to sit with wise old Andy, offload, and hear his thoughts on it all.

Wednesday evening was their regular pub night. But Shania, Ben and Toby were all in the pub along with Andy.

'Where were you last week?' Ben said, as Cassie bought a round for them all.

'Ah, I was, um, busy,' she said, trying to remember the excuse she'd given.

'Tired, you said,' Shania reminded her, with a frown.

'Tired, yes, I was. And I had a pile of jobs to do at home, kept me busy all evening,' Cassie said, covering her tracks.

'Andy had some feeble excuse last week too,' said Toby. 'Honestly I don't know what the world's coming to with both of you crying off on the same night. Anyway, no matter, the three of us managed to put the world to rights by ourselves, didn't we, chaps?'

'Certainly did. Well, now we're all here, cheers!' Shania raised her glass and they all did likewise. Cassie did not dare sneak a glance at Andy although she was acutely aware of him sitting next to her, the warmth of his leg beside hers although they weren't quite touching. When would she be able to get him on his own for another heart-to-heart?

'You all right?' he said to her quietly, in a moment when the others were having a lively conversation about the chances of Munster in a rugby match the coming weekend.

'Yeah, well, sort of. Kind of need to talk things through, again. Saw Dad on Monday. Was all a bit awkward.'

'Are you busy tomorrow night?' He said this in almost a whisper, his eye, Cassie noticed, on the other three across the table.

'No, nothing on.' She often attended a Zumba class on Thursdays, but not every week.

'Come round. I'll make you dinner, and you can talk all you like. You know where I live, right?'

She nodded. 'OK. I'll bring a bottle.'

'Andy, are you supporting Scarlets or the Red Army?' Ben said.

'What a choice! Red or red. Munster'll win. They're on good form this season. They'll thrash Scarlets, you'll see.'

'Nah, mate. Tenner says Scarlets'll beat them. Not by much but they will.'

'You're on,' Andy replied, shaking Ben's hand. And under the table, Cassie felt his thigh briefly press against hers, as though confirming their arrangements for the following night. She turned to Shania to start a new conversation before she said something incriminating. She still wasn't sure what was going on between her and Andy, if anything. Probably nothing, but he was certainly the best listener she knew, and that's what she needed right now.

On Thursday evening, after a long day at the sports centre, Cassie dressed carefully to go to Andy's. She, who was normally happiest in either a tracksuit or casual jeans and a jumper, tried on three dresses from her wardrobe discarding all of them, before eventually settling on a short skirt, thick tights and boots combination, teamed with a loose long-sleeved top. Casual, yet a bit more dressy than her usual look. She put on a bit of make-up, added a jacket and scarf, picked out a decent bottle of wine from the few in her wine rack and called a taxi to get to Andy's. He lived a few miles away. Too far to walk on a cold, dark November evening.

Andy lived in a small cottage on the edge of town – two bedrooms, front door right on the street, low ceilings and exposed beams. She'd been there only once before, when he'd had a party to celebrate a birthday – his fortieth, she thought. She wasn't far off that milestone herself. She remembered loving his cottage – the homely feel it had with its oak furniture, bright upholstery and open fire.

And yet as she pressed on the doorbell she felt nervous. What was he expecting this evening? A chat, he'd offer some advice, they'd share a meal and wine and then . . .? Come to think of it, what was *she* expecting would happen? Just that. The talk, the meal and then goodbye. Of course. He was her colleague, her boss, and she wasn't looking for any kind of relationship, least of all with Andy. No. It'd be wrong. She plastered a smile on her face as he opened the door, and stepped past him directly into his cosy sitting room.

'Cassie, good to see you,' he said, taking the bottle of wine from

177

her and kissing her cheek. 'Hope you like lamb hot-pot. It's that kind of day – I thought we needed a warm, comforting stew.'

'I love it,' she replied, hanging her coat on a peg by the door and then flumping down onto a sofa. 'Thanks so much for offering to cook for me. I've got nothing in. All this stuff happening in my life – it's made me forget to go shopping.'

'You need feeding up, then. Good job I have a treacle pudding and custard for dessert.'

Cassie laughed. 'You sound like my old Nanna.' And then she bit her lip. Tony's mother. The woman she remembered as a smiling, white-haired grandma who spoiled her at every opportunity, but who it now transpired was not actually her grandmother at all.

Andy seemed to have guessed why she had suddenly become subdued, and sat beside her, putting a comforting arm around her shoulders. 'Tough, isn't it? Getting used to this new set-up in your family relationships?'

She nodded. 'I must ask Mum who else knew. Did her parents know, did Tony's parents know? What about my Auntie Pam, Tony's sister? She always seemed to have a soft spot for me when I was a kid. She had three boys – my cousins, although now I realise they're not actually related – and she used to say I was the daughter she always wanted and never had.'

'Yes, I think you need to ask your mum exactly who knew and who didn't, and then with them decide whether it's time to tell all of them or keep it quiet, just between you.'

'And you.'

He blushed. 'Yes, and me. Cassie, I am humbled that you chose me to confide in. I hope I am able to help you through this.'

'You have, so far.'

He cleared his throat. 'So, if it turns out no one else knew about your parentage, would you want it to stay that way or be open about it?'

Cassie stared at an abstract picture in bright reds and oranges on the wall above the fireplace as she considered her response. The warmth of the painting echoed the colours of the dancing flames of the fire. It was an interesting question. Now that she knew, did she want everyone to? She shook her head. 'No, I don't think so. If Auntie Pam and everyone else have never been told I think it'd better to keep it that way. I don't see that much of them these days – only on occasional family celebrations – and I'd like to think we can still enjoy those the same way we always did. I kind of hope . . . once I've got used to the idea, I can forget all about it and things can go back to how they were.'

'That's in your power, then, if you just give yourself time.'

'Except whenever I look at Dad I see a man unrelated to me, and whenever I look at Mum I see someone who lied to me.'

'She didn't lie. She just withheld the truth. They must have thought it was the best thing to do.'

'She said they had always decided to tell me the truth, sooner or later, but just never did.'

There was a beeping noise coming from the kitchen. 'Ah, that's the hot-pot done. I need to take it out and let it sit a while before we eat. Back in a mo,' Andy said, as he sprang to his feet and went through to the kitchen.

While he was busy, Cassie relaxed back into the sofa, enjoying the warmth of the open fire. She could get used to visiting this cottage, she thought, then stopped herself. He was her boss, remember? A friend, but nothing more.

Andy returned to the sitting room carrying a bottle of wine and two glasses. He poured her one, and sat beside her on the sofa, facing the fire.

'Nothing like a good roaring open fire at this time of year,' Cassie said. 'I wish my flat had an open fireplace.'

'My aunt always had one when I was growing up,' Andy said. 'I loved it. So when I was buying a house it was a top priority.'

'Your aunt? Did your parents have one too?'

Andy looked away from her before answering. 'I didn't live

with my parents for most of my childhood. My aunt brought me and my sister up.'

'Oh! Sorry, I just assumed you'd . . . had a regular sort of upbringing with both parents. What happened to them, if you don't mind me asking?'

'I don't mind. It's a long story though, and aren't we supposed to be talking about you, putting your problems to rights?'

Cassie shrugged. 'We've got all evening.'

'We have indeed.' He smiled, and Cassie found herself wondering whether there was something in that smile – a hope, perhaps, that the evening would be a long one. 'Well. My dad left my mum when I was four and my sister was just two. Mum . . . struggled to cope, and then eventually my aunt stepped in and took both of us. I was about six by then. We stayed with my aunt until we left home.'

'What happened to your mum?'

'She's still around. I see her, about twice a year. She . . . wasn't really cut out to be a mother, I suppose. After Dad left – and I don't remember him at all; he moved to Australia and we never saw him again – she kind of went to pieces. Depression, I suppose, though at the time I just remember that she hardly got out of bed, didn't take me to school. I'd make sandwiches for the three of us, using whatever food I could find. The school called in social services in the end. We – Mel and I – were about to be taken into care when my aunt showed up. Auntie Mo was Mum's older sister. Quite a lot older – her two sons had grown up and left home by the time she took us on. Mel was four and I was six at that time, and Mo's husband had died of cancer the previous year, so she was on her own.'

'She sounds like quite a woman,' Cassie said, carefully.

Andy smiled. 'She was. I adored her – we both did. Mum's health improved, and after we'd been with Auntie Mo for a year there was talk of us going back to live with Mum.' He sighed. 'Being totally honest, I didn't want to go back. Even at seven I'd realised we were better off with Mo – we had regular meals; we were taken to school on time; we understood what the rules were in her house. And Mo was good at parenting. Every evening we'd have a bath and then story time before being tucked into bed. We'd never had a routine before, and I think kids need routine. Knowing what was happening, what was coming next – it helped us settle. Mel and I both have very happy memories of living with Mo. Families come in all shapes and sizes, don't they?' He looked sideways at Cassie. 'And I think we turned out OK. Well, Mel did.'

'And you did.' Cassie impulsively clutched his arm and pulled him closer to her, intending to kiss him on the cheek. At that moment he turned his face and she ended up catching him on the lips.

'Oops, sorry,' she said, with an embarrassed giggle. But he wasn't laughing. There was a question in his eyes, and then he leaned forward and kissed her back – just a quick peck but it was on the lips, and sent a shiver through her.

'OK, well I think dinner's ready,' he said, and the moment was broken. Just as well, Cassie thought. If that had occurred after dinner, after a couple of glasses of wine, who knew what it would have led to? And they would still have to work together. Better to just leave it there, still on terms that could be described as simply good friends. There was far too much going on in her life without the added complication of a relationship with the boss.

Chapter 20

George

28th May

It is strange but since admitting to Nathaniel that I lied and am not the murderer, I now feel more confined and constrained by prison than I ever did before. I cannot wait for something to happen, and the thought that outside these claustrophobic walls, people such as my brother are working to secure my release is what keeps me going now. I feel impatient to move on to the next step, whatever that will be. Before I was as content as it is possible to be in these circumstances, resigned to fifteen years of it, but now I want to be free to feel the wind on my face and the rain on my cheek. I want to ride over the fields, and walk up Fairy Hill. I want to stroll through the streets of Winchester, nodding to passers-by, and on a whim call into a coffee shop for refreshments. I want to spend my mornings sitting beside a window with a newspaper. I want to spend my evenings attending balls at the Assembly Rooms and plays at the theatre.

In short, I want to live the life of a young man of means – the life I was destined for, the life I should be living.

Today as I worked at the oakum I could not stop from sighing, and gazing at the tiny patch of blue sky I could see from my window, and every few moments drifting off into a daydream in which Nathaniel comes rushing in, face aglow, shouting that I should put aside my work, follow him, and be released immediately. Or one where my brother Charles arrives, bearing a new suit of civilian clothes for me and news that I am pardoned. Or one where none of it had ever happened, and Lucy and I had run safely down the hill that Sunday morning – no ankle had been twisted, no affair with my father begun, no need for Mother to poison her, and by now we were betrothed and making plans for our future.

Oh, these were pleasant enough daydreams but none has come to fruition yet, and of course that last one can never be. I did not pick my quota of oakum today and for that I am to be punished – half rations for three days. I do not care.

7th June

Well, something has now happened but it is not what I had hoped for. It occurred a number of days ago but this is the first chance I have had to write about it.

In the exercise yard, as usual, we were walking around in a line, at six feet distance from each other, no more and no less. There is an art to keeping in step with the man in front, taking the same size strides so as not to catch him up or lag behind. Usually I focus on the back of the head of the next man, and let my mind empty, but that day I kept raising my face to the sky and watching sparse white clouds flit across above us, and imagining the day when I would be able to see the sky from horizon to horizon, not bounded by the blackened prison walls. I was careful, of course, to keep half an eye on the line so I would not fall foul of Warder Plaistow who was on duty.

The man in front was of middle age, a wiry fellow with a sallow

183

complexion and only a few tufts of hair. His scalp, what I could see of it under his prison cap, was flaky and discoloured. I had not noticed him before, and assumed he was a new inmate or a transfer from some other jail. From the start he was stumbling rather than walking, his head hung low, feet shuffling and every now and again, an arm lifted to scratch at the sores on his head. He was clearly unfit and unwell. But I was preoccupied with thoughts of release and did not pay him much attention, until, about twenty minutes into our circular march, he collapsed and fell.

Plaistow was upon him at once. 'Get up, man! Up, up, I say!' He lashed out at him with his baton, striking the poor fellow on the shoulder and back.

I have seen this happen before, but not right in front of me like this. On the other occasion the prisoner in question got immediately to his feet and marched on, bruised but not beaten. But this time the prisoner stayed down, moaning, as Plaistow rained more blows upon him. It seemed he could not get up if he tried. The whole line had come to a halt, and everyone was standing in place, still keeping their distance from each other, but twisting to watch the proceedings with interest. Some men, no doubt, were glad of the rest, or the 'entertainment'. If nothing else it provided a break from the monotony of our days.

For a minute or so I too was rooted to the spot, watching but not reacting while the man moaned and Plaistow yelled at him, flecks of white spittle at the corner of his mouth. The warden then kicked him, in the ribs, and the moaning stopped. That silence, I think, was what made me do what I did next.

I threw myself down on top of the poor prisoner to shield him, making a cage of my body over his head and back. 'Enough! He has taken enough of a beating – leave him be!'

'Get off, and get back in line,' growled Plaistow. 'He has to be taught to stay on his feet. Off, I say, or it will be you who next feels the force of my baton.'

He aimed a blow at the man, at the backs of his legs where

I was not covering him. I shifted to try to protect more of him, and then, as promised, the baton came down on me. Once, twice, three times, and then I lost count as in a frenzy he hit my back, shoulders, buttocks, arms, kicking me at the same time. The pain was incredible but all I could think is that I was taking it and not the poor man beneath me, who was whimpering slightly but not moving.

And then, just as I felt I could take no more, the warmth and weight of another man was upon me, and another bent over my head, more on my legs, and I was shielded from the violence just as I had shielded the first man. Nathaniel told me later that no fewer than seven men, inspired by my act of bravery, had come forward to protect me. All of them also received beatings though spread across so many, each had only a blow or two to deal with, and escaped with minor bruising and cuts.

It came to an end when other warders and the governor, and Nathaniel himself, all alerted by the shouts of the men, came rushing out to the exercise yard and restrained Warder Plaistow. It took three of them, Nathaniel told me later, to drag him away from the pile of bodies and inside the prison. He lashed out at them too – thankfully his baton had been snatched out of his hand and he did no further harm.

They had to lock him in the cage in the governor's office, until he was calm enough to be released. Released, that is, from both the cage and his position at the prison. Nathaniel thought he should have been charged with assault and imprisoned himself. He said Plaistow would never again get a job in charge of men. I hope that is true, for the rage he showed was truly frightening. We may be prisoners but we are still human. Prison is our punishment for our crimes and we do not deserve to endure extra, which has not been decreed by a judge.

The man I had tried to protect – his name is Pinkton, Nathaniel told me – suffered badly. He was taken to the prison sickbay, and from there to a hospital outside. There was no fear of him escaping, for his injuries were far too severe. He had several broken ribs, a crushed skull, ruptured kidneys and a broken shoulder. I do not know whether he will survive. I pray daily that he recovers.

And what of me? I should complete this account by listing my own injuries. I am better off than Pinkton, and I will pull through, but I did not escape unscathed. I have cracked ribs, very many bruises across my whole body, a deep cut on the back of my head, and worst of all, a broken jaw, courtesy of Plaistow's boot.

I am in the prison sickbay, and bed-bound. The slightest movement of my torso causes severe pain and it is only today that I have been able to manage to hold a pen, balance an exercise book on my knee and write this journal. My jaw is bandaged tightly and I gain nourishment by sucking up thin gruel through a narrow hollow tube. One eye is swollen shut, and my head has been shaved around the cut to allow it to be stitched closed. I have been offered laudanum for the pain but am frightened of its long-term effects.

Nathaniel says I look a sight and he says it is as well there are no looking glasses in the sickbay. The mention of mirrors brought the sapphire-encrusted looking glass I'd bought for Lucy to mind. To think it was bought on the very same day I discovered her affair with my father! I wonder if it is still where I left it – tucked away in my clothing drawer at home – or has my mother cleared out my room, not expecting me ever to return to it?

9th June

Today I got out of bed and walked the length of the room for the first time since the beating. There is not much space in which to walk. The sickbay is a small room containing six narrow beds, separated by small bedside tables. Four beds are occupied besides mine at present – by men who seem to be constantly coughing. The occupant of the sixth bed died yesterday. He lay there, eyes open, skin greying, for an hour before he was noticed and his face thankfully covered by a sheet.

Every step of my walk was painful – my chest screaming at the movement. I tried also to speak to Nathaniel when he arrived but he could barely make out my words due to the continued swelling of my jaw. There is no news from Charles. The man, Pinkton, died of his injuries. My actions did not save him.

11th June

It gets easier. I can move around the sickbay now, and can speak intelligibly. The jaw bandages must remain in place for several weeks more to allow the bone to heal. The pain lessens gradually, day by day. Either it is lessening or I am becoming used to it.

12th June

I was visited today by Governor Freeman. He has entered the sickbay daily since I've been here, as part of his rounds, but this was the first time that he stopped by my bedside to speak to me. He put his hands behind his back and stood to attention, while I remained reclining on my bed. I am still not permitted to move except when the prison surgeon commands it, with an orderly at my side.

'Mr Britten, I understand you are making a good recovery after this, ahem, unfortunate incident.'

'Yes, sir, I am much better,' I replied.

'Then you shall soon return to your cell, and resume the regular routines of the prison.' He said this with a slight smile and a nod, as though I would rejoice at the news. 'In recognition of the seriousness of your injuries you will have only half-quantities of oakum to pick for the first week.'

'Thank you, sir.' It seemed the only reply expected of me.

He nodded, satisfied, and continued with his rounds. I

imagined sitting on the backless stool in my cell, bending over the oakum, teasing it apart, and shuddered. It would be very painful. Walking around the exercise yard in pace with the other men would be impossible. My only hope was for Charles to come with news. Nathaniel had written to tell him of my injuries but prisoners in the sickbay were not permitted visitors.

I feel lower this evening than at any time since entering the prison. I tell myself there is still hope for a release, and it may come soon, but with every passing day I find it harder and harder to hold on to those thoughts. Indeed I wonder if it was all a dream – Charles's visit and my confession to Nathaniel. Perhaps I never told him the truth at all. Perhaps none of it happened and there is no hope of release. I am here to serve out my sentence.

And then I begin to question what is the truth and what is not. It has been so long, and I become confused. Did I perhaps poison Lucy as I've always maintained? Am I the murderer after all? Why else would I be here? There seems to be no reality beyond the ever-constant pain, which surrounds me and engulfs me. I struggle to remember life before the beating, life beyond the sickbay. Life before prison is just a faint, hazy memory.

18th June

My goodness, the last entry in this journal seems like another lifetime ago now! So much has happened. I barely know where to begin. *At the beginning*, as Mr Smythe always said, and so that is where I shall start.

On the day after the governor's visit I received another visit – this time from Nathaniel, and he was excited. I knew that meant something had happened.

'Are you improving, George?' he asked. 'Can you walk a little way? You are wanted for an interview in the governor's office.'

I gaped. I have not walked as far as that since before the

beating. 'Well,' I said, 'I can try, perhaps with your support . . . Who is the interview with?'

'I shall tell you as we walk. It may help take your mind off the pain. I wish we had an invalid chair, then I could push you along, but sadly there is no such thing in this institution.'

'My legs weren't broken. If we take it steady I can walk.' I swung my legs over the side of the bed, stood up, slid my feet into my prison boots and set off with the chaplain at my side. A warder followed. Any movement of prisoners has to be accompanied by a warder at all times. Even when the prisoner is in such a state as I am.

It was a long walk, for the governor's office is in a different wing of the prison to the sickbay. I had to rest several times, leaning gingerly against the wall, catching my breath yet not breathing in too deeply because that hurts my ribs more.

'Tell me,' I said, as we shuffled along, 'what has happened? Who am I to see?'

'Your brother has done some detective work, following up on what he already guessed and what you told me. He talked to those witnesses and persuaded them to speak to Inspector Watling. It seems the inspector was at first reluctant to reopen the case, having secured a confession, but when your brother told him what he had found out and that you wished to retract, he had little choice. It seems that Watling is a diligent soul, and once he accepted that there was a question mark over your guilt, he began a deeper investigation to try to arrive at the truth.'

My stomach lurched at this, and I had to stop again. It was one thing for the case to be re-investigated to prove my innocence, but quite another if his questioning led to the full story. Nathaniel must have read my worries on my face, for he put a hand lightly on my shoulder and looked into my eyes. 'You must let justice take its course, George. You are not to blame and you shall shoulder the blame no longer, whoever it is you are protecting.'

I did not answer, but began again the painful shuffle along the corridor. The warder with us began mumbling complaints about our slow progress but Nathaniel gave him a look that silenced him.

At last we reached the governor's office, and I approached the door that opened to the cage within. Nathaniel shook his head.

'No cage for you, today. Come in through this door.' He led me through the other door into the office, and once inside, indicated a chair for me to sit down. A chair! One with a back and an upholstered seat! I realised it was many weeks, months, since I had sat on such a luxurious seat. I was still marvelling at this so it was a moment before I realised three more men were entering the office. The governor, Charles, and Inspector Watling joined the chaplain and myself. The warder took up a position outside the door.

'George, dear brother, it is so good to see you again!' Charles crossed the room and leaned over me as though to hug me where I sat, but just in time Nathaniel caught his arm and pulled him back.

'I am sorry, sir, you might cause him pain if you embrace him. I fear he is not yet fully healed.'

'I am healed enough to greet my brother,' I said, putting out my hand to shake his. Thankfully the shake was gentle. I could see on his face he was shocked at the sight of me – the grubby bandage still holding my jaw in place, the multi-coloured bruises around my eye, the pain that I feel must be permanently etched onto my face.

'You remember Inspector Watling, of course?' Charles said, indicating the policeman who nodded at me.

'Yes, I remember him well,' I replied.

The governor coughed. 'This is most irregular but it seems your case is to be reopened, and in the meantime, you are to be released pending the investigation. I shall let the inspector explain.'

Released! I could hardly believe it. I barely took in the inspector's words. I wanted to grin from ear to ear but my broken jaw would not allow it, so all I could manage was a kind of grimace. Charles grinned enough for the both of us.

Inspector Watling pulled out a notebook to refer to. 'You owe your brother a debt of gratitude. He persuaded me to re-interview members of your parents' household, and among them the maid-servant Maggie. She is a simple soul, but she does remember that day, and with gentle encouragement she was able to tell me that she sat with you in the church that morning. She also told me that a woman from the village whom she referred to as Ma Whiteley had entered the church while you were both there, and saw you. I was able to confirm this with Mrs Whiteley and the two testimonies together are enough to convince me of your innocence, despite your earlier confession. In addition, your father's groom John Lincoln witnessed your return to the house, after Lucy had already been taken ill. You cannot possibly have been the person who added arsenic to the hot chocolate and took it up to Lucy.'

Three witnesses! I knew that Maggie's alone would not have been enough but Mrs Whiteley's and John Lincoln's statements backed her up. 'No. You are right – I could not have done it and I did not do it. I apologise for my earlier lies.'

'Oh, George, why did you lie?' sighed Charles. I looked at him but did not answer. I could not be the person to tell him our mother was a murderer.

'No doubt because you were protecting someone else,' Inspector Watling said. 'And I have my suspicions who that might be. I have re-examined all the evidence and re-interviewed everyone who was in or around the house that morning, including both your parents, and the housekeeper.'

I felt myself pale under my bruises and bandages. I couldn't believe I had suffered so much for nothing, and that my mother might still have to endure punishment for her crime.

'Unfortunately,' he went on, 'I do not have enough solid evidence to secure a conviction. But mark my words – I have not given up yet.' He fixed me with a piercing glare, as though it was me he suspected after all. I felt only relief that he had not found sufficient evidence, and offered up a silent prayer that it would remain so.

'George, you are to be freed with immediate effect,' Charles said. 'The chaplain explained to me the extent of your injuries so I have arranged for you to go to a private hospital for a week or two to complete your recovery, and then when you are able to travel you shall come home at last.'

He didn't even try to keep the note of excitement out of his voice. All I felt was relief. No more oakum picking. No more would I be at the mercy of thugs like Warder Plaistow. No more would I be tied to the harsh, unvarying prison routines, designed to dull the senses and exhaust the soul. I could not speak. I simply shook my head in disbelief.

'He is tired, I think. We should not dally. Let us transfer him to the hospital immediately,' Nathaniel said.

With a pang I realised that leaving the prison would mean leaving behind Nathaniel and his friendship. It was the only thing that had kept me going. I looked at him with sadness and saw a reciprocal look in his eyes – sadness but also joy that I was to be released.

'I shall visit you in the hospital on my day off,' he said, as though guessing what I was thinking.

'A carriage awaits outside,' said the governor curtly. He probably wanted this over and done with, so he could return to his regular duties.

'I fear it may be a little uncomfortable but I shall tell the driver to steer as smooth a path as possible and the journey is a short one,' said Charles. 'Can you walk to the prison gates?'

Oh, I could walk to the prison gates all right. It took time, but the walk to freedom was so much better than the walk into incarceration. The sweet clang of those seven iron gates, each one unlocked to allow us to pass and then relocked behind us, with me being on the side of freedom each time, was as music to my ears.

I shall not dwell on the carriage journey except to state that it was exceedingly painful with every jolt sending waves of pain through my cracked ribs. I vomited twice and felt close to death by the time we arrived at the hospital. There, I was taken by invalid chair to a pleasant private room, where I am attended at all times, day and night, by a succession of competent, caring nurses. How very different it all is from my treatment in the prison sickbay!

It is in my hospital room, seated at a small writing desk, that I write this journal entry. A surgeon attends daily and is pleased by my progress. In another week he thinks I will be fit enough to manage the journey, by carriage and railway, home to my father's house. Nathaniel has visited as he promised, and Charles has been here many times too. My parents have not visited, although my father did send a brief note via Charles saying he was glad I had been released. I wonder what sort of reception will await me when I finally return home.

Chapter 21

Cassie

It was just four weeks to go until Christmas now, and Cassie realised she had an extra person to buy a present for. What to get for Bethany was a question she agonised over for ages. Something nice, special, not over the top but something Bethany would treasure. Cassie roped Shania into helping her with ideas, one morning at work when they were on a coffee break at the same time.

'Jewellery?' Shania said. 'Something pretty in silver?'

'I think she has quite definite tastes in jewellery,' Cassie said, recalling a chunky set of purple beads Bethany had been wearing on one of their meet-ups.

'Clothing? A cool leather jacket?'

'Too expensive. I'm on a budget.'

'An even cooler battered second-hand one?'

'Hmm, lovely idea and I can imagine her liking such a thing, but it is so personal. I don't think I could choose the right one for her.'

Shania nodded sagely. 'You have a point. Just trying to cast my mind back to eighteen and think what I would have liked.

Obviously she'll have iPods and phones and all that kind of thing, being a youth of today. God, I don't know. You'll have to ask her.'

So Cassie did ask Bethany, in a phone call that evening.

'You know what I'd really like more than anything?' Bethany said, sounding just a little hesitant. 'A day out with you. A whole day, pottering around the shops, having coffee and lunch somewhere, just chilling. Maybe even dinner at the end of the day. Wish you lived closer.'

'Well,' Cassie replied, 'such a day can easily be arranged. Why don't we meet halfway – not in London but somewhere neither of us know well that we can explore together? Where can you easily get to by train or bus?'

'Great idea! I can get anywhere, really. Pick a place.'

'OK! Well . . . how about . . . I don't know. Rugby?' Cassie remembered visiting the little town years ago. It had a good smattering of pubs and coffee shops, and parts of the famous school were open to the public to wander around.

'That's just down the road – easy to get to for me. But a long way for you?'

'It's fine – I'm getting used to driving up and down the M1! Right, I'll do a bit of research and text you a place to meet. I'll get up early and be there by ten-thirty.'

By the time she went to bed that evening, Cassie had planned a day out in Rugby, with suitable-looking cafés and restaurants flagged on Google Maps so she could see them on her phone. Bethany had said she just wanted company and chat for the day, and there were plenty of places in Rugby where they could do just that. Cassie resolved to buy her a present anyway – as they wandered around the shops they were sure to spot something she liked, and Cassie would offer to buy it for her.

* * *

Saturday rolled around at last, and it was a fine winter's day. Cassie didn't mind the drive up to Rugby at all – not with the prospect of the day ahead of her. She sang along to the radio for the whole journey, arrived in good time and found suitable parking. Rugby was a more compact town than she'd remembered, but quaint and inviting-looking in the winter sunshine. She arrived at the designated meeting place – a coffee shop in the town centre – fifteen minutes early but was not surprised to see Bethany already there. Her daughter always managed to arrive first.

They kissed in greeting, ordered coffees and a pastry each, and began chatting.

'So, you've talked to your parents again?' Bethany asked.

Cassie nodded, and told Bethany about the previous Saturday's visit to the Christmas market. 'It wasn't an unqualified success, to be honest. It's going to take a while to get used to this new relationship.'

'I know. I was totally prepared for you and I to feel awkward in each other's company to begin with, but we haven't, have we?'

'Not at all. We've just slotted right into a good relationship, haven't we?'

Bethany smiled. 'Do you think that's because we are close blood relations? That we naturally have an affinity for each other?'

Cassie shrugged. 'I don't know. The old nurture or nature argument, isn't it? Do we get on well because we share the same genes?'

'I think so.' Bethany leaned forward. 'That's kind of why I'd really love it if you decide to trace your real father. Wouldn't it be amazing if you just found you clicked with him, the way I have with you?'

'It would, yes.' Cassie was thoughtful. Was that the way forward? Find Jack Wilkinson, build a relationship with him, and hopefully in doing so, come to terms with her new knowledge and rebuild a relationship with Tony? Maybe Bethany was right and she needed to find her real father. 'I have no idea how to go about finding him, though.'

Bethany smiled. 'Easy. I can help you. I used an online family finding service, like I told you. Costs a bit, but they do all the hard work. You just tell them whatever you know about the person you want to find – name, dates, where they were last known to have lived et cetera – and they get on it. You can get the results in a few days; sometimes it takes longer.'

Cassie felt her stomach churn over. The idea of being able to be in touch with her birth father in just a few days was both exciting and terrifying. 'Well, I guess . . . send me the link, then, and I'll take a look.'

'Great! I am so happy you want to do this, Cassie. Honestly, you won't regret it. I've found it amazing to have two mums – you'll love having two dads too, I just know it.' She gazed down into her coffee cup for a moment, and when she looked back at Cassie there was a thoughtful expression on her face. 'Talking of two dads, I can't help but wonder about mine. I'm still wondering about trying to trace Arjun. When we talked about it before, I had the impression you weren't too happy about the idea?'

Cassie stared over Bethany's shoulder at a couple of teenagers who'd come into the café, laughing and jostling one another as they approached the counter. She wondered idly whether they were Rugby school students or not. Bethany's words had sent her thoughts spinning once again. She'd known that sooner or later this topic was going to come up again. Best to be upfront and open with her daughter, she decided. 'Um, to be totally honest with you, I'd prefer if you didn't.'

'Oh. Why, Cassie? I kind of want to find him, to get in touch with my Indian heritage, but I'd hate to do something you're not happy about.'

Cassie shrugged. It was hard to put into words her feelings for why she did not want Arjun to ever know about Bethany or have anything to do with her. 'I can't explain. I just . . . well . . . I've spent the last nineteen years trying to forget him, letting him get on with his own life. He left England – left me

– to get married and build his new life in India. The thought that, via you, he might come back into my life is . . . hard.' It sounded feeble even to herself. Bethany looked disappointed, downcast. 'But, Bethany, as you said to me about my real father, it's not up to me to stop you, if you do decide you want to trace Arjun. I'll totally understand. And I'll . . . deal with it, if or when it happens.'

Bethany gave her a small smile. 'Thanks, Cassie. Let me think about it. I don't want to upset you. I just wonder about him, about that whole side of things.'

'Of course you do. It's understandable.' Cassie reached over the table to squeeze her daughter's hand.

'Hey, do you have any photos of him?'

Cassie pulled out her purse. Tucked away in a pocket, behind her library card and Costa loyalty card was a battered old picture from a photo booth. She handed it silently to Bethany. It showed her and Arjun, heads touching, grinning, looking young and carefree. Arjun looked impossibly handsome in the photo, assured and confident, his life ahead of him.

Bethany smiled. 'He looks lovely. I can see why you fell for him.' She studied the photo in silence for a moment, as though imprinting every detail onto her memory.

'I have more photos at home, somewhere,' Cassie said. 'I'm sorry, I should have thought you'd want to see them. I'll dig them out and bring some next time we meet up.'

'Thanks, I'd like that.' Bethany handed the photo back. 'Do you know whether he had any children, or . . .'

'One, at least. A boy.' Cassie remembered Arjun sending a studio photo of a nut-brown baby lying on a fur rug, about three years after he'd married. She'd sent a 'congratulations' card back. Thinking about it, that was the last contact she'd had with him.

'I have a half-brother, then.'

Cassie hadn't thought of it like that. 'Yes, I suppose you do.'

'I wonder if he'd want to know about me. My half-brother, I mean. Would be weird, finding out about an older sister you had no idea existed.'

Cassie sighed. 'It's difficult, all these complicated family relationships, isn't it?' Some families were simply not straightforward. Andy's, too, was far from 'normal', whatever normal was.

'Yep.' Bethany leaned in towards Cassie and pulled her tight into a hug. 'But rewarding, as you and I have proved.'

The day progressed as Cassie had planned – with lots of chat, many coffees, lunch, afternoon tea. They wandered in and out of all the shops Rugby had to offer, and Cassie was able to buy Bethany a leather satchel she'd admired, as a Christmas present. When darkness fell in the late afternoon they decided on an early evening meal before splitting up to head homewards. They found a tapas bar with an enticing menu and sat at a table by the window, ordering a selection of small dishes to share.

Over dinner, Bethany asked about Cassie's genealogical research. 'I keep thinking about that beautiful mirror, and the fact George Britten left it to someone outside of his family. That chaplain must have really meant something to him, or done something special for him. Have you found out any more?'

Cassie had more or less forgotten all about the research ever since raising it had sparked *that* conversation with her parents. She shook her head. 'No, I've done nothing more on it. It's . . . not really genealogical research anymore, that side of the family, now that I know I'm not descended from George Britten.'

'True, but from what you said he sounds like a fascinating character. I'd love to know who he'd been convicted of murdering and why he got out so early. And didn't you say he'd also bequeathed a lot of money to some other person? Who was that, and why did he feel the need to support them? Oh go on, Cassie. There's so much to find out, and I'd love to know. Even though it's not our blood family.'

Cassie had to admit the mysteries of George Britten's will were still worth researching, if only out of curiosity. 'Sure. I'll get back to it when I can. In between finding my own more immediate ancestor, of course!'

The next three weeks on the run-up to Christmas were going to be busy ones, she realised.

Chapter 22

George

3rd July

Charles collected me this morning from the hospital. The nurses said a tearful and fond farewell to me, exclaiming that I had been the most pleasant patient they had ever nursed, and they wished me well. For my part, they have been the best nurses I could imagine, and my health has improved immensely in the time I have been under their care. I no longer need a bandage around my jaw. It has healed, although it is slightly out of alignment, giving my face a somewhat lopsided look. The bruising on my face has gone. Having faded from blue-black to brown, green and yellow over the weeks, I am now back to a healthy pink. I have been served tasty, nourishing food, which has helped to heal me; indeed I think I have put on more weight than I had before my incarceration.

I have no idea how much my care cost, but my dear brother waved his hand when I asked, and said I was worth every penny. Whether he paid the bills himself or had help from our father I do not know and dare not ask. My ribs hurt only when I cough, or if jolted severely, but I could manage the short carriage journey to the railway station without too much pain. Trains are far smoother than road travel, so that part of the journey was easy.

'Well, brother,' he said, as we alighted from the train, 'are you looking forward to your return home?' He seemed a little uneasy. He, of course, knew more of the atmosphere in our house than I did, and I wondered again what sort of welcome I would get. The lack of visits or even letters from my parents, both when I was in prison and in hospital, had unnerved me a little.

'Yes, I am. To be back in familiar surroundings, with my family around me and my possessions within reach will be wonderful,' I replied. We had decided to walk the short distance along the lanes from the station to the house. John Lincoln, who had been waiting for us with a pony trap had been waved away, after I'd greeted him and thanked him for his part in my release – his extra testimony. It was a warm, midsummer's day, the kind where the air hums with insects and Mother Nature's bounty is in abundance. I picked a few early blackberries from the hedgerows as we walked, savouring their tartness as though I had never tasted them before. How different to the thin tasteless gruel of prison, unpalatable unless you added a good pinch of salt from your precious saltbox!

Although these lanes were as familiar to me as the back of my hand, I was seeing them today as though for the first time ever, and I wondered at the skylarks singing, the heavy scent of chestnut blossom and the feel of the warm sun on my face.

'I must warn you,' Charles said, as we drew near to the house, 'Mother has been badly affected by this episode. She seems to think that *she* is the person the inspector now suspects, though why she should imagine he'd think that for a moment is beyond me. She has been quite beside herself with worry.'

'Was she pleased to hear of my release?' I had to ask, though I feared the answer.

Charles did not respond immediately. He turned his face away and regarded the hedgerow as we walked along. I waited patiently knowing he would not ignore or avoid the question. He would be simply framing the best way to answer.

'I am sure she was, what mother would not be joyful at such news? But I think worrying that she herself might be under suspicion has muted her excitement at your release.' His face was red, and he could not look me in the eye. I decided to question him no further, as it was clearly painful to him to respond. I would find out soon enough.

The remainder of the walk passed in companionable silence. I relished the exercise, the freedom, and the joys of being outside. I put Mother out of my mind.

As we turned up the driveway, Charles stopped and caught my arm. 'George, I shall always wonder but will never ask, who it was you were protecting by your false confession. Let me just say to you now that you are without doubt the bravest man I shall ever meet, and I am truly honoured to be your brother.'

I had no answer to give him, only a nod of acknowledgement, for fear I might weep and arrive in my parents' presence with tear-stained cheeks.

We were met at the door by dear Mrs Peters. When I saw her again I realised how much I had missed our little household, and found my eyes filling with tears, which I dashed away quickly. She made a huge fuss of me, taking my coat, exclaiming over the remains of my bruises, and offering tea, cake, coffee, chocolate – anything I desired. I must admit I blanched slightly at the thought of drinking chocolate in this house.

'Tea, Mrs Peters, and perhaps a slice or two of cake,' Charles answered for us both. I felt a little overwhelmed. Life in both the hospital and prison had been very simple and routine, and it had been some time since I had had to make a decision about what I wanted to eat or when.

'We'll be in the drawing room,' Charles told her. He turned to me, his eyes kind and sympathetic. 'Come on, brother.' He took my arm and led me through.

Mother was sitting on a sofa, near the window, with some stitching in her hands. Father was seated beside the fire, reading a newspaper. When we entered both looked up and smiled. For a brief moment I thought they were genuinely pleased to see me.

'Good afternoon, Mother, Father,' I said. I grinned and took a few steps forward, expecting them to stand and take turns embracing me.

'Charles, my darling, I am glad your trip to London was successful,' Mother said, ignoring me but holding out her hand to my brother.

'Yes, as you can see, here is George.' Charles sounded bemused that she was not more enthusiastic about my return.

'It feels good to be home again,' I said, still waiting for some acknowledgement of my presence from either parent.

'I am sure it does,' said Father. 'And we are pleased to have you returned to us, and very thankful to Charles for his part in it. I imagine you will not want to stay here for long. A week, perhaps. It will be pleasant enough to have you here for a week.'

I felt my mouth drop open. I thought I had come home to live, but it was clear I was no longer fully welcome. Before I had the chance to say anything, Father continued speaking. 'Now that you have lived away from home for a while we are certain you would not want to return here permanently. You will want more freedom than can be offered living with your parents. I shall settle some money on you, a modest amount but sufficient for you to set up home elsewhere.'

'Thank you, Father, for the offer of money. But when you speak of freedom, do not forget that I have had no freedom at all for the last few months. You termed it "living away from home" but I was in prison, Father, and then hospital. Surely you cannot think it is the same thing?' I was unable to keep the scathing tone from my voice.

'Do not speak to your father like that.' Mother laid down her stitching and looked at me properly for the first time since

I entered the room. 'You brought your imprisonment upon yourself, by your false confession. I can only assume you did so because you saw it as an adventure, a way to change your surroundings. And that's assuming, of course, that the confession was indeed false.'

I could not believe what I was hearing. Mother, of all people, should know why I made the false confession and she, too, was the one person who could be certain that it was false. I couldn't even begin to think of an answer but thankfully once more Charles came to my rescue.

'Please, Mother, Father. We are all together as one family for the first time in a long while. Can we not put the past behind us, and be happily reunited for now? There are, no doubt, questions to be answered and tales to be told, but those can surely wait. Mrs Peters is about to bring us tea and cake. Let us present ourselves to her as a happy family.' His face was taut with anguish, and I wondered what my own looked like.

Having not heard from Mother while incarcerated I had not expected a particularly warm welcome but her words had cut me deep. I remembered how, in prison, I had begun to believe my own story, and doubt my memory. If I'd heard Mother's words when I was in that mental state, it would have broken me. For now, I bit my lip. Charles was right. There would be time enough to discuss what had happened and try to regain my mother's love.

If I had ever had it, in the first place.

Mrs Peters entered a moment later, pushing a tea trolley laden with half a dozen kinds of cake and scones. I was overcome with gratitude – she at least had prepared for my homecoming, and was genuinely pleased to see me.

I write this by gaslight in my old bedroom. It has been good to return to this house, see Mrs Peters, converse with Charles, be reunited with my possessions in this room, not least the original journal Mr Smythe gave me. I have tucked the pages written

205

in prison and hospital into it at the relevant point, and I now continue writing on the smooth creamy vellum of the book itself. Tomorrow, I shall try to catch Mother for a talk, alone. She must explain herself.

4th July

Today dawned dull and rainy. Father had business in Winchester, and Charles has left to return to his own lodgings in London now that I am safely installed back at home, so Mother and I were left alone in the house. I was invited to Winchester but felt tired after yesterday's travel – I am clearly not yet completely recovered. After breakfast Mother retired to the drawing room, with her stitching in hand. I never see her with a book, or writing a letter, sketching or any other such ladylike activity, but she is talented at sewing of all kinds, and is rarely without a half-finished sampler or embroidered tablecloth in hand.

After perusing books in Father's study for a while, I went to join her, thinking perhaps we could have a long-overdue heart-to-heart talk. With no one else around, this was a chance to gauge her true feelings about what had happened.

She ignored me when I entered the room. I took a seat near to where she sat in her usual sofa beside the window. *Get straight to the point, George*, I thought, recalling Mr Smythe's oft-given advice, so I opened our conversation with the words: 'Mother, you know I did it for you, don't you? All of it was done to protect you.'

She put down her stitching and stared at me. 'Protect me? But why would I need protection?'

'I know what you did. And I know why. I cannot blame you – what Father was doing was . . .'

'You know nothing. You are wrong. I said yesterday – you probably did it yourself and are just fooling yourself.'

'But it has been proven I could not have done it. There are witnesses . . .'

She dismissed this with a wave of her hand. 'Pah. That girl Maggie. She hasn't two thoughts to rub together. I've dismissed her, you know. Useless creature.'

I didn't know this, but wondered why I hadn't seen her. Mrs Peters and a new girl, Clara, who was plump and plain, had served dinner last night and breakfast this morning. 'Poor Maggie. She did her best. It's not her fault she is simple. But, Mother, she was not the only witness, and that is why I was released.'

'I expect you bribed the witnesses. I don't blame you wanting to get out.' She nodded slightly at me, and picked up her sewing as though to signal the end of the conversation.

I was astounded. I leaned forward, my face inches from hers so she had to look at me and not at the sewing. 'If I'd wanted to bribe a witness, I would have done so *before* being locked up. I wouldn't have made a confession, would I? No, Mother, I *wanted* to go to prison to save *you* from such an ordeal. Being young, I was spared the death penalty. You, however, would have hanged for this.'

That comment struck home. She paled, and her hand, as she tried to make another stitch, shook. I felt a pang of guilt, but it passed quickly. All that I had been through to save her, and yet she wouldn't even acknowledge it, let alone thank me!

She composed herself and shook her head. 'It saddens me to say it, George, but you are deluded. I did nothing.'

'You asked me, that day when Inspector Watling was here, to listen in to the interviews and report back to you. You said yourself you'd hang for this. You as good as admitted to me what you'd done.' I hissed the words at her, and she cowered back away from me.

'Your memory of that day is false. I said no such thing.' But there was less conviction in her voice, and she wavered a little on the last word. Perhaps she wondered what I would do next. Would I denounce her to Inspector Watling? I could, of course, tell him what I knew. But I am not a vindictive man. While I now fully realised the futility of my misguided attempt to spare my mother, I would not do such an about-turn that she would be accused of the murder after all.

Indeed, despite it all, I hoped and prayed that the inspector would not find any evidence against her. I wished for her to get away with murder. Such is my love for my mother, despite her obvious lack of love for me.

I softened my voice. 'Mother, do not fear me. I will say nothing that could implicate you in this. I will keep your crime a secret for as long as I live, believe me.'

She looked at me, and I noted a glimmer of relief in her eyes. 'Then we shall say no more about this. However, I think it best that you find somewhere else to live, as your father has suggested.'

'I shall do so, as soon as I feel strong enough,' I replied. I no longer wanted to live under the same roof as her. I nodded, and took my leave.

As I left the drawing room, the doorbell rang and being near, I went to answer it, waving away Mrs Peters who appeared from the kitchen corridor. It was Inspector Watling. He shook my hand vigorously as I invited him in.

'Well, Master Britten, these are more pleasant surroundings in which to meet, are they not? I heard you had returned, and I am pleased to see you looking so well recovered from your beating.'

'I am not yet back to full strength, but I am much improved from when we last met.' I smiled warmly at him – the man who had secured my release. 'What can I do for you?'

'I came firstly to see how you are, and secondly to speak again with your father and mother. There are obviously still some unanswered questions surrounding the death of the maid. Now that you have been released I am afraid the gentlemen of the press are stirring up interest anew in the case. Be prepared that there might be some unpleasant pieces printed about you and your family over the coming weeks.'

'Thank you for the warning. It will probably be safest not to read the papers for a while, then. I am afraid my father is out this morning. Mother is in the drawing room.' I gestured towards the door, but hesitated to announce him. I did not want to return to her presence.

He must have picked up on the uneasy atmosphere in the house, for he nodded, and walked across the hall. 'Don't worry. I'll show myself in.'

I felt the need for some fresh air. A walk might clear my head and help me marshal my thoughts. I fetched a coat and hat, and set off down the lane towards the village. As I passed the track that led up to Fairy Hill I hesitated, wondering whether to go that way. But, fearing it might be too strenuous in my current state of health, I passed on by, and headed towards the church. A few moments' reflection in its cool interior might help ease my mind.

I was not alone in the church. A female figure was seated near the front. I slipped into a pew further back, on the opposite side, and closed my eyes in meditation. Being in a place of worship made me think of Nathaniel, whose wisdom and compassion I sorely missed. I had seen him only once while I was in hospital – his shifts at the prison not allowing him much time for visits. A chat with him would help me. I resolved to write to him as soon as I returned home. I would also write to my old tutor, Mr Smythe, who lived in London now and might be able to help me find lodgings. With the beginnings of a plan for the future in place, I felt a little restored, and opened my eyes again.

The woman from the front pew was now standing at my elbow. I started, having not heard her approach, then looked up and realised it was none other than Maggie, our one-time maid.

'Hello, Mr George, it is I, M-Maggie,' she said, stumbling over her words. She was twisting her skirt in her hands – a gesture I remembered meant she was nervous.

'Hello, Maggie. It is good to see you. Are you well?' I smiled kindly, hoping to put her at her ease. I wanted to thank her for her part in securing my release, but wasn't sure if she'd even remember what she'd done or understand the significance of it.

'I am well, I am, but I do not have a job no more, I don't,' she replied, her eyes wide and sad.

'Yes, my mother told me she had let you go. I am sorry for it. I hope you will find another place soon.'

'My ma be trying to find me work. I did like working at your house. Mrs Peters were kind, she were.' Her hands were still twisting the fabric of her skirt. I had the impression there was something particular she wanted to say to me, if she could find the words. Maybe I could try to prompt her, and bring it out.

'Maggie, do you remember speaking to the police inspector a few weeks ago? You told him about how you had seen me here in the church, the day before poor Lucy died. Do you remember?'

She nodded. 'I remember. I told him I seen you and I told him that Ma Whiteley were here too, I did. You was locked up, they said, and you shouldn't never have been locked up. I know I am simple in my head but I do know you shouldn't have been locked up, you shouldn't.' She nodded so vigorously her bonnet came loose and slid around on her head. She straightened it up and pulled the ribbons tight.

'I must thank you for that, Maggie. You did a good thing. Would you shake my hand?' I held out my hand to her, and, blushing profusely, she took it, squeezed hard and pumped it up and down so violently I had to suppress a gasp of pain as the motion transmitted itself up to my still-healing ribs.

'I know it weren't you who hurt Lucy,' Maggie went on.

'Yes, you know this because I was here with you when she was hurt,' I said, but Maggie shook her head.

'I know it weren't you, cos it were someone else, it were.'

'What do you mean?'

'She told me she were starting a baby. And that the baby's daddy was the master. I don't know how the master could be her baby's daddy when he is your daddy, but that's what she said, she did.'

I stared at Maggie. 'Lucy was starting a baby?'

'Yes. And she told the master she were starting a baby and he were cross. Proper cross, he were. That's what she told me, she did. He were so cross it must have been him what made her sick.'

'When did she tell you this?'

Maggie screwed up her eyes as though trying to remember. 'Don't know. Were before she died. Two days or three days before. She told me I weren't never to tell anyone.' She clapped a hand to her mouth. 'But now I have! You won't say nothing? I don't want to be locked up, I don't. You shouldn't have been locked up neither. The master should.'

I took her hand and stroked it gently. 'Maggie, you won't be locked up. I won't tell anyone what you just told me, I promise. You did well to tell me. It's hard to keep a secret by yourself.'

She pulled back her hand and blinked away a tear. She seemed less agitated now she had shared her burden with me. She smoothed her skirts and dipped a small curtsy. 'I should go now, Mr George, cos my ma will wonder where I am, she will. Till I get another job I have to help her at home, I do.'

'It's been good to see you again, Maggie. Take care, now.'

'Thank you, I will.' She skipped out of the church, humming tunelessly to herself. I felt glad to have cheered her up, but now I needed to reflect on the implications of what she had told me. If Lucy had been pregnant by my father, and he'd been angry when he found out, did that give him a motive to kill her? Could my father have been the poisoner all along, tiptoeing upstairs to add arsenic to the hot chocolate cup, and not my mother after all? Had I got it completely wrong?

Chapter 23

Cassie

It was late by the time Cassie reached home after her day out in Rugby with Bethany, and she had to work the early shift the next day. Even so, she fired up her laptop as soon as she got in, and spent an hour browsing the website Bethany had sent her a link to – the family finder site. There were testimonies from satisfied customers, all saying how easy it had been to use and how quickly the responses came back. Many also spoke movingly about how their lives had been enriched by finding their long-lost mother/ father/brother/aunt. It certainly looked easy, and although there was a fee it didn't seem much for the services they offered.

Experimentally, she filled in the form, entering Jack Wilkinson's name, the town where her mother had lived before Cassie was born, and her date of birth. It all seemed to be very little to go on, but the testimonies on the site had all expressed surprise and delight at how successful the company had been, tracing their family members despite the scarcity of information provided.

Her finger hovered over the Submit button. The next stage, if she sent the form, would be a phone call from one of the company's staff, to talk about her situation and explore exactly what she was hoping to achieve. The adviser would also then tell her how the system worked and what she might expect. She filled in a suitable time for a call – late Sunday, or any time on her next day off – Tuesday.

And then, without thinking too hard about what she was doing, she clicked the Submit button. When they rang she could always say she'd changed her mind. But she went to bed with a smile on her face. It had been a fabulous day out, and she was excited about having taken the first step towards tracing her birth father. Finding him would mean closure.

Being on the early shift on Sunday meant she'd finished work by mid-afternoon and had a long free evening ahead of her. Andy was on the late shift and Shania had the day off, so there was no one to suggest doing anything after work. That suited Cassie – she was planning to spend the spare time researching George Britten. It would help take her mind off waiting for a call from the family finder site, too.

As soon as she was home she made herself a snack and a cup of tea and settled herself on the sofa with her laptop and a notebook. Griselda jumped up and settled herself happily between Cassie and a cushion. Time to do some searches to see what she could find. She read back through her notes to remind herself how far she'd got – George had been in prison for the 1861 census but released early. He'd been charged with murder and only escaped execution because of his youth. She checked the occupants of his home address – the address he'd been at as a child in 1851. The census showed his father, mother, a housekeeper named Mary Peters, and a maid named Anne Baker. A groom named John Lincoln lived in a stables cottage on the grounds.

So how and why had he been released early? That was the question. Probably the best plan of attack was to check for newspaper reports. Cassie had already seen reports of his conviction in March 1861 but what about his release? She did not know exactly when he was released, but it had to be after the 1861 census, which was taken in April, and before the 1871 census. 'Just ten years to search. How hard it can be?' she muttered.

Might as well start at the beginning in 1861, she decided. She began a series of searches on the newspaper archive site, using search terms "George Britten", "Millbank", "release". It took a little while, working methodically through, but then she struck gold. An article in *The Times*, dated June 1861, gave the whole story.

George Britten, the nineteen-year-old who was convicted of murder in March of this year, was released today from Millbank Prison, his conviction having been quashed. Britten had earlier confessed to the murder of a servant girl named Lucy Carter who had been employed at his family home in Hampshire. Miss Carter died of arsenic poisoning, the arsenic having been put into a cup of hot chocolate.

However, new evidence has come to light: namely witnesses who placed Britten out of the house at the time the hot chocolate was prepared and taken to the unfortunate victim. Mr Britten's older brother Charles Britten, along with the detective in charge of the case – Inspector Joseph Watling – managed to secure George Britten's release after presenting the new evidence to the court. Britten was in hospital at the time, following an incident in the prison yard in which he sustained serious injuries.

It is not known why Mr Britten confessed to a murder he did not commit, but Inspector Watling told this paper that he believed the young man was protecting someone else. The inspector would not speculate on who might actually be responsible, saying only that he was glad that an innocent young man was no longer in prison, and that he wished Mr Britten all the best for a speedy recovery from his injuries. The investigation to find the true culprit continues.

Cassie read the article through a few times. So George Britten had confessed to a serious crime that he did not commit. He might have been hanged for it. Who had he been protecting?

Presumably not his brother Charles, who'd battled to get George's case reopened. Who, then? His father, perhaps? Cassie checked her notes – George's father was named Albert Britten. Had he been the murderer?

She ran some more searches. Now she knew the name of the victim – perhaps there'd been a later case in which the true murderer was tried and convicted. But she could find no more references to poor Lucy Carter in the national papers, nor in the local Hampshire papers. Albert Britten had remained living in his substantial Hampshire home for another twenty years along with his wife Augusta, until their deaths. So he'd clearly not been convicted of murder at any point. Perhaps it had been someone else – not a member of the Britten family – who'd poisoned Lucy. One of the other servants, maybe. But Cassie could not imagine George taking the blame for someone unconnected with the family, someone he was not close to.

'It's a mystery,' she said, stroking Griselda. 'And possibly one I'll never know the answer to. But at least we know why George was released from prison so early.' She wondered about the prison incident that had landed George in hospital with serious injuries. What was the background to that? She was building up a picture of this not-ancestor, now. She imagined a gentle, loving young man, with a deep sense of loyalty, who was prepared to go to prison or even the gallows to protect someone he cared about. Had George simply got caught up in someone else's fight? Or perhaps he'd once more been trying to protect someone. Another question Cassie would be unable to find the answer to.

She sent Bethany a quick email, outlining what she'd found out. She didn't mention anything about using the family finder website yet. Until she'd had the phone call from them and decided to definitely go ahead, she wanted to keep that to herself.

Cassie spent the rest of the afternoon writing up what she'd found out, so that at some point in the future she could present it to Tony. It was his ancestry, even if it wasn't hers.

And then at eight o'clock came the phone call she'd been both longing for and dreading, from the family finder website. A woman named Alison with a gentle voice and soft Welsh accent phoned. She confirmed the details Cassie had written on the form, and then talked through their processes. They used electoral rolls and other databases to try to trace a person forward from their last known address. Alison said that nine times out of ten they were able to find the missing family member within a week of first contact. After that, they would pass on details, and if required, would help arrange a first meeting. At all stages they would offer support, counselling and advice.

Of course it all came at a cost, but Alison didn't talk about the financial side of things, apart from to say that a detailed email would be sent as soon as Cassie confirmed she wanted to go ahead. Payment could be by credit card, and an initial payment was needed upfront.

Alison was obviously reading that part from a script, but her voice was so kind and gentle that Cassie found herself confessing the full story – how she'd always thought Tony was her real father, the bombshell he'd dropped as a result of her asking about genealogy, and how her own daughter had found her through the same website. Alison made sympathetic noises throughout, but then began winding up the conversation. 'So, I'll leave you to read through the email in detail, and when we've received your first payment we'll get the ball rolling. It's been lovely to chat with you, Cassie, and rest assured we will support you whatever you decide to do, at all steps of the process. You are in good hands. There's a phone number on the email if you feel like you want to ask more questions or talk anything through in more detail.'

'Thank you,' Cassie said. She felt a little overwhelmed by it all, but supposed that was normal and natural, and that Alison must have heard it all dozens of times. 'I appreciate it.'

'We're here to help. Have a good evening, now.'

Cassie hung up and immediately checked her email. Yes, the

message was there already. She read through in detail and then went ahead and made the initial payment. If she was going to do this, she might as well just get on with it. Jack Wilkinson. In a week or even less, she might have his contact details.

The response came in just three days. Cassie had decided not to tell anyone she had gone ahead with searching for her birth father – not her mother or Tony, or Andy or even Bethany. It felt somehow too personal. She knew Bethany would understand, when or if Cassie finally told her.

And so Cassie made an excuse not to go to the pub after work on Wednesday as she usually would – she felt she would not be able to trust herself not to blurt it all out in front of Shania, Ben and Toby. 'You're becoming boring in your old age,' Ben told her. 'We'll have to find a new drinking buddy if you keep crying off.'

'I'll be there next week,' she promised. Unless something else turned up. These days her life seemed far from settled.

The email was waiting for her on Wednesday evening when she got home. She opened it with shaking fingers, half expecting it to be just an admin announcement, perhaps asking for more money, or at best a progress report.

But it was far more than that. They'd found him. They'd actually found Jack Wilkinson, her birth father. The email contained contact details for him, and an offer to broker the initial contact if she wanted, and a reminder that she could phone to discuss the way forward at any time.

Cassie's heart was pounding as she read through. He wasn't far away. She could easily drive there and visit. But – his address made her gasp. This was something she hadn't expected or even contemplated. She stared at the details, reading them over and over, willing them to change into something more acceptable, something she could cope with, but the words remained resolutely the same. Jack Wilkinson's current abode was a prison, where he was serving a life sentence.

Chapter 24

George

7th July

Once again I barely know where to begin with today's journal entry. A calamity has befallen me, yet again. Oh how I long for and pray for a quiet life! Only a few short months ago my life was blissfully quiet: I was but a child, under the tutelage of Mr Smythe, with nothing greater to worry about than whether I would remember the Latin conjugations he'd set me to learn. Since then I've been in prison, released, badly beaten, hospitalised, realised that all along I may have been wrong about the architect of Lucy's fate . . . and now . . . learned something new that rocks the very foundations of my life still further.

I ramble in these paragraphs as I am trying to find a way to start. *Start at the beginning*, says Mr Smythe in my head, with an indulgent sigh and a shake of his head. Though I should no longer do what Mr Smythe taught merely because it is what he taught. I should do it because I know it to be the best course of action.

Very well. I will do so. I must return to the day when I'd met Maggie in the church.

* * *

I spent a long while in the church that day, brooding over what Maggie had told me. Lucy, pregnant with Father's child! She must have been in the very early stages. And she had told him about it. Had she made demands, I wondered? Perhaps threatened to tell Mother? Had she wanted money, or guarantees, or more?

Throughout these last few weeks while I have been convalescing the scales have fallen from my eyes regarding Lucy. She was a charming, beautiful young girl, but I see now that she was only after what was best for herself. Her early interest in me faded when she realised I was not the eldest son and would therefore have only a limited inheritance. With Charles away she turned her attentions to my father, and he, weak as he was, was taken in by her.

I wonder if she was indeed pregnant – by my calculations her affair with my father cannot have lasted more than a couple of weeks, from sprained ankle to death by poisoning; unless it had started before her accident. Perhaps she'd been intending to blackmail my father. Perhaps she'd been making it all up.

And had it frightened him so much he had committed murder to cover it up? Or as I'd originally suspected, had my mother's jealousy of the maid driven her to commit murder? Those seemed to be the only two solutions. Either way it seemed I was the son of a murderer. I did not like to dwell on this. I knew I could never tell Charles. While he'd said he suspected who'd poisoned Lucy, he had never told me what his suspicions were. And I would never ask, just as he had promised never to ask me who I'd been protecting with my false confession.

As soon as I returned from the church that day, I sat down to update my journal and write some letters. Firstly to Nathaniel, to tell him how I fared, and to tell him not to write to me at my father's house, for I knew I would not remain there for long. Secondly I wrote to Mr Smythe – a long letter that hinted at but did not fully explain all that had happened since he left my father's employment, and asking whether he could help me finding lodgings in London. For I have decided to try my luck in the capital.

I had a reply from dear Mr Smythe, my wonderful, wise and worthy friend, by return of post. He was gratified to hear from me, having longed to hear my news. He'd seen something of what had happened in the papers, but had not wanted to 'intrude' at such a difficult time. He knew, he wrote, that if I needed his help or advice I would turn to him, in time, and until then he'd wished to remain in the background. Now seemed to be the time when he could step forward and help his old pupil once more.

He is now married and with a baby on the way, making a living by instructing students privately in his own home, having left the school he'd initially worked at. He lives on the west side of London, not far from the river at Twickenham. He has a modest house but it contains a spare room, and, he wrote, he and his wife Lily would be honoured if I would become their lodger, for as long as I wanted. They would make the room ready for me at once, so I could arrive as soon as I desired.

On reading this letter I found tears running down my face. A true friend. Though once I might have resented his authority, and rebelled against his insistence that I learn about things that did not interest me, I now see that I became the man I am due to his influence alone. Not my mother's or father's.

I wanted to waste no time at all, so resolved to pack my things that very day and leave for London the following day. And so I set off around the house to make my farewells. I went to see the staff first, putting off the moment when I would need to face my father. I had still not decided whether to confront him with my new knowledge of Lucy's pregnancy.

John Lincoln and the stable boys were sad to see me go, but understanding of my decision. They shook my hand formally and wished me well. The new maid, Clara, I barely knew so there seemed no need to speak to her for more than a moment. She bobbed a curtsy and nodded at my news, then scurried off about her duties.

It was a different story with Mrs Peters. I found her in the kitchen, rolling out pastry to make a pie for dinner. When I told her I would be shortly leaving the house, for good, she burst into tears, wiped her floury hands on a rag and held out her arms to enfold me in a hug, just as she used to do when I was a child with a bumped head or scraped knee.

'Oh Master George, I don't blame you, but oh I shall miss you! You were always my favourite, you know? Your sweet, gentle nature has always been a breath of sunshine in this house. But you are all grown up now, and after all the unpleasantness, it's good that you can start a new life somewhere else. It has been difficult here. That police inspector, Mr Watling, keeps coming round and asking questions. I fear he thinks perhaps it was I who poisoned poor Lucy!'

I was shocked at this – I had never for a moment thought that Mrs Peters would be under suspicion. 'Why on earth would he think that?'

She dabbed away a tear. 'Because the key to the arsenic shed is kept in my rooms, I suppose. Only a few people would have access to the key.'

'But there's no proof the arsenic used even came from our store.' I was outraged on her behalf. More outraged, I realised, than at the idea it could have been Mother or Father who'd committed the crime. I hugged her tighter. 'It was not you, of course it wasn't. I shall speak on your behalf if Inspector Watling ever takes that ridiculous accusation any further.'

'If not me, and not you, who was it then?' Mrs Peters asked, quietly.

I shook my head. 'I do not know.' Given what Maggie had told me, at least my answer was honest. 'I . . . I can't bear to think about it.'

She hugged me once more. 'Then we'll say no more. If you are leaving, then perhaps I will too, in a little while. This household will not be the same without you. Where will you go?'

'I have written to Mr Smythe and he says I can lodge with him for as long as I want,' I told her.

She smiled at this. 'That Mr Smythe's a nice chap. I always liked him. I'm glad you're going there and he can keep an eye on you. I promised your mama I'd look after you.'

'Promised my mama?' I was confused. Why would Mother have wanted the housekeeper to promise she'd look after me, when Mother was here herself?

To my surprise Mrs Peters coloured up and clapped a hand to her mouth. 'Oh, Master George, I don't mean . . . I mean . . . I promised never to say . . .'

'Say what, Mrs Peters?'

'Ah, no, 'tis not for me to say. I promised . . .'

I took her hands and led her to a chair, bade her sit. 'Mrs Peters, now I am grown, as you say, and about to leave home for good. Pray tell me whatever it is you are keeping secret.'

She opened and closed her mouth a few times, reminding me of Maggie when she'd been battling with herself whether to tell me about her secret. At last Mrs Peters straightened her spine, took a deep breath and, still clutching my hands, told me the news that has rocked my life once again.

Mother is not my real mother.

Chapter 25

Cassie

The first thing Cassie did, on learning that her birth father was currently detained at Her Majesty's pleasure, was to google his name. She realised she could have done this before tracing him, after her mother told her his name. She might have found out about his crime back then, but would not have been sure that he was the 'right' Jack Wilkinson or not. Nevertheless it might have influenced whether she would have gone ahead with searching for him or not.

'Anyway,' she said to Griselda, 'we are where we are. Now then, Jack. What did you do to warrant a life sentence?' She was back on the newspaper archive website again, this time searching for more recent articles that mentioned the name Jack Wilkinson. After a little while she found reports of his trial and conviction five years earlier, with links back to reports of the original crime some ten months before. She read all these, one hand clasped over her mouth. It seemed Jack Wilkinson had been part of a gang of crooks, who had broken into a large house that belonged to a minor celebrity. Something had gone wrong and the three men had ended up fighting each other.

At some point Jack had pulled a knife and stabbed one of his comrades, then he and his accomplice had run off leaving the other man for dead. The crime was discovered when the homeowners returned from a holiday a week later. The dead man was identified and his known associates questioned, and Jack was charged with the murder. His only defence had been to say that the dead man had been acting contrary to their plan, and Jack had thought he'd be putting them all in danger of being caught. Wilkinson had showed no remorse, the report of the trial read, and the judge had not hesitated in handing down a life sentence after he'd been found guilty.

'Jesus. You killed your own friend. You were worried you'd be caught burgling a house and so you stabbed him to death.' Cassie shook her head incredulously. What sort of a man was he, this murderer whose blood ran in her veins? To think she'd been horrified that George Britten, who she'd thought was a distant ancestor, had been imprisoned for murder. She'd hated the idea that a killer's genes were in her. George had turned out not to be related, and also not guilty of murder in any case. But now, a much closer ancestor – her own biological father – was serving a life sentence for killing his mate. It was unbelievable.

Did she want to contact him? That was the next question. She checked visiting information on the prison website. Visits were permitted several days a week, but needed to be booked in advance. Should she go? Could she sit down opposite a man she'd never met and say, *Hello, I'm your daughter?* Look him in the eye, knowing he'd killed a man, asking him about his life, telling him about hers?

Cassie found herself becoming more and more stressed just thinking about it. There was no way she could make this decision on her own. And, she realised, if she did go to see him, she didn't want to go alone. Bethany was the obvious choice – both to talk it through with and to go with her on the prison visit, if she decided to make one. Jack Wilkinson was Bethany's grandfather.

She was on the point of lifting the phone to call her daughter and tell her the news. She would tell her soon, that was certain, but . . . did she want Bethany with her, if she went to see Jack? Was it right to put her beautiful young daughter in front of a convicted murderer in a prison?

'I can't do it,' she whispered, running her fingers through Griselda's fur. The action calmed and comforted her. Thank God for cats. 'I can't take Bethany. But I can't go on my own, either.' Her thoughts ran to her parents. She couldn't imagine her mother wanting to go. That would be wrong in so many ways. What about Tony? Have the man who'd brought her up sitting opposite the man who'd unknowingly given her life? Again, far too awkward for words.

She tried to picture herself alone at the prison, sitting on an uncomfortable chair at a bolted-down table, with Jack opposite and a stern-looking prison guard standing by the door. As the image took shape in her mind, she realised there was someone sitting next to her in it, someone calm and strong, who was unconnected to them but who'd have her best interests at heart. Someone who'd sit quietly while she and Jack talked, who'd drive her there and back again, who'd be on hand to mop up the inevitable tears.

Before she had time to think any more about it, she lifted her phone and called Andy, explaining through sobs and tears what she had found out about her birth father.

'Christ, Cassie. You sound in a real state. Stay put – I'm coming over. I'll be there in ten minutes or so.'

She had no chance to object, and as he hung up she realised she didn't want to make any objections anyway. She needed a shoulder to cry on, a sympathetic ear, a comforting arm about her shoulders. She looked around the sitting room – it was a mess, but she felt unable to do anything about it. She glanced in a mirror – she was also a mess. He'd have to take her and the flat as he found them.

Andy was there very shortly as he'd promised, clutching a bottle of wine. 'Thought this might help,' he said, and without waiting for her response he went through to the kitchen, opened the wine and found two wine glasses. He sat beside her on the sofa and handed her a glass. 'Right. Tell me once more what's happened.'

She did, managing to sound a little more coherent now that he was sitting beside her, the simple fact of his presence lending her strength.

'You really don't have a straightforward family, do you?' he said when she'd finished updating him. 'Thought my background was complicated enough.'

'So now I'm trying to decide – should I go and see him or not? And if I go, should I take someone with me?'

'If you don't go to see him, you might find you are always wondering what he's like. And, Cassie, although he's in prison and has done a bad thing, he won't be a monster. There's good and bad in everyone. He killed his accomplice – but we don't know how much he was provoked, whether it was partly in self-defence. You've only got a few short newspaper reports to go on. And, putting aside his crime, there will be other aspects to his personality. Some that you might click with.'

'You're sounding like Bethany.'

His eyes widened. 'Have you told her? I thought you'd only discovered all this today.'

She shook her head. 'You're right – I only opened the email from the family finder website when I got home from work today, and then I went googling to find out more about Jack's crime. I haven't even told Bethany I was definitely going to try to trace him. I don't think . . . I mean, if I do go to see him I don't think she should be there. I know he's her grandfather, but . . . she's young. I guess I want . . .'

'You want to protect her.' Andy smiled. 'Of course you do. It's natural. But listen, I don't think you should go on your own. I think someone should be with you – either waiting outside in the car or actually sitting beside you in the visitors' room.'

Cassie nodded, and looked up at him. 'Yes, I think it'd be easier not to be on my own.'

'Take me with you.' It was as though he'd read her thoughts from earlier. 'I'm not connected with this man in any way but I can support you. Promise me? If you decide to go, you'll let me go with you. Which prison is he in?'

'One in Warwickshire. A couple of hours' drive. Yes, I promise to take you. Thank you, Andy.'

He put an arm around her shoulders and pulled her in for a hug. 'You are very welcome. I'd do anything for you, you know that, right?' The last words were said in a whisper, his mouth against her hair, and she wasn't entirely sure she'd heard him properly.

It took her a few more days and a lot of soul-searching, but finally Cassie decided that she did need to visit Jack Wilkinson, find out what he looked like, what sort of person he was, and let him know he had a daughter. Give him a chance. Andy was right – if she didn't do it she would always wonder. You regret the things you *don't* do in life, she told herself. And so she agreed a date with Andy, and made an appointment with the prison for two visitors to see him. She was shaking when she received confirmation of the visit, and immediately called Andy.

'So, we're on for next Tuesday,' she said. 'Oh fuck. Am I doing the right thing, Andy?'

'I think so. But if you change your mind that's all right too. You'd only need to email the prison to say you're not coming.'

'Yes. I suppose so. Should I tell Bethany?'

She could hear the smile in his voice as he replied. 'Cassie, that's entirely up to you. You'll probably want to tell her eventually, but whether you tell her before you see him or after is your decision.'

'What would you do?'

'I have no idea. It's not easy. I suppose – I would call someone I trust and ask them what they'd do.'

She laughed. 'Well that's exactly what I've done, isn't it? Only the someone I trust is a bit useless and doesn't know what he'd do in this situation!'

He laughed too. 'But I hope that talking it through helps a bit, in any case.'

'It does, Andy. You're a good mate. Thank you.'

Tuesday rolled around slowly. It was only a week or so until Christmas now. Where had December gone? Cassie had barely thought about it at all. She'd phoned Bethany a few times but had decided not to mention going to see Jack until after the event. In any case, Bethany was busy with end-of-term activities, and her parents were coming home in a few days, in time for Christmas.

'I'm so looking forward to seeing them,' she told Cassie. 'So much to tell them. And they've had a shed-load of adventures in Australia – I can't wait to hear all the details and see the photos. Oh, and you must meet them. They've said they'd like to meet you.'

'Oh, er, of course!' Oh God. Cassie's stomach flipped. Another complex meeting coming up – face to face with the people who'd adopted her daughter and brought her up. Bethany had always said they were lovely and easy to get along with. So she'd just have to trust her. Anyway, before then there was another more momentous meeting to deal with.

Andy drove to the Warwickshire prison. The journey took a couple of hours, and they'd allowed time for bad traffic and a cup of coffee before the scheduled visiting time. They found a café not far from the prison – a dingy place with sticky tables, that served tea in cracked mugs.

'It'll do,' Cassie said, when Andy asked if she'd rather go some-where else. 'Frankly I'm not going to be noticing the surroundings.'

'Not too late to change your mind,' Andy said, for the tenth time that day. He was looking at her with concern as she took a seat near the café's window with its torn net curtains.

She shook her head. 'I've come this far. I'll go and see him. And I would like you to come into the visiting room with me, if you will.'

'Of course. Tea? And they do toasted teacakes – I quite fancy that. For you too?' Cassie nodded, and Andy gave the order to the hovering waitress.

Later, fortified by the tea and teacake, they drove the short distance to the prison's visitors' car park. As Andy switched off the engine he turned to Cassie and put his hand over hers on her leg. 'OK?'

'Nervous as hell. But yeah. I'm OK.' She unclipped her seat-belt and got out of the car, her hand feeling warm where Andy had briefly held it. She followed him towards a door marked 'Visitors' Entrance' and passed through it. They signed in at a desk, waited briefly with a few other people in a corridor lined with plastic chairs, and then were ushered through into a large austere room. It was just like she'd seen on countless TV programmes. Rows of functional tables bolted to the floor, with more plastic chairs set at each. Prisoners in grey sweatshirts sitting waiting, their gaze fixed on the door through which the visitors were streaming in.

Most people made beelines for certain tables, greeting their relative or friend, sitting down quickly and immediately chatting. Cassie and Andy stood to one side. Cassie was scanning the room, looking for a prisoner sitting alone, wondering if he'd even agreed to meet her. She'd given her name but no indication of who she was or why she wanted to see him.

A prison guard approached. 'Who are you here to see, miss?'

'Jack W-Wilkinson.' The name stuck in her throat somehow. The prison guard gave her an odd look, but then indicated a man seated on the far side of the room. He was leaning back in his chair, tilting it onto two legs, his arms folded across his chest. He was staring not at them, but at the large clock at the end of the room.

'OK, Cassie?' Andy asked, and when she nodded he took her arm and gently led the way. The man – Jack – didn't look round as they approached. It wasn't until they stood in front of him, pulling out the two chairs opposite him to sit down, that he glanced at them, frowning.

'Social services, are you? I told the last lot I ain't paying her any more money. The kid's not mine.'

Cassie gasped, her mouth flapping like a goldfish for a moment, until she realised he did not mean her. He knew nothing about her.

'No, we're not social services. We're . . . well, I'm Cassie Turner and this is my friend Andy.'

'Hello,' Andy said, with a small smile and a nod. Cassie noticed he half raised a hand as though to shake Jack Wilkinson's, but must have thought better of it because he turned the gesture into a scratch of his chin.

'What you here for then, if you ain't social services?' Wilkinson leaned yet further back in his chair. Cassie felt irrationally scared that the back legs would slip or buckle and her father would fall in a sprawling heap on the floor. Would she be expected to rush around the table and pick him up, check he wasn't hurt, offer sympathy?

'It's kind of awkward, Mr W-Wilkinson. I don't quite know where to begin.'

'At the start, love.' Wilkinson sniffed and wiped the back of his hand across his nose. Cassie was peering at him, trying to spot any resemblance between him and the face she saw in the mirror. He must have been good-looking when he was young, she decided. He had a strong jawline and straight nose, startlingly blue eyes. There were a couple of scars on his cheeks, and wrinkles around his mouth suggested he'd been a heavy smoker. But his profile was a little like hers, and the set of his mouth, and something about his eyes was familiar.

'All right. So – um – do you remember a woman called Shirley Callan? I think you'd have known her about . . . thirty-eight years ago or so.'

'Shirley who?'

'Shirley Callan. Slim, kind of darkish blonde hair – it'd have been long back then. Part of a group you hung around with . . . She was at a couple of parties you went to . . .'

'How do you know I met her at parties? I can't remember her. A looker, was she?'

'Pretty, yes.'

'Might have known her then. Doesn't ring a bell. Why are you asking?'

Cassie glanced at Andy who caught her hand under the table and squeezed it, in support. He gave her the briefest of nods as though to say, you're doing well, keep going.

'She's my mum,' Cassie said, watching Wilkinson closely for any sign of a reaction.

'But why are you asking me about her?'

'Because . . .' This was it. Time to say what she'd come here to say, and see his reaction. He hadn't been too warm and welcoming so far, but maybe all that would change once he knew their true relationship to each other. 'Well, because . . . she met you at one of those parties. She spent some time with you back then. You and she . . . dated, and then later, she found she was . . . pregnant. With me.'

Wilkinson shrugged. 'So what?'

'She says . . . she's only just told me all this . . . she says you're my f-father.'

Wilkinson was quiet for a moment, staring at her, and then slowly he tipped his chair forward back onto all four legs, uncrossed his arms and leaned on the table, resting his chin on a steeple of his fingers. 'You're my kid?'

Cassie simply nodded, and watched him as the news sunk in. Beneath the table Andy squeezed her hand tighter, and she made a conscious effort to suck in the support he was offering.

'So,' Wilkinson said, 'if we did a DNA test, like, it'd show up whether your mum's lying, right?'

'I suppose so, but . . . she doesn't lie. Why would she have made up your name?'

'How'd you find me?'

'A family finder website. Helps adopted people trace their birth parents.' Cassie found she did not want to use the terms 'true parent' or 'real parent'.

'Could be another person with my name.'

'You lived in Reading around thirty-eight years ago?'

'Yeah . . .'

'So that narrows it down to the Jack Wilkinsons who lived in that area at that time.'

'Hmm.' Wilkinson tipped his chair back again, crossed his arms and stared at the ceiling.

'Look,' Cassie said, trying to be charitable, 'I know this is all a bit of a shock. And perhaps . . . I should have written to you first. But I-I wanted to meet you.'

'And now you have, Carol.'

'Cassie.'

'Whatever. So what do you want from me?' He'd tipped forward again, leaning across the table, staring at her. 'I ain't got no money. Social services keep wanting access to my bank accounts and I keep telling them there's nothing there.'

'I don't want anything from you,' Cassie replied. 'Certainly not money. I just wanted . . . to meet you. Find out what . . . you were like.'

'Disappointed, are you, love?' He snorted a laugh.

'No, not at all,' Cassie said, sounding unconvincing even to herself. 'It's early days. But if you don't want me to come back again, I won't . . .'

Wilkinson grinned, revealing nicotine-stained teeth with a gap where one canine should be. 'Nah, you're all right. You come if you want. I get sod-all visitors in this place. Nice to see you.

Breaks the monotony, like. Hard to take in that you're my kid, though. I got a kid who's what, thirty-five?'

'Thirty-seven.'

He shook his head. 'Well, fuck me.' And then an expression crossed his face, that only later that evening, when Cassie was reliving the encounter in her mind, did she interpret as calculating. 'So, Cassie, *daughter*, you want to do something to help your old dad, do you?'

'If I can,' she said, hoping that the hesitancy didn't show in her voice. Beside her she was aware of Andy turning his head to look at her, but she didn't dare look back at him.

'Thing is,' Wilkinson said, 'I shouldn't be in here. Dunno if you know what I'm in for?'

'I do, yes,' she said carefully.

'It weren't me. It were the other fella – Jimmy – that stabbed Clarkesy. I-I took the rap for it. Cos . . . cos Jimmy would never have hacked prison.' Wilkinson sat up straighter, adopting an expression of martyred pride. 'I done it for him. Jimmy's soft, like. Wouldn't have lasted two minutes in here. So I went down for it, instead of him.'

Cassie glanced at Andy, who gave a tiny shake of his head as if to say don't go there, but she had to know more. 'What are you saying?'

'Saying I'm not guilty, that's what. So, daughter, here's what you can do for me. Get me a lawyer. A good one. You'll have to pay – I ain't got no money right now but I'll pay you back later. Get the lawyer to launch an appeal to get me outta here.' He reached across the table and touched her upper arm. It was the first physical contact she'd had with her father, and the realisation made her gasp. 'You'll do that for your old dad, will ya? Like I say, when I'm out I'll pay you back and everything.'

'I-I'll see what I can do,' Cassie said. She imagined herself talking to the Citizens' Advice Bureau to start with, to find out how to go about starting the appeal process. Maybe she'd have a chat with the governor of the prison. She could phone round criminal lawyers to find one who'd take on the case. 'Who represented you in court before?'

'Some bastard. Don't want him again. Useless twat.'

'OK, well, I'll see what . . .' Just then a loud buzzer went off denoting the end of visiting time, and the noise level of chat in the room increased as people pushed back chairs and said their farewells. Cassie wondered how to end this visit. Not a hug – that didn't feel right. To prevent it happening she put out her hand for a handshake. Wilkinson looked at her hand in confusion for a moment but then took it. His skin was rough and calloused. Skin-to-skin contact with her father, for the first time. Cassie gulped back a sob – she did not want to show any emotion in this place, or, she realised, in front of this man. 'Well, goodbye then. I'll try to do what you asked. I'll write.'

'Yeah, all right then. Me with a grown-up daughter. A looker too. Hey, you never said who this bloke is? Husband? Boyfriend?' Wilkinson indicated Andy who was on his feet, waiting for Cassie.

'My friend. Andy.' Cassie expected Wilkinson to shake Andy's hand and say something, but he didn't. He just grunted and turned away, shuffling towards the door by which the prisoners were leaving the room.

Andy caught Cassie's hand tightly and led her towards the visitors' exit. She glanced back once, just as Wilkinson went through his door, and then she quietly followed Andy back through doors and corridors, signing out at the exit, and crossing the car park. Only when she was in the passenger seat, handbag on the floor between her feet, seatbelt fastened, did she give in to the waves of emotion that were washing over her and let the tears fall.

'Come on. Let's get away from here, find a quiet café that's nicer than the last one, and have a cup of tea,' Andy said, starting the engine before he waited for a reply. Cassie glanced gratefully across at him and allowed him to take charge.

* * *

Half an hour later they were in a cosy pub in a small village on the route home. Andy had ordered tea and sandwiches as a late lunch, and they were seated at a table near an open log fire. Cassie had been to the ladies' loos, splashed water on her face and repaired her make-up. Her thoughts were racing around her head but she had Andy here to listen to her and advise her. Dear Andy. She realised she could never have got through this day without him. Even though he'd said nothing during the visit with Wilkinson (why could she only think of the man using his surname?) his quiet presence had lent her strength. He was a good friend. More than a friend, perhaps.

'So. What did you think?' Andy asked, after the tea had arrived and he'd poured them both cups.

She shrugged. 'I think ... it's too soon to know what he's really like. But ...'

'You didn't like him.' It was a statement, gently made, rather than a question.

'Not much, no,' she said, tears welling up again. A memory of the day she and Bethany had met for the first time in the London park came to mind. How different that had been! They'd instantly liked each other, and known they would have a good relationship. But right now, Cassie felt she wouldn't care if she never met Wilkinson again. She was glad she hadn't promised to. She could stay in contact by letter.

'You going to help him? Like he asked?'

'I'll make enquiries. I said I would see ... so I must at least investigate possibilities.'

Andy nodded, and she was reassured that she was doing the right thing. Maybe Wilkinson was innocent – of the murder, anyway, even if he'd been involved in the burglary. Maybe she could help, and by doing so build a relationship with him ... but did she want this? Or did she want to just quietly let the whole thing drop? Did she regret having ever traced him? She didn't know what she thought, right now.

Chapter 26

George

Mother is not my real mother.

My father's philandering ways, taking advantage of attractive young servants, goes a long way back, it seems, so Mrs Peters told me. She stood and made me sit in the chair she'd vacated, while she told me the full story. Mother had been pregnant, and her pregnancy had made her very sick. Father took his pleasures elsewhere, in the form of a pretty young parlour maid aged just sixteen. Her name was Martha Ellis, and the way Mrs Peters described her made me think of Lucy.

Martha had become pregnant, blossoming with me in her belly just a month or so behind my mother's pregnancy.

Mother's child – a boy – had been stillborn; the cord wrapped around his little neck. There was no midwife in attendance as there'd been heavy snow on the ground and the road from the village was impassable. Mrs Peters wept as she told me this. 'I did all I could, but the poor little mite never took so much as a single breath.'

Mother had fallen into a deep despair at this, made worse when little Elizabeth died shortly after. Meanwhile Martha's pregnancy continued to term, and despite Mother hating to see her husband's mistress still around the house, her growing belly testament to Father's infidelity, it seems he got his way and Martha kept her place. When Martha's baby – I – was born, Father paid her off, saying if she left and gave up all rights to her child, he'd raise it as his and Mother's own, replacing the one Mother had lost, hoping to take her mind off the loss of Elizabeth too. Whether he'd have done the same if the baby had been a girl was unknown.

And so it was that within days of giving birth my natural mother was sent from the house, with a bag of coin and a decent reference, having been persuaded that the best thing she could do for her child was to leave him with his father.

'We spoke for ages about what was best to do, Martha and I,' Mrs Peters told me, her hands gripping mine so tightly that she left red marks on the backs of them. 'What was best for you. And for her. Your father had made it clear she couldn't stay any longer, not with a small baby, so she'd have been out on her ear with no hope of getting another job, and with a baby to care for. She'd have ended up on the streets. This way she knew her baby would be well looked after and given a fine start in life, and she – she was only seventeen by then – could start again somewhere else. She made me promise, Master George, that I'd look after you. I've tried, Master George, I've tried to do as she wished. She were a lovely girl, your mama.'

There were tears in her eyes as she said this, and in mine too. I pulled her towards me into a tight hug. 'Mrs Peters, no one could have done any more for me than you. You have kept your promise to my mother. I thank you for it, on her behalf.'

And then I excused myself, and, it being a fine day and I in need of solitude, I went for a walk up Fairy Hill, and sat for a long while at the top of it beneath the rowan trees, looking out over the fields and farmland of my childhood, contemplating what I had learned. My mother had been a servant, seduced or abused by my father, then she'd effectively sold me to him. How

I felt about her giving me up I wasn't sure, but I understood what Mrs Peters had told me, that it had been the only course of action Martha Ellis could have taken. She'd done her best, and then she'd left with the money. What had become of her?

And it all explained the coldness Mother had always shown me. I was not her true child. She'd lost two babies around the time I was born. I felt sympathy for her, for that. It must have been hard for her. And of course I'd been a constant reminder all my life, of my father's betrayal of her.

As I sat there, watching swallows whirl and dive for insects above my head, I made more resolutions. This was the new, decisive, George Britten – a man who knew his own mind, made decisions, and then acted upon them. Firstly – I would confront my parents and demand the truth. Secondly – I would do everything in my power to track down my real mother. Mrs Peters might know something of where she had gone when she left here twenty years ago.

8th July

As I still intended leaving for London and Mr Smythe's residence as soon as possible, there was no time to lose to begin acting upon my decisions. Before losing my resolve I knew I must confront my parents. Or rather, confront my father and his wife. Augusta Britten, I realised, was no relation of mine.

I hobbled down the hill – still feeling the effects of my prison beating. Walking downhill was painful as it jarred my ribs. But pain was the last thing on my mind. Mother – no, I shall refer to her as Augusta from this day on – was in the drawing room with a piece of stitching, and Father was with her, reading a newspaper. Good – they were together. I wasn't sure if it would be easier or more difficult to speak to both at once, but certainly it meant I would get it all over and done with in one go. For I knew that this was likely to be the last conversation I had with either of them.

'Father, ahem, M-Mother, I wish to speak with you both on an important matter,' I began, trying to keep a note of assertiveness and adulthood in my voice.

'Not now, George. Can't it wait till after dinner?' Father said, while Augusta merely rolled her eyes. I had a sudden flash of recognition – that eye roll was the way she had frequently responded to anything I addressed to her. She had never loved me, and never would, and now I understood why.

'No, Father, it can't wait. Firstly, I want you to know that I will be leaving here tomorrow, and shan't be returning. I will write to you with a forwarding address at my earliest opportunity.'

'Tomorrow? So soon – I mean . . .' Father began, but Augusta interrupted him.

'Let him go, Albert, if he wants to. He'll be off our hands.'

'But, Augusta, he is barely recovered from his ordeal . . .'

'If he wants to go,' she repeated slowly, as though speaking to a child, 'let him.'

'Very well. Where do you intend going? I need to know, for financial reasons. Your allowance . . .'

'To London.' It was all I wanted to tell them at present. I had not decided whether I would even give them my new address. I cared not whether Father stopped my allowance – I would get myself a job, perhaps tutoring like Mr Smythe, and would pay my own way in the world.

Father nodded. 'Well, if that is all . . .'

'No. It's not all. I . . . heard something today. About . . . my parentage.' I stopped there, and watched their reactions closely. Augusta had returned to her stitching as though bored with the conversation, but at my words her needle paused, quivering, above the work. Father paled.

'Your parentage? What on earth do you mean, boy?' I recognised his tactic. Bluster, denial, he'd talk over me, he'd talk me down, make it sound as though anything I said was simply ridiculous and not to be countenanced.

'I heard that my real mother was a servant here, made pregnant by you, and then persuaded to give up her child to replace one you . . ?' I nodded at Augusta '. . . lost at birth. I want only the truth, Father. Confirm that this is so. I shall then leave tomorrow.' Running through my mind was Maggie's assertion that Lucy had been pregnant when she was murdered. Should I tell them I knew this too?

'Rubbish,' my father began, but once again Augusta cut him off.

'Oh tell the boy the truth, Albert. He's almost of age, and seems to want to go his own way now. What does it matter? After his spell in prison do we really want to be associated with him any more anyway?'

'So it's true?' I said, turning towards Augusta.

She nodded, her eyes cold. 'Your mother was a harlot, a slut I misguidedly employed as parlour maid. Your father's head was turned by her pretty fair hair and curvy figure, just as it was by your beloved Lucy, and any number of maids in between. And yes, she got pregnant, and I lost my baby and then my dear Elizabeth, and your father thought he could simply replace one with another, as though babies were interchangeable.' She spat out the last words, and I felt a brief pang of pity for her. She'd been expected to deal with her losses by bringing up another woman's child.

'We wanted another son, and after the stillbirth Augusta was told not to attempt any more pregnancies,' Father added. 'Adopting Mary's child was the best solution. You are mine after all, son.'

'Her name was Martha, not Mary,' I said quietly, but Father waved a dismissive hand.

'Martha, Mary, it's all the same. You've been brought up as ours. What are you going to do now – tell the world you're the son of a housemaid with loose morals? It'll do you more harm than me, I assure you.'

'I won't tell your secret. I don't care now, who my parents are. I am my own man.' It wasn't true – I cared, and I'd vowed to

240

myself to track down Martha if I could, but there was no need to tell him that.

'Well, that makes it easier. There'll be no further allowance for you. I shall disown you.'

I nodded, it was what I'd expected. 'And one further thing, Father. When Lucy told you she was having your baby, was that what made you kill her?'

I've never seen him go so red. I thought he was about to keel over in an apoplectic fit. 'Kill her? What do you mean? It was you put the arsenic in her hot chocolate. That's been established, despite what that Watling fellow now says. You've been lucky to get away with it.'

'It wasn't me. Three witnesses say so. It could have been you . . .'

'Or me.' Augusta put down her stitching and looked up at her husband. 'You've strayed one time too many, Albert. I overheard the girl telling you she was pregnant. I wasn't going to bring up another brat of yours. So maybe it was me who poisoned the girl. Who knows. The one thing that's certain is that it was one of the three people in this room. It's probably best if none of us ever talk of it again, to anyone. What's done is done.'

There was silence as we all looked from one to another – Augusta calm and cold, Father sweating and red, and I surprisingly calm on the outside although inside all was in turmoil.

And then I turned my back on these two people, one of whom was a murderer, and left the room. It was the last time I saw either of them. John Lincoln drove me to the railway station in the pony trap early the next morning, and I boarded the London train to begin my new life.

15th July

I write this long saga now in my small room at the Smythe residence, in the village of Twickenham. My room is at the front of the house, overlooking the street. Across the narrow road is the river Thames, meandering its way slowly and lazily towards the city. Trees line the banks, and a path winds its way among them beside the river. It is a pleasant place to stroll when the weather is dry. My room is sparsely furnished but clean and bright. I have a bed, made up with snowy white linen, a writing desk and chair under the window, a wardrobe and a small chest of drawers. There is a basin and ewer on a stand in the corner, and a hooked-wool rug on the floor. The curtains are worn but clean, and an embroidered sampler hangs on the wall reminding me daily that I should follow my dreams and trust my heart. I am happy and comfortable.

But I skip on too fast. I must write about the evening I arrived here, and the welcome I received. I caught a cab from the station, although it turned out to be such a short distance I might easily have walked had I known exactly where Mr Smythe's house was. He was delighted to find me standing on his doorstep, my boxes at my feet. I had a smile on my face, and I was determined not to engulf them with all my woes right from the start.

'George, dear lad! Come in, come in! Lily, he's here already. Lily!' He enveloped me in an enormous hug. He hadn't changed a bit – perhaps his whiskers were tidier and his jacket cleaner than when he lived with us; the influence no doubt of the small, pretty woman with dimpled cheeks who came bustling out of the back room, wiping her hands on her apron.

'Mr Britten, I have heard so much about you from Daniel, and all of it good. Welcome to our little house. It is your home for as long as you need it.' She smiled broadly at me. I had worried that she would have read the papers and formed an ill opinion of me, but it seemed that no matter what had been written about me, Mr Smythe trusted his own knowledge of my character, and his wife trusted her husband's judgement.

I was shown into a small, pleasantly furnished sitting room, and before long tea and cakes to rival Mrs Peters' were served. Within a quarter of an hour I felt relaxed and fully at home.

There was much to talk about with Mr Smythe, but as he said himself, there was time enough to discuss all that had happened at length. No need to go through it all on our first day.

Since then, I have relaxed, recuperated, enjoyed the company of Mr Smythe (he has asked me to call him Daniel, but I struggle to do so) and Mrs Smythe (or Lily, as she insists). Nathaniel Spring has visited us on his day off and he and Mr Smythe got on very well together. I watched the two of them chatting, and wished my brother Charles could be with us as well, and then I would have all my saviours in one room. Nathaniel, it seems, has acquired a lady friend named Emily whose hand he is going to ask for, in marriage. I am delighted for him. He will remain in his post at the prison; he feels he can do most good there. But he will be granted a larger, more pleasant apartment within the prison grounds, when he is married. For myself I could not contemplate ever entering a prison again, under any circumstances.

One more thing to mention to bring this journal up to date: Mr Smythe has asked around, and has found a position for me as a clerk at a solicitor's office, right here in Twickenham. I start tomorrow, on shortened hours until I am fully recovered and able to work full time. I am intrigued and excited at the prospect. I will be earning my own money, being useful, and finding my own way in the world.

All that remains is for me to do what I can to track down Martha Ellis. I have decided to enlist both Mr Smythe's and Nathaniel's help in this, although I have not told them the real reason I want to trace her; only that she was a maid who worked for my father some twenty years ago. They gave me sidelong glances accompanied by frowns when I said this, but neither questioned me and both offered to do all that is within their power to help.

Chapter 27

Cassie

The journey home after the prison visit was characterised by long periods of silence punctuated by Cassie commenting on things Jack Wilkinson had said or done, or what he looked like. 'That scar on his cheek. He's had a rough life.'

'I'd say so – given what he's in prison for,' Andy replied, his tone non-judgemental.

'He seemed very closed and suspicious when we arrived. Wonder what he meant when he thought we were social services – that comment about the kid not being his?'

'I'd guess his partner or ex-partner is trying to extract money, but who knows?'

'I could ask him, I suppose, when I see him again.'

'When?' Andy glanced sideways at her.

'If. I'm not sure right now. I'm not sure of anything anymore.'

'It's all right. You don't need to decide anything today. Give yourself time.'

Cassie smiled. 'Thank you, oh wise one. Honestly, where would I be without you?'

'No problem. Anything you need, any time, just give me a shout. OK?'

'I will.' And she realised it was true – she would. Any time. She took a peek at him as he concentrated on negotiating a tricky junction. He was beginning to mean a lot to her. Did he feel the same? Was there a chance they might get together? Even though he was her boss?

It was a couple of days later that she felt able to do anything about Wilkinson's request. She'd decided to contact his original lawyer and start there. Despite what he'd said about his lawyer being useless it seemed the best course of action. From newspaper reports of the trial she was able to find out who'd represented him – a barrister named Newton. By googling she discovered the chambers Newton worked at, and a contact number. She phoned and left a summary of her request with the legal secretary who'd answered the phone. 'I'll pass your message on,' the secretary said, 'and Mr Newton will call you back when he can.'

Cassie hung up feeling pleased – she'd made a start. She'd get some advice from Mr Newton and take it from there. She assumed she'd be billed for Newton's time, but so be it. This was her father they were talking about.

Mr Newton called back within an hour, sounding a little breathless as though he'd rushed back into his office and was about to rush out again. 'Got your message. I have five minutes, Ms Turner. You're enquiring about the Wilkinson case?'

'Yes. I'm . . . wondering whether it's worth him appealing the decision. You see, he tells me it wasn't him who stabbed . . . Clarke, was it? Mr Wilkinson says it was the other man – Jimmy someone? But Wilkinson took the rap to spare the other man from going to prison, says he'd never have coped . . .'

To her surprise Newton gave a short sharp laugh, which he quickly smothered. 'Ah. No. No chance of an appeal, I'd say.'

'But if he's retracting his confession . . .'

'Ms Turner, he didn't confess. He claimed he was innocent, and was found guilty by the court. The jury voted unanimously, as I recall. The thing is, and I'm sorry if this is going to disappoint, there was overwhelming evidence that Wilkinson was the man wielding the knife. I don't know how much detail you know about the case?'

'Only what I've read in a few newspaper reports, and the little that Mr Wilkinson told me.'

'Ah. Then you should know that there was CCTV at the premises where the burglary and stabbing took place. The entire thing was caught on camera, and it shows Wilkinson, clear as day, stabbing Clarke while the other fellow – Jones – stands back wringing his hands and shouting at him to stop. I've seen it, Ms Turner. There's no question that Wilkinson is guilty of murder.'

'But you defended him?'

Newton sighed. 'Everyone's entitled to a defence lawyer, if they plead not guilty. Even if there's incontrovertible evidence. I'd tried to persuade him to plead guilty and perhaps get himself a reduced sentence by showing remorse but he was having none of it – kept saying he wanted "the full works". He wanted his moment in court, for some reason, even though he must have known there was no hope.'

'Did he think perhaps he'd only be convicted of manslaughter?'

That laugh again. 'I don't think so. Again, the footage showed what the judge summed up as "a frenzied attack". Look, Ms Turner, I don't know your relationship to this man but if he's asked you to try to get the case reopened you are on a losing wicket. There's no chance, whatsoever. Perhaps you need to tell him that outright. He'll have to serve his time. Now, I'm sorry, but I'm due in court again in a few minutes, so I must dash. There's no charge for this phone call. Hope I've helped a little.'

'You have, thank you, Mr Newton,' Cassie said, but the lawyer had already rung off.

Cassie put her phone down on the coffee table and leaned back on her sofa. So that was that. Wilkinson had lied to her and tried to use her. He'd seen not a daughter with whom he might build a relationship in time, but someone who might do his bidding. Suddenly the future was crystal clear to her – if she kept seeing this man he'd keep asking her for more favours. Perhaps to bring things into the prison for him. Perhaps to put money into his bank account. Or talk to social services – sort out whatever the problem was with his partner and her child. Who might be Cassie's half-sibling, she realised.

No. It was best to put an end to this now. Before she found herself dragged into his murky world. She had done what she had promised him – she'd looked into whether his conviction could be appealed against, and discovered it could not. She was under no further obligation to him. All she needed to do was write and tell him the results of her phone call with Newton. And that was all. She would not include a return address.

She would tell Bethany the bare bones of the story. She'd also tell her parents. At the thought of Shirley and Tony she felt suddenly tearful. Tony. Dad. *He* was her real dad. The man who'd brought her up, who'd loved her unconditionally. The man who'd she'd been so cold towards for the last few weeks.

She wanted to call Andy, to tell him what she'd found out, but there was another call she needed to make first. She picked up her phone and called her parents. Tony answered.

'Dad? It's me. I need to apologise . . .'

'What for, love?'

'The way I've treated you lately. I'm sorry. I've been a horrible daughter.'

'Ah, it's been hard for you. Listen, I just want you to know that no matter what, I will always think of myself as your father. But if you did want to . . . you know . . . do something about finding your real dad then I'd support you – we both would . . .'

'Dad – *you're* my real dad. I know that now. I just needed time to process it all, I suppose . . .' Now was not the moment to tell him she'd already traced Wilkinson. That conversation should happen face to face, with her mum there. It could wait.

But one thing couldn't wait: 'I love you, Dad. Just wanted you to know that, OK?'

'Aw, love.' There was a crack in Tony's voice as he answered. 'Love you too, pumpkin.' The name he'd used for her as a child, which she hadn't heard in years.

Cassie told Bethany she'd traced Jack Wilkinson, over the phone. 'He's in prison. For murder. Frankly, Bethany, although I'm glad I know, I don't want to have anything to do with him.'

'Don't you want to meet him at all?'

Cassie had not told Bethany the full story yet. She took a deep breath before answering. 'I . . . did go to see him. And, well, let's just say it didn't go too well. I guess this happens sometimes. Not every reunification story will be like ours, Bethany.'

'I know. And . . . you know, when I traced you, I hadn't definitely decided if I'd contact you or not. It depended on what the family finder agency told me about you, I'd decided. And to be frank, if you'd have been in prison for murder, I reckon I might not have contacted you at all. I couldn't have handled going into a prison. It was bad enough being briefly in a police cell on that horrible night when you rescued me.'

'I'm glad I wasn't in prison then!' Cassie laughed. 'Not that I've ever done anything that would warrant being imprisoned, of course.'

'You're not cross with me for pushing you to find your father, then?'

'Not at all. You know what, in tracing Jack Wilkinson I not only discovered who my birth father was, but who my *real* father is. It's kind of brought closure – I've made it up with Dad.'

'Tony?'

'Yes. The only man I'll ever call Dad.'

'Aw, I'm glad. He's lovely – so's Shirley. We don't need the other fella, do we?'

'We certainly don't.'

There was a brief silence before Bethany spoke again. 'Also, I think now's a good moment to tell you of a decision I've made, about my own birth father.'

Cassie felt her stomach lurch. Was Bethany still thinking of tracing Arjun? 'Go on.'

'I've decided to leave him be. As you said yourself – it's completely different to me tracing you. You knew I existed. Arjun has no idea. He has a wife and family. I'd be such a disrupting influence on them all. It's simply not fair on him. So I'm not going to search for him.'

Cassie let out a deep breath. 'I think that's wise and very thoughtful of you. You know, I didn't really think about the disruptive effect when I traced Jack Wilkinson. If he'd been married with children . . . I guess I wasn't being fair either. I shouldn't have contacted him.'

'What's done is done, Cassie. It was me who urged you to find him. But regarding Arjun, I'm just going to imagine him out there in India with a swarm of children and a happy life. If you can spare a photo of him I'd love to have one to keep. A dad in a photo, but that's all.' Bethany paused a moment, before continuing. 'Oh, and talking of parents, of which we seem to have an excessive number between us, mine are back, and have invited you for lunch on Saturday. In London, we thought, so we can all meet somewhere central and still be able to get home after. Are you up for that?'

'Oh! So soon! I mean, lovely, yes, I didn't expect we'd meet up so soon but I'd love to.'

'Last chance before Christmas, Mum said. We can postpone it till January if you'd prefer but apparently they're off to Spain then, for the rest of the winter.' Cassie could practically hear the eye roll. 'Life's just one long holiday for them at the moment. Mind you, I'm glad they are making the most of their career breaks. They'll be back at work before they know it.' She gave a mock evil cackle.

Cassie noted down the details of where and when to meet – a restaurant in Soho – knowing she would need to spend at least five hours deciding what to wear. But there were a couple of days before she needed to worry.

She should spend any spare minutes working on her genealogy project – if she was to complete it by Christmas she needed to get a shift on with it. There was time after her phone call to make a start. First job was to decipher that unknown name on George Britten's will. Two short names. The second began with an E – that was clear. Enis, perhaps? By painstakingly comparing with known words in the rest of the document, bit by bit she pieced it together. Martha, and not Enis, but Ellis. Martha Ellis. Who was she, then, and why had George set up an annual stipend for her?

Cassie began searching for the unknown woman. There were several matches to people named Martha Ellis in the census returns of 1861 and 1871, and no way of knowing which was the right one. None lived in any place with a connection to George. Cassie tried searching the newspaper archives, but the only mention she found of a Martha Ellis was a brief mention in a London paper of someone by that name who'd been in court and then imprisoned for non-payment of rent. Again, there was nothing to connect this woman with George Britten.

A floral dress made of a clingy jersey fabric and a pair of knee-high boots, was what Cassie finally decided on wearing for the trip to London to meet Bethany's parents. She topped it with her trusty leather jacket and a bright, wide scarf. Her parents phoned early that morning, just to wish her a good day. She'd told them what was happening. 'One day, maybe we'll meet them too,' her mum had said. 'Some family occasion, perhaps.' Cassie had loved that Mum considered both Bethany and her parents as part of the family now.

As on that first meeting with Bethany, Cassie caught a train to London and arrived in plenty of time at the Pavilion, an Italian restaurant tucked away on a narrow Soho street. She wasn't surprised to see Bethany already there, sitting at a table with a middle-aged couple. Bethany was facing the door and spotted her, leaping to her feet and waving as Cassie approached. The couple turned round, pleasant smiles on their faces. Cassie experienced a momentary panic wondering how to greet them but once she and Bethany had hugged and kissed she realised both the others were on their feet and first Bethany's mum, then her dad, hugged her and kissed her cheek.

'Cassie, this is my mum, Jan and my dad, Adrian,' Bethany said. Cassie loved that she'd introduced them as mum and dad, and Cassie as simply Cassie. Made everything simpler.

'It's so lovely to meet you, Cassie. Thank you so much for coming,' Jan said. 'Beth's told us so much about you.'

'Ditto,' Cassie said, as she took the fourth seat at the table, and as Bethany started relating some amusing anecdote about their journey to London she took the opportunity to have a good look at Jan and Adrian. She judged them to be quite a bit older than her, probably in their mid-fifties. They were both fit-looking, as though they worked hard to keep in shape, and both were tanned, no doubt from having spent the last three months in Australia. Jan had a wide smile, curly hair that was part blonde streaks and part grey, as though she was gradually making the transition, and wore a pair of glasses with sparkling pink sides.

Adrian too wore glasses, behind which were deep blue eyes crinkled at the edges as though he'd spent too much time in the sun, or too much time smiling. Probably the latter, Cassie decided, as his smile seemed permanently attached. As was her own, she realised. Something about this couple made her want to keep a grin on her face.

'We were so glad,' Jan was saying, 'when Beth told us she'd met you and you'd got on so well. Have to admit we were nervous when she said she wanted to trace you. We only wanted to protect her, you see, in case she found out something she didn't like, you know?'

Cassie nodded. She did know, all too well, the dangers of finding out unpalatable truths about your biological parents.

'And we need to thank you,' Adrian added. 'Beth's been the best thing that ever happened to us. I know you must have had a terrible time, being pregnant so young with all your life ahead, but you did such a selfless thing giving up your baby. We felt we were the luckiest people on earth when we were first handed such a beautiful baby. We'd tried for years, then we'd been on the list to adopt for years, but all the waiting was well worthwhile to end up with this young lady.'

'Oh, Dad.' Bethany did a mock teenage eye roll. 'You're so embarrassing.' But she leaned against him and planted a kiss on his cheek. Cassie loved that their relationship was obviously warm and loving.

Just like hers with her parents. It was Christmas in a few days' time, and she was due to spend it with Shirley and Tony as usual, and she was very much looking forward to being surrounded by the warmth of her family again.

The lunch progressed well – a wonderful blend of chat, laughter and fabulous food brought to them by a smiling waiter. They ate three courses plus coffee, and ended up staying for nearly three hours. By the end, Cassie felt as though she'd known Adrian and Jan all her life, and Bethany was grinning so broadly Cassie feared she'd have jaw-ache. They found themselves together in the ladies' loos near the end of the lunch, Cassie on her way in as Bethany was washing her hands.

'Happy?' Cassie asked Bethany.

'God, yes. You like them, don't you? And I can tell they really like you. I'm so bloody blessed!'

'I like them very much, yes. I am so glad you were placed with them. So very glad.' With tears rushing to her eyes, Cassie gave Bethany a spontaneous hug. Bethany reciprocated, and a moment later both women were jumping up and down out of sheer exuberance.

'Is this a private hug or can I join in?' Jan asked, entering the small space.

'Of course!' Cassie said, extracting one arm so she could pull Jan into the group hug.

'Two mums. Two fabulous mums, I love you both,' Bethany was saying. Cassie felt too choked up to say anything more, and a glance at Jan showed she must be feeling the same.

'Away with you. Your poor dad will be wondering what's happening, sitting all alone at the table,' Cassie finally managed to say, and Bethany broke free to return to Adrian.

Alone with Jan, Cassie felt suddenly shy. 'She's a great kid. Well done.' It seemed inadequate to her own ears, but Jan apparently appreciated the words, for she smiled and nodded.

'Good genes.'

'Good parenting,' Cassie countered, and the two of them laughed.

Chapter 28

George

10th August

I have settled well into my room at Daniel's, my job as a solicitor's clerk, and my life here on the edge of London. I have had no contact with my father or his wife, although I did write to give them an address should there be any need to contact me.

Charles has been to visit. He lives across London, near to the Regent's Park in a modest house that is partly paid for by our father. He was curious about my choice of lodgings and employment, and I had to confess in the end that Father has ended my allowance. He was astounded.

'Why, George? Surely he cannot still think you are guilty. Do you want me to intervene on your behalf?'

I shook my head. 'No, Charles. I prefer to be independent of him now – I have my reasons for this.'

'But what of Mother? Surely she would take your side?'

If only he knew the truth! But he would not hear it from me. Charles was a good man, and I did not want to shake his belief in his parents, or damage his reputation by revealing that one of them was a murderer. And as for Martha Ellis – I did not mention her at all.

Charles brought news too, imparted to him by a letter from Father, of Inspector Watling's ongoing investigation. He had questioned the entire household once again. He had sought out Maggie. He had looked carefully at the shed where the arsenic was kept in case there were any clues there. He had 'bullied' – Father's word – Augusta and Mrs Peters, and been forceful too in an interview with himself. But he had gained no further clues and for now, the investigation was to be shelved.

I wrote to Mrs Peters asking if she had any information on where Martha had gone after I was born. She replied only that she remembered that Martha's parents were dead but she'd had a brother who'd married and was living in Southwark in south London at the time I was born. Mrs Peters remembered her writing letters to her brother, and there'd been talk of her going there after she left us. There was no address, but Mrs Peters said Martha had found it a huge joke that her brother lived 'just round the corner from the Queen's Bench Prison'.

I knew of the Queen's Bench – it was an old debtor's prison. It was a starting point. I imagined myself knocking on doors in the area, asking if they knew of a family named Ellis. It was just possible Martha's brother still lived there, and he surely would know of his sister's current whereabouts. Mrs Peters also told me that she had handed in her notice and was seeking employment elsewhere. She promised to keep in touch.

Nathaniel visited me again this afternoon, and I put my plan to him.

'George, I do not know why you wish to trace this woman, but be careful. If it was twenty years ago that she left your father's employ, it is quite possible that she might no longer be living. If she is important to you in some way, I would not want you to be hurt by what you find out.'

'I'm aware she might have passed on,' I replied, 'but if so I would like to know for sure, and then pay my respects at her grave.'

He frowned, clearly wondering what this woman was to me – this woman he believed I had never met. But he didn't ask – he allowed me my secrets. 'May I come with you, when you go to Southwark?'

I agreed. It would be helpful to have some company. I was nervous about the mission. And if by some chance we found Martha herself and the truth came out – well, I knew already I could trust Nathaniel with my life.

We have agreed to go next week, when we both have a day off.

18th August

I did not sleep last night, for worrying about the forthcoming day in which Nathaniel and I were due to begin enquiries in Southwark. I tossed and turned all night, imagining endless scenarios in which we found Martha Ellis alive and well, or discovered she'd been dead for years, or tracked down her brother who would not tell us anything about her. And yet I knew the most likely outcome of the day would be that we discovered nothing about her or even her brother. But I had to try. She was my mother, and I wanted to do what I could to find her. Whether for her benefit or my own, I was not certain. I hoped for both.

We set off early, meeting at Waterloo station and walking along the south bank of the river to Southwark. We had agreed while travelling to start on Borough High Street beside the Queen's Bench Prison itself, and knock on doors first in one direction then in the other, before fanning out onto other streets in the area. It was a rough part of London, and one in which I felt a little uncomfortable. My skin prickled as though there were ruffians waiting to pounce around every corner, thugs who would steal my purse and watch, tear the coat from my back and the boots from my feet. I voiced these fears to Nathaniel and was surprised when he laughed.

'George, my dear boy, you have survived a stint in Millbank jail, and recovered from a most severe beating. Hold your head up high, walk with purpose, and you will be safe.'

I was comforted by his words and glad of his company. We set off as we'd planned, knocking on grimy doors with peeling paint, which were answered by women in dirty aprons who'd never heard of anyone by the name of Ellis. Some doors were slammed in our faces. Some doors were never opened, although curtains were twitched and faces peered out at us.

It was mid-afternoon before we struck lucky – a middle-aged woman nodded at the name of Ellis. 'Yes, me ducks, there was a Samuel Ellis lived up the end of the road, last house on the left. Gone from there these ten years or more, though, I don't know where to.'

'Do you know if Samuel Ellis had a sister named Martha?' I asked, holding my breath for the answer.

The woman screwed up her face as she tried to remember. 'Think he did have a sister who lived with him and his wife for a bit. Seven children they had, and the sister helped look after them. Ten of 'em in that little house – more than's in mine, and we're on top of each other.'

'Do you know anything about his sister – where she went, what became of her?'

She was suddenly suspicious. 'Why d'you want to know? Who are you?'

'A well-wisher,' I said, hoping it was enough for her.

'Well I don't know no more than that. Got work to do now, so be off with you.' The woman took a step back inside but did not close her door, and there was an expectant look upon her face.

'Thank you. You have been very helpful.' Nathaniel pressed a couple of coins into her hand. I had not thought to pay for information, but by the smile it elicited I realised it was the best way.

''Ere, I thought of something more. That sister, she might have got in some trouble. I remember Ma Dunmore from number

257

twenty gossiping about her. She'd gone off and set up a business, making bonnets or some-such, all set up by her fancy man. Then he ran off with another woman and left her alone, only she couldn't pay the rent, and her brother couldn't afford to help her.'

'What became of her?' My question emerged as a whisper.

The woman laughed. 'Ended up in there, didn't she?' She jerked her head up the road, back towards the Queen's Bench. 'Funny, really, living so long in the shadow of the place then she ended up inside. Me and Ma Dunmore said it was 'er own fault, relying on a fella like that. Better off standing on yer own two feet, we said. Then old Sam Ellis's wife died, and he took the kiddies and went out of London, down south somewhere, Hampshire I think. Back to where he'd come from, leaving his sister on her own in the prison. They'd had a bust-up, brother and sister, over this fancy man. Sam had told her not to trust the fella, but she did, and look where it got her.' She folded her arms across her ample bosom at these words, as if to make the point she herself would not have got into such a pickle.

'Thank you again,' said Nathaniel, and he took my elbow and gently steered me away and along the street. I was too busy thinking about all I had heard to move of my own accord. Martha had poor taste in men, it seemed. Nathaniel and I left the area and crossed the river to a more salubrious part of the city where we found a coffee house. There we sat and discussed all that we had heard.

'The Queen's Bench is a debtor's prison,' Nathaniel said. 'I will be able to find out for you if she's still there. And then you can decide what you want to do next, if anything.' He looked at me with a question in his eyes, and I once more debated confiding in him.

'If she's still there, I will pay her debt,' I said. I'd always thought it wrong that debtors were sent to jail, and not released until they paid off their debts. How were they supposed to do that when they were in prison, unable to earn?

Nathaniel's eyes widened. 'You do not know how much it is.'

'No matter – I have some savings, and I have items I can sell, and I can work and save more.'

And that is how we left it for today, Nathaniel having promised to find out if Martha was still in prison as soon as he was able. I fear I will have another sleepless night tonight, as I ponder the day's events. The irony of my own imprisonment having been intended to spare the woman I thought was my mother, and then to find my real mother was herself behind bars, is not lost on me.

25th August

Dear Nathaniel. He was as good as his word, and within a week his enquiries as to the whereabouts of Martha Ellis had borne fruit. She was indeed still in the Queen's Bench Prison. I resolved to go to visit her as soon as possible. 'As soon as possible' was, of course, the very next day, which was happily a Sunday and my day off. While Nathaniel would have accompanied me once more, had I waited for his next day off, I resolved to go by myself. I pictured Martha Ellis as a young, frightened girl, and thought that if two strange men arrived at her prison cell she might find it disconcerting. And then I realised that if Martha Ellis was my mother, she would not be a girl. She would be a woman in her late thirties by now. Perhaps I would be the young, frightened child. Indeed, the idea of entering a prison once more, even as a free man visiting an inmate, kept me awake the whole night once more.

But I am an adult. I have turned twenty, now. I resolved this morning to be strong, grown-up, and to do whatever I could for Martha Ellis. I dressed with care, wanting to look smart, professional and in charge. I wanted to be treated with respect by the prison warders. Daniel wished me luck, as I left the house to begin the now-familiar journey to Southwark.

At the prison, after explaining my business I was shown into a visitors' room, which was furnished with a table and several plain chairs. There was no cage, thankfully. I waited perhaps ten minutes, feeling nervous. It is not every day that one gets to meet one's real mother for the first time. My palms were sweating and I found I had to keep wiping them on a handkerchief. I felt hot and longed to remove my coat and neck-tie.

At last a door opposite the one by which I had entered was opened, and a female warder entered, followed by a small, slim woman with fading fair hair and soft grey eyes. I found myself staring at her, my mouth slightly open, as I recognised in her expression elements I had seen thousands of times in my shaving mirror. Those were my eyes. That little furrow between them, above her nose, was present on my face when I was concentrating. Her hairline, with its widow's peak, followed the shape of my own.

She stood before the table, hands neatly folded in front of her, a question on her face. The warder took a seat at the side of the room. 'Well, sir, here is Martha Ellis. I must stay in the room, but you can go ahead now and state your business with her.' She settled back in her chair and closed her eyes, as though hoping to take the chance to have a nap.

If only it were as easy as stating my business! I confess I floundered, opened and closed my mouth a few times. I'd stood up as they entered, and finally I remembered my manners and bade Martha sit down.

'I am happy standing, sir,' she said, her voice quiet and with a Hampshire lilt.

I thought to remain standing myself, but then realised I towered over her, and not wanting to intimidate her I sat down and folded my hands together on the table. 'I am pleased to meet you, Martha Ellis. Have you been told my name?'

She shook her head. 'No, sir. I was told only that a gentleman wished for an interview with me. Truth be told, sir, I thought it would be . . . someone else . . .'

I guessed she was referring to the gentleman friend who'd set her up in business and then left her with debts. 'I'm sorry if I disappointed you. My name is George Britten.'

She gave a little start at my name, and the frown line between her brows deepened. She looked as though she was going to say something, but stopped herself.

'I think you knew my father,' I said, keeping my tone as gentle as possible, while inside my guts were in turmoil. I watched her carefully as she raised her eyes to mine, judging my age, wondering at my likeness to her, and then finally she nodded.

'Yes, sir, I believe I did. Can it be . . .'

'Martha, I am your son.' There, the words were out.

'Oh!' She clapped her hands to her mouth and stumbled a little. I was out of my chair and around to her side of the table before I'd even realised I was moving, helping her into a chair, and then kneeling at her feet. The warder opened one eye, then closed it again, clearly preferring to continue her nap than interfere.

'I only learned recently that Augusta Britten was not my real mother, and of what my father did. I am estranged from them now. They do not know I am here. I made enquiries and tracked you down . . .' I realised I was talking too fast, imparting too much information all at once, that poor Martha would find it difficult to take on. And I was right, she was shaking her head.

'Were they . . . cruel to you? Oh, I did not want to leave you, but he promised . . . I thought it would be best . . . Oh if he has hurt you I shall never forgive . . .'

It was my turn to shake my head. 'I had a good upbringing. I wanted for nothing.' Except perhaps maternal love, but I was not going to burden her with that. 'It is by my own choice that I am now independent in the world.'

She wiped away tears and looked at me once more, a small smile playing at the corners of her mouth. I had a sudden glimpse of the young woman she'd once been, the vivacious, pretty girl who'd gone to work for my parents, the girl she was before my father seduced her. 'You are a fine young man. You look like you have done well. I am pleased to meet you, Mr Britten.'

'Please, call me George.'

But she shook her head. 'No, sir. And you may not call me mother. We are better to remain as strangers to each other. You must not ruin your chances in life by being associated with a woman in a debtor's prison.'

'You will not be in here much longer,' I said with some passion. 'I will make sure of that.' I looked towards the warder, intending to ask how to go about paying off Martha's debts, but the woman's head was lolling and tiny snores were emanating from her open mouth.

'Do not concern yourself with my troubles,' Martha said, clutching at my arm. 'I would rather think that you are using your money to make your own way in the world.'

'I have enough. And I could never be happy if I left you in here.'

She smiled, properly this time, and gave a small but gracious nod of acknowledgement. 'Then I shall accept your money, as I want only your happiness.'

I pressed her hand. Her small, warm but calloused hand – a working woman's hand. I wondered if she too had to pick oakum or sew mail sacks. I was about to ask her when the warder gave a snort and roused herself. Seeing me still kneeling at Martha's feet she got to her feet and stepped closer.

'A visitor may not be so close to an inmate as to be able to touch her. Step away, sir. I shall have to ask you to leave now.'

I stood, as did Martha, and the two of us nodded at each other as we each left the room by different doors. I went straight to the governor's office where I began proceedings to secure Martha's release. Her debt was, by my father's standards, small. For me it was manageable, but would mean I'd need to rely on Daniel's hospitality and goodwill for some time to come.

And now, as I write this by gaslight late at night, reflecting on what the day has brought, I feel more settled and secure than I have ever done in the past. I know where I have come from. I know that the cold, unfeeling woman I'd called 'Mother' is no relation. My real mother is a gentle, caring woman who will be free from her prison cell within days, able to restart her life, as I am restarting mine.

Chapter 29

Cassie

Cassie had some spare time on the day after her trip to London. Time to return to finding out who was Martha Ellis and what was her relationship to George Britten? She looked again at the census returns, but with no idea where Martha lived or how old she was, she could not determine which entry was the right one. Same problem with birth, marriage and death registers – there were dozens. She'd already checked the newspaper archives.

Sighing, Cassie broadened her searches. She went back to the website where she'd found George Britten's will. It was a long shot, but maybe Martha had also left a will. It wasn't common for women to leave wills in Victorian times, but if they were unmarried or widowed and had money in their own name, they sometimes did.

She put Martha's name into the search box and clicked the search button, not expecting to find anything. But one result was returned. Someone with that name had indeed made a will. It was worth downloading and reading. As with all old wills, the handwriting was difficult to decipher but gradually Cassie made it out and there, on the first page, was a detail that made her gasp:

. . . and to my natural son, George Britten, I leave my milliner's business in gratitude for all that he has done for me, and in the hope that he will be able to sell it or install a manager and reap much income from it to repay him a little . . .

Martha's natural son. So Augusta Britten was not George's mother. Was Albert Britten his father? Cassie assumed so, as George had definitely been brought up by Albert and Augusta. She searched for Martha Ellis in earlier censuses, and gasped at the 1841 return – a Martha Ellis, aged fifteen, was listed as a servant living at the Britten's residence. She kicked herself for not spotting this earlier – she'd been so hung up on finding out about George's life from 1861 on.

Cassie leaned back in the sofa and stared at the ceiling. 'So, Griselda, we can see what happened here, can't we? Albert got a young servant girl pregnant, and then brought the child up as his own. Wonder what Augusta thought of that, eh?' And at some point George had discovered the truth, searched out Martha and made sure she was provided for if he died first. She, in turn, had made a will to leave whatever she had to him.

'Complicated family. Just like mine.' Cassie scratched Griselda's head, and the cat looked up lovingly at her, purring loudly. 'Much simpler to be a cat, eh?'

On the last Wednesday before Christmas the gang from work met up in the pub as always in the evening. Cassie felt she'd have liked a quieter night, perhaps with Andy in a restaurant, but there was no getting out of it – Shania was insisting. 'Been ages since you had a drink with us,' she'd said at lunchtime. 'Ben and Toby think you've completely forgotten about them. Andy said he's coming out tonight too.' She gave Cassie a sideways glance as she said this, and Cassie felt herself blush for no real reason. 'Is there something going on between you two?'

'Ah, no. We're just good friends,' Cassie replied. For the moment it was true, although she hoped . . . or did she dare to hope? . . . that in time they might become closer.

Work was very different this near to Christmas – the pool was closed for maintenance and had been drained so that grouting around the tiles could be repaired and the filters cleaned. There were still people using the gym, playing badminton and squash, and a number of Zumba and aerobics classes ran throughout the day. The sports centre had been decorated for the season, with a Christmas tree up in reception. The staff room had been festooned with tinsel and a glittery fairy hung from Toby's locker that he'd put up himself.

In the mid-afternoon Cassie glanced through to the empty pool and spotted the boys playing football in it. Toby was at a disadvantage, defending the deep end. She went through to the poolside, watched them for a moment, laughing.

'You'll be in trouble if Andy spots you,' she called out.

'Ha! He suggested it. He said it was OK as long as we took our shoes off, and we have, look!' Ben held up a shoeless foot, and then cursed as Toby took the opportunity to shoot the ball past him, hitting the shallow end wall.

'Goooooooaaal!' he yelled, thumping the air with his fist. 'Want to join in, Cassie?'

'No thanks. Your teams would be uneven, and Shania's taking a class.' She turned away, laughing, and remembering previous Christmases when she had joined in with five-a-side in the empty pool, with various different colleagues of years gone by. How long had she worked there? Possibly too long. Definitely too long as a general centre attendant.

That evening the pub was packed, and they had a rowdy time squashed around a too-small table in a corner near the pub's open fire. It was the usual crowd – Ben and Toby, arguing over who'd won the football; Shania, wanting to hear about Cassie's latest genealogy research; and Andy, sitting quietly next to Cassie.

'So you found out who those people were that your ancestor mentioned in his will?' Shania was asking.

Cassie nodded. She'd never told Shania, or anyone other than Andy and Bethany, that George was not actually her ancestor after all. 'Yes. He left money and that gorgeous jewelled mirror to the wife of a chaplain who helped him when he was in prison, and he left an annual stipend to his real mother.'

'*Real* mother?' Shania widened her eyes.

'Turns out, if I'm reading the clues correctly, that our George's father had a dalliance with a young servant that resulted in George's birth. The baby was left with his father. After George's brief spell in prison he must have somehow found this out, tracked down his biological mother – Martha Ellis – and then provided for her, for life. I think, too, that he may have paid off a debt for her and got her out of prison but I can't be sure.' Discovering a birth parent who was in prison – the parallels between George's life and her own were not lost on Cassie. But clearly George had managed to have a better relationship with Martha than she was ever going to have with Jack Wilkinson.

After a couple of pints Shania needed to leave. 'Another party to go to, darlings,' she said, waggling her fingers at them as she sashayed out. Ben and Toby were all for moving on to another pub, but Cassie shook her head.

'I need to go home and eat,' she said. 'See you after Christmas, hope Santa brings everything you wanted.' Ben and Toby blew her kisses as they finished their drinks and put on their coats.

'I'll walk you home,' Andy said, quietly so that only she could hear.

'I don't need you to,' she replied. It was only a twenty-minute walk to her flat, and she lived in the opposite direction to Andy.

'But you want me to, right?' Andy winked. 'Anyway, I was hoping to have a private word with you, and now seems like a good time.'

'All right, then.' They left the pub and began the walk to

Cassie's flat. The night was cold and frosty, and they could see their breath in the air. Cassie had her hat pulled down tightly over her ears and was glad she was still in her work trainers as the pavements were becoming icy. When she slipped a little, Andy caught hold of her.

'Hold on to my arm,' he said. 'Don't want you breaking something just before Christmas.'

'Thanks.' The warmth of his arm through her coat comforted her as well as steadied her. 'So, what did you want to talk to me about?'

'Ah yes. So, the thing is, I'm going to be leaving the sports centre. Probably at the end of January.'

'What?' Cassie stopped walking and turned to face him. 'But . . . you've always been there! At least that's how it feels to me. I can't imagine working there without you. You can't go! We'll . . . I'll miss you.'

'I've not been there as long as you,' he replied. 'Don't worry – I am not moving out of the area. I'll still be able to meet everyone in the pub on a Wednesday. A job came up at the sports centre over in Newbury. It's a bigger place, so managing it is a promotion. I applied a week ago, was interviewed yesterday and got the job. You're the first I've told.'

'Oh! Well done.' They began walking again, with Cassie still holding on to his arm. She was trying to imagine life at work without Andy there. She'd miss him, but would still see him on Wednesdays.

'So, anyway, this provides you, Cass, with a couple of opportunities.'

'Does it?'

'I'd say so, yes. Firstly, it's likely that Vicky will apply for my old manager's role and she'll probably get it. That'll mean there's a vacancy for an assistant manager.' He stopped walking and turned to face her. 'I think you should apply for it, Cassie. You'd almost certainly get it. You know that place inside out, you know what's involved in the job and you'd be brilliant at it. It's time you moved on a little.'

'But, I . . .'

'I know. You've always been happy as a general centre attendant. But, the promotion will bring in nearly twice the money for the same number of hours. It's more secure, too, as it's a job with set hours rather than ad hoc shifts – if someone else got the job who didn't know you, they might not give you your regular shifts.'

Cassie nodded. She'd been through this before – many years ago a change of management had meant her shifts were messed around for months before settling down. It had only been when Vicky started, and asked Cassie as the longest-serving member of staff, which hours she wanted to do regularly, that things got back on track. Maybe Andy was right. Maybe she should apply for the role. A few months ago the idea would have terrified her, but, her life had changed a lot in recent months, and she'd coped. She could probably cope with the job, too. 'Yeah. That's a good point, Andy. I think I will apply.'

'Good! I reckon you'll get it easily.'

'And what's the second thing?'

'What second thing?'

'You said you moving jobs opened up a couple of opportunities for me. The assistant manager's role becoming free was the first one. And the second one is . . .?'

'Ah yes.' He swung her round, catching her by the upper arms. 'Cassie, you know how I feel about you. I think you like me too, but I'm guessing you've kept your distance, and rightly so, because you don't think it's sensible for two people who work together to have a close relationship outside of work. Especially not when one's the manager of the other. So . . . well . . . if I've moved on, then we're free . . . should we want to, to . . . become closer. If you would like that, I mean.'

Cassie looked up at him in astonishment. As she gazed into his eyes and saw the longing there, she realised just how much she wanted him. He was right – it was their working relationship that had held her back. But here he was, in front of her, wanting her, and there was nothing to stop them. Shyly she smiled, and nodded, and he grinned and then dipped his head to hers, his lips meeting hers under the glow of a streetlamp. Despite the chill of the evening his lips were warm and full, and she felt herself melting into his arms as he deepened the kiss.

At last they broke free. 'Come on. It's cold, and at this rate we'll never get you home,' he said.

A thought struck her. 'I owe you a dinner, don't I? I was going to make a pasta bake. There's enough for two, if you fancy it?'

'I certainly do, thank you!'

They walked faster after that, hurrying to get into the warmth of Cassie's flat, but stopping every now and again to repeat the experience of that delicious kiss. Life was very good indeed.

Chapter 30

George, 1871

25th June 1871

It's been both shocking and amusing to reread this journal so many years later. Ten years later! Am I even the same person who poured out his heart in here? What possessed me, as a young man of nineteen, to take the blame for such a heinous crime, and go to prison for it? I have put that episode firmly out of my mind over these last ten years. I am proud of my actions as regards Martha Ellis, however.

Having found this journal, buried at the back of a drawer, I feel it is appropriate to bring it up to date, one last time. I will then put it away. Who knows what might happen to it in years to come? Perhaps after my death it will be found and pored over. I will keep it hidden during my lifetime. I owe my father and his wife nothing, but it would not do anyone any good to read here the truth about Lucy's death.

So let's see. Where did I leave off, back in 1861? Yes, that's right, I had moved into Daniel Smythe's spare room and begun a job as a solicitor's clerk. What a good move that was! I have lived happily with the Smythes for many years, and am only now preparing to move out into my own modest house. Their family has grown – they now have three children – and will welcome the return of 'my' room to allow the eldest, a dear boy named George whom I am proud to call my godson, to have his own room at last.

Indeed it is in the clearing out of my room and packing of my belongings that I have come across this journal, and the packing has been put on hold while I peruse and update it.

Nathaniel Spring has remained another constant friend. He has visited me often and the three of us – Daniel, Nathaniel and myself – have become quite a little gentlemen's club, eating meals out together, going for walks or rowing on the Thames, visiting the theatre or music halls. Charles joins us too, when he is available. I consider myself lucky to have such good and true friends. Nathaniel is now married, to a dear, delicate girl named Emily.

I secured Martha Ellis's release within a couple of days of meeting her, and am pleased to be able to set down here that she was able to restart her millinery business with my help, and is now an independent woman of means, employing two others and working from premises in Putney. Two years ago there was a change in the law that meant debtors are no longer automatically sent to prison. In fact the Queen's Bench Prison has since been closed and demolished. I wish the same could be said of Millbank. The very name of that place makes me shudder still.

I continued with my job at the solicitor's office, rising to become head clerk. In my spare time I studied law, and last year I was eventually able to become a solicitor in my own right, taking on my own clients. I am promised a partnership in my firm if I continue to do well. My earnings have increased many-fold since I began, and I have been able to save plenty for the future, as well as paying Daniel a fair rent (though he tried to refuse it) and loaning Martha money to expand her business. My savings have been enough to put down a substantial deposit on a house.

271

Charles kept me informed, over the years, of the well-being of our father and his wife. No one was ever prosecuted for Lucy's murder in the end. The investigation dwindled away to nothing, and was dropped when Inspector Watling moved to a different police force. Father and Augusta led a quieter life after I left. Their friends fell away, not wishing to be associated with the scandal; even my father's old friend Dr Moore, whom I had realised must be one of the few people who'd known my true parentage, had stopped visiting them.

Mrs Peters secured a post elsewhere and kept in touch with me as she'd promised. Augusta was unable to obtain another housekeeper as good, and has had to make do with only house-maids ever since, none of whom stay very long. Both Father and his wife have become bitter, Charles says, hating each other and hating their lonely lives. I find I have no sympathy for either of them, and Charles too has grown apart from his parents, visiting them only once a year out of a sense of duty.

The cursed silver and sapphire mirror, the gift I had forgotten I ever bought – I have found that too, deep in the drawer along with my diary. What will become of it? I must find a suitable recipient for it, one day. But I cannot contemplate gifting it to the woman I now love with all my heart. I will hide it away once more, I think, and bequeath it after my death to someone worthy. Lily Smythe, perhaps, or Emily Spring. It should not stay in my family. A year ago, Daniel's grown-up niece Louise, a quietly intelligent girl with brown eyes and an infectious laugh, came to visit. By the time her fortnight stay came to an end, I was deeply in love, and happily my feelings were returned. We wrote daily to each other, and since then she has visited twice more. On the last occasion, I proposed marriage and she accepted. We are to be wed on Saturday and I am the happiest man alive. We will have a short honeymoon in Margate and then move into our new house, which is not far from the Smythes', together.

Indeed I have come on a long journey since being the naïve, gauche young man who began this journal. I have learned so much about human nature, about what it is to love and be loved, what it is that makes a person who they are and what a parent truly is.

Soon, perhaps, I will become a parent myself, if Louise and I are blessed. I very much hope so.

Chapter 31

Cassie

The Big Day came around at last. As Cassie showered and dressed on Christmas morning she reflected on how her life had changed over the few short months since summer ended. A daughter found and loved, a father found and . . . ahem . . . not loved. Another father – Tony – reconnected with. She packed a bag with presents, chocolates and wine and set off for her parents' house. It was to be just the three of them – the way it had always been. They'd go out for a bracing walk in the morning. Mum would cook a huge turkey that they'd eat mid-afternoon. They'd light a fire as it got dark, and only then open their presents, while sipping glasses of mulled wine. Silly games and cheesy films in the evening, and then she'd sleep in her childhood bedroom.

Some things you never wanted to change, ever. Although, she smiled to herself as she navigated the quiet roads to her parents' house, maybe there'd come a Christmas when she wouldn't be alone turning up at Mum and Dad's. Maybe Andy would be with her. He was shaping up to be her first real relationship since Arjun. He'd called her that morning, wishing her a happy day, and making arrangements to collect her after she got back on Boxing

Day. 'Dinner at mine,' he'd said. 'And I'll make up the spare room for you.' She'd agreed, privately wondering whether making up the spare bed might possibly end up being a waste of time . . .

'Cassie! Christmas begins at last!' squealed Mum and Cassie staggered out of the car clutching overfilled bags.

'Oof! Let me come in and put this stuff down!' Cassie laughed, squeezing past Dad who was standing in the doorway of her parents' home. He'd hung back, she noticed. It was the first time she'd seen them since she'd made up with him on the phone, and perhaps he was still a little uncertain about their relationship. As soon as she'd dumped the bags in the hallway she reached out to him and pulled him tightly into a hug.

'So good to have you here,' he said. 'So very good.'

'Happy Christmas, Dad,' she replied. 'There's nowhere else I'd want to be.'

'Aw, love.' He squeezed her tight, and she felt the emotion coursing through him.

'Tea, Cassie? Or coffee? Or something stronger?' Mum was moving the bags into the kitchen.

'How about we go out for our walk now, if that fits in with the dinner preparation, Mum? We could swing by a pub for a pre-dinner drink.'

'Splendid idea!' Dad released her from the hug and reached for his coat.

'Yes, that fits in very nicely,' Mum said. She glanced at the bags of presents. 'I'll just put these under the tree, though, so it's all nice for when we get back.'

'I'll help.' Cassie grabbed one of the bags and went through to the sitting room, where the tree stood in a corner, its lights twinkling merrily. She added her gifts to the pile already there. Dad had set the fire ready to light, she noticed, and Mum had put little bowls of Quality Street chocolates on every side table. She grabbed a couple, eating one and putting another in her pocket.

'Oy, those are for later!' Mum said, catching her in the act.

'I'll have no room later, after eating your Christmas dinner,' Cassie said with a laugh.

The day was fine and clear, cold but not icy, and their walk took them through the village, up a hill to a point where there was a fine view in all directions. They passed many people while out – people walking dogs, families with sulky teenagers who clearly just wanted to get back to their new Xboxes, small children on new bikes or scooters, lone older men who'd presumably been dispatched so as to be out of their wife's way while she cooked. Everyone exchanged Christmas greetings.

'Don't you just love it when Christmas Day is like this?' Cassie said, as they paused for a rest at the top of the hill, standing beside a trig point and taking in the stunning view. Wisps of mist lay in the valleys, a few autumn leaves still clung to trees adding colour in a patch of woodland below. A dog came bounding up, sniffing and wagging its tail, as excited about the day as everyone else seemed to be.

Cassie's phone rang. She pulled it out to check who it was. 'Ah, Bethany! I'll put her on speakerphone.' She tapped the phone to answer it.

'Hey Bethany! Happy Christmas! You're on speaker, and Shirley and Tony are here too. We're up a hill, it's gorgeous. I'll send you a picture.'

'Happy Christmas, Cassie! You're also on speaker. Mum and Dad are here, and Gran and Granddad are coming later, along with my aunt and cousins.'

'Wow! Going to be a full house then! Merry Christmas, Jan and Adrian, and good luck with the hordes!'

'Ah, I love a busy house at Christmas,' Jan's voice said.

They all exchanged greetings, and made comments about the glorious weather (better where Cassie was than with Bethany as it turned out) and told each other their plans for the day. Adrian read out a couple of corny cracker jokes he'd saved from the previous night's dinner, and they all laughed. When Cassie finally hung up, her mother turned to her with sparkling eyes. 'They sound like lovely, happy people.'

Cassie smiled and nodded. 'They are. Bethany's lucky with her adoptive parents.' She turned to her dad and hooked an arm through his. 'And I'm lucky with my dad. Thanks for choosing him, Mum.'

'You're welcome, love. I'm quite glad I chose him too,' Mum said, poking Dad playfully on the arm.

'I'd have been on the scrapheap otherwise,' he said with a laugh.

They opened their presents much later as was their usual tradition. With a stomach full of turkey and Christmas pudding, with a glass of mulled wine in hand and the fire lit, an album of Christmas songs playing softly in the background – all exactly as Cassie had envisaged and precisely as she wanted it. She'd opened some great presents – new mugs for her kitchen, a pair of expensive trainers she'd been dropping hints about for weeks, a basket full of gorgeous toiletries. And now she was watching carefully as Dad opened the last of his presents from her.

He frowned as he discarded the wrapping paper and peered at the front of an A4 document wallet.

'I'll get it printed and bound properly for you. I must admit, it ended up being a bit of a rush. But I wanted to give it to you this Christmas,' Cassie said.

He opened the wallet and extracted the sheaf of pages within. 'Oh, wow, love. That's amazing.'

'What is it, Tony?' Mum asked.

'My family history. The Turners and Brittens, going back . . .' he flicked through the pages '. . . at least two hundred years, is it? Everything you've found out. You continued with the research then, even though it's not your genealogy. I'm really touched.'

'It is my family,' Cassie replied. 'You're my dad and your family is my family.'

'Thank you, love. Thank you so much. That's made my Christmas, Cassie.'

Whether he meant the gift or her words she wasn't sure, but it didn't matter. With a potential new job ahead, a boyfriend she really cared about, a great relationship with her daughter and her fabulous supportive parents behind her every step of the way, Cassie felt truly blessed. For the first time since her late teens she felt that she had a future to look forward to, and grow into. She was moving on at last.

Acknowledgements

This novel was completed, edited and made ready for publication during 2020's Covid-19 crisis, with all members of the publishing team having to get used to very different ways of working. Much credit is due to the entire team: the proof-readers, cover designers, marketing department and everyone else involved. From my point of view everything's gone really smoothly and it's all been just as normal. Thank you all – I love being part of the HQ family.

Especial thanks to my editor Abigail Fenton for her enthusiasm for this novel, and her insightful, clear and detailed notes on how to improve it. Thanks also to the eagle-eyed copy-editor Helena Newton, who spots the tiniest errors from a mile off. Novels are always a joint enterprise and this one is no exception.

As always my son Fionn and husband Ignatius were the first readers of this book, and deserve thanks for their comments which helped make the novel good enough to send to Abi. Honestly, first drafts can be so embarrassing; it's reassuring to have someone I can trust to help me past that stage.

Finally, thanks are due to all my readers: especially those in the Facebook Historical and Timeslip Novels Group, who are so wonderfully supportive and who helped decide on the title for this novel. Keep reading, all!

Dear Reader,

We hope you enjoyed reading this book. If you did, we'd be so appreciative if you left a review. It really helps us and the author to bring more books like this to you.

Here at HQ Digital we are dedicated to publishing fiction that will keep you turning the pages into the early hours. Don't want to miss a thing? To find out more about our books, promotions, discover exclusive content and enter competitions you can keep in touch in the following ways:

JOIN OUR COMMUNITY:

Sign up to our new email newsletter: hyperurl.co/hqnewsletter

Read our new blog www.hqstories.co.uk

https://twitter.com/HQStories

www.facebook.com/HQStories

BUDDING WRITER?

We're also looking for authors to join the HQ Digital family!
Find out more here:

https://www.hqstories.co.uk/want-to-write-for-us/

Thanks for reading, from the HQ Digital team

Keep reading for an excerpt from *The Secret of the Château* . . .

Prologue

Pierre, 1794

Pierre Aubert, the Comte de Verais, could see the mob coming in the distance, up the track towards the château, brandishing flaming torches, shouting and chanting. There were perhaps fifty or more men, in their rough brown trousers and loose shirts. Most of them were carrying weapons – farming implements, sticks, pikes. He clutched his young son close to his chest, hushing the child and trying to ignore the pains that shot through him as he hurried along the path that led away from the château, towards the village. The girl was ahead of him, holding the baby. They had to get the children to safety first; only then could Pierre concentrate on saving himself and his wife.

Catherine. His heart lurched as he recalled her white, frightened face as he'd hurriedly told her his plans. If she did what he'd told her, she'd be safe from the mob, and soon the family would be reunited and they could get away. Into exile, into Switzerland.

France had changed over the last five years or so. The old ways, the *ancien régime*, had gone. There seemed to be no place in this new France for the likes of Pierre and Catherine. In the past it had been their class who ruled, but not anymore. If this mob caught them, they'd be imprisoned, summarily tried, and very likely executed – by guillotine.

But the mob would need to catch them first. Pierre had received a warning and was a good way ahead of them. The men hadn't reached the château yet, and they wouldn't find Catherine there. She was safe for now, and he'd return to her later. It would all work out.

It had to. It was their only chance.

Chapter 1

Lu, present day

It all began one drunken evening at Manda and Steve's. We were all staying with them for the weekend, as we often did. Three of us – that's me (I'm Lu Marlow), my husband Phil and our mate Graham – had arrived on Friday afternoon, and Steve had cooked a stupendous meal for us all that evening. We'd all brought a few bottles of wine, and I admit by the time this particular conversation began over the remnants of dessert we may have all had a tad too much to drink.

'What are you going to do, now you're retired?' Phil asked Steve. Steve had been forced to retire early – given a choice between that or relocating to Derby. ('Nothing against Derby,' he'd said, 'but we've no desire to live there.') He was aged just fifty-nine. We were all fifty-eight or nine. We'd met forty years ago, during Freshers' week at Sussex University and had been firm friends through rough and smooth ever since.

Steve shrugged. 'Don't know. I didn't want to stop work. Not quite ready to devote myself to the garden yet.'

'He needs a project,' Manda said. 'Something to get stuck into. He's lost without a purpose in life. House renovation or something.'

'But your house is beautiful,' I said. 'It needs nothing doing to it.' We were sitting in their dining room, which overlooked the garden. They'd bought the house over twenty years earlier when their daughter Zoe was a baby. Zoe had recently sent Manda into a tailspin by moving to Australia on a two-year work contract. They'd done up their house over the years, turning it from a tired old mess into a beautiful family home.

'Yes, and I don't see the point of moving house just to give me something to do,' Steve said. 'More wine?' He topped up everyone's glasses.

'Can you get any consultancy work?' Phil asked. 'I've had a bit, since I got my redundancy package.' He'd done a few two-week contracts, and a part-time contract that lasted three months.

'Probably. But it's not what I want.'

'What *do* you want, mate?' Graham, who we'd always called Gray, asked.

Steve looked out at the rain that streamed down the patio doors. 'Better weather. Mountains. A ski resort within an hour's drive. Somewhere I can go fell-running straight from the house. A better lifestyle.'

'Relocating, then. Where to?'

'I fancy France,' Manda said.

'Yeah, I do, too.' Phil looked at me, as if to gauge my reaction. First I'd heard of him being interested in living abroad – we'd never talked about anything like that. We went to France or Italy a couple of times every year on holiday – always a winter ski trip (Phil's favourite) and usually a couple of weeks in the summer exploring the Loire valley, the Ardeches, Tuscany or wherever else took our fancy. Very often these holidays were with the other three people sitting round the table now.

'France?' is all I managed to say. An exciting idea, but my life was here in England. Even though there was less to keep me here, since Mum died. I imagined visiting Steve and Manda in France for holidays. That'd be fun.

'I like Italy,' said Manda.

'But we don't speak Italian,' Steve pointed out.

'We could learn . . .'

'Where in France?' Gray interrupted, leaning forward, elbows on the table. I knew that gesture. It meant he was Having An Idea. Gray's ideas were sometimes inspired, sometimes ridiculous, always crazy.

Steve shrugged. 'Alpes-Maritimes?'

'It's lovely round there,' I said. Phil and I had had a holiday there a couple of years ago, staying in a gîte in a small village nestled among the Alpine foothills. We'd gone walking in the mountains, taken day trips to the Côte d'Azur, dined on local cheese and wine and all in all, fallen in love with the area.

'It is lovely,' Manda agreed. 'But I'd hate to move somewhere like that and be so far from everyone. Bad enough having Zoe on the other side of the world but if I was a plane ride away from all our friends too – you lot, I mean – I'd hate that.' She sniffed. 'You know I hate flying.'

'We'd all come and stay often,' I said with a grin, 'if you got a house somewhere gorgeous like that.'

'We'd move in,' said Gray. I looked at him quizzically and he winked back.

Steve laughed. 'Ha! I'd charge you rent!'

'Maybe we should all just chip in and buy a place big enough for all of us,' Gray said. 'Sell up here, buy ourselves a whopping great property over there that's big enough for all our kids to visit us, and retire in style.'

There was laughter around the table, but Gray looked at each of us in turn. 'No, really, why don't we? Makes perfect sense. It'd be more economical overall – shared bills and all that. Property is cheaper there than here – at least cheaper than it is in the south of England. And imagine the lifestyle – we'd be out cycling and walking, skiing in the winter, growing our own veg. We should do it now, while we're still fit enough. None of us have jobs to keep us here anymore.'

'We could employ a cleaner,' Manda said, ever the practical one.

'And a gardener. And a chef.' Phil grinned.

'We could keep chickens and have fresh eggs every day.' Steve's eyes lit up. He's such a foodie.

'I'd get a dog.' I'd always wanted one.

'Can I have a horse? Let's get a place with stables,' Manda said, to a bit of eye-rolling from Steve.

'It'd need somewhere to store all our bikes,' Gray, our resident cyclist, chipped in.

'There needs to be plenty of spare rooms for guests. Our kids would want to come to stay.' Me, again.

'Imagine at Christmas! All of us together – we'd have a ball!' Steve said – actually, if he wasn't a bloke, I'd have said he squealed this.

We were all speaking at once. The idea had taken shape, invaded all of our minds, and yes, the quantity of wine consumed had helped but as the conversation went on, I could see it taking root. At some point Gray and Steve both pulled out their phones and began searching for properties to buy.

'You can get an eight-bedroom château for about a million euro,' Gray said, peering at a list of search results. 'That's about the right size for us five plus visiting kids.'

'We could afford that, if we all sold our houses here. That's two hundred thousand per person. Your place is worth, what, six hundred thou?' Steve looked at me and Phil.

'About that, yes. And the mortgage is paid off.'

'So you two put in four hundred, that's euro not pounds, and you'd still have a huge wodge of cash over. Manda and I do the same, Gray puts in two hundred.'

'Look at this place! It's got a medieval defensive wall!'

'This one's got a tower, like something from a fairy tale.'

'Rapunzel, Rapunzel, let down your hair!'

'Who's Rapunzel? Steve's bald as a coot, can't be him!' Manda teased.

'You, dearest! Always wanted you to grow your hair long!'

We were passing phones around, looking at the various large properties currently on sale across France. There certainly seemed to be a lot of intriguing-looking châteaux that were within the ball-park price range Steve had suggested. It was a fun evening, and as we indulged ourselves in this little fantasy of selling up and moving to France together we laughed and joked and I felt so happy and comfortable with my friends around me.

It'd never happen, of course. It was just a bit of a giggle, a way to spend the evening with lots of laughter. That was all. We were all far too settled in our current homes and towns. And I, for one, was not good enough at French to be able to manage living abroad.

We'd met during Freshers' week, the five of us. We'd all gone to the Clubs and Societies Fair, and had signed up for the Mountaineering Club. The county of Sussex does not actually contain any mountains of course, but the club arranged weekends away travelling by minibus to north Wales, the Lake District, Brecon or the Peak District for camping, walking and climbing trips. The first meeting of the term was at the end of Freshers' week, where first-years were welcomed and the programme for the term was laid out. I signed up immediately for a trip a fortnight later to Langdale in the Lake District. So did Manda, and we agreed to share a tent. By the end of the meeting we were chatting with the other first-years – Phil, Gray and Steve – and the five of us decided to go on to one of the student bars for a beer. And that was it. We bonded. We were practically inseparable from that moment on, sharing digs during the second and third years, although it wasn't till after university that Phil and I finally paired up, closely followed by Steve and Manda.

'No one left for me,' Gray had said, with a mock-tremble of his lower lip. He was best man at both weddings. And there was never any shortage of girlfriends for him throughout the years.

Melissa was the one who lasted longest. They never married but had two daughters together before splitting up when the kids were little. Gray shared custody of the girls with Melissa, having them for half of every week throughout their childhood. He was a great dad. Then there was Leanne who lasted a while, but Gray's commitment-phobia sadly finished that relationship in the end.

Phil and I had two kids as well – our sons Tom and Alfie. And Manda and Steve had their daughter Zoe. All were now grown-up, finished with university, earning a living, flying high and happy in their chosen lifestyles. They didn't really need us much anymore, other than for the occasional loan from the Bank of Mum and Dad.

So the five of us were all pretty free, free to do what we wanted with life. We were still young enough to be fit and active, although Phil was a bit overweight and not as fit as he ought to be. We were old enough to be financially secure. We were all recently redundant or retired. Our kids were grown-up and independent. We had no elderly parents left that need caring for – my mum was the last to go of that generation.

So I suppose if we had been at all serious about upping sticks and moving to France, it was the right time to do it. But of course we weren't serious, and in the morning we'd all be dismissing it as a joke, a good giggle but nothing more. At least I hoped so, as I lay searching for sleep in Steve and Manda's spare room that night. I didn't want to move to France.

I was the last one up next morning. That's not unusual – I've never been a morning person. The others were sitting in the kitchen, drinking coffee while Steve organised breakfast. All the men in our little group are great cooks. And Manda can bake amazing cakes, cookies and breads. It's just me who's a klutz in the kitchen.

'Morning, Lu,' Steve said. 'The full works for you this morning? Phil said you were still out for the count.'

'I was. And yes please.' I scanned their faces. Was everyone wondering, as I was, whether the conversation last night had been serious or not? Or had they all forgotten it after a night's sleep? The latter, I hoped.

Phil put out a hand and pulled me to a seat beside him. 'All right? There's fresh tea in the pot. Want some?' He didn't wait for an answer but picked up an empty mug and poured me a cup, adding just the right amount of milk. The advantage of thirty years' marriage is that we know exactly what the other person likes and needs. I smiled a thank-you at him and sat down.

'How're everyone's heads?' I asked.

'Surprisingly all right,' Gray replied. 'Think we drank about eight bottles between us so we've no right to feel good this morning. Not at our age.'

'Speak for yourself, Gray.' Manda gave him a playful punch on the arm. 'You may be knocking on a bit but I'm still only fifty-eight.' She'd always been the baby of the bunch – youngest by all of two months.

The banter was all very well, but I was dying to know. Were they about to start house-hunting in the Alpes-Maritimes? Or anywhere in France for that matter. I hoped not. Steve was busy flipping fried eggs, and Manda was taking trays of sausages and bacon out of the oven and putting them on the table. There was a bowl of cooked mini tomatoes, racks of toast and a pan of sautéed potatoes. I couldn't help but grin. A good old fry-up the night after a skin-full of wine was my favourite thing.

Could you even get bacon and sausage in France?

It was as we finished eating, as Manda was making more coffee and I began stacking plates to load the dishwasher, that Steve spoke up. 'So. This house in France. Are we going to do it, then?'

'Were we serious?' Phil asked.

'I was,' Gray chipped in, as he munched on the last of the toast.

'You're never serious,' Manda told him.

'Well' – he waved the crust of his toast at everyone – 'I was last night. Honestly, it'd be awesome. We could breakfast like this every day!'

'We'd be fat as fools in no time,' I said. My stomach gave a lurch. If they all wanted to do this, I couldn't be the one to spoil the party. Not now. It'd all fizzle out soon enough anyway.

'I'm up for it,' Phil said, looking at me with a raised eyebrow, and I swallowed and nodded. 'Er, yeah. Sure.'

'Manda and I discussed it this morning, while we waited for you lazy lot to show your faces,' Steve said. 'We think we could make it work. Manda needs something to take her mind off Zoe being away. Phil needs a healthier lifestyle. Sorry, mate, but you do. And you, Lu' – he nodded at me – 'need to do something for yourself, after all your years caring for your mum. As for me, I need a project. So I'm happy to do the legwork.'

No one was better than Steve at organising things. He'd been a project manager in a finance company for years and was good at it. And he spoke better French than the rest of us.

'What about me?' asked Gray. 'What do I need?'

'A new hunting ground,' Phil said, with a wink. 'Maybe you'd meet the perfect woman in France.'

'Mmm, I like the sound of that!' Gray laughed.

'Well then,' Phil said. 'Let's go for it!'

There was much cheering and clinking together of coffee mugs, and by the time I had that dishwasher loaded Steve had opened his laptop and begun a search, and a shortlist of potential properties was being drawn up. I watched them crowded around behind Steve and smiled. It would probably all come to nothing, but in the meantime I had to admit it was fun dreaming and planning. In the end the whole thing would no doubt just fizzle out, thankfully, but I wasn't going to be the one who said no to it. Not while they were all so excited.

Phil and I discussed the idea on our drive home later that day.

'Moving to France, eh? At our age! Great idea, isn't it?'

I bit my lip for a moment, not sure how to respond. It was one thing going along with the excitement when we were with all the others, but surely I should be honest about my misgivings with my own husband? 'Yeah. Lovely idea, but I can't see it actually happening, can you?'

Phil glanced across at me and frowned. 'Don't see why not. You know what Steve's like when he gets his teeth into a project. There's no one better than him at getting things organised and done.'

'Do you really think we should do it? Sell our house and everything?'

'Well, what's the alternative? Neither of us are working anymore. I'm not ready to just vegetate in front of daytime TV for the next thirty years. So, yes, I think we should put our house on the market as soon as possible. We've been saying we should thin down our possessions ready for downsizing anyway. This'll force us to actually get on and do it. And living with Steve, Manda and Gray will be awesome. It'll be like being twenty again – regaining our youth!'

'Ha. Except we are nearly sixty. But I agree, we do want to downsize and release some equity. So we might as well get on with sorting our stuff out. I reckon the boys will take some of the spare furniture. And it's probably time I threw out all their old schoolbooks and nursery artwork.'

'God, Lu, have you still got all that?'

I grimaced and nodded. 'In the attic. About five boxes of it.'

Downsizing. Not moving to France. That's all I'd agreed to, wasn't it?

So the following week I began clearing the attic, while Phil started on the garage and arranged for valuations from estate agents. We cleaned and tidied ready for the agent's photographer, and then put the house on the market. It felt good to make a start on this – we'd been talking about selling up for at least a year.

A week later we heard that Gray already had an offer on his place, and that Steve was away in France looking at potential properties.

'Already!' I said to Manda, when she phoned to tell us. I couldn't believe they were really this serious about it all, but it looked like Steve was, at least. My heart lurched. I'd accepted the idea of selling our family home, but moving abroad was a much bigger step, one I didn't entirely want to take.

'He spent days online scrolling through endless possibilities, then two days ago said to me it'd be easier to be "on the ground", and next thing I knew he'd booked a flight to Nice.'

'Didn't he want company?' I asked. I'd have thought he'd have taken Manda or Gray with him.

'I think his plan is to whittle his short list down to a proper shortlist – there are over a hundred on it at the moment – and then let us have a look at the details. Then if any really stand out and we're still all keen, we can go en masse to view them.'

'Sounds good.' The rest of us hadn't the first idea how to buy property abroad, but Steve would have looked it all up already, spoken to suitable people for advice, and would know exactly what he was doing. He was a born project manager.

'Lu, I'm so excited about this, aren't you?' Manda said. I detected a tiny bit of worry in her voice, as if she was frightened Phil and I might have had second thoughts. She was right – I'd been having second thoughts all the way through. But I refused to be the one to spoil things.

'Definitely! Just can't wait to get on with it now!' I forced myself to sound enthusiastic. Whatever happened, I was not going to put a dampener on it. There was still a strong chance the plan would fall apart.

'Phew! I told Zoe, too. She thinks it's a great idea. I was worried, you know, that she'd somehow think we were abandoning her . . .'

'But she lives in Australia – actually you'll have moved a little closer to her!'

'I mean more that when, or God help me *if*, she comes home to England, we won't be there.'

'No, but you'll be a short flight away. And she can come "home" to France. Home is where her heart is.'

Manda answered with a little wobble in her voice. 'You're right. It's the only thing that worries me, though. That our kids won't like it.' She took a deep breath. She'd struggled with empty nest syndrome ever since Zoe first left home to go to university. 'What do Tom and Alfie think?'

This was my chance. I could offload to Manda here, now, tell her my misgivings about the whole project, using the boys as an excuse, perhaps. She'd talk to Steve, and maybe it'd all be quietly put to bed, for surely if we weren't all happy with the idea, we shouldn't do it? After all, moving to another country is a big step, at any time of life. But no. I wasn't going to be the party pooper. They'd never think quite the same of me again if I did that now. And I was still convinced the plan would die a natural death if I just let events run their course.

I smiled, to make my voice sound happy. 'They're delighted. Tom sees it as a base for cheap holidays. Alfie's dictated we need to have a swimming pool, and a butler serving iced cocktails at all hours.'

'Fair enough. I'll let Steve know the new requirements.' We had a giggle about this, before going on to talk about Gray's house sale.

'Steve and I have said he can move in here if need be, if his sale goes through really quickly. Actually that'd give us some capital for a deposit, if we need it. It's all working out, Lu. We've got the skiing holiday coming up, then it's possible we might be ready to move in the summer!'

Well, I hoped Phil and I would be ready to move by the summer. But with luck, not to France.

If you enjoyed *The Forgotten Gift*, then why not try another sweeping historical novel from HQ Digital?

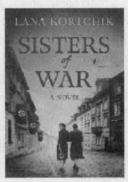